THE STEAL

THE
STEALING
STEPS

Nine Stories by
John Arden

In youth when I did love, did love
Methought it was very sweet:
To contract O the time for a my behove,
O methought there was nothing meet.

But Age with his stealing steps
Hath claw'd me in his clutch:
And hath shipped me intil the land
As if I had never been such.

W. Shakespeare, *Hamlet, Prince of Denmark*

Methuen

Published by Methuen 2004

1 3 5 7 9 10 8 6 4 2

Copyright © 2003 by John Arden

The right of John Arden to be identified as the author of
this work has been asserted by him in accordance with the
Copyright, Designs and Patents Act 1988.

Published in 2004 by
Methuen Publishing Ltd
215 Vauxhall Bridge Road
London SW1V 1EJ
www.methuen.co.uk

First published in hardback in 2003 by Methuen Publishing Ltd

Methuen Publishing Limited Reg. No. 3543167

ISBN 0 413 77334 5

A CIP catalogue for this title is available from the British Library.

Designed by Helen Ewing

Printed and bound in Great Britain
by Cox & Wyman Ltd, Reading, Berkshire

to ANNA TAYLOR of Huddersfield, poet,

in gratitude for so much chatterbox delight
and so many sparkish anecdotes,

above all for her account of a real-life 'Miss Fidelma',
choked with excess of memory and disregarded prophecy,
yet alive alive-o and unable to die,
like the Cumaean Sibyl in her jar.

CONTENTS

BARBARA

Woe to thee, O land, where thy king is a child!

– words of warning from the Preacher long ago in ancient Israel: words
to haunt England toward the end of the fourteenth century, with King
Edward III lying dead and Richard of Bordeaux, his little grandson, so
unconfidently perched upon his throne.

In those ugly nervous days there lived in the city of York an
unbeneficed cleric, a subdeacon, called Jacob of Thickpenny;
tapsters and ostlers and brothel-house abiders knew him as Clerk
Thickpenny the Rhymer. To be fair to him, he was a deal more than
a ragtag of an ale-cellar ballad-man. He scraped an irregular income
through the office for the dead and such-like devotions, which he
would sing at the behest of those who could afford them; from his
poetry and secular music he did now and then glean some veritable
success, it might be enough cash for a feast of roast duck and several
strong bottles, or even a new gown. He was an elegant performer
on the gittern and a much-admired old playmaker: indeed there had
been a time when mayor and aldermen called him in to rewrite the
Corpus Christi plays, and his work (as he reiterated ever after to all
who would listen) was a glory to the city – if you didn't believe
him, go give ear to the plays next summer and then ask your dad
what they were like before you were born. He was not as a rule
contradicted; grey-haired though he was, and pretty nigh toothless,
he still was reputed a most violent scrawny fighter who would stab
as soon as look at you.

At times he had been loosely accused of ill-conditioned thoughts
that bordered upon treason – maybe heresy as well, it was
whispered. The calumnies, however, were so vague that no one

took much notice of them. Until suddenly dire news came flying up out of the south, all of it horrifying, much of it true. The Kent and Essex rabblement, from their malice and envy, had taken prey of royal London (upon Corpus Christi day itself, who'd believe it? even as the actors of York were trundling around town on their glistering pageant-cars amid handclaps and cheers); moreover a violent multitude had seized the young king, and was now in the very act of dismembering his kingdom. Every nobleman, lawyer, sheriff, bishop, abbot and archdeacon in the north parts was remorselessly to be murdered just so soon as the rebel leaders could advance their banners this side of Trent.

As it happened, one of those leaders was well remembered in York by censorious and elderly clergy who shuddered to repeat his name: John Ball. An indigent, squalid mass priest, years ago driven out of the city for the virulence of his distemper against great men and civil propriety; and now, two hundred miles off, he had raised himself up as the prophet of insurrection to turn the world upside down and drag thousands of ignorant clodhoppers into death, doom and darkness. And all to the tune of a most perilous levelling song, which he would chant like a Bible text at the start and the finish of his murderous orations:

> When Adam dalf and Eva span,
> Who was then the gentleman? (*etcetera*.)

– verses, as was now revealed, that for months had been bandied from mouth to mouth, village to village, from Norwich to Ipswich and across the Thames as far as Canterbury, a species of password to a secret and heinous society, not only perilous but downright diabolical.

Was it possible that John Ball continued to have hidden dealings with his sometime associates in York? Had he not, years and years ago, been the brazen-voiced pot-companion of none other than Clerk Thickpenny? . . . No complacency, no delay, the matter must be thoroughly probed. So off went the diocesan summoner to fetch in the old poet: not to arrest him upon any specific charge, just to forcibly request on behalf of the archdeacon that he come and account for himself. The summoner was no stranger to Clerk Thickpenny: he had cruelly vexed him in season and out, extorting constant bribes upon the promise to keep quiet about Throstle Elspeth. This Scotswoman, a most marvellous singer, was the Rhymer's 'remedy', which is to say, his irregular wife: in official terms, his concubine, his clergy-whore, his tunnel to damnation, and moreover an inimical foreigner. Whatever she might be called, she was nearly as long-standing as his clerical status; she and he together had survived the great pestilence and the three plagues that followed it; they had shared their contented bed long before the present summoner came into the job. She was nominally attached to the household of the Earl of Northumberland, the great Percy: whenever he held festival upon one of his Yorkshire manors, she must gather up her gaudy skirts and trudge off to sing to him, either alone or in consort with other musicians of his train. For the rest of the year she could hire herself out to the communal or private gaieties of the city; if Clerk Thickpenny's drinking and her own fierce greed for the dice-box had not used up so much of her earnings, the pair of them could have lived in cleanliness and comfort. However, they preferred not.

They were known to have had four children: a pair of infant twins who died of the plague; a boy sent to Beverley to the alderman of the minstrels' guild, neither servant nor apprentice, but something of both, and accepted without premium as a favour to his parents; a daughter who took herself off at the age of fifteen with an itinerant Scots rope-dancer and now lived (so it was thought) in St Andrews.

Throstle Elspeth was a big woman, handsome, high cheekbones and a red face, her yellow hair striped whitey-brown with the years. She might have been five-and-fifty, it was hard to tell. She would drape her great bosom and her muscular forearms with so many garlands of cheap jewellery as almost to be taken for the sign-pole of a goldsmith's shop. But when the summoner arrived (an hour before dawn) at Clerk Thickpenny's lodging in the Shambles, a nasty loft beneath the gable of a tripe-scraper's house, he found her alone there in miserable pickle: she seemed not to have slept all night but huddled naked under a blanket in the litter of her bed, throwing dice left hand against right, and crooning some sort of dirge. She was plunged into black melancholy; he demanded the Rhymer's whereabouts; she spoke wearily between her fingers: 'He's no here. He's no anywhere, save maybe Scarborough, wad ye gang there and seek him? For he's no in Scarborough neither, save maybe four limbs and a toom wame and the een in his heid and they're blind or they're deid, I canna tell ye.'

This senseless-like speech caused the summoner to threaten her with his staff. When she fired up and invoked the protection of the Percys, he went well beyond threats, he flew at her in a fury of blows – 'Nay and it won't do: tha'rt a treasonous greasy owd breech-burner, and no more turdy words or I'll pass *my* word to them Percys they've a spying Scotch she-weasel in and out of their gates! Christ's Bread, they'll rear a gibbet for thee afore they've etten their dinners.' (Border treacheries were the first thoughts of many at this dangerous time; the panic throughout the city, with archers and billmen at every corner and chains across the river, was no less than when the Scots came raiding.) If he couldn't fetch Clerk Thickpenny, at least he would lay hold of the woman. He ordered up his cudgel-men to help. Between the pack of them she was so badly handled as to be unable to walk: they must carry her to the minster lockup on a hurdle. The archdeacon was disgusted and ordered ointment for her livid bruises, a bandage for her bleeding head and a mantle to make her decent; even then it was hard to question her. To begin with she lay helplessly retching, then she did nothing but moan, then she bawled and she cursed, and then at last, with a charitable cup of hot wine down her gullet, she managed to tell the tale.

A ridiculous tale but she stuck to it. In brief: for the past month Clerk Thickpenny had behaved like a man in a trance. Early in May he had been to Scarborough, invited by the notables of the fishermen's guild to discuss the shape of a new pageant-play for the first day of August, the feast of their patron St Peter, his miraculous escape from chains and gaol. Stages were to be built all along the harbour quay and on the decks of the fishing fleet, a gorgeous spectacular show with a marvellous fee for its deviser: the best opportunity he'd had for years. He left home in the highest spirits and returned after three weeks (so Elspeth lamented) quite beside himself with some inexplicable trouble, or ecstasy, she knew not which. He barely spoke of the pageant, could not seem to remember whether he was to work on it or not, spent hour after hour in bed, neither awake nor asleep, and then suddenly he'd pull his hood over his head and go out to walk the streets for hour after hour, greeting no one, stopping nowhere. Nor did he seek strong drink, which was a queer thing. Queerer still: upon the morning of Corpus Christi he could not be bothered to go to see even a single play of the sequence. His own plays: and not bothered. And then, that same night, in the sweltering June heat, he sat suddenly up in bed beside his Elspeth where she lay, his mouth open in a great cry as though his heart had that instant burst. 'Barbara,' she heard him call, 'sweet Barbara, love of my life.' He sprang to the floor, pulled his gittern from its hook on a rafter, snatched his walking stick from under the table, and scrambled out down the ladder, neither dressed nor undressed but all of a muddle of underclothes half-tied and his gown round his neck like a horsecollar. He plunged barefoot into the street and would have run straight to the city gate (which at that hour was fast barred; if he'd tried to go through it, he'd without doubt have been arrested and whipped for breach of curfew). Elspeth caught him up, pulled him back into the house, and told the disturbed tripe-scraper and his wife and his children and his apprentices and his maidservants to go to bed again and shut their blether: meanwhile she and her damned Jake would keep cool in the yard, impossible to get him up to the loft in his present state, maybe by morning he'd be showing a different face.

But no, it was the same face. He allowed her to dress him, never speaking one word – or never one word to *her*, for he did once again cry, 'Barbara,' with an intensity of yearning pathos, and then again, 'Barbara, eh Barbara, what cause not to tell me afore, all these years long gone and th'art nobbut i' Scarborough, in an arm's reach through all these years! sic a mickle dreary waste of it, years!' Whereupon he slipped her grasp and was out of the yard and its piles of stinking offal; into the street again, his gittern in its case at his shoulder; through the city gate upon the long road to Scarborough, lurching forward with his stick quite as though some malignant giant (with a mind to his destruction) had pressed the gift upon him of a pair of seven-league boots.

Now Elspeth knew who Barbara was: the woman whom her damned Jake had loved at the age of fifteen and lost for ever before he was twenty. She could not remember when she last heard him speak of her; but if in truth this Barbara was now to be found in Scarborough, and if he had seen her there or, what was worse, talked with her, *coupled* with her even . . . If he believed she could once again be his, why then, what remnant for Elspeth, the mother of his children? Had she lost him for ever? Was she not so much a forlorn woman as a dead one and damned, at the very onset of her wrinkled age? Unendurable – she would not endure it. She took but a few minutes to climb into the loft and collect her clothes and gear. A knapsack for her back. A wide straw hat against the sun. A purse at her belt for her day-to-day money. (Little enough in it; she didn't need to count. Times had been bad and her wagers unlucky.) Next to the purse a butcher's knife, broad-bladed and deadly, which she well knew how to use. After nearly four decades on the road as a singing-woman, she had made herself a hardy walker: she expected, within a mile or so, she would come up with her damned Jake and either turn him home for good or keep pace alongside him to Scarborough. If the latter, then she'd see what she would see.

But it seemed his tragic lust (if that's what it was) had made bowstrings of all his muscles and stirred a whirlwind in his lungs. For league upon league she was able to catch no glimpse of him, although those whom she met assured her he was ahead of her, on and on they had seen him march with his great surging strides like the tide-flow of Humber. Between York and Scarborough was by guess forty miles, and it took her three days. At the ale-stake in the town of Malton, and then again in a village called Staxton, she paid her reckoning by singing for it; despite weariness and rage and sorrow, she strove hard and sang well. But not without cost: it stopped her sleep, and next day the glaring heat and dust of the road came near to defeating her utterly.

From Staxton she took six hours to force herself the last seven miles into Scarborough. Sun-stricken, she thought: she should have rested through the noontide and not travelled until dusk, but it was too late to be wise, and at all events she was here. How to find him? Not hard: go straight to the harbour, he was bound to have been seen there by someone. The reek of fish and foul mudbanks was stifling. She spewed as she came out upon the quay. She staggered forward regardless and accosted a herring-boat skipper; she guessed he would know; and he did. 'Aye,' he grunted, 'aye. He came in, he went up, and I saw him. Baht hat, tha knows, baht speech, baht wit. *He'll* niver mek another saint-play, niver. Tha'rt best gang there uppards and find him.'

'Uppards', so it seemed, was a cluster of sailormen's hovels, wattle-and-daub and salt-caked thatch on an outcrop of the castle hill, higher than the rest of the town, tucked in just below the king's ramparts. She had to climb a series of steps cut in the rock, painfully steep; her heart throbbed, her eyes swam, she wondered for a while could she ever reach the top? When she did, she found people: a swarm of children, some ancient women who squatted on their doorsteps in the sunshine, knitting; a few men, even more ancient (one with a wooden leg and one with a hook instead of a hand); none of them would speak to her; they waved her silently onward, as though somehow afraid. Well beyond the last of the inhabited hovels, she found the ruin of a freestone house, part-fallen into the waves where some great storm had torn away the cliff. And there she found Clerk Thickpenny, her man. She wept and raged at the sight of him. He did not so much as look at her. No Barbara to be seen, nor aught else, save the children crowding in behind her, emboldened by her presence.

Within the ruin, among nettles, on a heap of collapsed roof-timber, he sat staring out across the sea. His gittern on his lap, he twanged the occasional chord. When he spoke, it was not to her, but easily and sweetly to Barbara; yet there was no Barbara. 'Allgates, dear love,' says he, 'never a sign of his ship, neither easterly nor south. Tha'rt assuredly i'th'right of it: he'll not be here while full tide, never in this wind, pet, nay: he's bound to tek his time sliding the coast from Spurn Head. Eh, sweetheart Barbara, six hours and more we've getten for the deeds and words of love. True love as it never was; true love as it ever shall be. Praise Jesu his sweet Mother for the grace of true love, for the grace of your naked limbs which never hereto, never, pet, oh never, no no no.'

He lay back on his pile of scantlings with unseemly abandon, slowly caressing his groin; on the side of his stringy old neck she saw a flaring red bite-mark. The children sniggered. Elspeth turned her face away: such an affront to herself and lewd beyond measure, altogether incomprehensible. Yet she could not just leave him ... He heaved himself up, he shrugged and shook his head, he picked out an air on his instrument. The saddest music she'd ever heard, she thought, and never in all their years together had she heard Clerk Thickpenny play it. Where had he learned it? Whose was the tune? The children sniggered and scuffled and pressed in beneath her elbows. Unwillingly she compelled herself to look at his face. She saw the tears stream down his grey-stubbled cheeks, his cracked lips trembling like cobwebs on a dewy thistle; and still he played on and on, gazing sideways through the broken wall as though into the eyes of someone who could not be there because not even the cliff was there, not any longer. All gone. All fallen down.

Such was her despair, she set her hand on her knife and would have plunged it into his heart, or into her own, she never knew which: but there came at that moment behind her the tramp of a man in seaboots, scaring away the gaggle of brats quick sharp. She turned; he was the skipper she'd spoken with down at the harbour. He saw her knife half out and shook his head. She let it drop into the sheath. She stood irresolute. He put it to her grimly: 'He's been here, sitha, he's been thus, for a night and best part of a day. What's to be done wi' him? More to t'purpose, what'll *thou* do? Th'art his woman, mek a choice.'

'Me? What'll I dae? Na, na, I'll dae nocht. For there's nocht that I can. His woman, d'ye tell me? I'm no his woman. Hae ye no heard the carl's ramblings? his woman is Barbara; God's wounds, let *her* look tae him! and I'd like fine to ken whaur she is.' She was sobbing, great gasps of misery, but she held herself bolt upright and once again she'd set hand upon her knife.

'Nay but there's no Barbara. She wor young, she wor swift and merry, sweet as spice, sharp as vinegar, and she's went.' He seemed

8

about to say more, but he saw she did not trust him. He saw that she thought he was trying to shield her damned Jake; his eyes clouded, his mouth tightened, he humped his shoulders.

'She's no went frae *him*,' snarled Elspeth, hand on knife. 'And forby frae me neither. I'm awa hame to York. I'll leave him to you and your slick fishers; dae what you will wi' him. Set his feet in a boat wi' a hole in it, shove him off on a falling tide, gif that's what seems maist canny. For me, man, nae mair of it, finish.'

He grew angry at her anger, hoarsely crowing at her to take herself off. 'If tha'lt not give us help, tha mun gang and that's it. Th'art no kind of woman for a man of his like. Gang then and mek prayer for forgiveness: I tell thee tha'lt need it.' He turned his back and left her. Entirely nonplussed, she turned *her* back and set herself homeward, stumbling blindly down the steps to hunt for the York road through a tangle of seaport alleys. Men and boys left off their work among lobster pots and nets to stare at her in silence. She might have been carrying the plague, the way they stood clear of her passage.

It took her five days to reach the city. All the vigour had gone out of her walking; she was devoid of desire to reach anywhere. She sought the loft in the Shambles for no better reason than that was where it was; short of the grave, where else should she be? She arrived at nightfall, went to bed, tried to sleep, failed: an hour before dawn she heard the summoner on the loft ladder, barking like a fox.

The archdeacon could not make up his mind how much of her absurdity he should believe. The whole story might well be a deliberate means to confuse the authorities and allow the man Thickpenny to escape. If so, it was all the more urgent to catch hold of the fellow and question him . . . And now, as though called upon cue, came a brand-new information. It was brought by a curate of St Michael le Belfry, the largest parish church of the city, where all manner of persons, great and small, mingled their prayers with daily business and rumour and news: the curate knew for a fact it was Clerk Thickpenny himself that made a most perilous rhyme, years ago, years, and had sung it to that devil of a John Ball, who'd now given it out in the south as a new thing altogether and the silly deluded people had taken it to their hearts. How did he know it? He choked with clumsy penitence: 'Ah Jesu, *mea culpa, mea maxima culpa*, wor I not sat i't'taproom to hear them? Nay but I sang treble to Clerk Thickpenny's tenor when John Ball wor roaring i't'bass: I'll not forget it, never, ah Jesu assoil me, I wor nobbut a young lad, nobbut fourteen year old.' They'd sung it, he said, as a catch; it dealt with Adam and Eve, and – The archdeacon told him sharply to be silent, that rhyme was already noted, the hapless curate was on no account to repeat it, or else.

Had it truly begun in York, from the invention of a cleric of York? Then the archdeacon must act with speed: the whole safety and reputation of the church in the north parts might depend upon his instant discretion. The summoner was at once sent to Scarborough, with an escort of armed horsemen and a letter to the port bailiff, a peremptory demand for the surrender of the malefactor. If the bailiff was not yet aware of the state of the kingdom, let the summoner inform him, with as much lurid detail as might seem needful; indeed, let the summoner put Scarborough most thoroughly in fear: *Clerk Thickpenny must be secured*.

The summoner did his duty. He found the town in fear already, the dreadful London news having arrived that very morning. The bailiff had barricaded himself in the castle and made no fiddling difficulty as to how far the king's officer could be overriden by the archbishop's: he sent down his catchpolls to do what the summoner told them. Elspeth's tale was shown to be true. The arrest was duly made. The fisher-folk, men and women, crowded around and looked on in some trouble of mind. Was bad luck being exorcised or was it only reinforced, when they saw the weeping Rhymer hauled handcuffed out of the ruin and dragged from top to bottom of the cliff-side steps as you'd drag an old bundle of sailcloth?

He was thrust onto a horse, his legs tied under its belly; the summoner's men set him off out of town at a bone-shattering trot. Slowly and sorely, over the next few days, they drove him on and on toward York. Now and then they knocked him about, at first to screw money out of him, and then upon the chance he might utter some sort of confession and earn them the archdeacon's praise. But he said nothing, save to ask for his gittern. Useless plea: it had been smashed in his tumble down the steps.

It may well have been his very mistreatment that brought the Rhymer back to his senses. Every jibe, every blow, fetched a glint more intelligence into his eyes; by the time they rode into Malton, he was looking about him with very nearly a full understanding. A most curdled understanding, certainly, a black brooding fury, combined with bewilderment as to how he had got there in the first place. For a while he kept silence, jogging painfully along with neck bent and eyes lowered whenever he thought they were watching him. Not far from the gates of York he suddenly jerked his head, and (of all things) began to sing: a harsh full-throated chanting that shocked them into genuine anger. They flailed at him with their riding crops. He wouldn't stop. What devil was in the old carl's voice-box, to bellow so sturdily from the midst of degradation and hurt?

> Fair are the fields in high summer,
> Green leaf on every hedge
> Would I had knuckles as free as the wind
> To bring blood from your cruel nose-ridge.
>
> *How much blood would flow?*
> Sweet Christ I think little or no.
>
> She being dead yet I've known she can live,
> As fair as the green summer leaf
> Maugre all falsehoods of ear and of eye
> Oh never she did, nor she never will, die,
> Ah, you foul trolls, you ride this road alive
> Yet worm-eaten beyond belief.
>
> *How many worms? and where do they crawl?*
> Score upon score, in your mouth, eye and nostril,
> Hundred 'pon hundred in cock, cod and arsehole.

When the summoner reported himself at the archdeacon's house, he was startled to discover that nothing any longer was as it had been. He found no sign of all of the previous urgent concern for his 'perilous and diabolical' prisoner: overnight a king's messenger had come galloping like joyous wildfire to tell clergy and laity throughout the north parts that the rebels were dispersed and his royal majesty, *Dei Gratia*, was safe. The chief commander of the revolt had been killed in a convenient scuffle, it was expected that the other leaders (including John Ball) would very shortly be gaoled and arraigned ... So how important was it to put up a great show over Thickpenny and his savage wife? They'd led no rebellion, they'd talked about no rebellion. Making rhymes, singing songs, 'years ago, years'? – not much of an indictment. Best give the pair of them a good vicious scourging and thereafter let them go. And so it would have happened without any more ado, had Thickpenny not cried for pen and ink. He had wonders to write down, he said. Moreover, he said it in Latin; so they must know, must they not? he was in his right mind. No, he would not tell it aloud: he would write. Only so could he be sure he had it exact. He kept on at them until they did what he wanted, and here are his words as he wrote them.

> In low Latin, arbitrarily interspersed with fragments of English [bold type].
> The postscripts were added by the archdeacon himself: they conclude in
> an agonized scribble.

These are not words of madness. They are truth but a strange truth, which harrows me to the core of my spirit even to think of it, and you may believe it or not as you will. I am old enough to know that time and again the truth is less easily believed than a lie. I also know, for the summoner has told me, that I am suspected of heterodox opinion amounting to collusion with this rebellion of **gode folk** (which is to say, the common people) in the southern shires, and that is why he has brought me here. I will not waste your time with attempting to prove my innocence. I am not innocent: for years I have made my poetry in defence of **gode folk** and to demonstrate my outrage at the injustices heaped upon them; if a man is to be hanged for that, you may hang me. I hear the name of John Ball. John Ball was an honest man, a good shepherd, and my friend. I maintain he is the same today as he was then, whatever arrogant calumnies are shot against his name. I know nothing about his doings in the south, but what I maintain I maintain and that is the end of all I will say upon all of that business.

So to come to the meat of the matter. In Scarborough these last days I have been living in a life not of this world; I do not mean a holy life, as of a saint in a fervour of prayer, but rather was I transported from the familiar proceedings of this diurnal **middelerthe** and placed within a realm of ... alas, I cannot delineate the nature of that realm: I can only write what I saw, heard and felt, and let you frame your own opinion.

If my tale is to convince, I must begin at my childhood. I was born sixty years ago, more or less; my father was a travelling man, tinker, cutler, bowyer, fletcher, horse-coper, horse-doctor, snarer of rabbits, who carried his manifold skills from village to village, farm to farm, manor to manor, all around the East Riding. When he found I was the only one among all his children to lack inclination toward any of his trades and that I lived only for music and verse, he begged for me the patronage of Sir Thomas de Wake, lord of Cottingham. Sir Thomas, in his liberality, sent me to Beverley to the minstrels' guild, to be bound apprentice to a lively practitioner. I became very happy in my new life. I pleased my master with my close attention to the art that he taught me, and before long he allowed me all on my own to sing songs and tell tales to his patrons: I was happy, and imprudently proud, as I accompanied him upon circuit as cocksure as a young poll-parrot of the plaudits of my audience. I grew warmly aware of the bright eyes of many maidens, but found myself scarce fit to converse with them; without my music and verse I had, it seemed, no words of my own. I was in truth even yet a tinker's oaf, a great **lurdan**, incapable of expressing in my own person the gallant discourse of love that I sang about with such confidence. The songs themselves began to fail, my performance infected by my shyness elsewhere, until my master deemed me lazy and took me abruptly to task. I suppose now that what was happening (which I did not fully comprehend) was my bodily alteration from boy into man: I found my imaginings full of uncleanness, heated dreams of girls' nudity and so forth. The more I thus pictured under cover of night these queer female creatures, the less able I was to greet them in broad daylight with proper courtesy.

And so it would have gone on until I ended as a beastly churl, haunting the bawdy houses, playing the ruffian with the crudest harlots. But one bright day in May, at the start of my sixteenth year, as I sauntered through Beverley market, gently humming a new song over and over to fix it in my mind, and delighting in the morning, I saw a girl I had noticed before (I cannot say today how many times) coming along from St Mary's church, and for a wonder she walked alone. Hitherto there had always been a mother or an elder brother or a maid at her elbow as she tripped upon her saucy toes in or out of the holy mass. I had not dared gaze overtly and yet I had poignantly noticed. She was small-shaped, neat-waisted, raven-haired, black-eyed, lovely beyond all. And she had noticed me, I was sure of it. So I found myself, that fine May morning, walking quietly alongside her. She turned her face to me and smiled. I cannot say how long we had walked before I was aware of the smile.

> Nor can I seye by what swyft sleye devyce
> Dame Venus, quene of mischeef, did entyce
> This maydenes fingres into myne: it felle
> Betwene us thanne so smothe, tonge can nat telle.

When we saw that we were walking quite shamelessly hand-in-hand, we at once became afraid we might be seen: we stole through the busy people into the shadow of the market cross and sat down on its steps behind a clutter of greengrocers' carts, well hidden and still hand-in-hand. We had not yet exchanged a single word. After a while we decided we should know each other's names. She was Barbara, daughter of a wealthy widow. Her father, a lawyer, had been the Beverley town clerk; she was scarce fourteen; no hope, none at all, she would ever be allowed to keep company with a minstrel's apprentice. Yet we knew from that moment, all in a glow, it was impossible we should ever break our unspoken compact. That is to say, *I* knew. She gave me to believe that she knew it too. I am not now so sure that she enacted a lie to me, even though for the great part of my life I've had every bitter reason to believe that she did.

Will you credit me when I tell you that for two full years and a half I frequented her company whenever I could, in deeply amorous secret, arranging meetings by means of her maid, deceiving not only her family but my master and his household, and yet in all that time I never lay with her carnally, nor did more than press her hand and kiss her mouth and now and again touch my fingertips (and once, indeed, my quivering lips) to the nipple of her most delicate breast? Yet it is true. She and I, in those days, were so foolishly lost in maze-like mysteries of poetic love, the theme indeed of every song I'd ever made, that we most drastically submitted to the chastity, the spirituality, of the lover's service of his mistress until such bejewelled time as she . . . As she what? Until such time as she thought fit **to lette hym in**. Of necessity by the slowest degrees.

There were hours when I wondered would she ever think fit? She laughed when I uttered my doubts, protesting that being a minstrel-boy I was more dangerous than I knew, that maybe she would do herself wrong to yield to a young sprig who thought first of his important verses and only after that would take note of a living girl of flesh and blood and uncertain temper – which indeed she admitted to be her most pungent vice. Besides, she said, she had her drawings, and the full attention of the master who taught her; if she learnt the accomplishment thoroughly it would be quite as important as any of my old rhymes. (Did I explain they were training her to make designs for embroidery? Beverley girls of her station were never allowed to be idle. She must work to enhance her value as the bride of some noteworthy citizen.) At this hint of her drawing master and his possible gropings and whisperings, I went wild with callow jealousy. I gripped her by the arm, leaving a wicked bruise; I would there and then have rummaged **hir coy & tendre cunte**; she broke away from me in horror; and I shook with an equal horror to recognise my filthiness. For weeks she refused to speak to me. I wept in corners. I tried to hang myself. And yet at length she reversed her countenance to be (so it seemed) as warm and as merry as ever she had been, and we basked in our love like two pigeons.

It so happened I fell ill. Burning headaches and delirium, I think a mixture of too much love stopped-short and too many venereal songs. They called it inflammation of the brainpan, shaved my skull and put leeches on my back. I had no choice but to lie in bed in my master's house, tended by his wife and her maid. I persuaded the maid to carry secret messages to Barbara's maid, telling her to tell her mistress how I was. The answers, several times, came full of affection; but of course it was not possible that my Barbara herself could come. And then there was no answer. The maid told me that Barbara had apparently left town. She told me too that Barbara's maid was in disgrace and not allowed out of the house. I concluded at once that our love had been revealed; I tossed and writhed in that wearisome bed until they thought I would never recover.

I did recover and walked the streets like a distracted little pedlar with no customers and nothing to sell. I hoped to meet . . . to hear . . . to find . . . I cannot tell you what I hoped; but suddenly one drear evening, taking shelter under a penthouse from a shower of rain, I saw Barbara's maid crouched down in the shadows next to me, and in a very bad way, the poor child. She told me through her tears that she had been imprisoned in the house, and then beaten by Barbara's brother until the blood came, and then cast out, so that all she could do to keep from starvation was to sell herself in mucky lanes. They had held her responsible for the runaway wedding, when the only thing she'd ever hoped for was that her mistress might run away with me.

'Wedding? In Jesu's name, what wedding?'

'Oh, but I'd made sure you knew? Alas, not a word from her till it was too late for me to stop her; she went off with the sailorman to Hull, they seemingly found a chaplain on a German ship from Hamburg, and he . . . Oh, Mr Jacob, how your heart must have broken. I am even more sorry for you than for myself.' Whereupon she offered her desperate young flesh to me and asked no payment, she had taken such liking to me all the days of those secret messages. And I, being so slain by her tidings, there and then took hold of her haunches and **steeryd** her all standing (first time ever in my life) on that wet and slimy doorstep. I even gave her some coins from the few that I had in my purse.

It turned out that I knew of this sailorman; a ship-captain in fact, from some far strand of the Baltic waters, and notorious. I had seen him once or twice along the riverside with Barbara's thick-necked brother, negotiating (I supposed) a mercantile contract. His name was Haukyn Grizzlebeard, one blue eye and one brown, old enough to be her father – no, grandfather! Men said he was a smuggler and probably a pirate; he lived wherever his ship was, Hull, Whitby, Scarborough, Tynemouth, Lynn, Trondheim or the islands of Frisia. A tall devil, narrow-faced, swarthy. I had never admired the look of him; and now of course I hated him. At last I went to Hull in a fury to find him out; and there he was, at nearly midnight, roaring among mates in a harbour-front tavern. 'Where's your wife?' says I, stuttering wildly.

He looks at me with quiet attention, blue eye shut, brown eye open. 'Where she should be, in my bed. She may be little more than a child, but she needs no squawking child to run after her. **Aweye, boy, else Ile mark yow.**' Not wise: I had my knife out and marked him before he could move, from the lower lid of his closed eye to the corner of his dirty mouth. First time ever in my life I'd used a blade against a man, indeed I failed to kill him, but his blood flew into my face all hot, it was enough. I was lucky to be able to run from that place unscathed; I was however light-footed, they were drunk, and I managed it.

Did I explain that Barbara was able to read and even write a little? At all events, she sent a tortuously-penned letter, slipped to me in the street by a ship's boy who didn't dare speak to me. She wrote:

> **Yonge sir, nevir Swete sir namore y-wis, bot Sowre:**
> **Lette thyne Knyf lette thee knowe why we shall nevir**
> **agayne have deallyngs. Ych hadde y-wysshed to have sent**
> **myne Sorrwe that unpardonwyse Ych went fro thee when**

thow was mortalle-seke, when all being hastif and thundersclappe, what else to doe? Oh bot myne Herte to-yerned in
swich sorrwe all ways; bot nowe towaard thyselven Nevir.
Ych am that Barbara that was thyne.

And a month or so after that, they told me my father was hanged.
He had been poaching the king's deer in Pickering Forest, silly old
fool. Why could he not keep to his rabbits? Thereupon Sir Thomas
de Wake sent word to my master that he would pay my apprentice
fees no longer: it was clear I was a boy of bad blood, unregenerate
and so forth (he had heard of my stabbing of Grizzlebeard), the
Wakes should never be seen to nourish such people. This was
calamity. I had two years to go before I gained my indentures; my
master could not afford to retain me unpaid-for. But he spoke on
my behalf to a priest of his acquaintance, and in the upshot I was
admitted to holy orders much against my will, and became as you
know me, Clerk Thickpenny – not very learned, but deadly
unregenerate, scorning the wrongs and foul inequities of this world.

As for Throstle Elspeth: in those days she was a long-haired girl
who sang with a troupe of women under patronage of the Countess
of Lancaster, travelling out of York here, up and down the Great
North Road. Her father had been a trumpeter in the service of a
knight of Dunfermline: this knight through affairs of state became
obnoxious to the King of Scots, and must flee for his life into
Northumberland. The only one of his people to follow him was the
trumpeter, a loyal man indeed but not sagacious. The trumpeter's
little daughter came too, over the hills in midwinter, strapped like a
cloakbag across her father's saddle. And then the father died, and
she must make her own happiness as best as she could in England
among the musicians of England; she felt always out of place, she
told me, even with lovers and good friends. As a minstrel-boy I'd
met her often; we were good friends. We joked and we tussled. A
formidable stark young creature, golden as a haystack and as huge.
Somehow, after Barbara (two years after? three?), she and I came
together. A welcome engrafting, surely, her unconscionable lechery
conjoined with my sorrow: why should either of us care I was

nowadays no minstrel but a cleric under rules? I made one most desolate song about Barbara and then no more:

> **Ho, ha-ro, wo!**
> **Lost love doth hurt myne hert-rote so,** *(etcetera.)*

A song I never sang to Elspeth. After that I am a poet of anger and strength and the sweaty contrary lives of the mere English, north and south. And so it all goes on, oh oh for how long? Call it two-score years – long enough, oh good enough, you will surely agree with me there.

And so they send for me to Scarborough. No omen, no augury, no nothing: I take the road with simple fervour, expecting friendship and good work and good money in my wallet. And that's how it is, until something else happens, something utterly other: how in heaven, hell or middle-earth should anyone believe it? Impossible, insensate. I'd not been there two days, I was walking the quay with fishermen to see where to place stages for their saint-play, all manner of folk on and off the crowded ships, bales of cargo swinging from cranes, barrels rolled down gangplanks, drunken deckhands hustled aboard so the vessel could catch the tide – in the middle of all this, Barbara. Dressed in black with a trim of silver braid, moving swiftly, gliding almost, through the press, and her face turned toward me, absolutely toward me – do you know, although she showed herself forty years and more older, the coiled hair beneath her kerchief shining whiter than wave-tops, she remained as neat and straight as ever she had been? No less lovely. No less loving. All rancour (so it seemed to me) forgotten, the smile upon her gentle mouth the very smile so sweet, so dangerous, that she wore at fourteen.

No sense to it, impossible, two-score long long years and she knew me and she smiled?

I broke away from those fishermen, I ran after her, crying aloud. Too late, I'd lost sight of her. Or was she ever there at all? We'd all been drinking through the noonday, I was making my own daft visions: forget them, I had work to do.

That work, day by day, became less and less effective. The guild began to fear they had picked the wrong playmaker. Not that I did not try, but my mind was all abroad: I could not concentrate upon St Peter, his doings amongst his boats, the disgrace of the cockcrow, his imprisonments, his crucifixion; even the glory of his vaunted popedom failed to kindle my ardour. For I must write for you what was happening: every day, somehow, somewhere, between the heaped-up cottages, the store-houses, the sail-lofts, the ropewalks of the seaport, and never very close to me, I would see her for barely an instant, all in black just as before, neat-waisted, small-shaped, walking away from me speedily with that saucy birdlike gait I so well remembered. Each time I saw her she turned her head to look at me, and she smiled, and . . . Each time I saw her I felt sure that she was . . . I must write, yet I hardly know how. Each time I saw her she was younger than the time before, until at last on the seventh day she was no more than, at a guess, between twenty and thirty? And this time her gown was white embroidered with gold and her hair in its golden net was as black as a raven. And this time she beckoned to me.

I must write that the fisherman's guild, with blunt forthrightness, upon that very same day had informed me they would find another poet to make their play. They paid me for my trouble and no doubt thought I would return to York. But I saw her. She beckoned. I followed. Up steps, along the cliff, past higgledy-piggledy cottages, ten or a dozen of them, to a fair stone tile-roofed house, newly built, bright paintwork still fresh on door and window-shutters. A small enough dwelling, just a ground floor and garret, but no mere fisher's house; a master mariner's, at least. Keeping all the time a few paces ahead of me, she led me to the door, took a key from her purse, unlocked, and beckoned me in.

The house-place with its long window was as well kept and cleanly as you would guess from the outside. There was a hearth with a seacoal fire, a square of costly carpet on the table, vessels of burnished plate ranged upon shelves, fragrant herbs among the floor-rushes: a species of small palace indeed, no less lovely to the eye than its mistress. I choked at the sight of it, the sweet scent of the herbs, the sweet scent of my Barbara: I could not venture to speak. But she spoke, softly, kindly, all those innocent words once again that she'd given me when we were mere children; she regretted all that had passed (she said), she desired to see me often, 'my man being far at sea,' she said, 'that lethal vehement man, my Haukyn, as splendid as a flaming peak of Iceland, who tore out my girlish heart and chewed it and gnawed it and reshaped it between his teeth.' Had he not given her leave (she said) to make me her guest, out of penitence for his sometime jealousy? And yet we must not mock him with it, for who could say when he would return? No, I was not to embrace her. Hold her hand, I might do that . . . She saw I carried my gittern – 'For the sake of our old secrecy, play to me, sweetheart-Jacob, sing.' I played her all the songs I had written for her in those days and the one I wrote afterwards. She asked for that one twice. I said nothing of Throstle Elspeth, nor did she. Then she led me by the hand to the door, and out. I was to come again tomorrow. With my instrument, my songs, and all my hopes . . . Hopes for what? The deeds of Venus? True, she was no longer the girl I remembered but changed (and how so? No sense to it at all) into a well-grown young woman of illegible deep meaning, while I myself was so direly and plausibly diminished after full forty years of it, **an olde hoorhede with yerde y-shrunken**, in a soup-stained threadbare cassock. And what age, in God's name, was her husband?

Nonetheless, the next day I went back, and the day after that: indeed the greater part of a week. I quite forgot to go to York. Each day then it was songs, honeyed speech and the touching of fingers, the turning-over of her pages of tiny drawings that she had made. While Grizzlebeard rode the waves, she limned in her loneliness these pictures to the tale of Troy, to the romances of King Arthur, to some strangely uncanonical Gospels – in short, to each of the books that she kept (so she said) at her bed's head. She had drawn lovers in firelit rooms, or among flowers in a forest, kissing, clasping, groaning and moaning: they were as vivid as a beetle's glimpse of the debaucheries of fairyland, but she would not let me talk about them. She showed me, that was all. By the same token, I thought it notable that she had in her house no crucifix, nor other usual image of any person of the Holy Trinity, save for one small dark carving of what I took to be the Blessed Virgin, crudely hacked long ago from a lump of driftwood (as I guessed) and not comfortable to look at. All I could see of the Christchild was two wide uncanny eyes peeping between the folds of her cloak **lyke unto a puddokke fro his hole**, while what should have been her feet seemed somehow more of a fishtail. Had it maybe been marred by woodworm? At all events, I was not to talk about it.

And then, at last, all my hopes. And how did she grant them but **hastif and thundersclappe**? all at once upon a Sunday morning as the church bells were ringing for Mass. 'Sweetheart-Jacob,' she suddenly breathed, 'it is time for you to take off my clothes, standing here, yes, here, here, in the embrasure of old Haukyn's window, here, here, shutters open in full heat of the morning sun. No one shall see us save the fishes in the tide; and you shall lie with me upon his window-seat where for hours on end he loves to sit like a cormorant on a rock, keeping watch upon the coastwise shipping – see, I have piled it with cushions.' Yet I had not unfastened more than one of the tags of her gown when she jerked strongly away from me, white-faced, gasping; her hand all-of-a-tremble pointed out between the window-bars. Weathering the castle point, in toward the harbour, crept a high-sided vessel of the sort they call **an almayne cogge**, red stripes on a black hull, and a great red sail. She cried out at it: 'See! it is his ship, **y-clept _Mary Gipsy_ of Flensburg**, I could never mistake it, old Haukyn comes home from his voyage! To be sure he regrets his jealousy: to regret, though, is not to forget. Ah but no knives! Just you take, dear sweetheart-Jacob, your road back to York, just go.'

She hurried me out of the house, stopping my protestations with her fingertips against my lips, whispering urgently that she would surely let me know when all was made easy and I must come to her again. 'How let me know? How?' Ah, she said, she'd find a way, I'd understand it when it came to pass. Which it did, in the middle of the night, her pleading small voice like a bradawl between my ears, to the fright and spitting anger of Elspeth. It is a fact, I reached Scarborough without halting for sleep even once, and my only food and drink was in mouthfuls from my hand as I walked. I strode into her house at sundown. She lay waiting for me, stripped.

Nought to tikkle hir tawny pelt   save a torcque of whyte dayeseyes:
And rose-blosmes whyte and reed,   full randomlich y-wrethed.
Fre-lymbed upon depe furres   by the herthe of a grete fyre
She gaf wellcome withynne hir warmthe,   so wylde was the streetch of
   hir arms.

No words, for hours, it seemed. Only her unutterable kindness. And then she whispered, just to mention that she had heard how the *Mary Gipsy* had weighed anchor in the Humber upon a northerly course; some time before tomorrow night (as she guessed) we would spy his sail again. 'Black sail tomorrow,' she said. 'For that will be his certain choice. Alas, it is the colour of his soul . . . But not yet, oh not yet.'

Whereupon, most amorously, she bit me hard into the neck: I bear the trace of her teeth even now, you may see.

They have told me Throstle Elspeth came into that house and saw us. If she did, I am truly sorry. But I did not see her, nor did I hear her. Which is all of a piece with the strangeness of the circumstance. At any rate, in that paradise I must have slept, must I not? for they have told me it was a full week before your summoner came to seize me. I woke to hear him shouting, as it were in a dream of vile bloodshed. I staggered to my feet, I think, and fumbled for my gittern. But the catchpolls had already gripped me. I had a sort of last glimpse of poor Barbara, appalling: it could only have been an illusion. She was spreadeagled open-mouthed upon her back, and beyond her, against the wall, the stooped shape of a sailorman in foul-weather gear, tarred jacket and hood. I say 'shape' because it was no more than a shape; when it lifted its head and I saw inside the hood, the face all fallen away almost to the bone of the skull, no eyes in the sockets, and grey-green bits of beard that hung from the grinning jaws like seaweed; while as for her, her bare body covered most horribly with blotches and weeping sores. She gave vent, I think, to sobs of pain and her eyes being mere bog-holes of pus.

Holy Rode of evir-ryghtwise Crist,   what rottennesse ransakkit hir so?

THE ARCHDEACON'S ADDENDA

Written the i July, Feast of Ss. Julius & Aaron of Caerleon, Martyrs.

As soon as he finished the deposition to which I subtend these lines, he demanded that his 'wife' be fetched to hear him read it – indeed, he said, his 'fornicatress', if that's what we preferred – she did not understand Latin, but she'd always been well able (until very lately) to read his heart from his face. He felt sure, with some improvised translation of needful phrases as he went along, she would follow his meaning. Without her, he would say nothing, not ever again, to nobody, not even if we tortured him with hooks. Devoured by curiosity, what else could we do but fetch her? She sat mute, her battered countenance a good match for his. He and she alike were filthy and in chains and much hurt; they avoided each other's eyes. He read the writing, slowly, without passion. As she listened to him she began to smile. A cruel smile, perhaps; at all events a knowing one. It was as though he were transparent to her and nothing if not familiar, yet she seemed to be astonished he was truly as he was. When he finished, she turned her eyes on him. 'Ah, Jake,' she growled darkly in her crooked Pictish jargon: impossible to transcribe it fairly into the tongue of Saint Jerome. 'Hard to say whether I hate you worse that you'd coupled with a phantom than had it been hot flesh-and-blood. I thought the latter, found the former, it drove me mad. As for now, I have no clearness as to you and your doings, none.'

I told her that he and she would be returned to their cells until I had had time to sift the whole business. I was not yet persuaded that either of them told me the truth. Those verses in his deposition were a bad sign.

Written the i September, Feast of S. Drithelm of Melrose, Monk.

I sent my secretary to Scarborough; he was there a month and found out nothing. The barbarous people were either in thrall to some heathen superstition or concealing a guilty secret. In the end I had to go myself. I brought two of the minster canons with me, to give the appearance of a tribunal of justice; we sat in the castle hall and held a solemn enquiry, sworn witnesses and threats of the gaol-house. We returned to York yesterday evening.

To begin with, I discovered no more than the summoner had discovered, no more than the woman Elspeth. Jacob of Thickpenny had indeed sat in the ruin of a ship-captain's house and communed with himself like a born idiot ... But little by little I dug out and dragged up all manner of bits and pieces of most untoward history; his disingenuous deposition began to make some sense. For the ship-captain, yes, was an outlandish man called Haukyn, said to be a Finn, thus by popular belief a sea-warlock schooled in spells and transformations; his wife, yes, was Barbara, supposedly a Beverley girl; he had lived at luxurious expense, building his house brand new, filling it with costly goods beyond all ever seen in the town; no one doubted that such stuff had come to him through bloodthirsty rapine. The people were afraid of him; they did not dare ask him questions; he was said to go to mass but rarely, if at all; to confession, it was said, never. Likewise his wife; the priest was afraid of them both.

And here is the first difficulty. It is all of forty-two years since this Haukyn arrived in Scarborough. He dwelt there no more than ten years, and then came a terrible ending, in 1349 if calculations are correct. He set sail in his ship, the *Saint Mary of Egypt* (that was indeed the name), giving out he was bound for Denmark. His wife, as she often did, voyaged with him. Woe alas! it was Good Friday. Impious, imprudent, ill-augured embarkation! ... Three days after Corpus Christi (these dates are exact) *Saint Mary of Egypt* was found drifting against a lee shore in Bridlington Bay, every creature aboard her a mouldering corpse, himself and herself and the men of his crew, struck down by the great pestilence, for was it not the second year of its outbreak? The Bridlington fishers who came to seek salvage took one look at them over the bulwarks. In fear and great haste they tossed lamp-oil onto the decks and threw a blazing torch in after it, and so set the vessel afire with all its grisly company. And little good they got of it. Willy-nilly the plague came to Bridlington, from Haukyn's ship or wherever else; it slew where it listed and ran north to Scarborough. And thence westward once more to York, where already it had wreaked (as we foolishly thought) its worst.

And here is the second difficulty. That house, deserted, shunned, thought to be accursed, was unroofed and flung down as long ago as 1362 in the great tempest of that year. Moreover, in this present year (1381) Corpus Christi was the very day before the night when the man Jacob felt a voice like a bradawl in his brain, and three days thereafter he was wrapped in the arms of the succubus. These dates are exact. It is clear he knew nothing of the death of his Barbara before hearing it from me last night; he received the news with ghastly visage but insisted that 'it made no difference'.

I write 'succubus' with intent. She had teeth, they were sharp, I looked close at his neck and I saw. Therefore she was no revenant, no wraith of his old love, for such spirits are intangible. Nor can she have been, as he stubbornly asserts, her miraculous reality, flesh and blood and still alive: only were she a saint from heaven could the phenomenon be possible. No no, it was a noxious DEMON! sent expressly in her false guise to deceive him to his ruin. (And yet I must wonder why? For Lucifer, I suppose, being an activated compound of each and every Deadly Sin, is like to be most slothful as well as malignant, and averse to needless effort. So what caused him to elaborate so complex a charade, if all that he meant was to bring old Jacob to damnation? Surely the silly wretch was already halfway there, with his spiteful little levelling rat-rhymes? A puzzle.) No, but I have argued with Jacob, and argued; it is impossible to persuade him. Nor, dreadful to tell, will the woman Elspeth accept it. She insists she knows 'the poor fool's heart from his very face', that he made his own Barbara by himself for himself *out of the power of his poetry*, wonder of wonders. Interpretation bad enough, implication even worse: that humankind constructs its devils to suit its private fantasy, by extension creates its God. Moreover she has ignored the creature's teeth.

Alas, the tale he told us was an adventure quite barren of God. Were he – and indeed she – a pair of infidels on a shore of Africa they would surely have made reference to their own eschatology, however idolatrous, if only to afford some moral proportion to the events they recounted. Whereas they are Christians and appear to have forgotten the fact. Forgotten all they were ever taught. Ah God, the woman Elspeth has caused me to wonder what indeed *is* a demon? Would I know one if I saw it? My administrative capabilities can put no order upon such ravelment. Ah God, what am I to do with this most questionable pair? Save to keep them and feed them at diocesan expense and pray over them daily until some ecclesiast more strenuous than myself may determine are they heretics? are they atheists? are they witchcraft people, heaven preserve us? and in the end, shall they be burned? How long until 'until'? – beyond that I am at a loss, indeed distracted.

There is another grave article to distress my spirit. It is said that the king's promise to pardon the lesser rebels has deliberately been broken, and that men are being hunted all over the south parts, chained, whipped, dragged at the horsetail, gelded and hanged. I know it is often asserted that 'we are not bound to keep Word with heretics or traitors', but – I know I cannot be sure any longer whose indeed *is* the Word, mine or my creator's, but – I know I am hideously crying all night long to the clouds of night, 'Who created whom, himself or myself, *who*?' For the first time in my life, my religion is overtaken, I am shaking from head to foot, my bowels are pierced with anguish.

Written the viii September, Feast of the Nativity of the Blessed Virgin.
Jacob of Thickpenny has died in his cell. He refused all food from the writing of his narrative onwards, accepting only a few possets piped into his gut at my violent insistence. He refused the sacrament of confession, whether from myself or from any other priest. He refused all talk of holiness. He refused all talk of anything. In the end he lay sleeping day and night among his straw; this morning the gaoler was unable to wake him. I am conturbed with remorse and sorrow: we were punishing him as yet for neither sin nor crime, we merely held him until ... Indeed no need, no need for this most fearful unhouseled departure. He has thereby rendered his lying soul to the Father of Lies. (Or so I would persuade myself, my conscience straining hard against wanton compassion.)

And worse: the woman Elspeth is also dead. Fast locked within her cell and nobody told her (I am sure of it) what fate had befallen the other. So how did she know? She stood up in her rattling chains 'like the tower of Lebanon' in the poetry of Solomon 'that looketh toward Damascus, fair as the moon, clear as the sun and terrible as an army with banners'.

'Aha, you damned Jake,' she cried, 'you have gone from me yet again. I followed you up before and I follow you now: and there'd best be no Barbara where you go.' She fell down upon her face, rigid, pouring blood from mouth and nostrils onto the flagstones. The apothecary made no bones of it: an apoplexy. There are those, he explained, who can compel such a seizure of their own strong will and despair. Thus it might have been with her. Indeed no need, no need. My bowels are pierced with anguish. Shall God forgive?

    Forgive. Forgive.

        Mouth and nostrils.

            Teeth in the neck.

Pierced.

BREACH OF TRUST

– but there's no knowing.
Very true.
We may, and we may not.
Right.

Futurity is dark.
As a cellar.
Men are moles.

R. B. Sheridan, *St Patrick's Day*

Nearly two hundred years ago, in a set of dingy rooms on the third floor of a Soho tenement house, a couple of industrious but threadbare playwrights wrote, slept, ate, talked, and entertained their bachelor comrades amid the stench of tobacco and brandy. The elder was Tom Longshank; the younger, Erasmus Grail. In theatrical or Grub-street or drinking-cellar circles they were understood to be fast friends for all adventures, arm-in-arm strollers and striders of the midnight pavements. 'Black Jack' Kemble, the actor-manager, cried out against them once in a spurt of rage, 'Two dogs upon one leash: make a grab at the one and the other will tear your balls off!' (They had come to his office, arm-in-arm, to revile him for his rejection of Longshank's new comedy. 'Picked from the pocket of Sheridan's corpse' had been his insulting critique. He very nearly found himself fighting a duel with the pair of them.)

Longshank was lean, lined and stooped; Grail's features were rotund and florid, deceptively boyish, his body thickset, his hair a red-blond sunburst. This physical contrast, together with the notable difference in age, only served to emphasise the strength of their attachment. In the autumn of 1820, when the attachment abruptly shifted its shape – by the intrusion of a third party, a most unexpected female – Longshank would have been about sixty years old, Grail twenty-eight or thirty. They had all the superficial appearance of ... what? Master and apprentice? Colonel and subaltern? Father and son? Any or all of these, take your pick.

Not that the 'superficial appearance' was seen in the same way by everyone. Some men said 'sodomy', a few others told a tale of the scandalous submission of an elderly yet hitherto innocent debauchee to his youthful preceptor in all manner of secret vice (sodomy perhaps included). Nobody ever showed any evidence for the truth of such rumours, although it has to be said there was *some* justification for them, at any rate for the speculations that created them. It was known that Grail and Longshank did pay their occasional visits together to whores' parlours off the Haymarket; they neither boasted about it nor deliberately kept it secret; but (just as they shared their lodgings) certain aspects of these lecheries were also, as it were, *shared*, in a veiled and rather depraved sort of way, which might have meant this, or it might have meant that, and who among their acquaintance could really be quite sure?

Nonetheless, however intimate the privacy of their enjoyments, as professional writers they never echoed one another, either in subject matter or style.

Longshank for many years was a regular protégé or unpaid employee of the late R. B. Sheridan, a sort of secretary-cum-stage-manager. After the great man's death he staunchly continued in his footsteps with well-constructed classical comedies. Whenever possible he had them produced at Sheridan's old theatre, Drury Lane; some of them were very nearly successful. Yet invariably they failed to supply their earnest author with the full satisfaction he craved. Nor were his audiences quite as pleased with the work as they should have been: every opening night, inevitably, there was the same scarcely perceptible flaw in the rhythm of their applause. They admired, but they could not enjoy. Good comedies frequently contain an ingredient of melancholy. Longshank's however were positively sullen; where they were satirical, they were sour beyond all expectation.

There was a reason for this, which Longshank only partly

understood and other people never thought of at all. Nearly thirty years before, when he was the same age as his friend Grail was now, he had travelled to Paris, burning with zeal for the new revolution. Back in England after six months of Gallic political delirium, he vehemently pitched himself into compacts and conspiracies to promote the radical cause – which is to say, by the standards of William Pitt's government, the *treasonable* cause. He did have the protection of Sheridan, as far as it went. Even so, he only contrived to escape Botany Bay by dint of a whispered warning from a sympathetic actress (who slept with a cabinet minister and kept her ears as wide open as her legs). There followed a change of name and a flight by post chaise to the wilds of the Pennine north where nobody knew him. For the next two decades of war against France, he lurked in obscurity as a resentful semi-outlaw, working where he could as actor or hack writer in one provincial theatre after another, brimming with hatred for the noisy wartime patriotism, the worship of Nelsons and Wellingtons, the continuous brassy renderings from the orchestra pit of 'God Save the King', 'Rule Britannia', 'Heart of Oak' or 'The British Grenadiers'.

'Oh God,' he used to groan into his hat as he stood in the wings, 'what would I not give for just a couple of bars of the "Marseillaise" or "Ça ira"?'

And after the war, when the Home Office sleuth-hounds had surely long forgotten him, he saw the political landscape even uglier than before; but he did not dare attempt any action against it. He had had too bad a fright. So the fright, and the hatred, and the groans and the resentful obscurity, all worked themselves willy-nilly into every play he wrote. Perhaps he should have given up comedy altogether, but high tragedy was beyond his powers and he knew it.

As for popular melodrama, a conceivable alternative, he affected a perfunctory scorn: 'Bellowing and bombast – transparently maudlin devices of plot – sword-fights as with butchers' cleavers in a hubbub in the shambles – tears and laughter tossed together more hideously rebarbative, oh yes! than a salad of damned nettles and dock leaves.' Words which made Grail rock with laughter until he hiccuped, for Grail in his vulgar way wrote nothing but melodramas, and upon occasions triumphed with them – not at Drury Lane, but on the boards of less reputable houses across the river, the Coburg or the Surrey. Playwrights there earned very little money although they did enjoy audiences of ruffianly gusto and actors of the most improbable versatility.

If sumptuous persons boasting elegant taste sat and smirked now and then in the side-boxes of these low establishments, it was not so much a tribute to artistry as an arrogant, wide-eyed wonder at the ludicrous diversions of the herd. Often, so it seemed, *intimidating* diversions. When Erasmus Grail was the playwright of the night, intimidation was hot and deliberate. He had never been so foolish as to actually join any seditious political club; Longshank's experience was more than enough to deter him. He preferred to parade his defiance in the theatre. He made certain that each of his insolent plays should celebrate some such hero as Richard Parker, intrepid bluejacket, naval mutineer of 1797, or a redoubtable heroine like Big Marianne the coster-wife, who led the women of the Paris market stalls when they hauled out King Louis from his lair in Versailles to face the rage and justice of the people.

Of course Grail upheld the blaring colour of his own writings against the austere drawing-room wit of Longshank's; and of course Longshank implored young Grail to show some decency and dramatic decorum. Despite all, they very deeply respected each other, and even respected each other's work, for both of them understood that their essential opinions were by and large the same, save for two points of difference. First, their manner of expression, and in truth that was no more than a personal taste. (In the same way, Erasmus fried bacon and eggs for his breakfast, and Tom devoured nothing but porridge.) And then, second, Erasmus was sanguine. Revolution, he believed, remained a possibility – for God's sake, a likelihood! – whereas Tom would mutter tetchily, 'No! Finished and done, man, defeated. All gone.'

It was therefore a huge surprise when the pessimist decided in his hoar-headed age to marry a young wife; and the wife that he chose was the very same bright-eyed, swift-laughing, enchanting little creature who not two months before had brusquely rejected the hand of the optimist. She was a Miss Twigget, actress, the soubrette of the Coburg Theatre stock company; she played servant girls and such; she was mischievous and arch, both on the stage and off; her christian name was Roseanna and her audiences adored her. Erasmus Grail quite lost his heart.

He first met her when she appeared in one of his melodramas as a bold and resourceful barmaid. He invited her to visit him, to clamber upstairs to the Soho third floor. She made no finicking demur, but took care to be genteelly chaperoned by a vigilant bosom friend. Erasmus introduced his giggling guests to 'Old Tom, my walking conscience', and gallantly administered cups of sweet tea and goes of cherry brandy and a dish of devilled bones with cress and cucumber on the side. 'Old Tom' was no less gallant; he bowed his lips over Roseanna's hand and assured her how much he had enjoyed her performance in Grail's play (where she misled the cunning thief-takers so that her truelove Dick Turpin could gallop away safe along the Great North Road).

'It meant a great deal to me,' he said. 'For don't you know, it's all quite true. A quarter-century ago, I had an adventure very nearly exactly the same. A brave girl saved *my* life. Thief-takers, oh yes. Spies and entrapment-men. I told it to ... ah, Mr Grail, and thereupon Mr Grail purloined it for his plot.'

Roseanna and the bosom friend begged him to recount the full story but he shuffled it aside with a kind of embarrassed diffidence, and then he excused himself. He had work to do, at his desk in the next room, would the ladies forgive him if he left them with ... ah, with Mr Grail? Of course they would, oh yes.

Later that night, Grail had it out with Longshank. What the deuce did the old bugger mean by all this 'Mr Grail' nonsense? 'You either call me "Grail" or you call me "Erasmus"; and don't you ever dare say to anyone ever again that I have *purloined* your damned memoirs! You told me that tale on purpose to enable me to use it in a play, like you're always telling me tales when they don't fit your own style of stagecraft; and you bloody well know that that's true.'

'True? – to be sure, oh yes. Just as *I* know it's bloody well true that you've been courting that little doxy for a matter of several weeks: I could tell it from the way you talked together. Yes, Mr Grail, weeks! and never one word of it in all that time to *me*. Breach of fraternité, breach of égalité, breach of all our co-operative customs, absolute breach of trust! D'you propose to make amends?'

Of course, before morning the angry spat was patched up, as such spats between them commonly were, with an exchange of apologies, grudging at first and then fervent. But Longshank took note that Grail did not offer to *explain* Roseanna Twigget in any detail, nor did he promise to invite her again to their rooms. Thus a subterranean spite, such as they'd never known before, was now inserted deep into the bachelor attachment; it would take more than fair words to uproot it.

Old Tom went very quietly up and down among appropriate theatres, he made a few enquiries at stage doors and green rooms. Without too much difficulty he soon discovered the whereabout of Miss Twigget's lodgings: Mermaid Court, a little entry opening out of the Borough High Street.

He then took to haunting those nooks and corners of Southwark that lay between Mermaid Court and the Coburg. A particular beershop attracted him, with a bow window where he could sit at his pipe and glass and look out upon Webber Street in both directions. And at length his small strategy fulfilled itself. It was a dark November evening of pouring rain and roaring west wind; Roseanna Twigget came hastening past, all in a bustle and flurry, no doubt on her way home from rehearsal. Her high pattens on the paving stones went click-clack-click, her umbrella went *whoosh*! as the wind caught it, and the wheel of a young buck's curricle splashed her with wet mud from ankle to collarbone. She floundered against a lamp-post and was astonished to find Old Tom at her side with an arm around her waist and his own umbrella open above her head.

'You'll allow me, I'm sure, Miss Twigget: your brolly seems to have blown itself clear inside-out and mine is a far stronger article

... I take it you don't perform tonight, as already you've left the theatre?'

No, she said, he had guessed it correctly, thank heaven! A night to herself was rare enough and very welcome, but oh, what a shame it was such filthy weather. 'The manager changed the bill at the very last minute,' she added. 'If he'd given us forewarning, I might have forewarned that slowcoach Erasmus; he and I could have had supper together.'

Thereupon, by implication rather than direct statement, Old Tom told Roseanna a lie: he let her think that he'd understood Erasmus to have said – though he admitted he could just possibly have *mis*-understood – to have said he'd be out of town for maybe as much as a day or two. In the meantime, perhaps Miss Twigget might do *him* the remarkable honour of going with him to find some supper – at some suitably respectable establishment – might he suggest the new chophouse in the Gray's Inn Road? They could catch a cab from the next corner ... She need not be afraid of how she looked: his own very long scarf would cover the muck on her dress. He was sure she would know how best it could be draped ... Oh yes.

This then was the first of several more or less clandestine meetings, but nothing overtly amorous was ever discussed between them. It is probable that Roseanna did not at first perceive how she was now the object of a madly treacherous courtship: Tom Longshank strove hard to hide the pungency of his newly aroused desire. He was in fact playing a strange double-role with her – Othello and Iago entangled together in the one contorted character. As Othello he spun her his yarns of desperate days among the revolutionists, his 'hairbreadth 'scapes', his 'disastrous chances', until she came, like Desdemona, to 'love him for the dangers he had passed'. And at the same time Iago would squat in his mouth, dropping curious little hints about Grail, who was given (he suggested) to equivocal behaviour that might be said to border upon the degenerate; and who (he suggested further) was notoriously unreliable, not only toward lovers and friends, but even toward his business associates ... 'Oh dear! my dear Miss

Twigget, notoriously, yes.' So she listened to Othello in a glow of admiration, to Iago with perplexity and some dismay.

She nevertheless continued to meet Grail, perhaps as often as three times a week. She did fear she was losing her taste for him, but she could not make up her mind to issue him an outright goodbye. He had promised to create for her a noteworthy part in his new play. He had so far written only two acts out of five. Until the script was finished, it would (she thought) be imprudent not to keep close to him. No question, she kept very close. One night she introduced him to her bedroom in Mermaid Court, where she thoroughly surprised him by her libidinous heat. She also surprised herself. Afterwards, she felt things had gone far too far, but he had been so importunate she could not resist. Her resistance, so she told herself, was always collapsing before such importunate scoundrels. One of these days they'd be making her pregnant despite all her tricks and dodges; she really would have to do something about it.

He finished his play in double-quick time, the manager assured her the noteworthy part was definitely hers, rehearsals were to begin before the end of the year, and everything should have been splendid ... except that nearly every night now Grail seemed to be in Mermaid Court, complacently accepting the frenzy of her bed; how dared the bloody man be so certain she was his? Suppose Old Tom was right about him: 'unreliable' – what might that mean? Should she not put him to the test? If she did not do it directly, it would soon be too late ... She gritted her teeth, stabbed her fingernails into her palms, swerved sideways on her dressing-stool as he bent over her from behind, his hands at her breast to unhook the top of her bodice – 'No!' she gasped quickly, angrily indeed. 'Erasmus, there's to be no more of it, not in this house, no. That vile old bitch my landlady is making demands: if you are to come here, I am to pay for you, I cannot afford it, I don't believe *you* can, my God she is extortionate! So where do we go? Shall I find myself, d'you suppose, a third lodger in your Soho garret, being slipped by way of friendship between the sheets of Tom Longshank?'

'What?' he cried, 'Roseanna! my love, what *do* you mean? Longshank, what, how? Nonsense!'

'It is by no means nonsense, as I can tell by the hang of your lip.

I've heard reports of your manner of life that give me no reason to trust you. I must ask you, Erasmus, without more ado, will you marry me, or not?'

Taken thus off-balance in the midst of his ruttish arousal, he might have answered very nearly anything. In fact he mumbled, 'Yes. Of course, Roseanna, yes. But . . .'

In reply to his reply her voice was an exact mimic of his. ' "But", does he say? "Of course", does he say? Each of 'em cancels the other. And I can tell by the hang of your lip that "but" is the word that shall signify. Erasmus, I'm truly sorry; hooks-and-eyes are finished with; drink up your wine, my dear, and scuttle.'

When she chose to be, she was formidable. He scuttled.

By what strange path through the labyrinth of her passions and her calculations did she arrive (upon St Valentine's Day) before the altar of St Mary Overy's, taking Tom Longshank's ring onto her finger, and swearing like an idiot to obey him till death did them part? She had a bad reason and a good one.

First for the bad reason, as instilled in her by Iago. While Grail was her lover she found in herself such wicked irritation against his friendship with Longshank, that she would happily do almost anything to split the two playwrights asunder. And the good reason? Why, of course, her discovery of her modern-day Othello: she fully believed Longshank to be a quiet heroic man who had acted for years with great courage upon his hazardous convictions. Grail, on the contrary, only wrote about his, and had never been known, ever, to put himself into genuine danger. If Longshank the married man would be anything like the modest yet acerbic raconteur of the Gray's Inn chophouse, then to live with him within four walls would be permanent entertainment. Obedience could be dealt with if and when it came up; she could not think it would make any great problem.

But what about carnality? The 'act of love'? Its consequences moreover? – childbirth? It surely ought all to be weighed one way or another when considering yes or no to wedlock. Unfortunately, Roseanna had not really weighed it at all . . . When Longshank proposed to her, he presented himself first and foremost as a refuge from Erasmus Grail and from all her toil and trouble with him. Implication once again, with very little direct statement ... Poor Old Tom, she understood, was worn out with the effort of keeping up with, and sharing on equal terms, the enigmatic 'depravities' inseparable from his years with Grail. He sought only a gentle and chivalrous relationship with the young woman whom he begged to be his wife.

She also understood him to be trying with some embarrassment to let her know there'd be very little sexual congress in their marriage (if any at all), and he'd never prevent her from following her own natural desires (provided she did it discreetly, and never, oh never, humiliated him). She was barely twenty-two; she'd already had three or four lovers but not one of them older than thirty; the lascivious potential of a grey-whiskered sixty-year-old wrinkle-skin was beyond her imagination; and besides, he let her believe he could find her an engagement next season at Drury Lane. She was cruelly deceived upon very nearly all of these points.

They set up house in the Soho garret. (Grail had taken himself off in a wild derisive snarl of bitter words.) She was right about one thing: there was no straightforward 'congress', the bridegroom could not rise to it. All he wanted to do was to sit fully clothed and stare at her while she spread herself naked across a huddle of red blanket on a ratty black horsehair sofa. He unhappily failed to find work for her at Drury Lane, perhaps because his own work was nowadays such a series of failures. He rarely reminisced with her or chatted, or offered her his sly *sotto voce* jokes. He was grumpy all day long, preoccupied with play-writing, even when he crouched over her to adorn her bare body with cheap jewellery and to fiddle with the braids of her hair. He would curse that none of his friends were trustworthy enough to be fetched up to stare at her with him. 'That squalid little renegade Grail!' he whined, hawking and spitting with malice. 'Why the devil ain't *he* here? Here's where he *ought* to be, here's where I'll wager he wishes to God he'd never left.'

At first she was sorry for him; she thought if she could manage to endure his behaviour with a cheerful sweet spirit, he'd surely be bound to improve ... And then, after thirteen interminable months, she suddenly decided it was time he understood how disgusted and bored she was. She let him know her thoughts. He'd been exceptionally cantankerous all that afternoon; he grinned at her, dribbling, before he spoke. 'You!' (in a deadly whisper) 'You, you filthy foulbed! D'you think I don't know all your goings-on in Monmouth Street? D'you think there's a stage door in London where they don't laugh and jeer about it?'

He went for her with his walking cane. A mistake: she snatched it from him and hit him and hit him until it broke; she left him curled up and sobbing in the ashes of the hearth. Nasty, pathetic old scorpion. But dear Christ, how *had* he found out?

Her dress thrown on all-anyhow, a veil across her face to hide the hot weal he had given her, she ran headlong down the stair and away – to where else but Monmouth Street? – and there, absurdly enough, into the arms of Erasmus Grail. He lived in a verminous kip above an old-clothes shop and spent four-fifths of his money on drink. He had grown so despairing-wretched since the day of her marriage that he was no longer able to write, at least to write anything any manager would be ready to pay for. Roseanna had been secretly meeting him for as long as six months; he was a refuge from the misery of Longshank, but otherwise no good to her at all.

Because she was a married wife, her entire income belonged to her husband. If she were to abandon him and continue to perform at the Coburg, he would instantly go to the courts and clutch hold of every penny that she earned. Grail could not keep her, Grail did not *want* to keep her, he sometimes mounted her with weary grunts, more often they just drank together and slept. As an intermittent mistress coming and going at all hours and sometimes not showing herself for weeks at a time, she seemed only to augment his despair. God knows what they thought they were about. (Unless indeed they truly loved each other: strange notion, but perfectly possible.)

She said, 'God, O God, Erasmus, I do not dare to stay with him a single day longer. Erasmus, I shall *kill* him! Or he will kill *me*. Think, think, man, what's to be done? I can't stop to talk about it, I've to get to the theatre at once, I've to act your bloody barmaid with a cheekbone like half a tomato. Curtain-up in fifty minutes, for God's sake, will you think and then *do* it?'

Did she mean Grail to murder her husband? If not, whatever did she mean?

At all events, there was no murder . . . A sudden death, certainly. For that very same evening, while Grail sat and soaked up the brandy, and Roseanna at the Coburg preserved the life of Turpin for the ninety-ninth time, Tom Longshank was felled by a coronary seizure onto the cobblestones of Greek Street, and that was the end of him.

So now she was free, and what would she do with it? Marry Erasmus? Live with Erasmus unmarried? Go away from Erasmus altogether? In the end she did none of these; because Erasmus went right away from *her*. He never told her why. He just disappeared out of London. In 1825 he returned from his travels, comparatively sober, to be told that Roseanna was set up in a Hampstead cottage by a theatre-loving banker with an 'interest' in Drury Lane. Grail took good pains to avoid her.

He avoided her for a score of years, until one day in front of the Sadlers Wells theatre he chanced to come limping along on his walking cane and stopped to read the playbill:

The Tragedy of MACBETH by Wm. Shakespeare
Mr Phelps as Macbeth!
Miss Twigget as Lady Macbeth!!

He threw himself into an attitude: 'Clytemnestra!' he roared, to any passer-by who might care to hear him. 'That's what she would play, if Phelps gave a damn for the Greeks. But he don't; so in default we make do with the Scotch lady! Sufficiently dreadful, oh I'll grant you, a terror to the heart. As I know. As I have known. I am her fragment.'

Roseanna, at that moment, stepped out of the stage-door entry. When she saw him, she went grey beneath her face-paint. 'Oh cannot you leave me alone!' she cried. And then: 'Why, you're Grail,' with a queer little whimper. 'Grail? And I thought for a moment you ... God, O God, Grail, I quite thought you were *him*.'

True, he was much changed, prematurely lean, lined and stooped, a dissatisfied bristle-haired solitary, too ill-tempered for female companionship. And yet this ageing Grail had become a strong public man, a polemicist, a Chartist orator; he had spent time in prison for incitement to arson and riot; he no longer wrote melodrama. 'I prefer,' he declared, 'to dissect the plutocracy by analytical comedy, though of course it's not so popular. I think I understand at last what Longshank was attempting, poor old sod.'

A GRIM ALL-PURPOSE HALL

If the people of the theatre are riddled with superstition, it is surely because their work is so desperately chancy. Even when subsidies and sponsorships appear to be constant (at least for the next half-season), and audiences keep coming and audiences keep clapping, good luck or bad luck always has the last word. No amount of rehearsal can assure a flawless performance from every member of a cast upon any one night; they are not marionettes, but men and women under threat of accident, emotional stress, sudden illness. A trivial sore throat can bring to an end not only a production but the very company that undertakes it; and as for sudden death...

So for hundreds of years the grotesque tales have gone about, consolatory, defensive, of good omens and bad omens, particular stages, particular dressing-rooms, tunes of music, colours of costumes, particular roles, particular plays – *Dr Faustus*, for example, where the Foul Fiend in person appeared upon the stage amongst all the enacted demons, and no one's been able to make a success of it since. Another one, *Macbeth*, blood, witches, apparitions and black bad luck, best never to mention it by name. A third play (with apparitions, a magician, and of course blood), John Webster's *The White Devil*, was notorious for a while around the mid-1890s: a genuine dread for as long as it lasted, but the malignant events that created that dread occurred only within a company of semi-amateurs, in no regular theatre but a grim all-purpose hall in an out-of-the-way London suburb; it was gradually forgotten. An obscure business altogether, and there were many who were glad to keep it so.

The month was November, the place was St Salome's Parish Rooms (so close to the Metropolitan Line between Latimer Road and Ladbroke Grove stations as to seem to have been built to give support to the railway substructure), the company was Mr Booth Willoughby's Antient National Drama Society, and the weather was incessant rain, soot-laden rain, black as the black London bricks. In those days Henry Irving sat on top of 'serious theatre' like the dome of St Paul's, monumental, awe-inspiring, echo-inducing; there were but two obvious routes to get yourself out of his shadow. You could go direct for social argument (Henrik Ibsen, G. B. Shaw, the Woman Question, three acts at a time of contemporary polemic); or you could strike at the great Henry from beneath his own armpit, presenting Shakespeare and Marlowe and Jonson and such, in uncut texts upon bare boards, with the meagrest of crowd scenes, correct 1600-ish costumes, and no music composed by anyone later than Harry Lawes. This latter route was Willoughby's, a theatrical fundamentalist, fiercely devoted to the true rhythms of blank verse and the pedantic versatility of a pair of doors, an inner stage and a sliver of balcony; and of course he always longed for all his company to share his zeal, rather than just perform the way he told them. He was however aware that to even the most idealistic actors the two routes now and then got mixed up. Miss Clemency O'Raw was a case in point.

She was twenty years old, slight and swift and large-eyed, of a darkling shot-silk beauty, never wearing the same expression from one moment to the next. She was not really an actress, having been trained as a singer in Dublin where she gained some reputation at charity concerts and the like. Upon one of these occasions she was heard by a man called Joachim Droit, of Belgian origin (so they said), a breathless and devil-may-care intellectual, an artistic propagandist; he owned a little theatre in Chelsea and risked all his money upon its work. He was among the first to present Ibsen, and was strongly reviled for it by conservative opinion. The fact was, his productions had lacked the vigour to overcome reviewers' distaste for New Drama. He badly needed actors of forceful personality. He was not as rich as people thought; the salaries of an experienced cast were beyond his reach; he was compelled to look out for novices. The tense excitement projected by Clemency from the concert platform went straight to his heart. Without hesitation he pursued her down the stairs immediately after the performance; gasping upon the Sackville Street pavement, he offered her there and then the crucial part of Hilde Wangel. '*The Master Builder*, my dear young lady, some believe it is his greatest play, rehearsals commence on Monday week, I shall pay for your fare to London, you shall stay in my house in Highgate and Mrs Droit shall be your chaperone, I do assure you, Mr O'Raw,' – (Clemency being accompanied by her father) – 'that all is most respectable to the highest degree. Ibsen, dear sir, is not to be mocked by concomitant moral frivolity. The young lady's mother also could stay in my house if required.'

Mr O'Raw, a bent-backed beanpole, sickly-looking, sardonic, chose not to comment. Clemency said abruptly, 'I have no mother, not here. Respectability is important. Ibsen is more important. For of course I have heard of him, my education has been enlightened.' – (a snort from her father) – 'Of course I shall come.'

And so she came. And she played the part. And Droit was enchanted. Unfortunately, critics were not. He had been so violently seized by the girl's personality that he had quite failed to notice how implausible was her appearance for a latter-day Norse troll-daughter. Under the crude chiaroscuro of the new-fangled electric stage lights (he'd have done better to have kept the old gas fittings) her features were not so much copper-coloured as dark chocolate. Imperial London knew a Eurasian *chi-chi* when it saw one, and scorned her absurd aspirations. Moreover, with defiant pride, she had told a newspaper interviewer how her mother, a Bengali nautch girl, which was to say a dancer-cum-courtesan, had lived with her father in Simla; how indeed she had done worse, she had *married* him; how her father in consequence had had to resign his post as headmaster of a school for the children of colonial officials; how the prejudice of race went hand-in-hand in England with the failure to give women the vote and the political subjection of Ireland, and how all three vicious attitudes were hot meat for the platter of Ibsen. In short, she overdid it, and alas, she embarrassed her patron.

'Poor Joachim,' she told him. 'You must not ruin your company for the sake of a silly girl's principles. I shall go.'

Droit, in dismay, attempted some sort of apology: 'I am aware it is most humiliating, *I* am humiliated, for today it is revealed how even those who forgather for Ibsen set such store upon the lordship of the White Man at home and abroad. I have seen it among my own sisters, in regard to the Congo. I beg you to remain.'

'Oh no,' she insisted, 'poor Joachim, I must go. My father would demand it. He would be sure I cannot stay with you any more than my mother could stay with *him*, despite the great love and respect.'

Droit fell silent at that; nor did his wife attempt to dissuade Clemency. Mrs Droit had proved a most careless chaperone, being a slothful valetudinarian who spent most of her time in bed; she never bothered how few or how many stray actors, painters, musicians or dress designers dossed down in odd corners of the house. She kissed the girl goodbye with a lightly affectionate grace, turned her head upon her pile of bolsters and drifted away in a doze.

One of the assorted denizens came down to the front door to make sure, if nobody else did, that a cab was called for Clemency, and that she was granted a proper farewell. His name was Rafael Sallins, he was a friend of Booth Willoughby as well as of Joachim Droit, indeed he claimed to be a friend of almost everyone of note in the business. He knew Oscar Wilde (at a distance) and affected Wildeish mannerisms, none too convincingly, for he was small, bald and grey-faced, thirty-odd years old, a bit of a dormouse, a bit of an owl, a bit of nothing in particular. He had few visible means of support; he would do a little acting when he could get it, which he sought to represent as a favour to one of his friends perhaps, rather than a professional necessity. Clemency mistrusted him; she felt qualmish at the sight of him, though of course she never said so and of course on this sad morning she was grateful for his kindness.

'Oh Miss O'Raw, God bless my soul, you should not leave us just like this. Do you know where you're going to go?'

'You have met Mary Heckstall, have you not? She was helping Mr Droit with the costumes. She most generously let me know there is a room to spare in her lodgings at Earl's Court, I am to use it until . . . well, until . . .'

'Until *what*? I suspect you don't *know*. I suspect you can do with some *help*. Tell you what, why don't *I* come with you? Come with you *now*? Lunch, before you're off to West Ken?'

'Lunch, Mr Sallins? Where? How? With you? I really do not think –'

'My friend Booth, Miss O'Raw, you have often heard me speak of him. He and I this very day will pick a bit of cold chicken, very probably in parsley sauce. You surely won't find it inappropriate to join us?'

The bit of chicken turned out to be a sparse array of sandwiches and lemonade displayed upon a buffet, in a dark narrow terrace house in a surprisingly dingy street somewhere between Stoke Newington and Canonbury. It seemed that Clemency was thus trepanned into an informal meeting of the Antient National, where plans were to be revealed for the winter season. The collation was presided over by the majestic Mrs Willoughby, all in black with a sort of starched purple shirt-collar right up to her jawbones, tightly-wound barricades of iron-grey hair, jet earrings reminiscent of flamenco castanets. At least twenty people were packed into the room; there was nowhere to sit down save for their hostess's throne-shaped chair. 'Booth,' she announced, 'will be amongst us once appetites are satisfied. Pray take your plates and fill them.' Even as they struggled for fragments of the lunch, he was suddenly in their midst with an armful of scripts, a drooping pince-nez, and a tightly-pursed narrow-lipped mouth. He murmured greetings to all and sundry without apparent enthusiasm, distributing his scripts like the medical man in a workhouse dishing out laxative pills.

Clemency thought it strange that such a drear personality should represent renaissance drama in all its gaudy colours, while flashy Joachim Droit was in charge (as it were) of the severities of Ibsen. What on earth was she to say to him, under his roof uninvited in this very awkward fashion? What had happened to Rafael Sallins? He seemed to have disappeared into the thick of the crowd somewhere. He hadn't even introduced her properly ... And here was Booth Willoughby, right in front of her, eye-to-eye. Worst of all, he was about to speak.

A short clearing of his throat, and then, peremptorily: 'I heard your Hilde Wangel. Great spirit, furious passion. You were blocked by the stodge of the translation; impossible to judge your true skill. Nonetheless, you can sing, for little Sallins says you sang in Dublin for your bread and butter, did you not? The German *Lieder*, I believe. Mrs Willoughby, if you please, persuade this young lady to sing. A test of moral courage quite as much as of voice ... Dear colleagues, the pianoforte.' To Clemency's terror, a lane there and then was made for her through the guests toward double doors thrown open into the next room, and a parlour was revealed with piano and aspidistras and black-and-silver striped cushions strewn all across the floor. Mrs Willoughby upon the piano stool already shuffled her sheets of music.

This was indeed nightmare, discoordinate, unhinged. There was nothing she could do but give herself up to the flood of it. She stammered the name of a song from her repertoire, 'Schubert, *Heidenröslein*, words by Goethe.' Mrs Willoughby found the songbook, found the page, a flourish of notes for introduction, head over heels she was into it, wrong key to start with, wrong speed to continue, but no: she would *not* stop till she came to the end, and so there!

As a rule as she sang she could tell good voice from not so good, but today she was too bewildered to be sure. The warmth of applause astonished her. Mrs Willoughby's parchment features cracked into a genuine smile and her husband made strange little grunting noises, clearly his mark of approval, for he turned to the company and declared that 'one so young, whose rendition in the original German should embody such precise and meaningful articulation, as well as rhythm, as well as harmony, must certainly be able to elucidate the tunes of the most complex Jacobean dialogue, all the more adeptly for her never having tried it before – Ibsen, badly Englished, is no sort of preparation. I shall offer Miss O'Raw the role of Zanche the Moor without further audition. So here, Miss O'Raw, is your script. You may say, do I cast you according only to your complexion? I say no, this is a *character*, and crucial to the truth of the play. Enjoy your luncheon.'

Skimming her eyes over what he had given her, she soon saw that 'the truth', wherever it might lie, would be rather far to seek. For she held in her hand nothing but a bunch of odd pages, a peculiar purple typescript run off from a wax on a patent copying-machine, no more than those few scenes in which Zanche appeared: no note of the overall plot or the nature of the other people in the tale, not even the name of the play. 'Do you suppose,' she faltered, fearing to take a liberty, this man and his wife were so very alarming, 'I might see the complete work? It will be hard to understand who I am and what I do unless I –'

'No, you do not need it. In my theatre the prime ingredient is the score, not the libretto, and I shall conduct it, bringing in every part or combination of parts where they fit themselves into the music. You will see how it comes once it goes. All of our company who have previously worked with me understand without question that I am to be trusted in this.'

'Trusted absolutely, Miss O'Raw.' Mrs Willoughby's taut voice was decisive and unanswerable.

'Absolutely, Miss O'Raw.' That was Mr Sallins, popped up from goodness knows where, a whisperer of mischief into Clemency's left ear. 'We none of us know the plot, you see, and now he's going to tell us.'

'I have no doubt we have finished our sandwiches, we shall all, if you please, sit down.' Mrs Willoughby swiftly marshalled them onto the black-and-silver cushions, or onto benches set against the wall.

Booth Willoughby, complete printed playtext open before him on top of the piano, launched smartly into his explanation. 'For those yet unacquainted with the soul of John Webster, macabre and temerarious, may I assure you that *The White Devil* is a snarling gallimaufry of adultery, murder and revenge. I say gallimaufry, because the plot is confused and has attracted hostile criticism, and will again, I am persuaded of it, however carefully we plan our stagecraft. Nonetheless, my dear colleagues, the poetry, the tune of the narrative, the verbal storm-and-stress, shall totally justify our effort to stage it. I believe it has not been attempted since the author's first production at the Red Bull in Clerkenwell in ... ah ... sixteen hundred and twelve, so what we do with it, for good or ill, shall be without question historic.

'Now then, the plot, succinctly. The Duke of Brachiano, an arrogant Roman nobleman, is infatuated with another man's wife. Brachiano is not yet cast, I had hoped for our long-standing colleague, Mr Solomons, but alas he is indisposed. We must see whom we can find. The wife, that is to say Vittoria, that is to say the 'white devil' herself, is Miss Jennifer Prosit, well known to all of you, our Cressida of last year. Her brother Flamineo, secretary to Brachiano, works upon her with all his wits to seduce her to his master's lust. Mr Sallins, if you please, Flamineo: a self-effacing caterpillar, yet on behalf of your master you hire a magician, hire a poisoner, murder Vittoria's husband, aid and abet the murder of Brachiano's wife. Zanche the Moor is Vittoria's maid and the confidante of her misconduct; a conniver, Miss O'Raw, a heinous but enticing slut, you'll discover her as we go along . . .' And so on, until he'd run through all the parts, fitted them into the story and fitted the actors to them.

Clemency was impressed. For all his rebarbative manner, he did have the gift to inspire. He knew what he talked about; and harshly, abruptly indeed, he would very soon see to it that *she* knew. (Oh dear, but he was not Joachim.)

There was now all around the room a voluble buzz, the whole company leafing through scripts, muttering dialogue scraps, comparing notes, counting lines. Under cover of the noise and movement, she edged toward Booth, nervously; so vital she must ask him this, for all she had heard from Sallins was that leading roles were paid professionals and small parts unpaid amateurs; she must at once discover where she stood, and yet she did not want to be perceived as a –

'Mr Willoughby, will there be . . . money?' She had blurted it out incontinent, goodness gracious, how he shot up his eyebrows!

'Money? Ah, yes, I daresay Droit was in a position to contrive you some small emolument. I don't know that I can match it, our resources are . . . Something, however, why not? I make no doubt that Mrs Willoughby will be able to . . . Yes, there will be something. You shall hear from Mrs Willoughby.'

All that remained was to fix the place and time for the first reading, next Thursday, and everyone to be word-perfect, 'if that is at all possible? Remember, dear colleagues, our old English playwrights were nothing if not masters of the word! Through their words we find their truth, again and again I insist upon it, the sole efficacious approach!'

'Sole!' echoed Mrs Willoughby, and thereupon the company dispersed.

No sooner had Clemency walked out of the front door than the first of the malignant events took place.

She had felt compelled to speak a short word of cordial thanks to Rafael Sallins, despite her mistrust, her puzzlement, as to why had he brought her here: his was not an easy character to read. They were still upon the Willoughbys' threshold, a step or two above the street. As she talked she evaded his insinuating eyes, preferring to look over his shoulder. And then she wished she hadn't, for there on the opposite pavement a large man was standing – no, strolling – no, *loitering* – yet he was no common loafer, he was garishly dressed, too garish for his years (no less than sixty, she was sure of it): grey bowler, chocolate-and-white checked jacket, yellow cravat like a horse-coper at Tattersall's. She saw his red whiskers (dyed whiskers, she was sure of it) round his beefy red face, and he seemed to be staring straight at her. And not for the first time, oh heaven. But never before in London. Oh heaven, had he followed her from Ireland?

She gave a gulp, a startled squawk, she abandoned the baffled Sallins in mid-sentence. An omnibus came clattering down the road from Newington Green, headed probably for the City but she didn't care where; she didn't even wave for it to stop but ran for its outside staircase as it passed her; she desperately caught hold of the rail and pulled herself upwards in panic, her toecaps catching her skirt at every step. She could feel a heavy personage lumbering and gasping behind her. She dared not look round but threw herself down on the first bit of bench she could find that had already somebody on it; for the life of her she must not leave an empty place beside her for this gross apoplectic pursuer. So of course he sat behind her and he panted all over her neck.

His voice (and how well she remembered it) was by no means

gross, but gentle and warm with the merest singsong hint of County Cork. He ought not to have been on this bus at all, but that's where he was. In default of an opportune policeman, what could she do but endure him? – deep-throated in her ear just like Sallins at the Willoughbys, with the addition of strong fumes of neat whisky. 'Miss O'Raw, this is dreadful, you must think me deficient of the most elementary decencies, but I simply don't dare plunge, d'you see, without some sort of introduction to 'em – that *was* Booth Willoughby's house? All those people in and out of it, they *are* his Antient National? Auditions, can you tell me, or has it all been decided? I'm only just off the Holyhead boat-train: I heard, d'you see ... I was told ... I thought first you were with Droit's people but they let me understand that you ... It's not possible you've forgotten me? How could *I* forget *you*? Why, Dublin, Miss O'Raw, when we sheltered from the rain? Begod I'm not a total shock to you, that *couldn't* be the way that it is.'

Nor was it: at least, not 'total'. But 'shock'? – another matter. For that 'sheltering from the rain' was a day she had wiped out of her life, an occasion of drastic error, of foul misunderstanding: she did her best to forget such words as 'forced', or even 'violated', or ... Whereas, from his present tone, he really seemed to think the whole merciless business had been no more than a clumsy rough-house of no consequence at all to a free-spirited bohemian girl. Or *was* that what he thought? If he did, why was he dogging her? One of the reasons she'd been so glad to leave Dublin were his regular appearances there upon street corners at all hours, loitering, staring, sliding away again like a conjuror's half-crown. And why now, today, this so sudden close convergence, both aggressive and evasive, oh whatever could he mean?

She refused to accept that he was concerned with the Antient National except as a pretext. Was he not a professional actor, a most competent veteran, adored by plebeian audiences all over Ireland for his ranting stamping vigour in patriotic melodrama? If he needed work from Willoughby, what prevented a direct request? Pretexts, from this man, she had reason to believe, could be very very dangerous ... His name, too appropriately, was P. J. Blood, and at last he was coming to the point, his soft voice surging into a maniacal series of sobs (and yet all within a whisper, keeping the other passengers well out of earshot: to be sure, he was most competent). Oh horror! could it be possible he believed himself in love? 'I swear to you, my dearest Clemency, I cannot live without you, yet I swear that I shall never again attempt to ... I only need you to consider me as a teetotal penitent old fellow who will utterly abjure his ... Sure, 'twas nothing but the drink, I am so bitterly sorry that ever I ... Begod I was all for Ibsen till they told me you'd gone off to the Jacobeans, Shakespeare I do know, but I've never read this Webster. D'you suppose I could manage to ... Jasus, isn't that the Dalston Junction railway station, if I don't catch a train here I've to go all the way to Broad Street! Never mind me, Miss O'Raw, I am a man from now onward of the sweetest moderation, save only for the passions of my heart!' As he rose from his bench, she ventured to turn her head for a non-committal glance at him, and immediately looked away. His protuberant blue-green eyes were glistening with tears. He pulled down the brim of his hat, bent his own head sideways, bent his big body to the staircase and bounced himself out of her sight.

The next sharp malignance manifested itself on Thursday at the first reading of the play.

The place was the upper room of the Hackney Mechanics' Institute. Clemency arrived early and no sooner had she opened the door than ... oh no, no fly in her eye, it *was* the man Blood, and there he was sitting there! in warm talk with the Willoughbys, expending his genial smiles upon everyone else who came in. Oh horror, he was Brachiano, and clearly for the Antient National a most wonderful trophy, despite his age, the nearest approach they'd ever had to an authentic leading man. Should she throw up her part? How could she? How would she live? She could never return to Dublin; she had thrust her independence so strongly in the face of her muddle-headed well-meaning old fool of a father that if now she were to concede defeat she herself would be an equal fool. Ought she to take Blood's remorseful vows on that omnibus roof as an honourable proof of amendment? Who should advise her? The Willoughbys? Impossible. They were absolutely basking in the sunshine of his talent. Might she go back to Joachim and put it to him? Ah no, her heart wrenched at the very thought. There was, of course, Rafael Sallins, but –

But during the luncheon-break she stifled her qualms and discreetly took Sallins aside. She bit her lip, lowered her eyelids, fidgeted her fingertips, and at once began to tell him things she had never dreamed she would ever tell anyone.

'Oh dear oh dear, my poor dear Clemency. Did you consider the police?'

'No. For they would say he did not actually do what I insisted he meant to do. And then they would say – and how could I prove them wrong? – that I'd seemed to encourage him. And then they would say he was a respected professional gentleman, elderly gentleman, Mr Sallins, and a damn good Catholic, isn't that the phrase? while I was nothing better than a ... well, Mr Sallins, will you look at me? I am no more Irish than I am Indian, but I clearly have all the vices of both nations, how else would a Dublin constable gain a clue to what goes on in my mind?'

'Has he attempted to speak to you today?'

'He has not.'

'Has he looked at you?'

'He has not.'

'He's looking at you now.'

'No he isn't.'

'He was before you turned to look at *him*. Perhaps though he just looked at *me*. Perhaps he really does wish to behave himself. He's been reading Brachiano most excellent well, not too intelligently but oh his brute power ... undeniable ... no?'

'Undeniable indeed, which is why I am so unwilling to –'

'Can you endure to be on the stage with him? I think you and he do not exchange dialogue; your chief conversations are with me and with Booth. So maybe the work need not prove intolerable. I owe it to dear Joachim to ensure you make the best of it here: the question is, have you the courage? On his behalf as well as yours, I can promise to keep my eye open, at the very first nonsense from Blood I assure you I shall –'

'Courage? I might have courage. You'd be surprised what I've dared all my life.' She was suddenly all afire and glaring at him. 'On *his* behalf? Whose? If you mean Joachim Droit, then say what you mean. Mr Sallins, I cannot talk to you if you use only these sidelong allusions, hints, innuendo, I cannot abide it, no.'

He apologized, effusively, averred he meant nothing but to convey Mr Droit's consideration for her, a certain guilt (he might guess) which Mr Droit was doubtless suffering as a result of Miss O'Raw's departure. Did she not know the profundity of feeling Mr Droit had developed for her during the days of *The Master Builder*? As to which, he would say no more; he'd keep his eye upon Blood and that was all.

Clemency, after hearing him, felt a partial relief: he had somewhat diminished the menace of Blood, but his other remarks left her troubled. All was not to be smooth in her young career just yet, but then how should it be? She had made her bed and must lie on it, as the world would inevitably tell her.

From then on, every day, rehearsals continued and at variable hours, several of the actors needing to attend to their jobs in real life – or should one say, *un*real life? – while the intense dedication of Willoughby, the novelty of his methods, consigned everything outside the Mechanics' Institute into a shadowy limbo which no one could or should take seriously. Even P. J. Blood fell under the spell, after a week or two of passive rebellion, vain attempts to assert himself as the no-nonsense professional, the regular old-style trouper who scorned intellectual analysis – 'All I want to know, dear boy, is how do I get off at the end of the act. Tell me my moves and my tunes will arrive on their own!' But he found the tunes did not arrive; in scene after scene his versatile voice strayed helplessly out of the road. These speeches were so tightly knotted, a quickset hedge of thorn interspersed with barbed wire, that he was glad to submit himself to Willoughby, to listen hard to Willoughby's *sotto voce* chanting of the verse, in short to relearn his business for the first time in thirty-odd years.

A number of the actors wondered, why exactly was he here? Was he privately sickening at the shallowness of his no-nonsense style, yet afraid to admit it, and aware at the same time that the plays which had made his name were sadly out of date and that he himself must very shortly sprawl beside them on the dust-heap in all the pathos of his mendacious red curls? Such thoughts occurred to Clemency; a plausible explanation, yes, but she still feared his main reason was herself. Did he hate her? Did he love her? How long would it be before he spoke to her once again? How long before he damned well *broke out* at her, and not only in words? She could still, as it were, feel the great grip of his fists on her arms, at her neck, between her thighs. At all events, it did appear he was no longer drinking. Let him only keep sober and all might go well in the end.

She found rehearsals a gruelling strain. Exciting, revealing, at times most highly satisfying, but she did not so easily catch the essence of Zanche as she had hoped; whenever she got it wrong, Booth Willoughby was quite without pity. Over and over again he would make her repeat herself.

'No no, Miss O'Raw, how often must I tell you, the voice lifted *up* at the end of the line, *up*! One more time, will you listen, your death-speech, you're about to be knifed in your ... your *lower abdomen*, Miss O'Raw! I do beg you to listen most carefully, not three syllables if you please to 'complexion' but *four*. When you've listened, you shall speak it correctly:

> I have blood
> As red as either of theirs: wilt drink some?
> 'Tis good for the falling sickness. I am proud
> Death cannot alter my com-plex-i-on,
> For I – shall – ne'er – look – pale.

One – two – three – four – *five*! For I – shall – ne'er – look – *pale*! Clap your hands in time with me, and as you clap them call the words!'

And so on and so on, for day after day.

And then again, there was a dreadful scene in Act Five where Mrs Willoughby, as Flamineo's mother, smacked Zanche in the face for making love to her son, while her other son, Marcello, no more than five lines later, took a cruel flying kick at the unfortunate blackamoor's bum. Between the pair of them, front or back, she nearly always got hurt, Booth as ever being more concerned for the pitch of her voice than the security of her skin. However, she progressed and she knew that she progressed; most nights she returned to Earl's Court to her bed, if not exactly happy, at least with some sense of achievement.

So: she was discovering how to cope with Booth's tyrannical stage direction, she was discovering how to cope with (or, at any rate, to evade) the potential erotic violence of Blood. But this small secret business of Rafael Sallins on behalf of Joachim Droit was another matter altogether, and she was dismally perplexed by it. First, it was quite unexpected: she had truly believed that all passages of romantic attachment between herself and the fervent Ibsenite had come to an end when she bit her lip, screwed up her courage and resigned from his acting company. She had done so upon principle, she was glad she had done so, she would never have done so had she intended to continue any sort of improper connection. She had small respect for Mrs Droit, but nonetheless there was a marriage there. No, she would not hurt it, or no, not deliberately; a swift access of warmth, impossible to foresee, so easily came and went between two souls (had it not? oh had it not?) without prior intention from either. So now she kept asking herself: why didn't she say this to Joachim the day she left his house? She spoke only of the ugly reviews they'd been reading in the newspapers, the sneers at her parentage, the mockery of her artistic pretensions. She must therefore have let him believe that if he . . . oh gracious goodness! . . . if he helped her (by means of Sallins) to gain entry into the Antient National, she would in gratitude be prepared to –

It only made it worse for her to feel a sly creeping thing in the depths of her brain, or her bosom, or her bowels, or *somewhere*, that persisted in letting her know his belief might be justified. But she would not do anything about it – no, not just yet – she would not let Sallins carry a message to Joachim (which is what he seemed to be offering), nor would she write directly to Joachim; and decidedly she would not go to Highgate, nor yet to the theatre in Chelsea. At any rate, not for a while.

The nearer to the opening night, the greater the tension, the agony indeed, of her personal conflicts. They began to derange not only the hours of her work but her limited spaces of leisure. She kept seeing P. J. Blood (or did she imagine it? invariably a quick glimpse of his disappearing back) in crowds on the street or the platforms of railway stations, or dodging between buses and cabs at the busiest crossings. Of course, it remained true that she did not have to confront him upon stage. In those scenes where he and she were both on together, she was able to slip the far side of Jenny Prosit (for example) and keep out of both his walk and his gaze – which was anyway only fitting: as Vittoria's maid, she had a duty to be inconspicuous. Unfortunately, she had also to indicate a greasy relationship with Flamineo. Sallins chose to forward this by closing himself upon her as they crouched in a rear corner of the stage, playing with her hand, stroking her neck – such a chilly damp touch, she couldn't bear it. Moreover, she was afraid she saw Blood taking note. Had it not been for all the Joachim nonsense, and her need to keep friends with little Sallins, she would have told the latter straight to *fuck off*. (Aha, when she wanted, her mouth could be as grimy as any soldier's of an Indian garrison, and she well understood the strength of such speech among people unused to it, the shock.)

By contrast, Zanche's blatant seduction of the Great Duke of Florence (Booth Willoughby) in the last act gave her no trouble at all, even as she 'simpered like the suds a collier hath been wash'd in', murmuring her dreams to him, arousing him to respond with a parallel prurience:

> ZANCHE   ...yet to say truth
> My dream most concern'd you ...
> Methought sir, you came stealing to my bed.

> GREAT DUKE   I was a-dreamt on thee too: for methought
> I saw thee naked ...
> And lest thou shouldst take cold, I cover'd thee
> With this Irish mantle ... Thou didst laugh

> Exceedingly methought ... And cried'st out
> The hair did tickle thee.

Booth played the Great Duke as a relentless avenger who'd assumed a fit of lechery for his own occult purpose, took care not to let it become real, and so fetched from his memory the right words and tone of voice, the whole time standing rigid, hands folded in his sleeves, with no more than the roll of his eyes and the curl of his lip to signal his use of the woman. Clemency was instructed to coil about him like a snake, but all she felt was what she'd feel if she'd wrapped herself round a lamp-post. Besides, with his usual obsessive director's trick, he kept stopping her to make her repeat her verse-rhythms.

She and he were running through this very scene on a freezing cold Sunday afternoon, while the Mechanics' Institute stove filled the room with its poisonous fumes. It was not quite a dress rehearsal; half the cast were in half-costume, to feel their way 'into the period' (as Booth put it), and for the dressmakers to check the look of the thing. Clemency had been given a very low-cut dress with a wide ruff above it close under her chin. Her breasts were thus all but entirely exposed, as it were through a little window, and she thought it would be thought 'unsuitable'. When she said so, Booth told her the costume was exact; it came from an old engraving and he showed her the engraving to prove it. Mrs Willoughby backed him up, averring that the classic theatre was no place for juvenile prudes. Offended and upset, Clemency went into the scene with such angry abandon that Booth had to push her away from him. He too seemed upset, to the unprecedented extent of forgetting his lines, stamping with frustration, sneering and shouting at the prompter.

And then came the third malignant happening.

Suddenly, from the small lobby opening out of the rehearsal room, where actors not immediately wanted would sit and smoke and play cards, there arose the most appalling hullabaloo. Little Sallins came tearing through the door, all in a ball like a hysterical hedgehog, his arms up to protect his head, while P. J. Blood behind him flung the wildest, widest blows at him with a thick, brassferruled ashplant cane. Both men were shouting, one in fear and one in rage; it was impossible to distinguish the words. Booth Willoughby instantaneously sprang at them; he had after all enacted scenes of fisticuff and clashing steel in good plays and bad throughout five-and-twenty years. He caught Blood's stick with both hands and wrested it from him, throwing it well beyond the stove out of everybody's reach. 'Don't tell me,' he cried, 'what this ruffianism is all about! I do not want to know lest I find myself forced to send both of you packing.'

Blood, for the moment, was unmanageable; he clearly hadn't listened, didn't listen, wouldn't listen: 'By God, Booth,' he stormed, 'just you hear what this snivelling little pisspot's been up to! He's after picking every filthy word out of the most scabrous nooks and corners of this perverted bloody play and snuffling them into her lugs! Why the very scene you're rehearsing this minute is the bucket where he draws his dirty water, don't think I haven't heard him, the slimy unnatural pimp, don't think I don't know who he's doing it for, neither! Not for himself, to be sure, he never rode a mot in all his life, oh no! because what *he* prefers . . . oh I'll tell you what *he* prefers, this Café Royal catamite —'

Only one phrase in the Irishman's tirade made any relevant sense to Booth. Although he was the smaller man, he seemed to tower over P. J., quelling him with his eyes and the knifeblade of his voice. 'I have undertaken this production, sir, upon the premise that *The White Devil* is pure essence of cathartic tragedy, infused with the harshest morality. If you seriously believe, together with the philistines, that the play is perverted, I am astonished you should continue to act in it. You need no longer do so. Any money that we owe you, Mrs Willoughby will see you paid.'

By this time the whole company had crowded in around them, and P. J. began to come to his senses. He collapsed into a chair, he was dribbling a little over the edge of his thick lower lip. Slowly, little by little, he faltered an apology, praising the play, praising Booth for giving him his chance in it, commending the Antient National as 'this truly wonderful poetical company of so many devoted troupers', and finally turning to Clemency with heart-rending appeal (and more than a hint of hard liquor): 'Miss O'Raw

is well aware of the veneration I have for her, and of the . . . of the
. . . of the *tact* I have maintained toward her during all our
rehearsals, may I plead that she plead with Mr and Mrs Willoughby
for leniency, just this once, knowing how agitated I have been of
late by the way my man Flamineo set me walking to my terrible
end, to the poison, the false friars, the strangler's knot to finish it: to
be sure he didn't plan it, but I'd never have shafted his sister if *he*
hadn't shown her the way. I'm sorry for my language, so; and I do
know, Miss O'Raw, it's no sound excuse, but I swear to you it's not
easy to play a part like the one I've been given, and still keep upon
two feet; I mean, am I old P. J. or in fact Brachiano? I do beg you to
beg them, let me stay, Miss O'Raw, because or else I'm a ruined
man, so I am, so I am, truly.'

She looked at him, stony-faced, for several moments, in dark
silence. 'Only,' she said at last, 'if you apologize to Mr Sallins.'

'Oh I'll do that, I will surely, oh I will. Mr Sallins, I'm most
mortal sorry for what I said, what I did. You're a decent man, I
know that well, and in the heel of the hunt a damn fine actor. I'd
never have gone for you if you hadn't been Flamineo so deadly to
the life that I . . . that I became I suppose you could call it confused.
There you are, sir: shake my hand.'

Thus disaster was averted, the company was kept together, and
Booth Willoughby was thereby prompted to make his own small
apology for his unwonted bad temper that evening. He had just
heard, so he told them, some miserable news. The William Hazlitt
Hall in Holborn would not after all be available to them for the
production. The trustees of the hall had been looking at the script:
someone had warned them that John Webster was both morbid and
decadent, and salacious into the bargain, and they preferred not to
give endorsement to his work. So what to do?

A day or two later, the early morning of the day of the first night:
Mrs Willoughby to Mr Willoughby in bed, a cup of tea in her hand
already, her other hand digging into her husband's left shoulder –
he is not quite inclined to wake up. 'Accepting his apology was a
bad mistake, Booth, bad. Please pay attention, it's already six
o'clock.'

'Good God, it's as black as the pit . . . Can't you see that I *had* to accept it? However we might try to replace him, without him the play would be collapsed. He performs his ferocious role entirely against the grain; he is an actor who loves to be genial. But was I to predict he would threaten manslaughter outside of the bounds of the script? No, he won't do it again, my dear, surely not, no.'

'You think not? We've never dealt with such an actor, and *he* never played such a hither-and-thither character in such a play ever before, all ambiguities, no villain, no hero, no clear black or white for him but black-*and*-white both together, I am telling you, you slow old man, that that's what's been eating his heart. And now that we must mount the play in a miserable dank cockpit among the gutters of Ladbroke Grove . . . O Booth, who on earth was St Salome? Do they really name a church after a girl who went and danced for a dead man's head on a dish? I think we have an omen, a bad omen, bad; I can't see my way to be rid of it.'

'I too was disturbed. I put the question to the vicar when I chaffered for his hall. It's not the same Salome. An Anglo-Saxon princess, wife of the king of Wessex, she inadvertently poisoned her husband when seeking the life of his . . . of his catamite, forgive the word: she was driven by unbridled jealousy and repented with an equal fervour. She took herself off to Germany, wandering the roads in rags and tatters, begging her bread for the love of God, and praying continually. The vicar called it a most beautiful story, so applicable (so he said) to the "perversities" of the present day . . . Did not Blood say "perversities"? I'm almost certain he said "catamite" . . . This really will not do: rain or no rain, I shall get up. We must be at the Parish Rooms by seven-thirty at the latest, or we'll never get the stage rebuilt. Dress rehearsal was ridiculous, with those pillars put where they are . . . I offered the vicar no comment. To tell truth, I had hated his story. But an omen? Surely not. She did go to heaven in the end.'

The audience was meagre and stiffening with chill. The rain rattled on the roof and seeped into the hall, while its vapour veiled the gas-lamps in green and blue wreaths. The three-sided platform stage, with its two gaunt wooden pillars, and its creaking, slam-banging, re-echoing planks, towered over the spectators like a gantry in a scrapyard – it had been made for the William Hazlitt, it didn't fit St Salome's, it had had to be foreshortened in all the wrong places – maybe not so much a gantry as an old-fashioned gallows. People did not like to see it; and therefore they were not best pleased by the actors who came bawling onto it, striving dreadfully to find the acoustic that would have reached them with such ease had they played where they'd wanted to play: the William Hazlitt was truly musical, Booth cherished its proportions, it was grievous to be deprived of it tonight.

From his very first entry, old P. J. was out of balance. He launched himself at Clemency upon *her* very first entry, where she comes to spread cushions for the adulterers' love-making. Having dragged Jenny Prosit to the floor before the cushions could be properly laid, he snatched one of them from Clemency's arms to fling it down himself; he heaved Clemency away upstage with a savage ejaculation (could she truly have heard him order her to *shift her sodding cunt*?); she staggered wildly into the crook of Sallins's elbow, and found him as startled as she was. And whatever about Blood's reconciliation with Sallins, something went very wrong with their partnership in the plot. It is true that Flamineo and Brachiano begin to gird at each other in the middle of Act Four, but much earlier in the production they were hiccoughing their exchanges like a pair of angry bravoes rather than acute confederates; so the quarrel, when it came, was altogether too strong, it quite doused the parallel quarrel between Brachiano and Vittoria, it seemed a build-up to a sudden murder to put an end to Webster's story there and then.

At the second interval, Booth Willoughby decided he'd no choice but to intervene. He detected great discomposure in the house. He could see Joachim Droit bolt upright in the front row, his large mouth wide open like a frog's and his hands at his fat cheeks as though to prevent them bursting. The man from the *Morning Post* was whispering scornfully to the man from the *Saturday Review*, the man from the *Saturday Review* had entangled his beard in his fingers and lowered his long head to the level of his shoulders. It was worse than embarrassing, it was an insult to the public: if

Booth could not put manners on these idiot actors at once, he might just as well shut up shop. Yet neither Blood nor Sallins was in the men's dressing-room where he looked for them, nor yet in the closet that claimed to be a green room, and no one seemed to know where they'd gone – they'd come off for the interval together and apparently had quite disappeared. So had Clemency. It was perfectly extraordinary: for where could they be unless they'd stepped into the yard? – heaven's sake, it was pouring with rain.

Nonetheless, across the yard was a silly little unlit bicycle shed, and incredibly, from inside it, Booth could hear their insensate wrangles, partly blotted out by the overhead bellow of a railway train hurtling to Paddington.

Clemency cried out, 'I was never your damned mistress, I was never the mistress of Droit!'

Blood cried out, 'Lies, you black bitch, you tell lies – is it one damned lie or is it two?'

Sallins cried out, 'And who's to prove the truth, when we all keep our own dirty secrets – *you*, you damned rapist? in God's name who are *you* to talk of lies?'

Booth strode across the cobbles through the rain, tore open the door of the shed, said simply, 'Five minutes, you're on stage in five minutes, why should *I* be your callboy? The only call you deserve is from the stokehold of hell, watch out you don't get it.' At which point came another train in the opposite direction, pouring cinders and smoke into the yard, and no more words were uttered. All four of them sneaked back into the hall once again; all four of them seemed thoroughly ashamed.

The end of *The White Devil*, as with most Jacobean tragedies, is a cumulative slaughterhouse. To understand what took place in St Salome's Parish Rooms, we first need to lay out what should have taken place in the play, thus:

Brachiano is induced to organize a tournament. The agents of the Great Duke of Florence put poison in his helmet; he is carried screaming to his bed:

> On pain of death, let no man name death to me,
> It is a word infinitely terrible.

The friars who come to render him the last rites are his murderers in disguise; they pour curses into his ears; as he bellows in torment for his beloved Vittoria, they throttle him with one of their girdles.

Thereafter, Flamineo (who has stabbed his own brother in a fit of rage and seen his mother in consequence go mad) walks alone through the palace, overcome with melancholy. He meets the ghost of Brachiano, in the accoutrements he had worn for the fatal tournament, but carrying, instead of a sword, a pot of lilies with a skull in it. Flamineo dares to jeer. But his bravery fades away when the ghost, without a word, throws soil upon him from the pot, holds up the skull at him, and vanishes. So he's now without a master, he must fend for himself; he goes at once to Vittoria to demand the arrears of money that Brachiano owed him. She refuses:

> I give that portion to thee, and no other
> Which Cain groan'd under having slain his brother.

Zanche is with her. In what appears to be an access of implacable madness, he forces the two of them to a queer sort of suicide-pact. They shall each hold in their hands two pistols, one aimed at him, the other at each other:

> These are two cupping-glasses that shall draw
> All my infected blood out . . . Shoot, shoot!

They shoot, but only at him, not at themselves; he falls (as they think) mortally wounded; they run to him and tread upon him in triumphant malice.

> O I smell soot!

– he groans,

> Most stinking soot, the chimney is a-fire . . .

> There's a plumber laying pipes in my guts, it scalds;
> Wilt thou outlive me?

Then he leaps to his feet, yelping and crowing with his own malice:

> The pistols held no bullets ... I live
> To punish your ingratitude ...
> Trust a woman? Never, never; Brachiano be my precedent: we
> lay our souls to pawn to the devil for a little pleasure, and a
> woman makes the bill of sale.

After that, the bestial finale. The Great Duke's agents enter and seize them, rope them all three to the pillars, drive daggers and swords into their bowels. No one left to mop up the blood but the young son of Brachiano: this child runs in weeping at the head of his guards, upon the very last page of the script, to send off the murderers to 'the rack, the gallows and the torturing wheel'. *Finis*.

So that was what ought to have been. Now then: what was.

The first scene after the interval contained neither Sallins, P. J. nor Clemency. It lasted some ten minutes and Booth was onstage for the first five of them. When he came off, stage left, oozing murderous designs towards the hated Brachiano, he began to look about him for the (by now) no less hated Blood. But seeing the latter sitting quietly, back turned, at the make-up table in the dressing-room, he thought he need not speak to him; instead, he cast his eyes round for little Sallins. Little Sallins was on a stool just inside the stage-right entry-door: he had the first speech of the next scene and seemed to be ready for it in a sober enough fashion. Clemency was beside him, with Mrs Willoughby, Jenny Prosit and several others, a processional entrance about to take place. Booth could not wait to see it. He had a very quick costume change and a make-up change into the bargain: a couple of minutes into the scene the Great Duke was to reappear disguised as a blackamoor, even blacker than Zanche. So why wouldn't Blood get up from in front of the mirror and allow him to sit down?

'Mr Blood! I need the table. And you should be with Miss Prosit, the procession is already forming.'

'Aha. So it is.' P. J. turned heavily round on his stool, blinking toward the backstage passageway. 'So it is. I hadn't heard it. But I don't go to my death just yet?'

'No sir, of course you don't. The next scene but one, you go to your death. I beg you, sir, catch hold of yourself.'

'Mr Willoughby, you're a good man. Let no one tell you different, here, there and everywhere, for all of their damned lies.' He rolled himself off the stool, picked his plumed hat off its peg, and plodded out to make his entrance like a man under extreme fatigue . . . Fatigue or not, he drove himself through the next part of the action with a crescendo of energy, handling Flamineo's fratricide with white-lipped fury, wielding his sword in the tournament like a windmill in a hurricane, writhing and roaring on his deathbed with all the force of the hurricane itself. The audience responded to him: all of a sudden the failing play had come to life, the other actors on every side of him were infected by his power, the noise was terrific, the echoes in the roof of the hall even drowned out the trains on the railway.

At the very moment when Brachiano must succumb to the strangler's knot, Booth Willoughby (who was not in the scene, but was just about to enter) felt a touch at his elbow: Barney Bosco, his stage manager, thin spiky features twisted with worry. 'Mr W., the pistols. D'you know where they are, sir? I don't seem to see them. They were there on the prop table, there. Mr W., did *you* move 'em?'

'No I did not. They cannot be far away. Pistols do not walk. Take your time, Bosco, look carefully. Deuce take it, you delay my entrance.'

A whole crowd had to rush upon the scene through both doors, it didn't matter that he brought up the rear. Very shortly he and Clemency were at grips in their seduction scene. He was immediately aware the girl was shivering from head to foot. She had always been nervous, but this was excessive. She had to talk of her dream that he came stealing to her bed; but she talked as though this *was* the dream, the oddest sort of lecherous murmur he'd ever imagined.

In the very middle of it she laid her hand under his cloak between his legs.

For a moment she outrageously aroused him, and then she damned well *hurt* him, and then at once she glided off for her serpentine exit, with her enigmatic half-line 'and wash the Ethiop white': God alone could decipher what she thought Webster meant it to mean, or whether it was Zanche talking, or whether it was Clemency herself. There followed an episode of women winding the corpse of murdered Marcello, Flamineo's brother. Zanche had a dirge to sing; the script gave her no words; Booth had cannibalized a few from another of Webster's plays:

> Who seeks to leave a living name behind,
> He weaves, he weaves but nets to catch the wind.

This was to be chanted several times over in melancholy diminuendo, until interrupted by Mrs Willoughby as the grief-wracked mother. Altogether contrary to what she had done in rehearsal, Clemency grew louder and louder at each repetition, an outcry of feral threat: Mrs Willoughby had to screech to get her voice into the scene at all.

And almost immediately afterwards, Brachiano's ghost walking in upon Flamineo, its face streaked livid white with greasepaint: there was something very odd about the way the old actor placed his feet. Altogether contrary to what he had done in rehearsal. Everyone in the audience noticed it, or said the next day that they'd noticed it. He was wearing heavy jackboots, and yet he seemed to trip on his toes like a ballet dancer while holding his arms out wide, wrists upward turned, flowerpot raised in the right hand, the rope-knot that had killed him dangling from the left. There was also a strange noise, as though he whistled between his teeth . . . It sounds comical, but it was not comical, it was – (somebody said it, aloud at the back of the house) – 'vile'.

Sallins's jeers, when the soil was thrown, the skull shown, were downbeat when they should have been upbeat, he lowered his voice on the line-ends, exactly as *not* instructed by Booth, he never did it before, why the deuce should he be doing it now? Booth, listening hard backstage, ground his teeth and wrung his hands, all his work coming unravelled yet again, just when he thought the play was saved and on a clear run to the last few murders, on a clear run to a standing ovation, catastrophic. And here (yet again) at his elbow, the white-faced Barney Bosco, no longer just worried but shattered, incomprehensible, gabbling, 'Oh Mr W., Mr Blood's never going to be able to come on for his ghost scene –'

'What's the matter with you, man? He's onstage this minute, I saw him, I even heard him. *Whistling*, if you please! Inexcusable.'

'No, Mr W. No. Oh please, Mr W., come this way. I popped in to give him his call and . . . and here's what I found, sir –'

As he spoke he had brought Booth, all but manhandled him, across the passage to the men's dressing-room. The room was empty save (impossible!) for the bulky form of P. J. Blood, on the stool before the dressing-table, fallen back *across* the dressing-table, tongue out, eyes bulging, the noosed rope-knot encircling his throat, so close it disappeared into the folds of his thick neck, a fearsome garotte. It was looped up behind him round a hatpeg in the wall beside the mirror: his two hands clutched the end of it, as though by main force he had contrived to haul it taut. His cheeks were half-smeared with white make-up; the greasepaint-stick had rolled across the table under his armpit. Upon the floor near his right foot, his property flowerpot, overturned; soil, lilies and skull spilt out across the grubby linoleum.

In addition, a most lamentable indecency. The codpiece of his puffed-and-slashed leather breeches was unlaced, his private parts hanging out of it, engorged, almost as though . . . as though somebody's hand had . . . How could Booth not think of Clemency's hand, Zanche's hand, not ten minutes ago? and how illegible, how blank, had been the stare of her wide dark eyes as she took herself out of his sight.

Barney Bosco said, 'Is he dead, sir, I mean, *quite* dead, dreadful accident? Oh my God.'

Booth said, 'Come out of here. Shut the door. Lock it, Bosco, damn your eyes, find the key and bloody *lock* it. I've got to get back on the stage. There's nothing we can do till the play's over. Over and done, oh my God.'

He had nearly missed his last appearance, the Great Duke making sure that the killers will finish the bloodshed, a very brief episode with no more than four lines for him; he flustered his way through it like a blind man in a hailstorm.

Over and done? – why, yes, a good deal sooner than even Booth could have guessed. The lengthy final sequence, Vittoria and Zanche, Flamineo with the pistols, the high-flying melodrama and death, went awry, every bit of it, from the start. Sallins was inaudible, mouthing the speeches with frantic exertions of his lips, nothing emerging but gurgle and spit. Jenny Prosit seemed to have forgotten most of her words; when the prompter tried to help her she overrode him and swept ahead, omitting one line after another. She jumped straight from Flamineo's entry with the weapons (four single-shot handguns in a baldric slung over his shoulder) to land herself at random in a declamatory couplet that out of context made no sense:

> Millions are now in graves, which at last day
> Like mandrakes shall rise shrieking.

Clemency managed to get two or three of her own lines in, hopelessly trying to bring Sallins to his suicide pact so that some degree of plot might make contact with the public; but after her unaccountable aberrations with Booth and with the dirge, she was not so much acting as gasping and lunging and clinging to a pillar for support. Suddenly Sallins burst from his trance, exultantly calling out about 'cupping-glasses', thrusting the pistols into the women's hands – 'Shoot, shoot,' he kept exhorting them.

So they shot and he fell and they trampled him as it says in the script. And Jenny exclaimed, as it says in the script, 'What, are you dropp'd?', and he could not at first reply because his mouth was full of blood and he vomited it all over the stage. Then he spluttered some broken words, fragments of the image of the plumber ... Then, and with a terrifying clarity: 'Blood, damned bloody Blood, dead man's dirt thrown over me. O Clemency, you can best tell why.' Then Jenny understood he was really and truly gone – he,

Rafael Sallins, not any more Flamineo – and she screamed her realization to the roof. Clemency had known it already. She was on her knees in the pool of blood, doing her best to smooth out his poor little face for him before its horrible distortion became fixed with rigor mortis.

The detective inspector from Scotland Yard, a sour-tempered fellow called Legrade, Lestrange or some such, was anxious not to waste time on the case. He finally pronounced that Blood had made away with himself; the grip of his hands on the rope was more than sufficient proof; a pity, though, he had left no suicide note to confirm matters, and it *was* most unusual for an elderly man to find the power and sheer hardiness to drag the noose tight by his arms' strength alone and no leverage but the hatpeg, which was not really high enough to be of much help . . . Self-hanging, the inspector had often seen. Self-strangling: not only rare but *unnatural*, he thought.

The question of Sallins and the pistols was more difficult. He had indubitably died from a bullet in the left of his breast. Which meant that it had come from Clemency's pistol, even though she was sure she fired wide. Booth had told both her and Jenny, most earnestly, to be sure they fired wide: with firearms, he'd insisted, you could never be too careful. The pair to be pointed at Flamineo should have held blank charges of black powder and wadding, detonated by explosive caps: this would make a realistic noise, there would be smoke, flame and stench, and the audience would scarcely notice they were not authentic period matchlocks. So who loaded the fatal weapon?

As the inspector said in confidence to the Willoughbys, a week or so later, 'I thought at first that mulatto girl might have had her own notion, y'know? wicked-looking wench, I'd not put a murder past her if she thought it'd suit her ends. Add to which a cross-reference from a colleague in the Special Branch, political section, y'know? the man Blood was known in Ireland to have been an active Fenian several years ago. They could never actually prove it, so they never tried to prosecute, but they kept him now and again under surveillance. By the same token, the girl was observed at political meetings in Dublin, Parnellite stuff, y'know what I mean?

Home rule and all that. Seems her father pulled her out of the convent where he'd put her to school after bringing her from India, he told the nuns they were 'political poltroons', sent her off to take classes in the Erse language. Seems he speaks the Erse language himself. *Fringing* on rebellion, is the way my colleague had it, not quite the full sedition, but not so far from it. Except that they do know that she and Blood in Dublin used to go to the same meetings. What d'you make of that, then?'

'I had no idea,' cried Mrs Willoughby, 'that the British police kept such – such malevolent dossiers; we might just as well be in St Petersburg. Inspector, this is shocking.'

'Shocking,' contributed Booth. 'And moreover, I'd say, pointless. Or why did you not arrest her?'

The inspector was unabashed. He knew his soft-headed liberals, he didn't even need to despise them. 'Oh we thought about it, don't delude yourself. But there seemed to be no way she could have manipulated the loaded pistol into Mr Sallins's baldric so he'd give it her without error, even if she *had* loaded it herself, and we couldn't make out where this could have taken place. Your man Bosco said he charged two of the guns with blank, and at least three people saw him do it. It's true that they did disappear (as you yourself, sir, confirmed), and we don't know where Mr Sallins found them when he came to make his entrance. He and Blood did have that quarrel a few days previous; maybe Blood somehow put the bullet in? And they quarrelled over the girl, so it seems from what was heard. Which adds a complication, but, once again, no proof, neither for politics nor ... nor for amorous passion, if you'll excuse me, ma'am, amorous, there's also the funny business of the old fellow's breeches. I'd put no impurity past her, if she thought it'd suit her ends.

'I was tempted to class it as a second case of suicide, by proxy, y'know what I mean? – Sallins gives a gun to a woman; he wants her to kill him. But is she aware of it? Maybe not. Pity we've no clue to the motives. Which is why, when all's said, it's been made clear from ... from higher up ... that we've no choice but to write it down as accident. It's scarcely a plausible story, but it could lead the inquest to give non-committal verdicts, keep it quiet and bob's your uncle, probably all for the best.

'My own view: a pair of murders. And *cherchez la femme*. But who am *I* to have a view? At the Yard it's the Commissioner that lays down the law ... Yes, ma'am, you have been known to meet him socially, somebody told me ...

'And it still don't answer the question: when P. J. Blood in the dressing-room was doing himself in, oh God, then who was it that walked upon stage in facsimile of Blood's costume, to mark (you might say) Rafael Sallins for his death?'

Despite the timely tact of the Police Commissioner (a most cultivated gentleman anxious to bring no scandal to the arts), the Antient National dissolved itself. What else could it be expected to do?

As for Clemency: once she was certain she was no longer being watched by detectives, she went to Joachim Droit and put it to him straight – why had he not helped her in her fearful ordeal? It was no sort of excuse to plead he was so devastated by the sight of the death of Rafael that he'd lost all his capability for many, many days. He owed it now to Rafael (she told him) to back up the messages that Rafael had been bringing her. If he wished to run away with her, abandoning his wife, why then – she would agree. Provided only that they went today.

'Ah, Clemency, not quite today.'

'Ah, Joachim, then in that case, not quite at all, ever ... Goodbye.'

She was not seen to act upon a public stage again. Did she return to her music? If she did, it wasn't in London.

SECRET CHATS

This old man, mortally ill, propped upon a heap of pillows, dictates gaspingly but clearly to a serious young woman, a charitable volunteer of some sort; she has come to the Hospice for the Dying to give ease to his last few days. He is Mr Abel Jenkins, self-styled man of letters, but described by many others, far too many others, as a waster, a sponger, a conman, a treacherous voluptary, not so much a genial libertine as a tomcat on the prowl with needle claws and teeth like carpet-tacks; but today he is dying and he needs, so he has said – no, it far exceeds 'needs', dammit: he might 'need' a cup of tea, he might 'need' a bedpan, that's not it! – no, he craves, he requires, he demands that his well-intentioned visitor should instantly take down his memoir, as quick as she possibly can, before he proves unable to finish – in short, before he's finished. Quick sharp!

You do have the shorthand? I especially asked for shorthand . . . Good. So there we are: memoir. Which means memory. How can I be sure I truly remember it? – such a long long time ago. But it is a tale that is part of me, has been part of me for eighty years, not so much a memory as a *growth*. I cannot be carried under the arch of the crematorium and let it lie there untold, so hard, tight, convoluted inside of me all in a knot, just waiting like the rest of me for the fire. Because it's made me what I am and nobody knows it and everybody blames me, oh God. Do they think I made myself, this ugly piece of craftwork? Will you look at me as I lie here, nugatory, vacant, vile? But to whom can I tell it? Never to my gooseberry-eyed red-haired grandchildren, chuckleheads every one of 'em, they'd just sit with their ill-chosen spouses in their

semicircle round this bed and they'd gawp, not the least understanding. But you, you're a stranger, no reason to like me, no
reason (not yet) to dislike me, it's much the same as talking to that
Grecian plaster statuette in the hall here between the rosebowls,
that Demeter or Psyche or whatever she is; yet you, if you're a
plaster cast, you're a plaster cast with the shorthand and the good
conscience to keep on writing it, whatever the words may mean
that this horrible old man gives vent to, because you are, are you
not? a worker of good works, and moreover most classical to look
at, highly Grecian and desirable, were I young. I was once.

After all my piddling poems and loveless little scraps of dead
fiction, it's my final attempt at literature, maybe my closest
approach to it? Let's get on.

I'm talking of the time when I was no more than eleven years old,
because I do think it possible that if there *is* such a state as the
Afterdeath, then is it not also possible that every one of our ... our
mistakes ... shall be reckoned against us, even those that we made
as a child? Not a question, do you see, of the gravity of the ... the
mistake ... but rather of the depth of the shame that we felt at the
time? *My* shame at what I did at the age of no more than eleven was
the worst I ever knew throughout the eight decades that came after
it. And I did nothing, said nothing, to achieve any brand of
forgiveness, not then, not later. So what about today? I don't
believe in clergy, it'll soon be apparent why not; I confess it instead
to my Psyche, my Demeter, straightfaced, round-throated, beautiful, and she, without comment, is about to write it down, and
anyone can read it who wants to. Just to tell it, that's all that I need,
and conceivably the shame will dissolve.

Did I say the worst shame? It was also the last. Ever since,
throughout my life, now and then, for this and that, I've felt
embarrassment, even regret, after some of the things I've done. But
never again shame. Some people lose their faith. *I* lost my ... what?
My morality? Oh I don't like that word. Shall I say instead, my
objective self-assessment? ... 'Judge not, that ye be not judged'?
Which means, don't judge others. It means do judge yourselves;
and I haven't, I couldn't, I didn't even bother to try.

Let's get on with it.

They'd put me into this boarding school. They put me in during the Great War, and two years after it ended I was still there: I mean the first of the Great Wars, Lloyd George and the Kaiser, Passchendaele, all of that, and my father had been killed in it. A solicitor's clerk in 1914, he joined up and they made him a corporal. Within two-and-a-half years he slipped off some duckboarding and drowned in a communication-trench mudhole, no sort of hero, all he did in that war was to do what he was told. But I couldn't think such a thought at the time, to me he *was* a hero; his silly little death broke my mother all to pieces, she had no other children, the family saw she was incapable of coping, they one after another stuck their hands in their pockets and pulled out enough cash for the cheapest class of prep school and there I was: Dryghtskerry House, Private Academy for Young Gentlemen, on the black shale cliffs of the coast of north Yorkshire, where the shore turns as it were to the left and the view out to sea is direct in the eye of the wind blowing all the year round from the Arctic and the waves are never blue, never green, but a bleak trenchant grey from one end of the year to the next.

It was a school of no quality but specious pretensions: we had to wear these Eton suits, d'you know what I mean? – no you don't, you've never heard of 'em – wide white starched collar, short black bum-freezer jacket, tight pinstripe trousers and would you believe a bowler hat? The headmaster – more precisely, the proprietor – was a smooth-spoken clergyman, tall, bald and hunched, a pair of golden pince-nez on a glittering golden chain: the Reverend Hugo Pellinore. Every day he would cane little boys on the bare bottom, for almost anything we did – which is to say, not only for bad behaviour, but common-or-garden playing about, talking, laughing, fidgeting; in short, just for being little boys. He was a one-man reign of terror and every time he whipped us he quoted the Bible. I cannot think he set up that school for any other purpose than his pleasure in the use of the cane. Which we all thought was just as it should be – that that was what necessarily must happen at a proper English school, it was manly to be proud of our weals. We were brainwashed as well as thrashed, and nobody's parents cried 'Stop!' In truth, nobody *had* any parents, it was that sort of school: they were dead or incompetent, as was the case with me; they were abroad in the army or colonial business; they were archaic throwbacks to the high-Victorian storm-and-stress, who positively desired their sons to be whipped and had packed 'em off to Dryghtskerry of deliberate intent. 'Stiff discipline,' they'd ejaculate, 'ha! it never did *me* any harm!' Such schools were written about often enough, sixty years ago and more, in boys' comics, novels, autobiographies, the accounts of 'em so frequent you could call it a literary cliché: but that doesn't mean it wasn't true. These places did exist – oh I'm sure they still do, does anyone ever inspect 'em as they deserve to be inspected? – and they poisoned their pupils' lives. Depraved little despotisms, impervious to outside influence unless somebody told, and who would tell except one of the children, and who would believe him? – all of 'em brainwashed, children and families alike.

It's not only what happened to the children: amongst the arbitrary adults within those lairs, those dens, those warrens, almost anything might ... might *go wrong*. Even if it went so wrong that the newspapers, the police, could not be kept out of it, the full story would always stay hidden; the place itself of its very nature was a hiding place.

Mrs Pellinore, school matron to save an additional salary, must have been twenty years younger than her husband, as I'd guess, thinking back on it. At the time I wouldn't have known; anyone over twenty-five to a child might just as well be fifty. Name of Griselda, a boisterous harsh creature like an unmanageable pony, all shaggy hair and disorderly hoofs. She delighted to send boys down to Pellinore to be whipped whenever she detected 'misbehaviour', which was most days of the week and twice on Sundays. She and he between them touched a nerve of occult cruelty in the cellarage of my heart; I have never been able to be rid of it. She'd give us juniors our weekly hot baths, ten of us at a time squealing and splashing in a roomful of steam; when she saw Pellinore's red stripes across our buttocks she'd pass her neighing comments with the coarsest jocularity and expect us to laugh when she laughed. Then we'd scuttle off to bed for furtive murmurs in the dormitories, fantastically speculating by what strange incantations the bald

Hugo had wooed his mare. She'd enough hair for both of 'em and not alone upon her head or under her armpits: a boy called Westwood swore he'd seen up her skirt as she sat beside the cricket field in a deckchair; it seemed she was quite without drawers. The shape and texture of a grown-up female distressed him immeasurably – and us too, when he told us.

The teaching staff was Pellinore himself (Scripture, Latin, Greek), two or three assistant masters and Miss Elderbroom, a melancholy grey lady who looked after the youngest class. Miss Elderbroom was permanent, the assistant masters came and went; nearly every term at least one of them would be replaced, sometimes all of them. They were either breezy, young and fatuous or sourly middle-aged: they left no great mark on my memory, until I'd been at the school, for how long? – four years? five? – at any rate I was eleven. Autumn term and just the two of 'em, Mr Latrappe and Captain Varley. The latter had turned up in the middle of the previous term to take the place of ... of Mr Somebody, I don't remember the name, who left in a hurry after smashing all the glass in the Pellinores' conservatory (with a brandy bottle, we heard it said). Varley stayed on throughout the long summer holiday. So did I. So did a number of other boys – parents in India and so forth, my own mother in a nursing home – a common enough convenience for which Pellinore charged a very moderate additional fee: he needed a member of staff to help with the supervision, and the captain appeared to have nowhere else to go.

I think it likely that in those days almost every private school had a captain or a major; they'd come out of the war in a terrible state of the shakes; as a rule they'd no idea how to teach, but the titles of their rank looked good on a prospectus; unfortunate gulls, they were fit for nothing better. Captain Varley, for example, had not only served in France (where he'd been blown up by a German shell and had 'all his insides rearranged'), but after the armistice he'd volunteered for the intelligence department of our garrison in Ireland; for a while he commanded a squad of what he called his 'bold black-and-tans', 'catching murder by the throat, sending vicious little hobbledehoy rebels to their well-deserved and bloody ends'. At any rate, that's what he told us during the long clifftop walks upon which he had to lead us as a holiday-time substitute for regular lessons and games. One of the vicious rebels had put a bullet from a Mauser pistol into the captain's left thigh – it was still there, he let us know – which was why he had to walk with a stick. His face twitched uncontrollably as he narrated his adventures; his curious little smudge of a ginger moustache worked up and down and backwards and forwards like a horsefly on a window-pane. Sometimes he would take us down to bathe, in Dryghtskerry Cove immediately below the school grounds. This was not so much fun as you may suppose. The beach was all ridges of rock and it faced due north, so that the sun even at midday never got into it: a dismal little gulf with too much slimy seaweed. We bathed without togs, except for the captain; *he* wore a bathing-suit, an elegant dark-blue affair with short sleeves in the prevalent style and a regimental badge at the breast; we could take a good look at his Mauser scar, a horrid livid pit in his flesh, hacked about, he let us know, by a useless drunken surgeon in Dublin. For a special treat he would allow us to stroke it with our fingers, his 'mousehole', as he called it: we were all, as it were, in the same exclusive club. Honourable wounds . . . oh yes. Because he did make his jolly jokes about marks on our bums, though with none of Griselda's damned malice; and in any case the holidays meant not so many whippings, if only because Pellinore was off the premises a good deal of the time.

Altogether we liked and admired Captain Varley. At least *I* did. Up to a point. He was almost the sort of hero I was sure that my father had been; had my father survived the war he would no doubt have told me exactly the same sort of stories.

I should mention the 'secret chats'. Once or twice or more often, in the long holiday evenings after we'd gone to bed – the Pellinores having driven off in their motor car (for the booze and the jazz-dancing, so we scandalously supposed, at a posh hotel in Scarborough or York) – the head boy, McAllister, a noxious great lout of fifteen who was permitted to go to bed when he chose, would come into the dormitory and fetch another boy out. 'Old Varley again,' he'd whisper, 'come on.' Never to me, I may say: I was too young. It would be Armitage or Kenyon, one of those fellows in the fifth

form who'd be seniors in a year's time; whichever one, he'd stay
out of the dorm till we'd hear the car wheels on the gravel. If we
asked where they'd been, they'd wink and look so bloody superior:
'Why, where d'you think, you silly snotter?' ('Snotter' being school
slang for a junior.) 'Captain Varley wanted a chat. About my career.
We understand one another, the captain and me, if only you knew
what I meant. He's going to wangle me a place at Sandhurst when
I'm old enough, so there.' Or some such taradiddle. It was all quite
transparently false. But as for the truth, we were unable to imagine
what on earth it might be. I don't know about the other snotters,
for myself I was made most uneasy and preferred to forget about it,
to assume it hadn't happened, to avoid as far as possible the fifth-
formers with their sniggering, their sidelong glances, their hints of
knowing more than they ought to.

So that was how it was till the end of the holidays, when the rest
of the boys came back and we were returned to our own proper
dormitories where fifth-formers did not mix with juniors. If the
'secret chats' continued, I was no longer aware of them and was
glad not to be aware. Certainly nobody talked about them.

*At this point in Jenkins's narrative, the young shorthand-writer,
under some degree of stress, and oblivious of the discipline of her
craft, looks up from her notebook and says, 'Ah!' He asks her what
the devil she means, interrupting him so recklessly. She is at once
apologetic, though not as apologetic as perhaps she ought to be. Her
name is Sylvia Briggs and she has very strong views on the sexual
abuse of children (not that she knows much about it). She insists
upon suggesting that if that was the sort of thing that went on at
Dryghtskerry, it might very well explain the dysfunctions of his later
life. 'All of 'em?' says he, and he's winking and blinking and
chuckling, a rattling rough chuckle like dried peas shaken about: is
he laughing at her or at the thought of his own dysfunctions? 'All?
And if so, why would I exhaust myself talking and talking the whole
damned business through at so bloody damn nearly the end? For
godsake, Sylvia Briggs, nothing, nothing is that simple. Why must
you young people be always so damned absolute? Wipe the tear out*

of your eye, you sweet compassionate creature, take your notebook, take your pencil, do your job.'

Mr Latrappe. Max Latrappe. From Canada, so they said. The new master. And we didn't like him. He made his entry upon a motorcycle two days after the beginning of the September term, under a roaring red sunset with wild bursts of black rain and his bike kicking up the gravel like the bow-wave of a destroyer. A few of us saw him from the window of the junior dorm (the only upstairs boys' room with a view of the front of the house); he was furiously ringing the bell and hammering on the door, shouting at the top of his voice. 'Hugo, are you there? Where the hell have you got to, you damnable toad-in-the-hole? For God's sake, man, send a slavey to unbolt this bloody door. I'm as sodden as a floormop. Hugo! Hugo!' In his goggles and leather helmet and his waterproof cape he might well have been a messenger from another world. All we could make out was his great height and the hump of his shoulders; when the door was at last opened, he seemed to have to stoop to pass through it. It was not one of the maids who let him in, but Griselda herself: we heard her voice for a brief moment, swift and angry: 'Less noise or you'll wake up the school. To you from now on his name is "headmaster", and I am the matron. It's perfectly disgraceful of you to come here in this –' Whatever else she had to say was lost in the sharp volley of coughs with which he drowned his own words, and the slam of the door as he went in.

Now we didn't know that night he was Mr Latrappe; we'd no notion *who* he was, except that he was clearly an unusual excitement. For the whole of the next week we saw neither hide nor hair of him. And then, upon the following Monday, there he was at morning prayers, standing in cap and gown behind Pellinore and Captain Varley, overtopping both of 'em, although Pellinore was tall enough. He had his face slightly turned away and his fingers at his waist intertwined and writhing about. Altogether as sanctimonious-looking as Pellinore himself. (Varley at morning prayers used to glower at the ceiling as though challenging the Lord God to give an answer if He dared.) Pellinore finished reading about the goodness of the Good Shepherd, he gave out his list of boys to come for punishment after dinner, he told us that Captain Varley would no longer be taking Maths, and that French would resume, as would Saturday evening carpentry class, and Mr Latrappe would be in charge of all three.

'Mr Latrappe is from Canada. He doesn't know our English ways. But I have made clear to him the way we keep discipline. If you try to take advantage of him, I shall take advantage of *you*, are you listening to me, Jenkins? No you are not.' No, I wasn't, or not completely, I was staring too hard at Mr Latrappe's chin, trying to work out was he in fact growing a beard or had he just forgotten to shave? I was added to the list to be whipped after dinner, which gave me a whole morning to run in and out of the boghouse with my usual looseness of terror, so Mr Latrappe's first French lesson went altogether over my head. All I can remember is the message he wrote on the blackboard before he spoke a word to us:

Monsieur MAX LATRAPPE.
Votre nouveau Professeur, de Québec, Canada,
ou on parle toujours Français.
Dans ce classe, nous parlons seulement Français.
Nous ne parlons point Anglais, comprenez-vous?

And from then on he had us reciting verbs and things in French; he refused to speak English, but sometimes he forgot himself; his English had a very foreign accent, quite different (I thought) from the voice I had heard on the doorstep; he snapped the boys off sharp if anyone tried to ask a question; he never smiled, not once; he interrupted himself continually with his irritating, half-suppressed cough. In short, it would have been a dreary enough lesson even if I hadn't had to squat in such a puddle of fear.

Two hours later, in the punishment queue outside Pellinore's study, I found myself next to Westwood. We were desperately trying to be brave, we must talk about anything in the whole wide world save what was going on behind the door (the first little victim was already inside there; if we didn't talk we could *hear*, which was appalling). Westwood was clever at French. He said, 'Did you know that "classe" is feminine? So why didn't Max write up "*cette* classe"? Do you think he don't know his own language?'

But just then the first victim came plunging out amongst us, scarlet-faced, bawling and ashamed to be bawling; he tore away upstairs in his agony, not even able to tell us the number of cuts of the cane the beastly man had given him. Pellinore that day was being savage beyond all precedent. Neither Westwood nor I could think any more about French, we just bit our lips and trembled and hoped that bowels and bladder would hold fast.

Yet afterwards don't imagine we forgot what had been said; we returned to it often under less fearful circumstances. For we were puzzled by this Max, his perpetual downcast morosity, the accent that wasn't there and then it was there, the blackboard mistake, the curious feeling we had that he didn't care to even *attempt* to instruct us, he was just going through a series of meaningless routines which happened to involve a class of boys but might as well have been carried out in front of three rows of cabbages for all the difference it made to him. He proved himself without doubt the dullest teacher I'd ever sat in front of. Yet he *was* growing a beard and it was coming along very well. With his shaven upper lip and his long lined lantern-jawed face overswept by a nodding forelock of dark hair striped with grey, he was something after the style of the photogravure of Abraham Lincoln in our history book. I can't think he was very old. I'd say in hindsight much the same age as Griselda, maybe thirty? thirty-five? The odd thing about him was that he really did look as though he ought to be interesting; and he wasn't. Which in itself was of interest, at any rate to Westwood and me.

Westwood suggested he must be neither Canadian nor French, for what sort of name was 'Max' if it wasn't notoriously German? – clearly the man was in England on an espionage mission from what was left of the Hun High Command, Hindenburg, Ludendorff, to reconnoitre the coast for a new Great War of Revenge. My own opinion was less international and more immediately personal: I felt there was a connection – oh sinister enough! – between Max's strangely delayed first appearance before the school and the uncontrolled flagellations that followed it so swiftly. Pellinore had quite lost himself in a delirium of punitive glee, while his regular measured homily with a text from Solomon's *Proverbs* ('The rod and reproof give wisdom: but a child left to himself bringeth his mother to shame,' etcetera.) had slipped into incoherent gabbling of 'rod', 'reproof', 'shame', 'shame', 'shame', over and over again. What, a full score of whistling cuts for a moment's lack of attention at morning-prayer announcements, even more if the cane hadn't shattered in his hand? – none of us had ever known him so wild. Max for some reason was driving him mad. It could well be a tale of the most fascinating blackmail. Oh yes, and what about those cries upon the doorstep the night that Max arrived? 'Toad-in-the-hole'? Unbelievable: we had to find out.

So the pair of us met by stealth on a drizzly afternoon behind the outside boghouse, where we talked the matter over for the twentieth time and then made a solemn covenant: we would turn spy ourselves and unmask this ill-omened newcomer, we would follow him all over and eavesdrop, we would if necessary purloin his letters (except that he never seemed to get any), if he went away for any well-signalled number of days we would creep into his bedroom and search. We portentously clasped hands upon it: our most perilous secret. And we'd start the wicked business that very weekend.

I say 'we', but I soon saw I did nearly all the spying on my own. Westwood was very good at interpreting the intelligence I brought him, once I'd got him to agree that Hun generals were out of the question, and that in truth we were investigating Pellinore as well as Max: whatever was going on, they were both in it up to the neck. But Westwood as a sneaking eavesdropper was no good at all. He was incorrigibly garrulous, even in the most hazardous situations, and he was also far too timid. As for myself, I'd always thought I was a species of coward (at football, for example, I kept well clear of rough play and strenuous kicks), but now I seemed able to dare almost anything. The fact was, I had nothing to lose. If Pellinore were to catch me he couldn't whip me any worse than that Monday, or I'd surely be dead and he'd hang and he knew it. Could I face a repeat performance? Well, I'd survived the first one; even though I hadn't boasted of it like some of us had, being too much aware of how demeaningly I'd blubbered; even though there'd been oozing blood, a horrible ghastly glue to stick my underdrawers to my skin, as I found out hours later towards the end of the afternoon, and I'd blubbered anew to undress myself. But I remained so furiously angry at the whole squalid injustice, that I really didn't care if he flayed me alive – *provided I first threw open whatever disgrace he was hiding*, and oh yes, there was a disgrace, I was convinced of it, oh yes. In the smoulder of my rage I could not fret over possible failure. Westwood, of course, had more imagination than I had: he did *not* think flaying alive was an acceptable option. Yet he didn't attempt to deter me, and he listened to all I told him with gratifying admiration.

By God but I was proud of that. I was suddenly feeling, without fully understanding it, a rich glow of leadership in my veins. By God but I felt it too soon.

For some weeks very little happened. I stalked Max Latrappe whenever I could, but he never seemed to go anywhere or meet anyone at all out of the ordinary, except now and then when he mounted his motorbike and leaped away out of sight along the high moorland roads. Because I couldn't follow him, I could make no deductions: his excursions might be strongly significant or they might mean straight nothing. Westwood would not admit they could possibly mean straight nothing. He said, 'We must keep a proper log, and analyse. Date and time of departure, time of return (if it's not after lights-out), state of the weather, state of Pellinore – where is he, when Max goes off? Does he ever say goodbye to him, or make a point of saying hello when he comes back? Because if Max is on some sort of message having to do with what Pellinore's up to, there should be some sign of it – Oh crumbs!'

'What? What's the matter? Have you thought of something new? Don't sit there on your tuckbox just sucking your teeth. Come on, man, give give give!'

'I may be quite wrong, but ... We said we were watching Max, we said we were watching Pellinore, we really said nothing about Grizzel. Where is *she* when Max goes off?'

'Oh crikey-crumbs, Westwood, no I never thought of it! Where *is* she? On the days he goes off, it's about two in the afternoon, if he hasn't any after-dinner classes. When Grizzel takes the car out, and Pellinore's not with her, as a rule it's between two and half-past. Why on earth haven't we noticed if it's on the same day? Or on some of the same days? Or ... Next time, no fizzing error, we fizzing well make sure of it, because ... Do you think they could be meeting?'

'Of course they could. But why? She's never a word to say to him except to bark at his heels – "Mr Latrappe, if you *don't* mind, there are some juniors here waiting to be told what to do." "Mr Latrappe, have the goodness, please, to keep those boys' muddy boots out of the hall." "Mr Latrappe, where *is* your laundry? I have spoken to you about it time after time, it really is *most* inconsiderate." ' Westwood was a famous mimic and we rolled about laughing from one end of the boxroom corridor to the other. (If Pellinore had caught us he'd have whipped us yet again with no mercy: I'm astonished even now to think back upon how careless we were.)

So we watched for another fortnight, setting all our observations down in a notebook which Westwood kept in his locker, entitled, if you please, E. W. WESTWOOD, MOST SECRET, DO NOT OPEN! At the end of that time it did seem that we might have been right. Max on the motorbike had gone out upon three afternoons; Griselda in the car had gone out upon six afternoons; three of them had been the same as Max's; on each of those three she had come back much later than on the other three, in point of fact about an hour after Max came back. We did not see them talk together upon any of those three days, not even the most run-of-the-mill school-business conversation, laundry, boots, and such. They might almost have put themselves under a vow of avoidance for those particular periods of time, and yet not for the rest of the fortnight. Aha, so very strange, but how could we follow it up?

And then, a day or two later, while we were still at frustrated odds over the possible implications, came the even stranger incident of the Scattered Sunday Walk. Captain Varley was conducting a bunch of a dozen juniors along the dirt track that led to Norseman's Head lighthouse, about two miles from the school, a favourite route with super views of coastwise shipping and all sorts of scope for the captain to be reminded of wartime episodes. We should have been an orderly column, but we had jumbled ourselves together into a small milling crowd the better to hear his complex narrative of how the Sinn Féiners last winter had tried to scuttle a Royal Navy gunboat in Dublin Bay, and how he and his faithful batman had foiled them. As this muddy lighthouse road was normally devoid of traffic, the captain did not try to reorganize the ranks; he was in any case too deeply plunged into the thrill of his own yarn.

The wind was blowing in from the sea, freezing our ears, making it hard to hear the story, and impossible to hear Max's motorbike until he was all but right on top of us.

He came roaring over a hump of moorland, rocking zigzag between heather and gorse, down the line of a narrow sheep path that ran into the lighthouse road at just about the place where the walk had come to a halt for Captain Varley's dramatic climax. Or rather, Captain Varley had come to a halt; he needed to flourish his stick to make vivid his sentences; he didn't care to risk his bad leg on the slippery ground if the stick was not ready to support it. So picture us, if you will, open-mouthed in a ring all around him and Max Latrappe at full throttle with nowhere for his handlebars to turn. As I've already told you, we scattered. Captain Varley was unable to scatter: he skidded on one foot, fell upon his knee, sprawled among wet grass and sheepshit, bellowing words and frantic phrases that we all knew were forbidden, though we may not have known quite what they meant. Max swung his heavy vehicle left to right, right to left, desperate to avoid carnage: he too skidded and fell. Into thick gorse which broke the impact, but cannot have been painless. The bike went wildly onward, freed from his control, flailing through more of the gorse, carrying away a barbed-wire fence, shooting out of sight over the edge of the cliff. Two hundred feet down it hit the nearest of the greeny-black ridges that gave their name to the cove, the Dryghtskerries. At that stage of the tide great waves were rolling across them; when we cautiously peered over to find how things were, we saw only the front wheel rearing up above the foam like the figurehead of a storm-broken ship.

By the time Captain Varley had dragged himself to his feet and called us to order, anxiously counting to see were we all present and unhurt, Max Latrappe on hands and knees had begun to laugh, a huge cackle of raucous hilarity, such a thing as we'd never heard from him. Then he stopped it as abruptly as he'd started, jumped up (groggily enough) and was off down the road to the school at an astonishing swift run. We all, including the captain, stood stock still and gazed after him, blankly. 'Now look, chaps,' (the captain, in a small shaky voice, very nervous now the danger was over) 'just forget, if you please, what you might have heard me say; and I think not a mention to the headmaster? Awkward sort of business, really: best leave it to me to have a word with Mr Latrappe and we'll see what we shall see. Very well then, about turn, back to the school, left-right-left. Teatime in forty-five minutes.'

Ever since Max's first day as a master, it was obvious that he and the captain did not get on. They seemed civil enough to each other; but they also walked warily, the captain now and again dropping obscure little sarcasms, pretending to be jokes, about 'rough trade in the colonies', or 'trapping for warm pelt among the Iroquois', which Max did not laugh at. But then Max until this strange Sunday had never laughed at anything. Even so, I'd not expected the sheer virulence of the quarrel I overheard not long after tea. Deliberately overheard: I was very much on the prowl, and anywhere Max went was the place for me to be, just supposing I could do it in safety.

On Sunday evenings we endured two hours of 'Bible Study' prior to bedtime prayers. For the first hour we had to memorize a given chapter in rigid silence; for the rest of the session we were interrogated upon it by Pellinore in his frostiest cane-threatening mood. Sometimes his place was taken by Miss Elderbroom, who was devout but not vindictive. She really did believe in a God of Love, poor lady, and she would not refuse you 'permission to leave the room' if you convinced her it was urgent. (Pellinore more than once had boys actually pissing in their seats, he was so strict about 'self-discipline' when Holy Scripture was open in front of us.) Upon the Sunday of the Scattered Walk Miss Elderbroom, thank heaven, was in charge and I easily got leave to slip out. Already, on our way into the classroom, I had heard Varley snarling at Max: 'A word with you, a word, in the masters' room, *at once, please*! Don't you dare try to put me off!' The masters' room was down a passage as you went to the inside bog; it was not really dangerous to make a slight detour; the door was none too solid, you could hear any raised voices inside, and by God but they *were* raised.

Varley was reviling Max for evasion of duty: why did he never conduct the Sunday walk? 'You know bloody well I have my gammy leg, you know bloody well we're supposed to take it in turns, you long streak of Irish shite! And how dare you fart about in the very *midst* of my walk on that bloody great crud of a machine, showing off to the brats. Jesus Christ I'm bloody glad it went over the cliff!' – and so on.

Max, in high coughing crescendo, tried for, and at length obtained, an interruption: 'Wait a minute, hold on there – hold on a fucking minute, man! – what the hell d'you mean, Irish? Will you say what the fuck you're intending to say? Irish? Who the fuck said *Irish*?' Not a trace of his queer Frenchy accent: pure English, and the foulest-tempered English you could hope for anywhere short of a barrack room, though Max (as far as we knew) had shirked rather than soldiered in the war. I didn't understand the 'Irish' business; what the captain said next made it no clearer.

'Don't tell me about Irish. Don't tell me about Dublin, Christmas Eve in Grafton Street, hey? when you'd half-moon fucking giglamps and a 'tache across your face the size of a carrion crow, and who called you Fergus O'Brien?'

'My name is not O'Brien, never has been, what do you mean?' The queer accent was beginning to slip back into place.

'No and it was never Latrappe, till you came here out of nowhere. I've been wondering three weeks where I'd seen you before. I could *have* you, you shitty bugger – internment, that's for certain, I'm not sure I couldn't get you as far as Jack Ketch, that's to say if I was able to –'

Able to do what, I never heard; because Max once again had launched into his extraordinary laughter. It thoroughly knocked the captain off the railroad of his rage, his response was so deflated and fatuous, a sort of miserable groan.

'Laugh? Oh of course, laugh. Why, anyone can sodding well laugh, but –'

Max's cockerel whoops and hoots continued, hawking and spitting and screeching, freezing my spirit as I heard him, until suddenly I heard something else. Footsteps along the corridor, quick hard-heeled tap-tap tap-tap, Griselda upon her rounds, drawn to the masters' room by the racket, oh crumbs, oh crikey-crumbs, oh please dear Jesus, help me! how could I *not* be discovered?

There was a broom cupboard, I sprang into it; I knocked some stuff down inside it, frightful row from a tin dustpan, but Griselda was intent upon the furious pair of masters; she had no ears to spare for a mere delinquent pupil. I heard her fling open the door and create instantaneous silence. She spoke quietly and with cutting finality. 'You are aware that it is Bible Time and that many of your loudest words will have gone through to the boys' prep-room? I couldn't pick up all of them myself but those that I did hear would not suit Miss Elderbroom. Nor her charges, I sincerely hope. How fortunate the headmaster's indisposed. Captain Varley, you at least should know better. Officer-and-gentleman? – what *do* you think it means?'

A humiliated mumble of apology from Varley, as he limped upon his stick, fast as he could go, down the stairs beside my cupboard and away. She began then on Max; but oh with what a change in her voice. Angry, to be sure, but sorrowful and yearning, and shamefast (I'd say), all mixed up together, and a strong deep throb behind it, neither anger nor sorrow nor shame but a quality quite new to me and darkly unwelcome. 'What can I call you but a man of no good luck, a most damnable idiot, both on your bike and off it? Was it *you* that made that hideous noise? Was it a laugh, or what was it? Oh I do not want to hear it from you ever again. I had the handyman go down and take a look at your bike, he says even at low tide there'll be no getting it up, it's jammed among the rocks and that's the end.'

'I can't afford another one, not on what Hugo pays me; but it's surely not the end.' No accent, no shouting, a curious echo of her own low urgent tone. 'Consider: it is not impossible. If we can't meet out there it'll have to be here.'

'*Here*? You've gone mad.'

'Clearly not within the schoolhouse. But what about the carpentry shop? I teach there every Saturday at half-past seven, the handyman unlocks and gets things ready a couple of hours before time, Hugo never goes there. Varley never goes there, we can bolt the front door in case any of the boys turn up early, if they do you'll be out at the back before I move to let them in. Of course it won't be perfect but when did we ever find perfection?'

'Do it,' she said, harsh and blunt; at once I heard her footsteps, tap-tap-tap to the stairhead, and his going the other way, coughing now and then, to the left. So I sneaked back to the classroom and Miss Elderbroom asked me if I perhaps had an upset stomach? She was always kind-hearted and never suspicious; I felt my cheeks all on fire as I fumbled for chapter and verse through page upon page of *Deuteronomy*.

Westwood was shockingly complacent: he showed no surprise whatever. 'What did I tell you?', was all he said. 'They're plotting together, I knew it. But we'll neither of us know any more unless you find a way one of these Saturdays to hide in the carpentry shop. Golly, what a go! I bet you don't. I jolly well bet you don't dare.'

I had never been great friends with Westwood, until he lighted on this Max adventure. Thereafter I'd had the thrill of having him look up to me for my unexpected pluck. But now he was presuming on it. He thought I wouldn't dare to evade a dare, did he? Well, he could think again. I said, 'No I don't dare, unless *you're* in there with me. Oh don't be such a scab, such a rotter, such a beastly little funk, you and I made a covenant, and I'm jolly well going to hold you to it.'

He giggled and cringed and shuffled; but I forced his agreement. Then I wondered was it a sensible tactic? If he couldn't keep quiet he'd ruin everything. But I did need his company; this was real spying and dead dangerous. I'd already given myself a horrid fright in the broom cupboard, I couldn't possibly handle the next stage all on my own.

We had to wait several Saturdays before we got a chance. But when we did, why, it wasn't too difficult. Saturday was a free evening, except for those boys whose parents paid for the 'extras', carpentry, music, watercolour painting. Mr Jackson, the music teacher, came in by train from Whitby; Miss Elderbroom taught painting. All those, including myself and Westwood, who were not enrolled for 'extras', were supposed to spend the time 'doing revision' in the library under the care of Captain Varley; depending on his mood, this could be a loose enough process. And on this particular Saturday, the captain arrived late, looked tired, reeked of liquor (as I heard some of the older boys whisper, but *I* wouldn't have known); he sprawled in his chair with a racing journal and his feet up on a table. He didn't bother about whispers and fidgets, nor had he checked who was or who was not in the library. Not much of a library, of course; how could it be when a brace of pinchbeck Pellinores had put it together? A dingy sort of boxroom really, L-shaped, with tattered books on a half-dozen shelves, together with a congregation of desks, chairs, globes, blackboards, wall-maps and charts, superannuated clutter not quite fit to be thrown out but of no current use in the classrooms. Which is to say, an easy place for two small spies to dodge away from. So we dodged.

Ms Briggs is amazed. 'Now I wonder, Mr Jenkins, do you mean me to think it's all true, or do you exaggerate? If that headmaster would ill-treat you as despicably as you say, I can't think how you could run yourselves into so much extra danger?' He rumbles, as it might be with contempt: 'Oh what would she know, what would Sylvia Briggs know, of everything a child might dare in such a . . . such a noisome little stewpot?' She observes him suspiciously; once again she hears his chuckle deep down in his withered throat. 'Oh yes, our knife-edge courage was fun for us,' says he. 'Even funny. Even then, we had a giggle. Westwood and I, giggling. Even then, under most terrible threat. But you, am I right? you'd far rather it was a pack of lies, over-the-top fiction and no need for yourself to be hurt by it. Not what you thought you'd be here for, am I right? Not quite your usual? the serene closing-down of quietly concluded lives? Because mine is not concluded. Don't you see, girl, I have caught hold of it, all of it at last, all of a sudden one great handful in no more than an hour, necessarily compressed, and thus, if you like, exaggerated. So believe what you choose; let's get on with it.'

The carpentry shop was way out at the back of the school, the far side of a cobbled yard, in one wing of a great range of outbuildings. Dryghtskerry House boasted a foxhunting, steeple-chasing past: but the Pellinores kept no horses, just the motor car in the old coach house and stacks of discarded furniture dumped here and there among the stables and harness rooms. The carpentry took up no more than a portion of the far end of the largest stable. Westwood and I tiptoed tremulously in there the very minute the handyman was finished; he'd lit the stove and a pair of paraffin lamps, he'd made sure all the tools were laid out, he'd finally gone off to his supper. There was plenty of room for us to lurk, among worm-eaten tables and chairs and an elaborate antique sideboard with a vast tarnished looking-glass perched on top, which was jammed into a corner. But it was hard to find the strategical spot, as we didn't know what Max and Grizzel would be doing, or where they'd be doing it, or even if they'd be meeting here at all. It was after all a good while since we'd heard them lay their plans. We'd already reached the end of November, the evenings were teeth-chattering cold, so we thought they'd stay next to the stove. If so, the only place where we could see them without being seen would be down on all fours beneath a table. The whole of this part of the room was in black shadow; it did look as though we'd be safe enough, the more so as a back door was only just behind us.

It led into a harness room which led into the coach house and so out into the yard; we put our heads through the opening to check the escape route was clear, no furniture in the way, no gardening tools or buckets and such; everything seemed safe and sound. But just as we crouched down to creep toward our hiding places, in from the yard comes Max all swift and eager, throwing off his coat, pulling a roll of tarpaulin from under a workbench and laying it on the brick floor, spreading travelling rugs on top of the tarpaulin – at least, that's what Westwood was later to claim that he saw. For, curses! I wasn't able to get under the table in time; I had to drop between two chairs over against the sideboard, and the area round the stove was completely out of my sight. But I could hear Max well enough; he was moving about, dragging things and coughing in little bursts; and then I heard him shut the bolt upon the door where he'd come in, which was queer if he was expecting Griselda; and then I heard him mutter and fidget, and then immediately behind me such a sudden diabolical din that I very nearly squawked out aloud.

Of course! and I should have thought of it, for who else could it be but Grizzel? – at the entrance to the coach house, as she hauled open by main strength the double doors upon their rusty old hinges, jumped back into her car, drove it in, jumped out of it, swung the doors shut again, *slam-bang-crash*! and then the heels of her far-too-well-known shoes tap-tap tap-tap tap-tap straight through to the back entry of the carpentry shop, straight through towards me between two chairs.

For eighty years until this day I have never been able to work out how it was she didn't see me.

I suppose she must have come there expecting nobody but Max, and expecting him so fervently I could have danced all over that sideboard with a battleflag in my hand and I wouldn't have caught her attention. For she was speaking to him even before she was inside the room. I couldn't quite catch what she said, it was a fierce throaty murmur like an angry cat asserting itself, and I heard him respond to it with a series of breathless gasps, not at all the same thing as his coughs; and then 'Zelda', he kept whimpering her name, at any rate this shortening of it we'd never heard anyone use; and then she gasped back at him, 'Harry, Harry, oh Christ, Harry, Jesus Christ oh dear Harry, whatever will we do?' (Harry? Hadn't Varley said his name should be Fergus? And what *was* this run of blasphemy? Pellinore's cruelty and his back-to-front collar had long ago combined to turn me into a little atheist, but nonetheless I was truly scandalized. Could she possibly talk like that, could her husband talk like that, when they were shut up in their private rooms alone?) 'Oh Harry you bloody fool, this is *impossible*.' After that, nothing but unaccountable sounds, cat-sounds and dog-sounds and horse-sounds (from Grizzel), and a bumping and stretching, a sort of rolling, and a pulling-about of cloth; I heard a pocketful of money falling onto the floor, and what I guessed was a shoe or two kicked off against the wainscot.

At this point the piss-willy Westwood crawled altogether out of the place. He did it very deftly; the first I was aware of his defection was the accidental knock of his foot against the doorpost as he slid past it. I turned my head and saw the movement, a lizard-like disappearance into the darkness behind me. He told me afterwards that he could not bear to see what he'd been looking at, it was all he could do not to burst into his giggles, it was beastly, it was rude, 'all bare,' he said, 'both of them, it was worse than the cricket field,' and did I think (with a giggle) it was the sort of thing that Varley and his fifth-formers carried on with? because if it was ... I told him to shut up, he was a scab and a rotter and a funk, how could I think anything when I hadn't been able to *see* anything? and I didn't believe *he* had, so let him not bother me any more. Not true: I hadn't seen much, but I had indeed seen something, far too queer to share with anyone, let alone such a treacherous ass.

For as I huddled to the clammy floor-bricks, shuddering cold and all of an itch with the cobwebs and sawdust, listening to what I couldn't properly make out and didn't really want to hear any more of, such a cramp got into my neck I absolutely had to wiggle it, let them catch me at it, I didn't care.

Well, of course they're far too busy for anything but their own ... their own ... whatever ... But the movement for the first time turns my eyes up toward the big looking-glass. And the looking-glass, leaning forward on its horizontal pivot, can reflect a tight corner of the space between workbenches and stove, well lit by the oil-lamps, but nothing below eighteen inches above floor level.

To begin with all I can see is one of Grizzel's legs, in a brown woollen stocking, sticking straight up into the air. Then her other leg shoots up and kicks convulsively. She cries 'Christ oh Christ!' and both legs disappear. After which she stops her noise, and so for a while does Max. Nothing now but the bumping and stretching, and the quick heaving-up of first his head then hers into the scope of the looking-glass. I can just see her nape, bent forward, half-hidden in the thicket of her dark hair, which falls out of its usual bun and tosses its full length down her back and over her shoulders. I can see her spine, likewise half-hidden as far as the narrow of her waist. Seems to have no clothes on above her waist and a rucking-up of garments around her waist, I can't see any lower. Is she *sitting* on him, astride? Looking down at him? Looking wildly upwards and away from him again? Looking almost straight into the looking-glass at *me*, and bouncing and somehow *striving*? The looking-glass doesn't let me see quite how.

I see her bring her wristwatch to her eyes. She says, 'God, it's after five past seven; the brats'll be coming any minute for their carpentry.'

He says, 'Let me get up then, I can't do a damn thing unless you let me get up.'

She says, 'I can't stand or I'll be seen above the window-sills, you should never have lit the lamps, how the hell can I get dressed lying down?'

Then both are out of view together. The looking-glass shows me nothing but travelling rugs shaken, tarpaulin held up at arm's length to be banged into its folds, and finally the pair of them standing, fully dressed, strangely dishevelled, and turning away out of the light. Which meant they turn nearer to me: their two pairs of feet are almost within my reach. If I dared to look up (but I don't), I'd need no mirror to see their faces; they're towering immediately above me. I hold my head in my hands and try not to listen, but I must.

And yet if I hadn't listened I'd never have known anything, after the first unaccountable shock of a beast with two backs on an old stable floor with no apparent reason for it. I was not yet aware of – how shall I say? the *usual* reason – of the savage carnal need and greed, day-in day-out, that drags us unendingly together in pairs, no matter what our names are, our pretensions or our duties, our promises to other people. Nor could I foresee that this was no more than what *I'd* be doing not so many years ahead. (Insatiable and vicious with it, that was me, at a late stage of my teens; my mother's brother was to call it 'moral turpitude' the day he had me hauled into court. Out of the bounds of this story, forget it.)

As I say, if I hadn't listened, I'd never have known *how*, I'd never have known *why*, I'd never have known *because*. Better if I hadn't known, better if I'd stayed as pig-ignorant of it as Westwood – 'rude', he said, 'beastly', that was all he saw before he fled, all he would ever remember and no doubt laugh at in later life – whereas for *me*, whereas for *my* memory, it was something far more desperate, oh you do understand? for this, exactly this, is why you're writing it, I'm not going too fast for you? I'm afraid I go too fast for myself.

Because suddenly, as they stood there, Max began to talk. So urgently, allusively, elliptically, that I could not properly follow him, and yet afterwards I could not forget him. The whole shape of what he said to her sank into my mind like a tune of music. It made little immediate sense, and afterwards so many times I've thought about it over and over and of course inadvertently reshaped it (although I did check certain names in the history books), so that what I dictate to you now is bound to be – I won't say 'inaccurate'. *Your* word: 'exaggerated'. No help from Griselda: her growing interruptions confused me at the time as much as they clarified.

'Oh Zelda, my only Zelda, this ought not to be happening, you know it, I know it, we say it to one another every week, damnably stupid, abominably dangerous, I mean why do we do this, I mean why did we put ourselves where we had to be doing it, no good luck for either of us, I mean oh God why the hell did you ever marry Hugo? I mean, I know that I've asked you before, and before, and before, but oh God –'

She was cramming her hair up (without hairpins, which she seemed to have lost on the floor somewhere) under her sombre brown felt hat, a school matron's disagreeable hat, no hat for a woman who played the way she played in stables. 'You've asked and I've answered, a hundred times, a thousand, he was your brother, he still is, who else but the nearest available? he told me he ... he ... he *desired* me, that was his word; if in the upshot he thought the child was his, why not? how was *I* to know it would be dead within six weeks?'

'*My* child. And fuck you for not taking better care of it.'

'Of course yours. And how could I know about care when

nobody knew where you were all those years? And in the upshot, Damascus – how was I to know you weren't dead? I went out of my mind. The War Office thought you were dead.'

'They told lies to prevent the scandal. All of it filthy politics, every decency of warfare entirely forgotten, relations with the Arab chieftains, and beyond the Arabs, the French, and the French, and the French, I've explained it a hundred times to you and to bloody Hugo.'

'Bloody Hugo perhaps believes it, *I* don't, not a word of it. You killed a Turk, he was a prisoner, you should not have killed him, it's preposterous you desert from the army for that. They were killing men all the time in the chaos of we-bloody-win and you-fucking-lose. None of us know how cruel we are, how foul and how filthy, till all of a sudden we're in a panic and by then it's too late, God *I've* been in a panic ever since I met *you*, the greater part of seven years. All right he was an *important* Turk, but I still can't see the shape of it –' She was sitting on the edge of the table where Westwood had hidden himself earlier, her skirt above her knees; she was fingering a hole in her stocking with one hand and (I thought) pushing him away with the other.

Max had begun again the moment she said 'killed a Turk', very likely he never heard the rest of her stuff, about cruelty and so on – which sank into *my* ears even though I was still listening to *him*, very odd I can remember both of them, both talking on top of each other, but as I said, it's a tune of music, I've had all of my life to pick it out, unravel the counterpoint note by note. 'Did I *say* he was a Turk? Did *anyone* say he was a Turk? Did the War Office send a telegram to inform you he was a Turk? Because oh no, he was an Arab, for the first time I am *telling* you, so shut up, if you please, and listen! He was Ahmed Ibn al-Mu'azzam, he was one of the coalition that had made the revolt against the Turks; Intelligence at the last minute passed the word he was a Turkish agent, hugely paid, had been, still was and would be, to destroy the coalition, break it to fragments in the hour of victory into murderous tribal war.

'He had to be eliminated, the Arabs couldn't be seen to do it, even better if they never knew about him or else they'd go blind with suspicion and start their murdering anyway (that's what they told me Colonel Lawrence had said, why should I not believe 'em? Oh God was he not the expert?); so he had to be killed by Turks, *my* job to find enough Turks to make sure it got done. "Up to us to do the dirty work, why the hell else d'you think we're here?" That's how they put it to me. "Dear boy, you've to swallow your conscience: if possible, without indigestion." There were prisoners in those festering dungeons'd perpetrate anything for the right sort of reward: I made the promises, Serjeant Thackeray found the weapons, we both of us drilled 'em till we saw they'd got it right, we hid behind the curtains while they did it, we shot 'em down bang-bang-bang the instant they'd finished; everything completed according to . . . oh no but it was not! Not according to any orders that anyone had actually *written*, and that crafty bastard Thackeray sent in his report to say so, and in fact as it turned out the poor bugger al-Mu'azzam was no more a Turkish agent than I was. Intelligence had got it all wrong and who would they blame for it but me? And what the hell were the French going to say? So . . . so . . . so what else could I do but go on the run, they'd have had me in front of a firing-squad if they'd caught me, you do see that? Or buried me for years in a military prison? What good would I have been to you there?'

'God's sake, you were no damn good to me even *before* you went to the war, disgracing yourself at Cambridge with somebody else's money and no more than half a yard in front of the police – you still haven't come clean on the whys and wherefores of that. I needed a man who could give me a living, not just to stuff me brim-full of an ailing baby and bugger off. Hugo at least is a businessman, for all his nasty collar and hypocrisy, this school makes its profit, don't pretend you don't benefit, it's a sodding good hidey-house for you, and myself between your legs to take up where you left off, in spite of all I hate you for, in spite of your everlasting lies . . . oh you sly lying bastard, one word from me to Hugo of who was the child's father, of what we did then and what we've done since, I could finish you, collapse you for ever, gestrafed, kaput, *fucked*; so why don't I?'

'Why don't you – ?' he began to say, but broke off in a splutter of laughter. There was a slight noise, a scraping, a kind of scratch, from behind me (I thought) in the harness room: was it Westwood coming back? Because if it was, I didn't want him, I should never have insisted he ever came. Or maybe it wasn't in the harness room, was it not more likely Griselda? She kept irritably shifting her position on the table, she couldn't cope (I thought) with Max and his torrent of words. I could hear him showering spittle as his laughter ran on and on, shooting up all of a sudden into yet another of his dunghill screeches, which almost at once became an overpowering eructation of gobbets of phlegm, a vomiting into his handkerchief; the worst I'd ever heard from him. It even made Griselda speak tenderly – 'Dear Christ is that *blood*? Oh my dearest, why didn't you tell me it was that bad? If only I'd known –'

'I've had it for ages, I'm not on my deathbed just yet.'

'But have you been treated for it? A sanatorium, or at least perhaps a –'

'They say Dartmoor is sovereign for such conditions, kills you even quicker than Switzerland. Never mind about that now. I want you to listen, and listen quickly, we haven't much time. I told you what I've just this minute told you because it seems to me Varley is about to find things out. Has *begun* to find things out. He knows about Dublin. But then *I* know about Dublin, as well: I know that in Dublin he somehow blotched his record – interrogated maybe the wrong man once too often with a cosh in his hand or a knuckleduster, I can't say, but they cleared him out of it, the bullet in his leg was just a pretext, at any rate he won't want to go to Dublin to pursue me. But then they cleared *me* out of Dublin: that punctilious jack-in-office Childers got wind of Damascus, or part of the story at least, and it's not beyond imagining that Varley can get wind of it too. I suppose he still has his black-and-tan friends, I suppose they might write him letters – some of them at least will be literate.

' "Sheer filth," says Childers to me in the basement scullery (would you believe?) of a regular Monto brothel house, "ordure flung in the face of our peculiarly splendid cause, to have one of us revealed as a freelance assassin on behalf of the British Empire, and *using*, what is worse, our clandestine campaign as a means to conceal himself from justice. It's no part of my business, nor that of General Collins, to turn you over into the hands of our enemies. General Collins, by and by, wants you dead, he's afraid you'll go and blab to save your skin; I'm inclined to think you won't, I know more about your sort than he does, I know a damn sight more about the dilemmas, the contradictions, the red-hot hooks and pincers, you must have come up against in Syria ... so no, I don't believe you are a swine ... you just look like one, that's all, and we cannot have you with us. Change your name once again, O'Brien, get out of the country on the ferryboat tonight, keep your mouth shut and think yourself lucky." Ha! the considered voice of the brand-new Republic of Ireland, such as it is. So it's as well you're made aware of exactly how I'm placed and just why I can't stay here much longer.' (She gave an almighty great moan like a lost calf crying out in the fog; the hand that had seemed to be pushing him was now tugging him to her in an access of grief.) 'It's not as though Hugo ever wanted me here anyway, even with what little he knows of my reasons; as it stands he's ashamed to give me up, but ... Next week, next month, next term after the New Year, when he hears the full story, what then?'

She made little gulps in her throat as though she tried to answer him; but before she could frame them into words, there was a clatter of feet outside in the yard, a clamour of voices: the carpentry class, precisely punctual! and the carpentry shop fast-bolted and herself in the butt-end of it with her coarse face all swollen with tears, her hair coming down out of her hat. They jerked themselves, those abject adulterers, in opposite directions: they might have been a pair of startled mice. He to the front door to undo the bolt before his pupils got their hands on the latch, she through the back door, almost treading on my legs, desperate to lose herself in the coach house.

Max, breathing heavily, and sounding (at least to *my* ears) like a burglar caught red-handed, blurted out his routine orders to the class, enjoining them abruptly to take their tools, find their wood, make sure they had the right calibre of nails, and all the rest of it. There were now a dozen seniors and half a dozen juniors all over the floor-space, busying themselves hither and thither: oh golly, I'd to get out of there that instant, but how?

Only because I was precious near paralysed with fear, I acted just as though I was brave. I quietly stood up in the shadows, I stepped out of the back door, quietly. The door was within arm's reach; it was easy for no one to notice me, the room being full of boys, and myself (for a moment) no more than another boy amongst them. Max had his back turned, fumbling in a cupboard for the aprons his class must put on. I took care not to shut the door behind me. As little movement as possible, in exactly the same manner as Griselda – or Westwood indeed – a succession of well-lubricated exits – smooth oil of pure terror, and it sped me without hindrance through the harness room into the coach house.

I paused inside the coach house; important I should not overtake Griselda; I crouched down behind her car to watch her, how she went. (There was a splinter of cloud-muffled moon edging through a glazed panel, very grimy, above the lintel of the double doors.) I could see her stoop to take her shoes off and then pad upon stockinged feet toward the wicket in the left-hand door: she opened it quickly and quietly, closed it behind her quickly and quietly, silent strides across the cobbles of the yard.

No less silent than Captain Varley, who rose up in the gloom beside me, seized hold of my neck with one hand, clapped the other across my mouth, shoved his lips and his moustache into the hollow of my ear. 'Now, laddie,' says he, in a voice like the tide in a seashell, 'not a word or a cry or I'll tear your throat out. You and I must have a chat. But not here. I've left 'em at their revision far too long as it is. Into the schoolhouse, the masters' room. At the double – *move!*'

He held me in the same angry grip until we got there. He overflowed with a waspish ferocity he had never before shown in his dealings with us boys, whatever about his fury against Max. He thrust me roughly into a chair, shook a baccy-tawny finger an inch below my nostrils – 'Not a word, not a cry, or I'll *do* it, with one hand!' – and he was off down the passage to the prep room. I could hear him there quelling the wildly unsupervised buzz, I could hear him taking names for headmaster's punishment tomorrow, I could hear him limping back at full speed. He hung a notice on the door, TUTORIAL SESSION: DO NOT DISTURB! He locked the door, sat himself heavily down in front of me and poured himself a drink. It looked like water; I daresay it was neat gin. He stared me out of countenance for several minutes. His haggard face was twitching more vehemently than usual, he seemed to find it difficult to begin. He said, 'Now laddie,' two or three times, breaking off to clear his windpipe. At last, he ejaculated, 'Good! I think now we know where we are. You thought fit to listen, at the back of the carpentry. So did I, from the harness room. I'd caught that boy Westwood running in from the yard, you see; he told me you were there, insofar as he could tell me anything: the silly child seemed half-stunned. So I went to find out and I found. Just the end of it. Half a minute, no more. You must have heard more than I did. And none of it too pleasant for a clean young chap like yourself to experience. Let me tell you a few things that might . . . might help to . . . *explain* the experience. Here we go then, good.'

He launched into a long story of his work in Dublin Castle. As usual he unfolded it with picturesque vigour; in my breathless relief that I was not being sent to Pellinore, I listened to him completely entranced.

He began by explaining what he called the Tricks of Terror, how this evil fellow Collins, a self-described 'general', eaten up by hatred for Britain and by fanatical adoration of the Boche, had recruited a most ruthless murder gang for outrages all over Ireland, attempting to reverse the result of the late war, the war (Captain Varley emphasised) in which my father gave his life for no other end but to keep the world clear of all such men as Collins and their very brutish deeds. He described some of the deeds – as for example, no longer than a week since, the early-morning butchery of gallant British officers as they enjoyed their Sunday lie-in before church, fourteen of them all told, spread out across the city of Dublin, and all within the space of an hour! A dire treachery that only succeeded because Collins had corrupted (with trinkets and small coins and, dreadful to relate, kisses) the very housemaids in the officers' lodgings. Unbelievable? But nevertheless he was just the type for such foul play, a tamperer with servants' affections, a wheedler at back doors, a sort of up-to-date version of the snake in the Garden of Eden.

Now fragments of this had previously formed part of the captain's stories, but never quite so systematically laid out, nor exuding such moral intensity: no longer a passing entertainment but living history with strong purpose.

He worked toward that purpose in a curiously crablike manner, switching away from Dublin just as Dublin became thoroughly gripping. 'And the rest of it?', he snapped. 'All the rest of what you heard, just now amongst the carpentry. You see, what we have here, laddie, is the essential raw material of basic intelligence; it's your job to communicate, as clearly as you can. Fire away.'

I did my best. Attempting to avoid any account of the close dealings of Max with Griselda, I found myself stumbling among thickets of atrocious incident, Turks in a festering dungeon, Serjeant Thackeray, bang-bang-bang, and who was to eliminate whom? He soon interrupted me. How much did I already know, he asked, from what I'd heard, or what I'd read, about the war in the Near East? General Allenby? Colonel Lawrence? The Arabian revolt?

I knew a fair amount, I said, of the adventures of Colonel Lawrence, disguising himself as a sheik, blowing up the Turkish railway, but –

'Not much else, I daresay, h'm? The political campaign? The undercover work? Except these few hints from Mr Latrappe just this last half-hour, h'm? Espionage, assassinations, knives in the stinking alleyways of the native bazaars, Arab boys who'd sell themselves to anyone anywhere, and thereafter sell your secrets which you'd never known you'd lost?' He developed the theme of 'lost secrets', concentrating upon the necessity for spies (whether ours or theirs) to construct deceitful lives for themselves, to tell all sorts to everybody (to our side as often as their side), to 'lie in the same bed as a venereal vampire, a reptile that chewed at your guts'. He became excited at this thought, specks of foam seeped from the corner of his mouth, he did not appear to hear me when I asked him what 'venereal' meant.

He harrumphed, jumped to his feet, paced the room, swung his stick from side to side like Mr Punch. 'Now look, laddie,' with a harsh gargle at the back of his Adam's apple, 'you saw what I saw in the carpentry. Break a man's heart, but I'm damned if I let it. Least said, soonest mended. And we're both here to mend, understood? Ah yes, though: but how? Damascus won't do. He's supposed to be dead to save their faces, why would they want to resurrect him?

'But Ireland's another matter. Now look, laddie, while I was stationed there – and I've told you all a good many tales about that, h'm? – much of our duty was the sifting of all the data that came in from informants, truth against lies. I'm sorry to say a high proportion was indeed outright lies, cooked up to get a reward for some drink-sodden gurrier or gouger or bowsie or gobshite from the Dublin slums, or else, and far more dangerous, deliberately provided by Collins's men to mislead us. Vitally important we took no action until we knew our information authentic; we didn't want to put a bullet into one of our own agents, h'm? Couldn't risk moving entire squads to seal off an empty warehouse only to find the rebels had been holding their illegal parliament in a wide-open hotel at the far end of town, which did happen, let me admit to you, though it's not generally known and it's best you shouldn't spread it about.' (In nearly all the captain's tales was a titbit 'not generally known'. After Dryghtskerry, so I've been told, he went to work for the *Daily Mail*, special correspondent from the far-flung shores of empire, where there was no one to challenge his accuracy.)

'But a smart young chap like you,' he cajoled me, still striding up and down four paces each way, pausing for emphasis at either end of the room, 'will appreciate that unproven information, upon which we could not act, might nonetheless turn out valid, that's to say in the long run, and provided we didn't forget we were holding it. So you see, we had a rule: do not destroy data. And then we had a second rule, logical consequence of the first: every morning, every evening, take a browse through your out-o'-date files, you never know what you might not turn up.'

What did turn up, explained the captain, was a folder of pictures, some of them taken by army or police photographers, others cut out of newspapers: views of crowds at public meetings, football matches and the like, everyday street scenes, portrait groups of schools or athletic clubs or charity committees. In every picture, at least one face (sometimes more than one) had been haloed in red crayon. 'Red,' explained the captain, 'for acute suspicion. On the back of the picture, name of the chappie, reason for the suspicion, name of the informant providing it.' The face, as you'll have guessed, of one Fergus O'Brien was there, very clear in a wide perpective of Christmas shoppers in Grafton Street: he was carrying a stringbag full of parcels wrapped up in patterned paper, he wore a wing-collar and a homburg hat, combined (as you'll have guessed) with half-moon specs and a soup-strainer moustache. He looked like a senior bank clerk fetching home the childrens' presents. On the back of the photograph an informant had written, 'Could have organized murder attempt against lord lieutenant, 19 December '19?' Captain Varley couldn't remember the name of this informant, but he did remember observing that it was a name that 'failed to carry immediate credibility'. So at the time he'd taken no great note of O'Brien. The moustache and glasses stuck in his mind as being possibly a disguise. Something else stuck in his mind, no disguise but a physical characteristic impossible to conceal: the unusual hang of O'Brien's left hand as he balanced his limbs against the weight of the stringbag in his right hand.

'Now, laddie,' breathed the captain, sitting down very softly in his chair, 'have you ever noticed Mr Latrappe on his way into class with a heavy pile of exercise books under his arm, have you noticed how his other hand curls up and turns over from the wrist?'

This could not have been more exciting. I quite forgot what Max said to Griselda about knuckle-dusters and coshes, or if I didn't forget, I dismissed it as the unworthy smears of the enemy: I was hearing the inside story, I was in the confidence of the Secret Service, how should it matter to me that the Secret Service had shifted his chair a good foot-and-a-half nearer to mine, or that the Secret Service had a breath like a dog kennel and was tapping with his fingers along the top of my thigh? All I could think of was – when would I find out by what tremendous dramatic device the inside story would reach its conclusion?

But there was no dramatic device; in the middle of his tale he just came to a full stop and barked: 'I suppose it crossed your mind you should tell the headmaster?' I goggled. He showed all his teeth in a slow, cunning smile. He dropped his voice. 'Oh, oh, but tell him *what*? Should we speak to him of *Mrs* Pellinore?' It was not possible I could sit still; yet where could I move to? I was jerking about in an uncontrollable spasm of fright. And then it was his turn to jerk: 'God, boy, what are you up to? Sit straight in your chair. Good Christ is he having a fit? – here you are, boy, drink this!'

It was his own half-empty gin glass; I certainly needed it, for how could he think I'd tell any such stuff to Pellinore? Unless the captain himself didn't know ... And *if* he didn't know, wasn't it right that I should ... *Now*? I choked, spluttered, recovered myself, this was a new sort of fright altogether, but I had to say it, hadn't I?

'Sir, it's not just Mrs Pellinore; sir, it's Mr Pellinore himself; sir, Mr Latrappe is his brother!'

He was beyond question taken totally by surprise.

'Brother, brother, what? 'Oh no, are you sure, quite sure?'

He had to repeat himself several times; I replied to him several times, trying hard to get a grip, avoiding (as before) the black incomprehensibility of 'who was the child's father' and the even blacker chasm of her legs in the air one after the other and her bouncing about astride and the ugly gurgles from her wide-gaping mouth. 'Why,' says he, finally, wearily, as though making up his mind toward a new and more complicated state of affairs, 'why, this, if you have it right, boy, so entirely alters the ... alters what I thought was the –'

He falls into such a deathly silence I feel I must somehow break it. All I can think of is the question I've asked already and got no answer. 'Please sir, what's venereal?'

He doesn't look at me at all, but begins, after a moment, to speak, wandering from whatever point he might have been trying to make in regard to the headmaster or Max. His words are directed more to himself than to me, almost inaudible murmurs about ... about, I suppose, Mrs Pellinore, because he calls her that just once, but otherwise she's the 'Dynamo-Tartar': a remarkable pair of words if I'm hearing them correctly, but I don't think I do, he's mumbling so low in his throat. (If, as I nowadays guess, he alluded to the fearful fable of *Vagina Dentata*, he was a better-read man than most would have given him credit for: damn his eyes, do I misjudge him?) At all events, he rambles on through his sour complaint against her, how he's lagged and limped after her for months, all summer and autumn, like a randy old dog with his tongue hanging out, how he's known she was in heat but never for him, oh no! how she's given him 'fuck all but the wind from her fundament and only then when she blew from the north-east. They all think that because I . . . They all think a man's got no interest in women, just because in default he has now and then chosen to . . . And then, and then,' he mutters and whimpers, 'oh and then, just like that, here he is on his bloody great crud of a machine. I suspected from the first day I saw him and saw *her* with her eye upon him, eye.' He rolls his own eyes in a grotesque ogle, glaring into mine at a distance of less than a yard. Which seems to bring him back to where he is, who I am, why he's found it needful to talk to me. 'Aha!' he suddenly cries, interrupting himself with a sort of relief, 'we are prevented. Tomorrow, why not tomorrow? Let's brood on it overnight.'

So, we were prevented, by the bell for the juniors' bedtime. It came clanging through the corridors, with Griselda like a town crier augmenting its clamours – 'Hurry along now to your dorms, no foolery or talking or the headmaster gets your name in the morning, quick sharp!' – two dozen pairs of feet up the carpetless stairs and myself toiling after, abruptly dismissed by the captain, frantic not to be last. Any night, if she felt like it, last boy up could be reported: last boy up was very frequently whipped. As it chanced, the last boy wasn't me; a harmless little fawn of a child called Blenkinsop being the one to be entrapped, his name taken, his sleep turned to apprehensive nightmare. But I slept no better than he did. I had dreams about Grizzel, her gleaming eyes, her tossing fetlocks. I don't care to think about them, even today, God I *dread* to recapture those dreams: in my present state how can I contemplate what she did to me in those dreams, what she insisted that I did to her?

In between the waves of dream, sweeping in on me throughout

the night, I was well enough awake to make up my mind that whatever Captain Varley wanted, I could not, I would not, oblige him. My adventure with Westwood (indeed, at the crucial moment, *without* Westwood, the little creep) had sickened me of the whole business. I was fearfully unprepared for these grown-up emotions, unmanageable and vile. The captain's inside story from now on was no mere romance by Max Pemberton or Percy F. Westerman; it was a tangible physical entity in the depths of a dark wood, a species of lurking Jabberwock, if I moved it would pursue me, if I spoke it would throw itself on top of me and suffocate me, if I tried to resist it would without remedy devour me.

Next morning, Sunday morning, the only decent breakfast of the week, sausages. Captain Varley served them out to the juniors; I wasn't at all hungry, and he himself ate nothing, seemed poorly, left the room before the meal was over. Passing me where I sat at a corner of the long table, he stooped and spoke softly in my ear: 'After church, laddie, the library, another chat; don't talk about it.' I saw McAllister, from the top table, looking across at me with a peculiar expression. It worried me, I can tell you, nearly as much as all the rest of it: to be noticed by McAllister was at once to enter jeopardy.

No light reading being permitted on the Sabbath, the library was out of bounds, so it was easy for the captain to be there with me unobserved. When I came in, he was already seated with notepad, envelopes and fountain pen in front of him, his fingers tapping a tune on the table top. 'Good,' he said. 'Here we are; take it up where we left off, h'm? Have you given it some thought overnight?'

I stood there without a word. He asked me again, and not a word. Again, and again, and never a word. I may perhaps for a moment have stammered a little, but then I bit my inside lip till I tasted the blood in my mouth, so stubborn I was to hold my silence. I must have appeared as stupid and mulish as only a distressed little boy can appear. I thought he would have hit me, his twitch so extended itself from his face to his neck, to his shoulders, to his arms. He clenched his fists and banged the table.

Then he bethought himself and tried a new tack.

'No,' he said, gently enough. 'No, laddie, it's not your fault. Mine, in fact, for seeming to fling the full burden of it onto you. But you see, we do have a very dreadful kind of fellow buried (as it were) in an ordinary decent English school, blackmailing (no doubt) the headmaster by his family relationship, and corrupting (you can depend upon it) the wife of the headmaster so she becomes ... becomes ... well, the type of lady you don't need at your age to talk to or even hear about.' He paused, looked at me thoughtfully and then suddenly shot me a question: 'Which of these people do you *not* want to get into trouble?'

This was such an unexpected thought that it quite destroyed my silence. I gasped, 'Trouble, sir? No! I didn't think *they'd* get in trouble, but ... Mr Pellinore, sir, when he's really angry, he'll give a fellow as many as twenty cuts. Mrs Pellinore, sir, she'll laugh when she hears it happen, I've seen her outside his study after dinner when we're standing in line there for ... Mr Latrappe, sir, he never had me hurt, never sent me up for Mr Pellinore's punishment, however mad he sometimes got with some of the others, it's only that he ... that he ... he expects us to know more French than *he* does, oh oh oh it's not fair!' By this time I had collapsed into regular blubbering, and d'you know, that bloody pervert had me sitting on his knee, and to this day I don't really know what he did with me, but somehow with his hands all over my body in and out of buttons, he soothed, smoothed and frotted me, yes he did: I didn't think at the time there was anything wrong, maybe in point of fact there wasn't, or at any rate not in specifically criminal terms.

Nonetheless he did soothe me, and all the blood in my young veins felt strangely and deliciously warm.

Never mind if it annoys, Ms Briggs must make her comment. She positively does not *believe that when he says 'delicious', delicious is what he means. His experience was invasive, aggressive, traumatic; she really must* not *allow him to remain in denial, she really must –* 'Shut up,' *he says.* 'Wait.' *He's not yet at the point of his story.*

The captain put me onto my feet again and spoke quietly and briskly of practical matters. 'Mr Latrappe has never had you hurt, because Mr Latrappe has never dared draw attention to his very clear abilities to hurt all manner of people in all manner of very cruel and dreadful ways. I cannot tell you for sure whether the man called Fergus O'Brien was or was not involved in the attack on the lord lieutenant. But if he *was* part of that gang, then it's a matter of moral certainty that innumerable other outrages can be laid to his charge. Attacks upon policemen, repeated ambush of military vehicles, the abominable massacre of magistrates, clergymen, old ladies, fishermen, farm labourers, only because of their devotion to king and country and the loyal information that they gave to the authorities. That's what he did, you see, and then when the going was good they slipped him safely out of it. Never mind what you might have heard him say in the stable last night, Sinn Féin would never have chucked him on such a ridiculous pretext, no no: he has been sent. For a highly nefarious purpose. D'you supposed we can unravel it?'

I think I must have said something to the effect that – oh sir, couldn't, shouldn't, wasn't it possible, the police be fetched in to unravel? He didn't seem to like the word 'police' in my mouth, yet he clearly had been waiting for me to utter it, if indeed I did utter it. This whole conversation was as though I was hypnotized, and (again) to this day I don't really know how it was he persuaded me to do what I did.

'Important,' he said, 'that *you* should write the letter. Multitude of reasons why it couldn't come from me. Confidential. Security. Any role I have here of necessity *covert*, if you know what that means? I have certain responsibilities of my rank, you understand? even though invalided-out. Besides, if they read it from a brave young English boy, it'll help it to carry immediate credibility, the raw material, d'you see? of basic intelligence. Credibility implies we may have to twist the truth, oh no more than an inch or two, no harm because it's all on behalf of the greater truth, which after all is all part of the game – we don't fight secret murder by Marquess of Queensberry rules. Jolly good. Sit quiet for five minutes, stick your nose in a suitable book.' I found a *Pilgrim's Progress* on a shelf and examined the etchings in it for about twenty minutes, scarcely able to think, scarcely aware of where I was or what was to happen. The captain, breathing heavily, wrote and crossed out, and wrote and crossed out, and crumpled sheets of notepaper into his pocket. At last he looked up at me with a crooked but triumphant grin: 'Y'know, I don't think I'll have you copy it; instead, I'll dictate it. That way, you can make your own spelling mistakes, it'll show itself more authentic. Take the pen, take the pad, tilt your handwriting back to disguise it, and not a word of talk till we're finished. And then I'll explain it. Here we go.'

And here's what he had me write, every syllable burnt into my memory:

Dryghtskerry House School. **URGENT & CONFIDENTIAL**

To the Chief Constable, North Riding Police, Northallerton

Dear Sir,
I spoke to Mrs Pellinore about this and she says I ought to write to you on patriotic grounds, but if I'm at all scared I must beg you not to find my name. If anything goes wrong, you see, that husband of hers will whip me within an inch of my life. And she'll have to deny it. So I beg you as an officer and gentleman to protect me. One of the masters here is an Irish rebel and murderer. Also he was a traitor in Syria in 1918. I know all this because I heard him telling Mr Pellinore about it. He is Mr Pellinore's young brother Henry, although we all have to call him Mr Latrappe. Mr Pellinore is hiding him in the school while he makes plans to assassinate in England. He said to Mr Pellinore that he knows they have his picture and dossier in Dublin Castle. Could you please telephone Dublin to see if they really have? The name they know him there would be Fergus O'Brien and whatever he's done in Ireland it should certainly get him interned. I want him interned. He is terrifying Mrs Pellinore, he makes her cry, she says he wants to
[*fornicate* crossed out, *copulate* crossed out, *rape* crossed out]
do things to her, I'm not sure what the words mean, but it's horrible. She won't write to you herself, she says she has a duty to her husband.

Yours truly, and in danger,
A Young English Boy (aged 11)

'But sir, this isn't true, I never spoke to Mrs Pellinore, sir, I never did at all, and she never said to me that I ought to –'

'Shut up. If you wail like that you'll be heard all over the school, dammit.'

'Sir, you promised you'd explain?'

'Yes I did and I told you we were going to twist the truth. So wipe your eyes and pay attention. Y'see, laddie, it don't do to make a lady the villain; Mata Hari, fair enough, she was foreign, but an *English* lady – oh dear no! Not if we want the bobbies to treat the data with respect. In any case, d'you see what it means? When they come to make enquiries, the first one they'll go to will be her. With some damned embarrassing questions. She won't know how on earth to answer them. Even though she's not shown as a villain, she'll be blushing all down to her boots. Dear oh dear, such degradation. Don't you tell me, laddie, you don't want to see her degraded. Jesus Christ, but *I* do. Dragged through the mire where she'd drown all honest men, if she could, if she could: oh dear, she'd drown *me*, no doubt about that.' For a moment he seemed to relapse into his 'Dynamo-Tartar' confusions of the previous evening; but he pulled himself out of it, pulled himself out of his chair, and hobbled at great speed round and round the room.

'Envelope, envelope,' he snapped. 'Sit to table, boy, write the envelope.'

'But sir, sir!' I pleaded. 'They're bound to know I wrote the letter, even when it's sloping backwards, if they use ... won't they use ... g-graphicological an-alice?' (I had the phrase, or thought I had, out of Sexton Blake.) 'Oh sir, scientific comparison with everyone else's writing throughout the whole school, and when they know it was me, won't they ask me and ask me till I admit only half of it's true and then they'll not believe *any* of it and ... Oh and Mr Pellinore, sir, won't he surely, oh but he will –'

'Wait, boy – what you say is remarkable good sense. Graphological analysis, my God, science! D'you know I hadn't thought o' that, too much on my mind to see things straight. Too much. So what do we do? What the deuce do we do, boy? Ha! And aha! I know what we do. I'll go and I'll *type* the bloody letter, in the masters' room, the bloody typewriter, why the deuce didn't I think of it before!'

'But sir, if you type it, I don't see how it's going to look as if –'

'As if you're the one that wrote it, ha? Aha! then we'll clarify: and here's how we do it. We'll add a few words more, at the bottom, take your pen, I'll dictate.'

A postscriptum, and it said:

> PS: I sneaked into the masters' room to type this on the machine there so that
> you won't be able to tell from my handwriting it was me.

'And I'll type it shocking badly, bloody near indecipherable, two
stuttering forefingers like a half-wit gorilla. And then I will type the
envelope, and then I will find a stamp, and then I will post it, and all
we've to do after that, laddie, is crouch: cats at a mousehole, bloody
well crouch there and wait.'

*He shoots out a palsied hand all covered with liver spots; he grips Ms
Briggs by the wrist; it is not a very strong grip but it shocks her, so
unexpected, like the dart of the tongue of a chameleon. She'd give
anything to shake it off. Yet she does feel a delicacy, considering the
circumstances. She lets the hand lie there; she asks him what's the
matter? She implies he should not continue if it agitates him so
much. He says, 'You are sweet'. He says, 'You are compassionate'.
He says, 'At this point I must ask you what should I have done?' She
tells him she'd rather not tell him, it's not for her to – He tightens his
grip. His fingernails cut into her flesh. She winces and tells him that
if she must tell him, she believes that most people would think it
right to denounce a terrorist, but wait! in her own short lifetime so
many terrorists who weren't terrorists at all, and political and media
prejudice, police malpractice, what about that? and all those unjust
judges. So maybe he was wrong, although perhaps he had no choice?
But most certainly he was wrong to – 'To write lies, you mean to
say? Peculiar twisted lies about that twisted peculiar woman just to
suit Captain Varley's neurasthenia? So would it have been better
had I written the truth about her? Answer me that then, Sylvia
Briggs.' But she can't. He leaves go of her, he lies back, he continues.*

I must thank you, Sylvia Briggs, for the benefit of the doubt. But
although I said 'hypnotized', the captain was no Svengali: I did have
the choice, I could have refused, I knew very well that I should
have refused. But then, there was the matter of *trust*. I trusted the
man Varley, whatever his 'secret chats' and his twists and his
twitchings, for no better reason than he *was* a British officer and my

father a British officer – non-commissioned, but nonetheless a leader of men into battle – and the captain had been wounded and my father had died. Whereas, with Max Latrappe, no trust in the fellow at all: why not? For no better reason than he was the first grown-up man I'd ever heard – and indeed to an extent *seen* – in the throes of the two-backed beast with a bloody great grown-up woman – and the woman was Griselda.

During the next seven days I kept out of the captain's way, nor did he come near me, nor did he speak to me, save the odd insignificant question in his English or History lessons. Even so, he did stare at me; and I found myself staring at him. Boys began to notice. It was not only embarrassing, it was dangerous. McAllister seemed to think I was in some way encroaching upon his territory, his privilege, his prerogative, or something. Together with Armitage and Kenyon he would lie in wait for me and torture me. I won't tell you how, I don't want to remember it: it was filthy. Nor could I understand why. D'you know they wouldn't tell me why. They'd just hurt me, humiliate me, and run away sniggering.

I'll tell you who I didn't stare at: I didn't stare at Griselda, I didn't stare at Max – I didn't even *look* at them, no not for a whole week. I had to look at Pellinore, we all had to, anyway, always, or he'd smarten us up with his cane. More by token, within that week I was booked for his punishment four times. On the Monday, then the Wednesday, and then (would you believe?) on the Friday, dear God, twice. In short, the one week in my life of the greatest depth ever of physical pain and of course the expectation of pain, I cannot tell you which was worse.

I began to wonder, had all that business in the library been no more than another of my bad dreams? But during the last two or three days of the week I noticed policemen, on bicycles, on the road in front of the school. They would pedal slowly past the gates in pairs, two heads under tall helmets turned up towards the windows, a careful, deliberate glance, nothing overly significant, but I hadn't ever seen them there before. They did seem to appear quite often, every four hours, maybe; I couldn't really tell, having no chance to keep a consistent watch. I didn't know if anyone else noticed them

– the captain? or Max? Or maybe they had always patrolled the road like that and I'd never happened to see them?

And then, Max Latrappe caught hold of me.

A bitterly cold morning, snow the night before, turned now into ice, iron-hard upon the road: we were walking home the three-quarter mile from Sunday church, a bowler-hatted, woollen-gloved crocodile, prayer books in our right fists, big boys in the lead immediately behind the two Pellinores, small boys trailing behind, Max and the captain like sheepdogs guarding the flanks, and Miss Elderbroom to bring up the rear, hand in hand with Bateson and Gooch (the two smallest in the school, aged five-and-a-half and six, unhappy little beings). As we picked our way up the steep street of Dryghtskerry Staithe, not so much a village as a sordid cliffside straggle of fishermen's hovels, Max suddenly seemed to slide across the cobblestones directly toward me. He saved himself from a fall by grabbing hold of my elbow, causing me to slide in my turn: he contrived to manoeuvre me in one adroit movement out of the crocodile into the narrow alleyway between Mrs Hordle's grocery shop and the side door of the Captain Cook pub. 'Stay there,' he said swiftly. 'Lean against the corner of the wall. You and I must have a chat.' To Miss Elderbroom, just then passing the end of the alley, he said, 'Jenkins slipped on the ice, he may have sprained his ankle. I'll take a quick look and have him home safe and sound, don't worry.' He waited till she was out of earshot, and then continued, behind his hand, in a dark insistent whisper, broken as ever by his damned coughing: 'I'm not interested in the likes of Kenyon or Armitage, let alone that dirty cornerboy McAllister, but I *am* interested in *you*, and I don't think it's any too late. Not yet. So we'll follow up to the school by the back lane, along here, and I want you to listen very carefully. You don't have to answer me, if you're embarrassed, if it's painful: I shall quite understand.'

He kept his hold on my elbow like a constable conveying me to a Black Maria; he walked me round behind the pub up the flight of stone steps that constituted the 'back lane'; he talked all the time about Captain Varley, very hoarsely, very earnestly. He knew (he gasped) that effectively I had no parents; Captain Varley was in no wise a suitable substitute; I really must be most careful how far I confided in him; on the other hand he himself (Mr Latrappe) would always be ready to listen to me, upon anything that might perhaps trouble me. He had (he gasped) observed the captain looking hard at me on several inappropriate occasions, he had observed me peering across rooms at the captain as though I needed to catch his eye, he had also observed the captain deliberately ignoring me when he might have been expected to speak to me. All this (he gasped) added up in his mind to one question: was I involved with the captain in anything 'not quite right', anything I might be ashamed to talk about, anything (not to put a tooth in it) *beastly*? – he felt sure I understood him. For the captain was almost certainly carrying on in a way that could get him sent to prison. And if he did get sent to prison, the boys he was involved with would be grievously involved with Mr Pellinore's punishment, whether or no the police decided to let them alone. He thought it likely that if *I* were involved, at this stage and at my age, I'd be a more or less innocent party; even so it was not impossible I would soon be most direly corrupted.

Yet another bewildering shock, and after so many already! and how was I going to respond to it, except by a feeble 'oh sir, I don't know'? And then, after a moment, 'Sir, sir, are you going to tell them about ... about ... are *you* going to tell them about anything? – the *police*?'

He said, 'That depends. A most highly serious business, Jenkins. One would have to know more of it, Jenkins, a great deal more, one would have to be certain, one couldn't take the risk of it –' (he clicked his tongue indecisively, swerving away from whatever words he might have been about to utter) 'I just thought it necessary to give you a short breath of warning, that's all, obviously of warning but also of ... support and potential ... ah, potential comfort ... it is dreadful for a man, for a boy, for any age or shape of human being, to clench some ill secret to their heart and never to dare to deliver it. I feel sure you understand me.'

We had by now reached the entry to the school playground; he dismissed me among my classmates with a private pat on the shoulder and a public reassurance as to my ankle. Sinn Féin murderer or not, he had without doubt been speaking very kindly to me; he sincerely seemed to wish to save me from something.

Captain Varley was no more than part of it: my main thoughts and fears were directed toward McAllister and his gang. I knew now that Max was aware of them: perhaps I really should go and talk to him about them, had he not said he would listen? But oh, if I did, how could I ever keep silent about ... about ... Oh please, gentle Jesus, how *could* I?

Did I say the shock bewildered? So how d'you think I felt when it suddenly struck me (in the middle of Sunday dinner) that I ought to go direct to the captain and tell *him*? It was as though I was battered from one wall to the other like a ball in a fives court; it was as though I had become imbecile in the instant of a handclap: for was it not probable that Max's gentle words were a treacherous deception, the first strike of his counter-attack against the forces of the crown as incarnate in Captain Varley?

Nonetheless, for the next two hours (which is to say the pudding course of dinner, followed by thirty minutes scuffling about in the frozen playground and keeping clear of McAllister, followed by our departure in a high wind upon our regular Sunday walk, conducted unusually by Pellinore himself) I could *not* make up my mind whether to go brazen-faced to the captain or not – which means, I suppose, that my *trust* was not quite what it had been.

Yet the letter irrevocably had been sent. With the captain I had pledged my oath to crouch against the mousehole, implacable. Our noble task. Our plain duty. And here I was, beginning to wish I could find some way to repudiate it. Here I was, beginning to hope it might not be too late to turn everything around and ... and ... why, be back just where we were, before ever any thought of that dark unhappy carpentry shop!

Pellinore, on the few occasions when he took the walk, would choose for his companions a pair of boys who would not be in the worst of his bad books; they must listen to his prosings all the way along the road and back again. That Sunday I was one of them, not having been whipped since Friday. The other was Westwood, with whom I was scarcely on speaking terms. We walked at the rear of the column, so that Pellinore could keep his eye upon everyone else's behaviour. A blustering, uncomfortable afternoon: he was in gruesomely jovial mood with his anecdotes from Roman history and his screwdriver questions; he seemed to think we knew all the books of Livy cover to cover. Thus (on the very last leg of the walk, just about to re-enter the playground gate): 'Westwood, boy, *your* opinion, as Jenkins seems entirely nonplussed – if Romulus had not killed Remus before the wall of the new city was finished, how do you suppose he could have dealt with him once he'd finished it? It's a question of practical politics. In a few years' time you'll have the vote. Remus, for example, might be a ... ha! ... a treasonable socialist candidate. Ha ha ha. Well?' Westwood was still dithering, his mouth going open and shut like a stranded fish, trying to work out what on earth the man was getting at, when the boys at the head of the walk came to an abrupt and disorderly halt; we all bunched up behind them; Pellinore began to expostulate, venting his usual threats, but he stopped because he saw – Because the first thing he saw was his wife, with her hair about her ears, running across the playground towards him.

At the main porch of the schoolhouse, behind her to the left, a long black touring car stood parked on the gravel, with a flat-capped policeman at the wheel. Another copper beside it, holding open the rear door. Behind the car, a whole bunch of them in helmets and capes, standing with their bicycles. Upon the steps of the porch, Max Latrappe coming down between two more, large men in bowler hats and heavy overcoats. We could see the handcuffs on his wrists. We could hear him cough and cough. We could hear Griselda's cries. We could stand in a wide-eyed cluster watching how she flung herself sobbing upon Pellinore; we could realize how Pellinore was no longer aware of any of us; we could (after a moment) take note of a group of seniors, at the far right of the playground, kept back against the wall by Captain Varley; we could observe the upper windows, servants' faces, white and staring, Miss Elderbroom wringing her hands in a torment of uncertainty.

The moment he saw Pellinore, the larger of the two large men strode rapidly to meet him, even as Pellinore thrust Griselda aside and hastened in the direction of Max. 'I am Chief Inspector Piker, Mr Pellinore; I take it you *are* the Reverend Pellinore, headmaster of this school? Be so good then, Reverend, to send all these lads out of it, it's nowt at all to do with them, and those others in the corner there with your subordinate, we don't want them here either. Get along, you lads, go!'

'D'you hear what the officer says?' cried Captain Varley. 'All boys out of the playground: this way now, quick sharp!'

'I'd also be obliged, sir, if you'd put some sort of stopper on the lady? It'd be useful if we could hear ourselves think.'

We had scarcely made the first move to obey the captain, when Max, halting suddenly halfway down the steps, stiffened himself upright, flung open his mouth and uttered an astonishing bellow: 'I see you there, Varley, *you* did this, *you*! Oh yes, to shut my mouth, you dungbucket stench of an imperialistic pederast, you did it to –' *Imperialistic pederast* made no sense to me at the time; it's sheer hindsight guesswork that that's what he really did say; but whatever it was, he never got it finished, let alone in any sense explained. At the height of his execration he broke off – mouth wide open, mouth shut! – to make his instantaneous escape.

Why was he not handcuffed to one of the detectives, if they believed themselves to be arresting a dangerous rebel, in all likelihood armed? I'd say surely for that very reason. For they themselves (as it soon appeared) were equipped with revolvers, deep inside their overcoats. Unaccustomed to shooting people, they'd need both hands free for the business.

At any rate, he ran.

He ran absurdly, with his wrists clamped in front of him, but he ran very fast. He had taken the last four steps in one leap; he tore zigzag through the playground, through all of us indeed, scattering us as he came; he sped through the gateway, over the road, and onto the cliff path that ran towards Norseman's Head, a path strictly out of bounds to every boy in the school: no fence to shield it from the brink, a notoriously perilous place. Police came pounding after him, but he had the advantage despite his handcuffs: he was slighter, longer-limbed, and was wearing neither overcoat nor cape, only a light cardigan over his collarless shirt. The pursuers were also hampered by all the boys still in the playground: I could see Mr Piker and his colleague pulling pistols out of their breasts, but how could they shoot in the midst of such a panicky crowd? Thrusting clear of the playground, they did fire some shots, they really, actually, fired some shots, I saw and heard them fire shots, it would have been like a cinema film if the films were at all realistic: in fact it was just *crack-crack* with no more drama than a broken plate, because none of the shots hit any sort of mark, neither Max nor anyone else, and if somebody had told us these fellows were firing blanks I could never have said that he lied. Uniformed men in the meantime were running every which way, some of them jumping on their bicycles and pedalling furiously out along the lighthouse road, I suppose to cut Max off where the road joined the cliff path; but he wasn't going to give them the benefit.

Because of course he must have realized he could not possibly escape. A mortally sick man, in frost-bound winter, manacled, with not one friend in the entire countryside, doesn't stand a chance in hell and he knew it. He threw his arms straight out in front of him and jumped off that cliff as though from a diving-board.

We all saw it. We could none of us truly believe we had seen it; but we had. It was infamous, demented, accursed.

I fell weeping to the ground between Westwood's stupid feet, and Westwood bent down and put his arms round my shoulders to console me. Console me for what? *He* didn't know; *I* didn't know; his face was as wet with tears as mine was. And nobody noticed us at all. Nobody out of an entire prep school of malevolent little tykes paid any attention to two of their number hugging in the playground like a pair of soft girls and blubbering shamelessly. Incredible, but it happened. Dryghtskerry House in one short moment had been transformed into an open wound: who among its company should have eyes for anyone else?

Nevertheless I do retain certain camera-like images, swift glimpses of adult persons at that moment of terror and horror, passionate gestures fixed forever in the darkroom of my mind: Griselda tearing after her lover with a wild, desolate roar of anguish; she'd have jumped the cliff herself if a copper hadn't grabbed her round the hips: Pellinore standing all askew, front to back, with his feet toward the house and his face toward the heaving sea and his wide-brimmed clerical hat screwed up tight between tumultuous fingers; his pince-nez on its long chain had somehow got entangled with the hat; he broke the frame and cracked a lens and never noticed: Captain Varley, yellow-faced and bent across his stick, sidling like a strip of cloud behind some of the taller boys, and then behind the gatepost, and then altogether out of sight behind the house.

That evening the school handyman spread it about that Max did not fall straight down into the waves: he bounced and banged from one ledge of the cliff to the next until he smashed himself onto the north-western spine of the Dryghtskerries, half under the surging water, half out of it, just like his toppled motorbike. He died a considerable distance from the ruin of that motorbike; but the same merciless ridges did for both of 'em.

That was Sunday afternoon, just before tea. Miss Elderbroom took charge, decisively took charge, which for her was most uncharacteristic; but then the whole day was uncharacteristic, it was a day quite abstracted out of time. She gathered the school together as though for Prayers and Assembly, indeed as though she herself were headmaster. She told us that after tea we would have Community Singing for a portion of the evening; she would then read to the juniors from *The Jungle Book* while the seniors could choose their own books from the library, any sort of book. She thought, under the circumstances, we could do without Bible Studies.

The Pellinores and Captain Varley were not to be seen anywhere about the boys' part of the schoolhouse. At intervals we were aware of a muffled but agonised howling from somewhere at the far end of the building: we guessed it was Griselda, and we shuddered in horrified delight. The handyman let us know that the police, helped by experts from the Whitby lifeboat crew, had hoisted Max's corpse up the cliff by means of an ingenious tackle. The corpse had been carried away in a police van to wherever such iniquities were dealt with: a very special kind of corpse, a criminal suicide, macabre. We were not allowed to see any of this. Mr Piker and other plain-clothes coppers were in and out and up and down asking questions of the servants for the rest of Sunday and most of Monday. They did not question any of the boys, with the exception

(Westwood told me; I didn't want to know) of McAllister and one or two seniors, who weren't with them for very long and wouldn't talk about it afterwards. Helmets and capes pervaded the grounds, and the masters' room was kept locked, with a constable in the corridor outside. Miss Elderbroom was with the detectives in Pellinore's study for nearly an hour; she came out of it biting her lips, and was unusually angry with anyone she met for quite a time afterwards. More reading and more singing filled up the greater part of Monday. No lessons. A long walk in a sleety squall, well away from the cliffs, was made adventurous by the sudden eruption into our ranks of three pickpockety-looking men in trench coats and squashy hats. Miss Elderbroom called them 'gutterpress' and drove them off with her umbrella. Of course the whole school was buzzing with rumours, Westwood oustandingly prolific, though none of his fantasies came anywhere near the truth.

The handyman passed the word that Captain Varley had gone away before dawn. A lad from the saddler's shop at the top of the village had fetched him by horse and trap to the first train for Scarborough and York. He forgot to tip the handyman, who was sure he wouldn't come back, he'd had such heaps of luggage with him and was so bloody-blasted surly with everyone, particularly the police at the gate ... The police, yes ... Particularly ...

Once again an interruption from Ms Briggs. She thought, she really thought, that that small piece of news must without doubt have dissolved any remaining atom of trust Mr Jenkins might have felt toward the captain? She was sorry for butting in, but he seemed to have come to a halt, and she really did think it was psychologically crucial to make the point clear, whether or no there'd ever be any readers of what he'd dictated, or whether ... Himself and the captain: it was the end, wasn't it?

The end, yes indeed, of my trust. Oh indeed you are quite right. And not only my trust toward the captain. My entire basis of trust, for the whole of my life, was quite utterly undermined. Slowly, over the next year or so, I came to understand that I was never ever again going to place my trust in anyone, not for anything, not for love, not for money, not for any useful secret I might conceive within my breast. Let me tell you, there've been *hordes* of secrets. Let me tell you, furthermore, I've never let anyone put trust in *me*. Which no doubt will be the reason why my piddling poems and my loveless little scraps of dead fiction brought me nò reputation, except as a sort of cult among a certain crowd of hole-in-the-bucket avant-garde, throwbacks to the days of *Ubu Roi*, artistic bloody charlatans I did my best to ignore, except now and then to prey upon 'em, fitting 'em up with dud projects and bogus exhibitions, insolvent magazines, gaudy public-relations schemes which somehow never got through to the public, but all of 'em feeding nicely into one or other of my bank accounts.

He attempts, for the third time, to chuckle. A very feeble noise; he can't keep it up. He chokes and splutters, but carries on speaking.

Not a lot more to tell. After breakfast on the Tuesday Miss Elderbroom made an announcement. We were to start our Christmas holidays a fortnight sooner than arranged. (God, how we cheered!) Telegrams had been sent off to all parents and guardians; the day would be spent in packing; the next morning we would all be on our ways, driven to the railway upon a specially-ordered char-à-banc, provided the roads were not too icy for the horses' hoofs, provided the parents and guardians had replied to the telegrams; and we were all to wrap up well, the char-à-banc had an awning but was otherwise wide open to wind and weather. She added, 'You must remember, boys, everything you have here, clothes, books, toys, sports equipment, you must pack! Mr Pellinore is not going to ... That's to say, he doesn't know ... Mr Pellinore has not yet decided when the school will reopen for the Lent Term.'

I suppose I should have realized she knew it would never reopen. But I'd not quite finished with trust, and I still had the notion that most grown-ups would say what they meant, and mean (on the whole) what they said. Especially such good grown-ups as Miss Elderbroom. We all used to mock her behind her back, calling her the Old Floorbrush and suchlike; but I think we well knew she was good, the only good one at Dryghtskerry; we knew.

Anyway, the school did close and my irritated relatives sent me off to another establishment, not so far distant – Dryghtskerry in fact had played cricket against it. Quite a number of Dryghtskerry boys found themselves there that January, including Westwood, silly weed. It was as bad in its own way as Dryghtskerry, but the headmaster was not cruel. Only weak, and too tolerant of bullying and of beastliness and of general this and that, which did me no good, no good at all, damnation. Out of the bounds of this story, forget it. But what I *don't* want forgotten: all the likely and unlikely tales that floated in to the new school not long after we got there, most of them via Westwood, tales about Dryghtskerry we otherwise wouldn't have known.

We heard that the Pellinores were no longer together. Neither of them had been prosecuted for harbouring a suspected rebel, but the word had got out and their names were as murky as muck. He lived in York now, giving crams for exams and getting drunk because he couldn't find anyone to whip; she'd gone to London and sold drugs in a nightclub.

Miss Elderbroom went into partnership with the wife of a Darlington doctor; they set up a modest kindergarten for children under the age of eight; they never whipped or even slapped their little pupils.

At home with his family, that nasty young devil Armitage let slip an incautious word about Captain Varley's 'chats'. The matter was relentlessly probed; his parents went to the police (who already had an inkling, thanks to Max in his handcuffs on the doorstep); the captain thought fit to travel south. To the steaming hot jungles of Kenya, according to Westwood, where they were all on the run from Queer Street, as was very well known.

I began to have a dream, a cold clear frightening dream, which stayed with me at this new school night after night for a whole year, and then faded away until . . . until . . .

* * *

The man I always think of as Max Latrappe, which is to say Henry

Pellinore, comes staggering out of the sea, swarming the clefts of the Dryghtskerries, heaving and wheeling all that's left of his motorbike. His handcuffs are snapped in two, but the halves of them are still locked on each wrist. Blood masks his face and drips from his beard, blood mixed with seawater, blood from the huge wound in his head mixed with blood from his mouth as he coughs. He and the bike are garlanded with glistering seaweed and he speaks to me, not harshly, coughing, snorting snot from his nostrils, weeping.

'Oh my dear Abel, dear boy: I was so sure it was Varley who betrayed me, but now that I am dead I know it was you. Despite which, it is possible I may be able to make you laugh. I laughed just three times and nobody, nobody, could understand why.

'One, because Varley told stories to you boys that I knew were a pack of lies, and as far as I knew, he didn't know that I knew.

'Two, because when he knew that he knew about Fergus O'Brien, he didn't know that I knew about McAllister and his gang.

'Three, because Hugo found out long ago that Griselda's dead baby was mine; it was only to stop me telling her that I knew that he knew, that he let me stay hidden in his school; Brother Judas, didn't he yearn every day to hand me over?

'When I knew about McAllister and I did not have proof, oh my dear Abel, why could you not have helped me to find it? And that letter which you wrote – If you'd written the full truth as you knew it, you could surely have praised yourself the whole of your life. As it was, you were as filthy as the rest of us. Oh my dear Abel, dearest boy, you'll surely never find reason to praise yourself ever again.'

* * *

Can you believe it? The dream came back to me, no more than a week ago, the night of my seizure, when they brought me to this hospice. Which is why I have you writing all my torrents of quavering words; oh sweet and warm young woman, my delicious and most *trustworthy* Sylvia Briggs, just for you to be here at my bedside, that dream came back and came back! I have suffered it every night I've been here. But now, I think, not any more. Call it a birthday, not a deathday. And there we are. Finished.

He lies back in the bed and closes his eyes. She is anxious to say something, offer a consoling comment upon all that he's told her, but he seems not to hear, seems not to feel her soft hand. She puts up pen and notebook into her briefcase and goes softly from the room. In the foyer she takes care to observe the statuette; she had not noticed it before. Neither Psyche nor Demeter, she concludes, but Aphrodite stark naked, with a furtive, cruel smile upon her face. An odd little flaw in the workmanship adjacent to the right eye looks exactly like a wink. Was old Jenkins aware of this? She concludes that he probably was, and that he meant her to take it as a sexual proposition: the best he could do, given his age and state of health.

MOLLY CONCANNON
& the Hag out of Legend

There was a woman called Molly Concannon. I was in no way a friend of hers, but a few people I knew in Galway would talk about her, often: she was a character. She lived about ten miles from town in a half-modernized, half-derelict cottage, on a low-lying marshy peninsular running out into Loch Corrib. She drove a half-derelict *deux-chevaux* Citroën in a notoriously dangerous manner. She had been a teacher in a girls' secondary school and had taken early retirement. For 'health reasons', she sometimes said. I heard that at other times (usually when she had been drinking) she would attribute the retirement to the malice of the nuns who ran the school. Her own malice was as notorious as the virulence of her motoring. She wrote poems and short stories which achieved occasional publication: they seemed to be saturated in begrudgery and guilt but it never was quite made clear whom or what she was begrudging or why she felt guilty.

She also wrote book reviews for a local newspaper. She was usually 'disappointed' by other writers' work; very rarely she chose to praise it, and then she went entirely over the top, hailing some obscure and crosspatched author as the most stimulating discovery since Colette or Mary Shelley or maybe Djuna Barnes. She maintained her personal pantheon of literary 'greats', incongruous and inconsistent, which she did not try to justify; she simply asserted their overwhelming qualities. If your taste ran with hers, good! If it didn't, the more fool you.

People sneered at her, but had to admit she did have a talent. Her conversation was extravagant, whether vicious or girlishly enthusiastic. She buttonholed individuals, in the street and in cafés and bars, and embarrassed them dreadfully with long tales of academic conspiracies against her literary advancement, or with far-fetched accounts of this publisher or that critic who had said such wonderful things about her latest piece of writing that she was sure to be nominated for that prize or this and thereafter be as famous as she deserved – 'And *then* you'll see me swagger down Shop Street!' she'd yelp.

I talked one day with a man who had talked with a woman who had been talking with Molly; and to Molly, so he said, had been vouchsafed a remarkable epiphany. She had somehow uncovered, in a queer little corner of Galway, a gorgeous old, old woman with the most wonderful memories; incontinently she (Molly) was about to encapsulate them in what was only bound to be a wonderful, wonderfully gorgeous book.

I thought, 'That'll be the day'. Molly had never written a book. Even her longest story was no more than six pages. Was it possible she possessed the energy? She certainly did have bad health.

And then I thought, 'If she means it, she's bloody brave.'

And then, 'Piss and wind. She's bragged like that before.' On thinking it over, I couldn't remember that she had. At least not in such straightforward terms, not to so precise a specification.

And then, a week later, I met her, in Middle Street in what was then Bewley's Café; she put out a little gloved paw at me and held me by the forearm as I was passing her table with my cup and saucer; she grinned at me as though she'd known me all her life, and wheedled and steered me with ancient-mariner glamourie into a chair beside her, fixing her sharp grey eyes upon mine from behind her bifocals and never taking no for an answer.

As usual she was wearing her bright-red belted plastic mackintosh, with a grey tam-o'-shanter on her crisply-cut short whitey-brown hair. If it wasn't for a bit of a twitch at the mouth and an intermittent tremor of the hands, she looked clean, cared for and presentable (which was not always the case). But I did think she seemed unwontedly *aged*. Something was wrong with her teeth.

And of course she'd already been drinking, elsewhere than in a café: her sentences went round and about.

Nonetheless, the old woman. There really *was* an old woman. And really old, that was the point: Molly kept insisting on it. She swore that her 'Miss Fidelma' was ninety-five and no joke, a recluse and a cantankerous one, and yet in her own way a 'species of goddess', a 'hag out of legend', the 'ruin of incredible beauty', holding hard to very nearly all of her faculties and well able to talk and talk and talk with exact articulation – although not altogether along lines of conventional logic. She could also remain silent for days at a time – whether sulking or suffering, or merely taking a rest, was not to be discovered. Her silences were illegible – 'and at her age, that's her privilege, wouldn't you say, Arden? Wouldn't you?'

Fidelma McLeddy, daughter of Fergus McLeddy of Utica, NY.

Never married (so Molly had deduced) but far from celibate; born in America and expensively educated there by some very high-class nuns; quarrelled with the Church at the age of fifteen; came to Ireland the same year, already mixed up in some complicated way with the Republican Brotherhood and the 1916 Rising; intelligence agent for Michael Collins in the War of Independence; ditto for the Republicans in the Civil War immediately afterwards; hardline Communist during her years in the Soviet Union (ah, but which years? Molly hadn't yet got the dates out of her); Trotskyite (or was it Anarchist?) in Spain; double agent among and against the Nazis in World War II . . . and God alone knew what she did in Europe and Latin America for decades after that, only all the time, *all of it*, she'd been writing 'these gorgeous poems, would you believe? and for Christ sake, not one of 'em published!'

And then, the men (and women) she'd had some class of a love affair with. A list like Leporello's in *Don Giovanni*. 'D'you know? I won't accept that more than a quarter of 'em are lies. Exaggerations, maybe – I mean, how the hell would she have had the time? But dammit, Arden, they're plausible – even *you* couldn't weasel your pedantic little way out o'that, if you'd heard it the way she tells it – one in six may be outright famous – Trotsky himself, in Mexico? – who knows? Bert Brecht? The Countess Markievicz?

Dare I say the Countess Markievicz? ... But to my mind the *poetry's* the key to it; I'm reclaiming her as a poet whom no one's ever heard of; and mind you, she wrote in Irish as often as English or even sodding French ... Oh, if only I could *accurately* work out when and where.' Chronology, she informed me, was not the most vitally surviving talent of this antique Semiramis.

And yet it did seem that Molly was little by little extracting from her the bones of a biography. Well, perhaps not a biography: was 'memoir' the more correct term? Perhaps not even 'memoir': a series of reminiscent 'impressions' might well be the best she could get.

But –

'But,' she said. And then, after a long pause, 'Oh yeah. Did I tell you? She refuses, absolutely refuses, to give me permission to write? Cantankerous, that's her. Cantankerous and unpredictable, and as arbitrary as a midsummer thunderstorm. I have to listen to her, and remember, and pretend *not* to be remembering, and talk it all down into my tape recorder as soon as I get home. Pathetic.'

From which the inevitable conclusion: Molly could utter no book until Miss Fidelma was dead. But on the other hand, if Miss Fidelma died too soon, there would never be enough material for a book. The memories were oral and random; the poems were written down indeed, but literally all over the place, fetched now and then out of drawers and cake tins and unexpected little pockets or purses, on fragile scraps of yellowed paper, shown briefly to Molly and then huddled away again. I gathered that Molly used to go to Miss Fidelma's house – a single-storey two-room box in an alley leading down from Prospect Hill – every day to sit and chat and run messages for her, as it might be a charitable visitor, a 'lay nun' on the social services round. After the first hints of book-writing, which met such a chilling rebuff, Molly had not ventured to return to the subject. But she was sure that Miss Fidelma knew well what she was after; she was sure that Miss Fidelma was cruelly teasing her.

I gathered it had all begun on a pouring wet evening three months or so earlier, when she had found Miss Fidelma staggering home down the alley from the shops with a bag full of groceries she could scarcely lift and no umbrella. Molly had offered her help, had been tumultuously invited in to tea, and had sat and listened for hours to weirdly erotic recollections of Alexandra Kollontai and of V. I. Lenin in his prime. 'We laughed and laughed together; she said of course I must come again. Which I did, and kept on coming. Now you know. Oh Jesus, d'you suppose I'll ever get the book made? Ever, ever? God, but I get so depressed.'

After that, for half a year, Molly dropped out of sight. Into hospital, I heard later, where she had to submit to a series of gynaecological and gastric operations. 'Minor' operations, to be sure: but they cannot have done her much good. When she eventually resurfaced in June, she was quite lame, she was haggard, and ghastly pale. I remembered her as she had been the first time I saw her, twenty years earlier, a brilliant little dragonfly, sanguine and vivid, a sort of emblem upon two legs of nature's vitality at its most creative, a sort of –

(Oh, leave it alone! We all of us fall ill, we all of us have to grow old.)

I came upon her one day in Eyre Square: she was walking very slowly, arm in arm with a tall gaunt astonishingly upright figure in black. They both had their sticks and it was not quite clear which woman was supporting which. I immediately assumed the tall one must be the famous Miss Fidelma. Somehow I felt I ought not to confront them: I dodged behind the transplanted renaissance porch-structure that forms a focal point at the head of the square; I saw them and was not seen.

They walked, very slowly, round the fountain, black coat and red coat, rigid black hat and soft grey cap, just too far away for me to hear what they were talking about. But without doubt they were talking, both at the same time, and both with remarkable energy.

Molly was stooped over, and her cap pulled well down across her brow; I could not see her face.

But Miss Fidelma's face was notable.

Hawk nose, sunken cheeks the colour of dried brown apples, no apparent eyebrows, a small knowing smile of an intimate mouth that no doubt contained false teeth for it certainly did not *munch* as

do so many ancient mouths, and a pair of deep dark eyes that may
have been half-blind (Molly had said they were half-blind) but
nonetheless kept flicking and flashing in every direction as though
everything was in their view and everything was watched and
weighed and marked down for judgment behind that uncompromis-
ing wide mottled forehead. A few wisps of white hair escaped
from below her hat rim; a thin plait of it, tightly wound, lay over
the turned-up overcoat collar like an old-fashioned Chinaman's
pigtail.

I heard her suddenly make a noise in her throat: a barking,
baying, gargling noise, which I took to be a laugh. And then Molly
laughed too, with her usual shrill yelp. And then the two of them
turned in their tracks and aimed their slow walk toward the
pedestrian crossing by Richardson's pub. And so up the right-hand
pavement of Prospect Hill, and presumably to Miss Fidelma's little
home.

I began to think, compulsively, of *biblical* people. Of the
prophetess Deborah, perhaps, fetched out by a younger acolyte
under the palm tree between Ramah and Bethel to give instruction
for the war against Canaan. Or perhaps of the queen Jezebel, led
upright to her dressing table in Jezreel, preparing to paint her face
for the better defiance of Jehu. At all events, I thought, Molly's
'catch' was a splendid one: and I hoped, almost fervently, that the
book she was planning would not be aborted.

That autumn I had to leave Galway for more than a month; as often
happens with such trips, I discovered when I returned that a crucial
event had taken place in my absence. Six copies of the *Galway
Advertiser* on the mat with a heap of letters, clogging the gap
between front door and floorboards; half an hour to look through
this pile of bumf (most of it junk mail) and make mental abstracts of
its chief contents; an hour and a half before my eye caught a
smallish headline buried in the middle of one of the *Advertisers*.

GALWAY WOMAN'S LINKS WITH HISTORY
Lonely Death of a 'Great Survivor' Spurs Revolutionary Memories

'Great Survivor' being a quote from 'Ms M. Concannon, well-known local writer and friend of the deceased', who had discovered the body, or so the paper said. Miss Fidelma had 'passed away', so it said, 'in the armchair beside the fireside'; and Molly, who held a key to her house, had walked in upon her, all unsuspecting, to find her 'sitting there as she always sat, staring towards the door, her eyes wide open in welcome, her hands spread out to gesture "Hello".'

No references to any poem or any hope of a book. Molly at this point was playing her cards close to her chest: when all was said, why shouldn't she? The book was to be *her* book, nobody else's. Fair enough.

I rang Molly to offer belated condolences and to play nosey-parker; she did not answer the phone, she did not call me back in response to the message I left on her recording machine. After that, I minded my own business, and neither saw her nor heard anything about her. Maybe she was in hospital again?

Towards the end of November, an unseasonable burst of fine weather: I was invited for a 'Sunday spin' with some neighbours in their new car round the coast of Connemara and inland through the hills and valleys of the Joyce Country. We stopped off in the failing light at a remote thatched pub along a twisty bit of road a mile or so short of Maamtrasna. Maamtrasna of the horrible murders, more than a hundred years ago, when several innocent men went to the gallows. As the others didn't mention it, I refrained from spoiling the jaunt with macabre comment.

There was a great turf fire in the cramped little bar: comfortable for a while, but then it became oppressive. The chimney smoked in an adverse breeze. My head began to ache with the close atmosphere. I excused myself from the company and went out for a breath of air. I found it already dark this side of the valley, although across the river atop the shoulder of the opposite mountain the sun still struck vehemently, laying its huge patches of orange and gold along the ridges. I felt an urge to climb those ridges for at least a part of their long slope, to place myself there in the glow of the sunset, to stare at it directly for the few minutes before it ended; I trotted downhill to the bridge, over the water, and off the road up a steep narrow bohereen for a couple of hundred yards. It was deathly quiet, except for the occasional scoffing sound of some mountainy sheep behind the bank. The only building in sight was the pub I had left behind me, electric bulbs in pokey windows gleaming bright through the dusk. A car swung down the road, horn blowing at the bend, tail lights disappearing in a matter of moments behind a fold of black hill.

And then, at the very end of the track where it ran up onto the open moor and was closed off by a makeshift barrier of cut boughs and strands of barbed wire, I came to a cottage. A cottage in total ruin full of brambles and nettles, two broken stone gables and fragments of old wall connecting them. There remained in the front wall a pair of eyeholes of window-gap and a doorway like a yawning mouth, through which I could see all the way across the valley to the glare of the last few moments of fierce red sun. A quarter of the disc had already sunk behind the hill; the rest of it would be gone before I could regain the pub; I stood there and dazzled in its rays.

It can only have been about half-past five, but it seemed to be much much later; a feeling almost of midnight, I can't explain why.

Nor can I explain why I was not really startled to see and hear a woman in the ruin of the cottage, even though she sprang out of it like one's notion of a banshee, with a moan and a low screech and the flurry of a tattered red garment. Somehow she seemed to belong there: an icon of old slaughters, a shade of everlasting lament from the famine years.

But I *was* startled when I realized she was Molly Concannon. She saw me and blinked at me. Stopped short, fell silent, blinked at me.

'You,' she said. 'What are you doing here?'

'Me. What am I doing here? I mean, what are *you* doing? Why?'

'I came for a drive. And then I went for a walk.'

'Where's your car?'

She made a vague gesture. 'Somewhere. That way. Below. Miles away, who knows? Does it matter?'

'Molly, have you had an accident? Your mack's all torn and . . . God! is that blood on your face?'

'Thorns,' she muttered. 'Barbed wire. Fingernails. I don't know. I don't want to talk to you. I came here to be alone. I came to think about death.'

Death? I guessed she must be drunk, or else having a nervous breakdown. I wondered ought I run back to the pub and fetch some help, or phone for it. Was it perhaps an ambulance situation? At the least I should ask the others if *we* could bring her home; I was sure she wasn't fit to drive.

'It's not on my face, the blood.' (She was mistaken, it was.) 'On my hands, that's where it is: hands.' (But her hands were gloved. This was nonsense.) 'Don't leave me. I have to talk to you.'

The last shred of sunset caught her sideways across her brow, causing her right-hand spectacle lens to flare. Her hair was thrust out like a furze bush; she seemed to have lost her cap; she spoke rapidly and awkwardly out of one side of the mouth, as though a dentist had been at her gums, freezing them with a local anaesthetic.

I decided to let her talk, while I pondered what to do next. She sat down in the gathering dark and bent herself into a bundle, pressed against the cottage door-jamb between the brambles and an old iron pot-oven that lay at the base of the wall. A great deal of what she said was unaccountable rambling, about unmarked famine graves all over the western hills, about the rubbish in the bohereens (on my climb up there I had indeed passed the wreck of an abandoned car and what I took to be the relic of a refrigerator), about the end of all life at the edge of ocean and how from the ridges above us she thought she'd seen the edge of ocean and knew that it was *final*.

Suddenly she came to the point.

'Fidelma died. You know that? She had to, you see. Because when I was in hospital they kind of . . . kind of fucking let me know that *I* was due to die. Six months or a year at most. The hell with it, they didn't say so; but I could see it in their eyes; they knew it, they bloody knew it. She wouldn't let me write. I couldn't wait till she was dead. She was going to live for ever and I was going to die. Christ, man, how could I find the time? Did you hear how I told them I found her?'

I muttered something silly: yes, I'd been away, but I had seen the piece in the paper, hadn't Miss Fidelma been sitting in her chair? Heart failure? Not surprising. After all, she was ... ninety-odd, wasn't it? They *do* die, at such an age. Isn't that what we call the 'human condition'? Isn't it?

I don't think she heard a word I said.

'At last, you see, I persuaded her to dig out all her poems for me. I mean *all* of them. And a diary. Volumes of it. A whole heap of it. All written in little account books, year upon year. She laid it all upon the table and then she began ... oh God she began ... to shove the lot of it into the fire. She cried out I was a horse leech. "Give oh give!" she kept repeating, imitating my very voice. "Why, you're not called Concannon at all! Does not your Bible tell you that *Give* and *Give* are the only names of the daughters of the horse leech?" She sneered and she gargled and she barked and she laughed. Such a very wicked woman, such a bitch, such a hag, such a monument of malice: I had no choice but to stop her breath.'

'Stop her – ? Molly! You don't mean that you – ?'

'Cushion. Took a cushion off the other chair. God, she was strong and I was scarcely strong enough. Did I tell you, my operations. But when I'd finished, her eyes were open, her mouth open: all I had to do was lay her back where she was and spread out her arms before they got stiff. No blood, of course, that was the beauty of it. Which is odd, because nowadays –'

She rubbed her little gloved paws together like the Lady Macbeth of a school play. There was the moon coming out from behind a cloud: I could just see her peaky white face peering up at me from the shadows and twisting itself at me, nostrils, lips, teeth, chin.

'No, I had no choice. Could I have persuaded her to stop burning the manuscripts? Maybe. But suppose I had? How was I to know she wouldn't do it again, the very instant I left the house? I told you she was arbitrary. Arbitrary and so fucking *unreliable*, so she was. You'd have done the same, they'd all have done the same. *And* it was just as well. Because, d'you know, she didn't leave one line of a fucking will or sodding testament! That useless old cousin of hers, that half-wit of a next of kin, didn't *she* get the fucking package, house, money, everything? *And*, if I'd not attended to it, every single bit of paper with any shape or size of writing since way back to Patrick Pearse and Tom Clarke.

'But, you see, I did attend to it. I went straight to my own house, returned with a suitcase, piled the whole of it into it, put it into my car which I'd left up Bohermore not half-a-hundred yards away, went back yet again to *her* house – and lo and behold, I found her there stark dead!

'And nobody, nobody, had any suspicion at all. Why should they? All her cash, all her jewels, they were all where they should have been, when "next of kin" came creeping and scraping. "Next of kin" knew fuck all and cared fucking less about diaries, about poems, as well I was aware or I'd never have tried it. Ignorant old trout. When I say "ignorant old trout", I am quoting Fidelma: I know in my heart *it was as she would have wished*. How dare you imply that it wasn't?'

I had implied nothing of the kind. I'd remained entirely silent. But now I felt I had to speak.

'So, Molly, you can start, can you not, to make your book?' I talked very quietly and easily, keeping my distance – humouring her, I suppose one would say. 'Or probably you've started already? You must surely have sufficient material to –'

She astonished me with a sudden shriek; she leapt to her feet and blared at me, a tumult of falsetto frenzy, a 'speaking with tongues' as at a charismatic cult meeting. Her voice was so swift I only caught half of it, and half of that was filthy swear words. But this much was the gist (and then I heard no more of it, for she fled): she had motored down to Dublin with the suitcase in her car to spend several days in the National Library checking dates and references; the car was broken into in broad daylight in Ballsbridge while she negotiated a bed-and-breakfast; the suitcase was stolen; the Garda Síochána informed her they were very very sorry but she 'hadn't a chance in hell of ever seeing it again', such being the present state of the capital.

'Nothing left, oh fucking nothing, and then ... on my hands ... it hadn't been there before ... it's been *given* me, instead. Sti ... Stig ... Stig Stig Stig ...'

At last she was able to articulate 'Stigmata!' Howling it out again and again, she ran away from me down the bohereen, away under the hump of the hill out of reach of the new-risen moon: the black of the accursed valley swallowed her up. Just like that: clap.

MOLLY CONCANNON
& The State-of-the-Art Development

It was widely said in Galway that Molly Concannon, of all people, could never have attempted a 'terrorist-type crime'. Yet that's what they were going to charge her with, under the Offences Against the State Act, for which the Dublin Special Court, needing no jury, was liable to rustle up the most exorbitant sentences. It was less than a year since George W. Bush had announced his War Without End On Terror. Official Ireland was anxious not to seem to run contrary to American inclinations – to say nothing of its own inclinations, despite all the blarney of the Peace Process. Even such a shabby little grey-haired mouse as Ms Concannon, retired schoolteacher with literary leanings, must at least be unmercifully investigated, whether or no they might in the end have to let her go. The place and the circumstances of her arrest were an oddity: ten miles from the city of Galway, at the very gate of the lakeside cottage where she'd spent most of her adult life. A few years ago she had thrown this property on the market and disappeared from the district in inexplicable haste. When arrested, she had with her a stolen white van full of stolen computer stuff, an allegedly illegal foreigner of Middle Eastern appearance and a loaded automatic pistol.

So why would she not be a Subversive? She herself was an oddity in her place of current residence, a standoffish blow-in, not at all friendly to her neighbours there. She had arrived, knowing no one, in a desolate dreary townland on the fringe of the Border, and had rashly and incompetently bought a plot of land. She set about building a bungalow without (it seemed) enough cash to finish more than half of it or enough common cunning to prevent the contractor cheating her. His cheating was as notorious as his jerrybuilding: Ms Concannon, all unaware, became quite a figure of fun. That's when she took to drinking, said some of the neighbours. Others said no, she was at it already; hadn't she lost her job in Galway because of the drink and licentious behaviour? They said too, she had a guilty secret. In this, they were not far wrong; though none of them could do more than guess at what the secret might be.

The officers of the Garda Síochána in Galway, who'd intercepted her as it were at a venture, found nothing against her outstanding in their records, no connection with paramilitaries, or any other doubtful hangover from her local past, except that – 'Hold on there!', an instant of excitement among the filing cabinets – it was remembered she was reputed to have had something to do with the sudden death of an old woman who in turn was reputed to have owned a most valuable cache of historical papers. Alas, no more than a rumour and it did not make good police sense; the death was not suspicious; no papers turned up anywhere; Ms Concannon showed no sign of having unexpectedly enriched herself.

Yet once she was in a cell there surely had to be at least a morsel of plausibility about the whole business, some consistency in the Book of Evidence to give confidence to the prosecution, or else –

Special Branch did some searching and built up the bones of a story, approximately as follows:
It was in fact that very rumour about the old woman that had caused Ms Concannon to flee Galway in the first place. It had reached her nervous ears with a ping like a mosquito, biting straight into the quick of her brain. She found herself quite unable to continue her writing, whether book reviews for the *Connacht Tribune*, or poems or bits of stories. She went in and out of hospital for nearly two years (the Psychiatric Unit, a voluntary patient), and then, without warning, cut her ties with everyone she knew in Galway – none of them were really friends – and clattered away in her rust-eaten ghost of a *deux-chevaux* Citroën under cover of darkness to the borderland estate agent who sold her the building site.

Her secret of course was that she *had* killed the old woman – or rather, she thought she had, which made her of course a murderess even though she might not have been one. She had certainly stolen the papers, but almost immediately the papers had been stolen from *her* by an ignorant thief who broke into her parked car without a notion of what he laid hands on; she hadn't even had the time to look them through from top to bottom, let alone collate and edit.

She was a ludicrous mess of guilt-provoked deprivation, and not at all well. She sorely lacked a companion in the ill-built bungalow which she strove to make into a home, while the dishonest contractor went to court to get even more money out of her, more money than she could possibly pay. It looked as though what little she had would soon all be spent upon lawyers. She had always hated lawyers: what use to expect a cheat to protect her from a cheat? Maybe she should kill herself? Had it not been for the north-westerly view from her ill-fitting kitchen window, she would have cut her throat with the breadknife. But she stared every day at the landscape of woods, valleys, mountainy hills, regular mountains; green, grey, russet or purple, according to the time of year, the wind and the rain, the position of the sun. She loved it, and lived.

All but for one part of it, the view to her extreme right. Here she could see masts and skeletal watch towers, and helicopters among the hills like malevolent dragonflies: their angry little antics reminded Molly every day that what she was looking at was the 'Six Counties', the two-thirds of Ulster still *under British rule*. When she thought of such a thing she ground her teeth and muttered to herself in Irish (a reaction sometimes noted by certain of her neighbours). The less she saw of County Fermanagh the better; so as far as possible she compelled herself to ignore the politics of the landscape and to enjoy it for its own sake, soothing herself, preparing herself for the end of her life – not indeed by suicide but by natural declension. She was scarcely as old as she looked. But she did feel she was probably finished.

Thus she is thought to have dwelt in her half-finished half-house in no more than a half-state of existence through the fag-end of a wet summer and six months of the autumn running on into storm-torn winter. Until spring and a bright spring morning, winking sunshine, fresh breeze, white clouds in blue sky: and in the field below her field, cataclysm and havoc, devastation and wreck. Two yellow bulldozers she saw and she heard, and an orange mechanical digger, not a furlong from her wheelie-bin at the corner of the house. In bare feet and trailing nightgown she ran out of her door all the way down the slope through nettles and thistles, through a gap in the wall at the bottom, over a dry ditch into the midst of the site-clearance gang, crying out for whomever was in charge: no blame to them if they thought she was mad.

A portly man of thirty, red-haired, in green wellingtons and red safety helmet, assured her that *he* was in charge, not just the foreman but overall boss of the job, Eamon Brady of Brady Construction, Castlebar, taking a squint at the first morning's work. What work? Didn't she know? Why, the Greenview Hotel, Conference Centre and Leisure Complex, it had been in the media, foundation stone to be laid by the Minister for the Environment, his commitment already given, greatest bit of state-of-the-art development the region had seen for years, so wasn't it great? He handed her a glossy brochure: on the cover was a computerised mockup of a glittering sprawl of building five storeys high at one end and eight at the other and nearly as long as the valley.

'But . . . but nobody told me . . . I hadn't the least idea . . . there's been nothing in these fields but sheep . . . intermittently sheep . . . how could it happen?' Her voice trembled, her whole body trembled, her white feet were bleeding into the dew.

He gave her a calm smile from underneath his bunchy moustache. 'We're after pegging the site more than a week since. I'm surprised you wouldn't have noticed.'

'Pegs? How should *I* know what are pegs?' (Had she been so blind drunk, not seven days before, that she never saw these pegs put in?) 'But you don't have the planning permission, don't dare to try to tell me you do, I'd have been bound to see the proclamation, I do read the local paper, and your entrance gate's beside my boundary wall – there!' she yelped, 'just over there! No such a thing as a proclamation, not anywhere near the gate, no! and I've been here half a year and before that a whole twelve months I had that ruffian at work on my house, no proclamation!' she stormed, 'no proclamation, no such a thing!'

He told her easily that the notice of planning permission applied-for had indeed been up according to law, where the corner of the site met the road in the valley.

'But that was no good, I never go upon that big road below, too much traffic, too much noise. It should have been where I would see it. How else could you expect me to put forward my objection? And what about the newspaper?'

He told her that the announcement had indeed been made according to law, in the *Longford Leader* and the *Western People*, not his fault if she hadn't seen it.

'One of them's forty miles away and the other is nearly seventy, why on earth should I read such papers? God, d'you know what *you* are, you're a cute fucking hoor and a shit-headed cheat, and you needn't fucking think I'll let this pass because I won't!' She spun round in a shuddering fury and tottered away from him, up the field, over the ditch and so home.

She seems to have brooded tipsily, within doors for three full days, while the work on the site grew in noise and intensity and the view from her window became a poisonous prospect of petrol-fumes, dirt, abomination and desolation; and when it was finished there'd be no view at all, just a horrible great block of eye-hurting glass and leering balconies, upon every one of which every half-wit in the land with money to pay for it would sprawl in a deckchair and ogle her ravished privacy. At sunrise on the fourth day she sprang into her car: able no longer to cultivate solitude, she must at once take action. She drove incontinent to the county town, where she hurled herself into the county offices and slammed on the 'Enquiries' counter with the palms of both hands. The startled girl behind it fetched her at once to the Chief Planning Officer and shut her in with him smartly. If *he* couldn't deal with her who could?

'Let me try once again to explain, Ms Concannon. There is a statutory time for putting in your objection to planning permission, the relevant legislation makes it perfectly clear that if that time elapses without any objections, the planning authority may award the permission at once. The plans and specifications from the Greenview company complied with all our guidelines, and to be

frank the county authority is very glad of the proposed development. We regard it as a great asset, a burgeoning opportunity for
the region.' He reminded her that the national boom had significantly passed its peak. It was everybody's duty to actively nurture
any symptom of continued growth. 'Of course there will be some
nuisance, there always is with building work; but as soon as the
contractors are finished, all the nuisance will be all over.'

'All over me arsehole. There was deliberate ... deliberate ... no
proclamation ... neither in the local paper nor ... not anywhere
near my house. If that's not a cheat, what is it?'

He was genial and courteous, despite Molly's coarse fury, her
broken words, the tears that blotched her scrawny cheeks. He had
the plans of the Greenview brought to his desk, he showed her how
not one window was less than the statutory distance from hers – oh
no though, he apologized! maybe there *was* one, in the fire-escape
stair-turret at the south-east corner of the tower; he would call in
the contractors to have it carefully re-measured, and he was sure
Mr Brady would be happy to use obscured glazing in that particular
instance, if it would relieve Ms Concannon's mind?

'I know,' she said, 'I do know a shit-headed cheat when I see one,
and what about my *view*? – the lake, the green fields, for God's
sake, the mountains, oh Jesus, the ... the lambkins – why aren't
there lambkins?'

'I know,' she insisted, 'I do know from ... I heard it years and
years ago that guidelines, guidelines for an architect, I do know
about architects, he has no choice but keep to them and they do *not*
allow windows to stare into windows at total expense of my
privacy. How d'you explain *that* away, hey? Five fucking storeys
and eight in the tower at the end. Eight, can you imagine, and my
little house just a bungalow.

'Not fair,' she said, 'not fucking fair. Let me tell you, you're
worse than the Brits: let me tell you, you're fucking dead.

'I shall write to my TD,' was her final announcement, as she
limped out of the office with lofty disdain. 'You shall hear from my
TD. He has, I understand, the reputation of a helpful gentleman: I
don't care if he don't belong to the government, all the more reason
he will *not* let a lone woman be persecuted.'

She went home and composed a most eloquent letter to this parliamentary deputy, one of three in the constituency. She knew something of him (she thought). A one-issue independent, she had voted for him only a month ago in the general election, for his campaign for a local hospital: he might not (she thought) be 'in league, like the rest of 'em, with the filthy developers.' He laid specious claim to environmental pretensions; he would be grateful for her continued franchise; she might (she thought) have hopes. She did her best to make the first paragraph (at least) of her letter both moderate and likeable:

> Please be clear about one thing from the start: I raise no objection to a rural hotel, as such; even five-star, I might even stay myself in that class of a premises (supposing I could afford it, which I can't). My dismay is upon a question of principle. I was not forewarned, not ever, never, no sir, I was not!

He was Deputy Eugene Gilmartin, a long, soft-voiced, willowy creature with a soft grey beard; his clothes were pleasantly informal at his weekly clinic in the private bar of the county town hotel, blue jeans and a T-shirt with a smiley-face logo. He had Molly's letter in his hand; he listened carefully and took notes.

'I would of course, Molly, have the utmost sympathy with the loss of your view. Such beautiful countryside between here and the Border, and surely you would have chosen your site with that at the front of your mind, surely. But of course it is a fact that none of us are legally *entitled* to a view. We live in the real world, we cannot control change, a world of change, Molly, choice, competition, development. Let me assure you the Greenview project would be a most progressive local initiative, a three-county participatory co-operative: a partnership, in short, between public authority investment and regional business input. The obvious advantages: touristic and ... ah ... corporate, time-share apartments, you know, and seasonal conference bookings? I do suppose, though, had it been possible for you to have raised your objection within the specified date limits, that something of an amendment of the plans, toward your ... well, your convenience, your amenity, your ... in short, your *view*, might well have been finalised. As it stands, I can write, and will write, to the Minister –'

'What Minister?'

'– for the Environment, of course; we might – it's just possible – get some of those more immediate balconies moved? But don't hold out too many hopes. I'm sorry.'

Molly was beyond expostulation; foul language and frenzied stuttering were no longer of use to her, for without doubt this man was not to be trusted for anything. She sat silent for a long, smouldering minute. One supposes that this was the identical minute when she stopped being a Victim and became a Subversive ... unknowingly? who knows? she rose to her feet. 'Why, you yourself, you're a shareholder yourself,' she breathed. 'Would ya look at the white face on ya! sure you don't dare deny it! Why couldn't I foresee it? I'll not waste my time, that's your lot, you're fucking dead.'

It might also have been *her* lot, save for a chance meeting almost at once in the lounge of the same hotel. A face she had known in Galway. A young woman, sharp-featured, crop-haired, blonde. Not certain of the name, but a journalist, surely. A half-suckled student journalist, unlicked and ignorant, but ambitious and therefore very possibly an answer to her problem. Molly pointed an awkward finger at her from three tables away: 'You interviewed me once ... no you didn't ... I wouldn't see you ... wanted to talk about my poetry ... poisonous rubbish, all of it, no damn good and anyway ... anyway I'd given up writing it, I'd not been any too well. You are Nora Tyrrell. I know that. You're still a freelance, struggling?'

'Struggling, sure. Not a freelance. I'm a staff writer on the *Intelligencer* here, d'you read the *Intelligencer*? – as local rags go, it's not too bad.'

'It's shite.'

'You're dead right, but I mustn't say so. I'm only into the job since November. Can I buy you a drink?' Nora Tyrrell recollected there was some mystery about Molly Concannon. If now she could get that interview it might turn out to be something more than the usual literary sludge. Nora Tyrrell had the cut of a tough little cookie from a 1930s Hollywood comedy, but inside herself not quite. She knew that she needed a stroke of good luck or she was stuck in her dreary job in this dreary decayed county until she died.

And immediately Molly obliged her by surging full blast into her copious tale of catastrophe. The brandies she swigged down, one upon the other, did not seem to discoordinate the vigour of her speech – that is to say, not more than its day-to-day shapelessness. Nora Tyrrell was both professionally sympathetic and genuinely appalled. The Planning Officer, she said, was well known to be bought and sold; almost certainly he himself would have recommended that thug Brady to stick his notice out of sight. 'It's a marvel he gave *you* the permission for your bungalow, how much did you pay him?'

Molly was startled by this one; it hadn't occurred to her in the least; and suddenly she saw what had happened. 'Jesus, I dunno, the contractor paid him off of course, and I paid the contractor, the scheming sod must have buried the charges in my overall bill, I wonder what else he buried? Oh shite, what a ride they did take me for! ... Now tell me, girl, this Gilmartin, would you say he's as bent as he looks?'

'Yes.'

'Oh God, then who *isn't*?'

'Only because the whole county's half-dead from infrastructural malnutrition, there's the more scope for exploitation, all of 'em are at it, what else can I tell you?'

'Do you write this for your paper?'

Nora Tyrrell dropped her eyes. 'No,' was her first word, the rest trailed away inaudible.

'You're afraid and you don't bother, or they won't print it anyway?' Molly's eye was like a cockatoo's, any second there'd be claws out and a cut from a vicious beak.

'I tried. To begin with. Till it was put to me very candidly that I was writing for a local paper, it exists for nothing at all but to serve local interests, its advertisers are local businesses, what possible use is it to any of 'em if it makes'em out to be ratbags and sleazemongers and the scuff of the country? It was put to me very candidly that I'd one more chance left to find the sort of stories that

I *ought* to be finding. So there you are: I *am* afraid, and to bother about it's pointless.'

'Oh-woe-woe-woe,' groaned Molly. 'I've drunk meself very nearly too drunk to drive home, and nothing, I've got nothing, I'd at least had the hope I could get you to write it up! At least you can tell me where I can go to find someone who will.'

Nora Tyrrell, without much conviction, said maybe not a journalist, conceivably a solicitor ... She thereupon emboldened herself and went on to flap her mouth, boasting and bragging that by remarkable chance she happened to know the 'only honest lawyer in Connacht-Ulster. And at least for two days o'the week, he's ... like ... *brave*. Point of fact, I live with him, come home with me, I'll introduce you, you'll have to come anyway, we can't have you driving in drink.'

But the lawyer, however honest, however brave, was of no practical use to Molly. He said simply, 'You haven't a chance. It's a matter of law, not justice. You didn't really think the courts dealt in justice?' Molly (for a wonder) decided not to take offence. He seemed a kind man, despite his brusquerie, quite young but almost dwarfish and as ugly as a punctured football, puffy and wrinkled at the same time. Of course, as a lawyer, he was not to be trusted.

The three of them spent the evening listening to CDs of Irish traditional music, drinking various mixtures, swopping anecdotes of corrupt practices in high places and smoking illegal substances until Molly fell asleep on the sofa. Nora Tyrrell took her shoes off for her, found a duvet to put over her, and went up to bed with the lawyer. Next morning when they came downstairs, they found no Molly; only a note on the kitchen table:

6.30 am: left early because I can't sleep knowing my little car is on its own in the car park, anything could happen it, and *did* happen once in Dublin, damn their lights and livers! but thank you both so so much so much for hospitable great generosity, I truly didn't mean to impose and now I'll have to think up what the hell to do next. *Law, you say,* NOT *justice.* Well, hell, we shall see.

Regards, M.C.

Molly holed herself up in her bungalow for weeks, tippling and fuming (one may deduce). Yet first thing every morning she was seen at the post office with a budget of outgoing letters to all sorts of public persons. Only one of them is known to have reaped an answer, and that from a deputy of the government party: he regretted he could do nothing for her, for reasons which she already knew. ('Long past the stated date; regulations were not to be by-passed by *anyone*; or did she want *everyone* to seek to slip through loopholes?') Horror-story. He added a bite-sized moral.

> This is, as you know, a Border County. People-friendly infrastructural development can only fortify the Peace Process, so crucial to us all – as I am sure you will be happy to agree.

The result of the election had apparently laid it down that all voices in the region should stand to be counted in favour of the Greenview project and its likes. Or if there was dissidence, Molly never heard of it – how could she hear anything anyway, with Brady Construction's daily sound effects just yards outside her windows? Would she ever get used to such loathsome cacophony?

Against all her exhausted inclination, she pulled herself together and actually took practical steps. She went down the back road to a small farmer with whom she was still upon reasonable terms. She knew he did odd jobs, and she asked him would he put up a fence for her between her bungalow and the building site so that workmen could not see her and she could not see workmen. (There'd been certain low gestures: when she retorted with the first words that came to her mouth, handfuls of mud were thrown against her washing line.) The finished fence was over six feet high, a wavering line of stakes with green strips of mesh stretched between them, exactly the sort of stuff Brady Construction hung on its tall scaffolding, more or less impervious to impertinence. The neighbour, sad to say, charged her more than she'd expected; she tried to avoid a quarrel, but her tongue ran out of bounds. Then she paid him every last cent, made a point of not thanking him, went indoors and slammed the door.

Let it be said that two or three years since, before she suffered her breakdown, she would never have shown such ugly petulance;

she used to be sweet and insinuating to anyone she deigned to notice, even those who might take advantage of her.

The final setback of the TD's letter ought to have meant the end of her struggle, for the fence was no more than amelioration of defeat. And so it would have been, had she not had two visitors, unannounced, unexpected (but observed by her insulted neighbour and eventually reported to the Guards): Nora Tyrrell and legal friend. The friend's name, Molly remembered, was Cormac O'Croinin. Months had gone past since she'd met them in the county town. She made haste to clear away the barricade of an old bookcase which was all that held the door shut in a southerly wind. She brought them in and sat them down and fussed. Nowadays, when she wasn't tipsy, younger people brought her up short; she felt unimaginably old and remote, although not so long ago she'd faced classes of teenage girls every day without confusion. In a burst of unaccountable crankiness she hid away her brandy bottle and brewed a pot of tea; she cautiously waited to see who would speak first.

The opening comment, deliberate and well prepared, characteristic of a solicitor, came from Cormac O'Croinin as he looked out of Molly's window into the wind-rippled green mesh two or three yards from the glass. It seemed to astonish him. 'I asked Nora to bring me up here so we could see things FOR OURSELVES.' He had to shout the last two words against a sudden explosion of noise from a pile-driver or some such at the top of the site.

'*I* cannot see,' said Nora Tyrrell, 'how you'll be able to continue to live here.'

'*My* bit of field, *my* house, *my* furniture, *my* choice. And moreover my own choice to have closed up my own lovely view.'

A swift ironical edge to Cormac O'Croinin's smooth voice. 'What would you say if they offered to buy you out?'

'Who?'

'Basically, I suppose, the Greenview company, no doubt through an intermediary. Maybe Brady Construction would have an iron in the fire. If you persist in your complaints, you could be quite a nuisance to their public relations: they'll know you went to Gene

Gilmartin, they'll suspect you've been to others, Councillors, TDs
– you have, haven't you, as well as him?'

Molly laughed, and appeared at first to receive his remarks as
lightly as he'd tried to deliver them. 'I wrote letters. Have written.
He was the one that saw me. Only one to condescend. Do you tell
me, they talk? *Me*, I'm a hot subject, speculation in all the pubs? Do
you tell me they've come to *you*, to come to *me* hot-fucking-foot
with a treacherous offer, to evict me, that's all it is; coerce me to
evict myself; oh you blackmailing sod of a cunt.'

'Ah,' he murmured, 'treacherous? Not at all. Not on my part, at
all events. Sure, I bring you the offer as requested, don't I do this
sort of thing for a living? and I certainly don't advise you to even
consider it. I told 'em you'd respond in the negative and you have;
and there's an end to it, okay?'

'Is it?' Molly narrowed her eyes at him. Why had he never
mentioned that Greenview were his clients? 'Why?' she snapped.
'You hid it. Made sure I was thoroughly pissed and you hid it.'

'Dammit, Molly, NO!' He suddenly lost patience, or pretended
to do so. 'They're not my clients, never were; but of course they
knew that *you* were, of course you were seen with Nora on the
steps of my house, d'you suppose in broad daylight in a flagrant
little town the like of ours any visit of any consequence is secret? So
their legal man rings me, and requests me to ring *you*, but you're
not (so it seems) on the phone, so here I am in person and Nora
came along for the ride.'

'And for friendship,' cried Nora Tyrrell. 'For the crack, for the
curiosity. And you really do mean to stay put?'

'Didn't I say so?'

'Really, truly? No going back on it?'

'Didn't I say so, didn't I say?'

'Oh you did indeed, Molly, but there's more to be stormed over
yet.' Cormac O'Croinin was nothing if not seductive. 'For we came
here to bring you not only that very dodgy offer, but also an item
of news which may or may not please you. Greenview Developments plc, for a number of technical reasons, are making quite large
amendments to the design of the hotel. None of them affect *your*

problem, I'm sorry to say. I mean, they haven't decided to do away with their balconies. However.'

'However? However what? Playing games? I don't need games.'

'No, this is no game, Molly. To alter their architecture, they must reapply for planning permission. Why, it throws the whole thing open again. And you now have the chance to put in your objections; here I am to help you write them, if you think you'd require help, which I doubt. So what about it?'

'What's the catch? There *is* a catch. I can tell it from the tone of you. If this was as good as it sounds, it'd sound even better than it is, and it don't. What's involved that you haven't told me?'

'Ah. Yes. Involved. Now it's not very much, Molly, but the principle is disgusting and you may not be willing to go along with it. The new legislation demands a fee of twenty euro for every objection, and if you're overruled and you choose to appeal it – why then, you've to pay more than six times as much. It's outrageous.'

'Outrageous,' ejaculated Nora Tyrrell.

'Outrageous!' roared Molly. 'Unchristian, perverted and base! Twenty euros, they shall not have one. They shall not have one *cent* for their insult to my privacy! And you have the nerve to tell me of it as though you were bringing good news. Oh, I cannot bear with you, go away, go away back to town.'

Three days later they were back, with (they said brightly) a total change of subject. Molly nearly shut the door in their faces. But she was so short of friends and so hungry for conversation, she could not bring herself to refuse their company. She even went so far as to break out the brandy bottle. Cormac O'Croinin sat wordless, while Nora Tyrrell went through the motions of a worried young writer in need of advice from an old hand. She rambled at length about her work on the *Intelligencer*, and the editor's vicious attitudes: for example, his absolute support for the War Without End and the use of Irish airports to maintain it; his absolute refusal of a debate in his letters column on the grounds that September 11 had discredited bleeding-heart civil-libertarians for ever and a damn good thing too. And then again, asylum seekers. What was Molly's view of asylum seekers? Of the government's dispersal scheme? Did she know there were a near two hundred of them in bed-and-breakfasts up and down the town, and three-quarters of them black? while a strangely nasty brand of unprecedented racism was already augmenting itself –

'Both covert and overt, demonstrably coordinated for occult political purposes. Arson attacks. Murder. One of these days. We don't joke.' Cormac O'Croinin came abruptly into the conversation as though relieved to talk about something other than the job problems of his trull (as Molly was now privately defining her).

'They've started deportations,' continued the trull with a strange earnestness. 'And that gall-bladder *Intelligencer* praises them. Evicting decent quiet people right out of the country the very instant they've begun to feel at home here.'

Molly refused to show herself impressed. She chose to pretend that she'd always maintained that bogus asylum seekers deserved to be sent packing; then she stopped herself, bethought herself, cried out, 'Aha!' A cunning grin overspread her features. 'Aha,' she cried again, 'I catch you! And you thought, you little bitch, you'd catch *me*. "Eviction" was the word, hey? You remembered what I said the last day! Sauce for goose, sauce for gander: if *I* cannot bear to be shafted, why should I let *them*? Okay, girl, you've made your point. And what am I to do about it?'

She knew now it was for this (and this only) that they'd come; she felt wretchedly helpless though very much put upon; she sat back in her chair, growled between her teeth and listened. A long tale from Cormac O'Croinin of a particular asylum seeker, a Kurdish woman called Fatima with no husband but a child, a little girl; she was maybe a widow, maybe the husband had become displaced in the vortex of terror and flight from Eastern Anatolia, more probably there'd never been a husband, the woman had become pregnant against all the rules of her people and none of them as a result would lift a damned finger to help her. At all events, here she was in Ireland, with no English and a bloody great deportation order staring her in the face. He had tried to advise her, but the story she told him (through the deadly disapproval of the male Kurd fetched in to interpret) was all over the shop. He knew no way to make any sort of case for her against the ice-floes of bureaucracy. He was sure she was not 'bogus' – whatever the word might mean – but he didn't know *what* she was: all he could comprehend was her ghastly distress. Every day in the midst of her hurtling narrations the word 'torture' cropped up, again and again. Things had been done to her that should never be done to anyone; but the Department of Justice refused to believe her. 'Inconsistencies', they said, 'discrepancies' in her account, dates, places and so forth; therefore she was 'bogus', therefore she was a crafty liar, therefore she had come here to thrive illegitimately at taxpayers' expense and the only thing to do with her was to pack her off to Belgium (her last continental foothold) and let the Belgians handle her however they thought best. Back to Turkey, very likely, and more torture, but that would be no skin off anyone's nose in the department and no one in the department could be blamed. There were laws here and laws in Belgium; she had broken them, *of course* she had broken them; why, she hadn't even arrived with adequate ID, let alone a proper document from a consulate in Ankara. Cormac O'Croinin knew no way to prevent her being plucked from her officially-designated hostel by Immigration and Gardaí at some ungodly hour in the morning (*any* morning, maybe tomorrow, maybe not for a whole week) and whipped off to Dublin and onto a plane for Brussels before a single soul could hear of it.

Therefore, said Cormac O'Croinin, she needed a – 'A safe house,' Nora Tyrrell came chiming in upon him. They both of them, in chorus, repeated the phrase; and then sat in silence and looked anywhere but at Molly.

'Not this place,' yelped Molly, flabbergasted. 'She'll be a Moslem, trousers and petticoats all together, it won't do. I drink.' This sounded like refusal. Under ordinary circumstances it certainly would have been. She was selfish and timid and not at all ashamed of it. But nothing was ordinary. Tyrrell and O'Croinin had seen her great green fence; they were thoroughly aware of the state of her mind.

'Sure you could hide a full score of 'em behind that ... that Shakespearian arras.' Cormac O'Croinin's voice was a bottomless pit of treacle-dark cajolery. 'Kurds and Romanians and a brace of

Nigerians, but all we ask is just the one. At worst no more than a long weekend. So strong a chance, with a day or two in hand, to assemble further evidence, crucial evidence, *crucial*, to get going on a further appeal for her –'

'Oh God but she has a child with her.'

'The quietest wee child in the world.' Sentiment and compassion now from Nora Tyrrell, very likely entirely sincere. 'A changeling child, really. Oh your heart would go out, Molly – lord, I know that mine did.'

'Whatever, whatever, whatever made you think that *I* would be – How *could* you bring yourselves to exploit me, exploit my most hideous grievance, my need for revenge for most manifest injustice – Moral blackmail, it's disgraceful: if I agree I'm as weak as water, if I refuse I'm a dead rat in a ditch. All I can say is – Why me? oh why me, why me, why me?' She was up upon her slippered feet, grinding her teeth and scurrying round the room in a repetitive widdershins circle, leaning forward and bobbing her head and feeling before her with outstretched fingers like a blind woman. Above her mantelpiece was a picture, a large coloured print stuck to the wall with bluetack, Bruegel's *Massacre of the Innocents*, Spanish troopers in a Low Countries village filling the snow-covered street with nightmare, grabbing babies out of mothers' arms, fighting with mothers and fathers, breaking down doors to get at more babies, cursing, swearing, jeering, while their narrow-faced greybeard of a general sits his tall horse behind the bloodshed, surveying it, every foul act of it, in grim conscientious silence: he knows what must be done for the good of the state and ensures that it *is* done, as speedily as possible. Molly came to a halt and pointed.

'Those women had no warning. This Kurd of yours, she has had. Should I call meself lucky I'm here to maybe . . . maybe what? back it up for her? Get her out of it, off the street, out of the horsehoofs (will you *look* at 'em) and the snatch o' the drawn swords? Jesus, you do not make me a happy woman today at all; but then when did a lawyer ever make a good woman happy? Just not in your trade description, don't pretend to me it is. Oh but I ask you again, why me?'

This odd little speech was nothing less than Molly's acceptance, for as soon as she had uttered it she coughed, snorted, spluttered and got down to logistics as though work for a resistance movement had been the mainspring of her life.

That night, several hours after dark, an efficient, long-limbed, middle-aged woman drove up to the bungalow in a pickup truck and introduced herself as 'Bríd, from the Refugee Support Group'. From somewhere in the gloom behind her (she'd put out the lights of the truck and there was no moon) came a piteous wail, instantly hushed by an anxious female voice in an outlandish and guttural tongue: Fatima and child, beckoned forward by Bríd into Molly's chaotic kitchen. Mary Virgin upon the Flight into Egypt, thought Molly, hastily draping her own dark anxieties in mythological garb – 'reconstruct it as an episode from an old master, as it might (why not?) be Bruegel, only way to get through it, get over it, absorb it into the system without intestinal collapse,' so she told herself, and put the kettle on for a midnight pot of tea, while Fatima unselfconsciously began to change the little girl's nappy.

Bríd handed Molly a paper with what appeared to be instructions as to how to help with the child, and how to understand Fatima's more urgent needs without the use of language. There was also a number to call in case of emergencies; as Molly had no telephone it might not be of much use. Bríd promised to come at the same time on Monday night (tonight being Friday), or, if not, somebody else would, possibly Sam, or maybe even Deirdre – Deirdre? Sam? who? This peremptory Bríd, nearly six foot high with her carving-knife profile, was most sweeping and offhand, but the farewell kiss that passed between herself and Fatima was deeply affectionate, and the cuddle she gave the little girl was quite tragic. It was as though they were her own family, never to be seen again.

It cannot be said that the fugitive Kurd was an easy person to have about the place. She kept trying to talk to Molly in violent and emotional bursts of what was clearly meant for English but was almost entirely opaque. Molly tried to talk to her in simple phrases, loudly repeated, mostly questions, such as, 'Your little girl, she was born *here*? ... No, not here in *this* house ... This *country*, yes ... Ireland? ... Ireland, *here* ... Turkey, *there* ... You come through

Belgium, yes? ... (Oh fuckit, what *does* she understand?) ... How *old*, your little girl?' This last question *was* understood, and answered by a finger display; three years and three months, Molly gathered; though the child looked a good deal younger than that and spent much of the daytime huddled into a pile of cushions and blankets in a corner of the spare bedroom, not running about, not prattling, not even crying, heart-breakingly beautiful as she crouched there, with her great big dark eyes like pools in the depth of a forest, and curls of the softest jet-black hair to frame her sad little face. Her name was Balkis (Queen of Sheba? even wiser than Solomon, Molly seemed to remember from some book or other she'd read years ago); her silence was clearly not a permanent condition, and may indeed have been but a token of wisdom, because as soon as they were all settled down for the night, Molly could hear her through the jerry-built bedroom wall, laughing to her mother and chirping like a bird, while Fatima sang songs and told stories and altogether (by the sound of her) seemed to discover a gaiety not to be shown to Molly, or at any rate not until they knew each other much better. Nor was there going to be much time for such knowledge, maybe it was as well there shouldn't be, maybe Molly was no more than a staging-post upon a weary woman's weary journeying, and ought not to expect any more than she would get.

Perhaps Fatima was beautiful also; it was hard to be sure, for her features strained and twisted with acute anxiety whenever she and Molly were floundering through one of their efforts at conversation. When they weren't, she was always busy, suckling Balkis, attending to Balkis's spoon-food, or her nappies, or washing her own clothes and Balkis's, or scrabbling for this or that in one of her suitcases. She did indeed wear trousers together with 'petticoats' and wrapped her head indoors and out in a great kerchief of printed cotton: white and yellow flowers on dark blue. Her other garments were as elaborately patterned. Molly thought, if there was to be any question of evading police in public places, a more indigenous style of dress might be better; Fatima's complexion was not so very dusky, she might easily be a Connemara Irish woman. Delicate matter, it was up to Bríd to deal with it. Molly most certainly was not going to venture.

On the Sunday evening, warm sun after a gloomy afternoon, no wind, and best of all, no workmen on the Greenview site, it was possible to bring Fatima out of the house. (Saturday had been windy and wet, enough to keep anyone indoors, even without the security imperative.) To Molly's surprise, as soon as they were upon her scrubby grass-patch, concealed from the back road by a cluster of hazel and blackthorn, with a pair of deckchairs fetched from the lean-to, and Balkis installed in a laundry basket like a watchful little household sprite, Fatima went inside again and reappeared with buckets of water, one after another. She unwrapped the kerchief from her head and let down her night-dark hair, a wonderful plaited rope of it that hung to her very hips; once she had unwound it from its plait, it spread all over her bared shoulders, veiling her breasts, twining about her arms as though she caused them to be caressed by slender benevolent serpents. With solemn deliberation, she dipped the hair into the water, and indeed ducked her whole head into the water; and then she wrung the hair out, and dipped it again, and dipped it again, shaking it in a bright shower across the grass to create a miniature rainbow, which the little girl could see (and was obviously expecting to see), for she clapped her hands and crowed, unheralded display of vigour and joy.

Molly laughed and Balkis laughed.

And then Fatima danced, rolling her head in circular jerks round and down and round again till her hair shook in front of her like a thundercloud. She made srange vehement noises with tongue against palate, siren-like ululations which might have been lamentations or might have been the cries of love or might have been no more than an attempt to amuse the child: how could Molly have any notion? Then the dance stopped, all of a sudden; Fatima all of a sudden decided her hair was dry enough; she sat down to steep it in oil. She fetched a tin of vegetable oil from one of her shopping bags, she scooped it with her hands and poured it and rubbed it into hair and neighbouring skin until hair gleamed under the sunset like polished ebony, and skin like cloth-of-gold.

Molly sat stone still, eyes fixed, flushed face all running with sweat, hands trembling, body and soul possessed by an unaccountable erotic glow – she had not felt such inner heat since . . . no, she must not calculate since when . . . so much pain, so many troubles, to strangle all sensual surges before they'd even formed themselves and yet . . . and yet, now, in the midst of this painful and troublesome emergency –

Such thoughts were ridiculous; they were impelling her, so she feared, towards the hidden brandy bottle, which wouldn't do at all. So she stayed where she was, stone still, and wondered about Fatima (as she'd been wondering since Friday midnight); not so much the question of the truth of this young woman's history, but, far more important, Fatima's *view* of her history, as to where she had been, where she was now, where she might be in the future? Not even as a schoolteacher trying to fathom some fraught teenager had Molly felt so baffled.

She watched her undress Balkis and rub her all over with oil; she watched her press the child to her shining breast to suck; she watched a pouting-mouthed bald-headed man, and a squat woman in a mackintosh, with heavy spectacles and a pudding-bowl haircut, stand quietly among the hazels and watch all that was going on.

It took Molly rather more than one shocked moment to understand what she saw, how she had, in all her carelessness, been crept upon by a pair of spies. Fatima looked up, followed her gaze, by contrast took no time at all to understand, and sprang to her feet with a shriek like a dog beneath the wheel of a tractor. Clutching Balkis tight to her chest, she ran directly into the house and then out of the house by a wild leap through the window on the far side (the back door, as ever, refusing to be opened), she tore her way between the strips of mesh on Molly's new fence, she scrambled over the drystone wall into the Greenview field, among the debris and detritus of the building-works, upon the instant out of sight of either Molly or the spies.

Himself coming down through the mesh to the drystone wall, as he peered from left to right for any sign of the vanished fugitive, Bald-head said sourly, 'Not good. Miss Concannon, not good at all;

you know well you are in breach of the enacted legislation, and if we are not able to recover the . . . ah . . . the alleged illegal and child, a serious charge may very well lie in your direction, yours. Have not the Guards answered, Janet? begod they take their time.'

Pudding-bowl had a mobile phone against her ear; even as he spoke she started gabbling into it, waited for five seconds to hear a response and then shut it into a pocket of her mackintosh. 'I'm after telling 'em, Mr Flynn, to have their car on the main road below, so they're set to intercept if she chooses to go that way.'

'Like they were set to intercept that Nigerian last week; yet they lost her for us for all that.'

Thereupon Molly did what she told herself afterwards she'd never done before (she refused to remember the old woman in Galway lying dead in her armchair): she acted upon impulse with no sort of forethought whatever. She dodged behind Janet and under the elbow of Flynn, round the house and across the gravel to her Citroën beneath the lean-to.

The two spies, whatever they were (immigration officers? social workers? racist vigilantes? not even the Guards could be sure who employed them), were caught on the back foot by her sudden move. They came running in front of the car as she pulled with frantic fingers at the choke. Flynn made a jump for the handle of the driver's door; in his other hand he clutched a briefcase. Both of them were thrown to the ground as the car floundered forwards. Hands, forearms and knees were lacerated. Janet's spectacles were smashed. Flynn's briefcase lay open on the stones, a swirl of loose documents scattered all around it by the force of its fall. Molly gave vent to a most cruel cry of delight, gritted her teeth in bitter tenacity, and stamped on the accelerator all the way round the long hill to where the far end of the back road ran into the main road – a matter of three miles or more, but if the Guards were not yet in position, it might just be possible to do it. On the way she passed the spies' car parked close under the roadside bank. She drove near enough to make a long savage graze of its paintwork, an act very likely deliberate, needless malice, and imprudent, for it did damage to her offside headlight. She swept left into the main road, another mile, another mile-and-a-half, recklessly in and out of the streams of Sunday traffic running home for the family supper, until there, on her left again, the temporary entrance to the Greenview project – where a tattered barefoot Fatima, exhausted and desperate, Balkis still strained to her breast, staggered down through the gathering dusk toward Brady Construction's site hut.

Molly had anticipated no such person as a grubby old weekend watchman to come plunging from his site-hut door, thrusting his arms out dead in front of her to bring her to a halt, then turning upon his heel, up the hill to meet Fatima, to arrest her? to lay hands on her? no. For at once he stepped aside and beckoned her down toward the Citroën: the bravura of a traffic cop waving ambassadors into Phoenix Park for an audience with the President. Molly already had the passenger door open, she pulled Fatima and Balkis inside, wrenching her steering wheel to drive straight out of the site with no more than a grateful wave to this improbable watchman, but he ran to her window and rapped on it; he made urgent signs to speak to her. She had no time to lose, she wanted him gone and her car on the road again. Yet he might have something important, she did not dare ignore him.

'Well? Is it important? We *must* be on our way. Please.'

He was a man of discomfortable appearance, tall, stooped, with a lined and greyish face, a long cleft chin with coarse grey stubble that was almost a beard but not quite, and a black patch over his left eye. His clothes, too, were discomfortable for such fine weather, or indeed for a man who had just emerged from a Portakabin with no windows open: he wore a sort of hooded duffle coat, muddy-blue in colour and very dirty, and a broad-brimmed grey slouch hat. His wellington boots looked enormous. 'One moment, missus, that's all.' His voice had a northern twang, harsh, slow, rattling deep down in his throat. 'One moment and we're all right, okay? Now, d'ye know my name? Ye do not. So I'll tell ye. They call me Hood, Cathal Hood, and I watch things. Would yous believe me when I tell ye I watched all that went on, above there, this last hour, so I did? Would yous believe me when I tell ye the polis are on the way here, and that's the rowt they'll come by!' He flung his arm out in a general north-westerly direction. 'That's the rowt, so don't yous take it. Neither you nor your eastern princess. *Your* rowt lies backward, backward the road south. Try your offside light a quick minute, there's a strand hanging loose: aha! ye're all in order, the glass may be gone but the bulb is sound. Oh but I'm trustable, missus:

amn't I auld Cathal Hood,

ne'er for the bad and aye for the good,

though there's some say vice-versa, no truth in 'em at all, on your ways, missus, go!'

If he didn't tell the truth, why would he lie? And yet without doubt there was something very queer. She took the risk and she took his advice. She drove a devious zigzag miles and miles to the south and east, until she found herself without design among housing estates by night, suburbs of Mullingar, the midland metropolis; she was abominable hungry. Should she also be frightened? She had indeed met no Gardaí. The rising moon showed her a featureless block of building, a meat-processing plant; in a side road behind it, a lock-keeper's cottage at the edge of a canal, unexpectedly picturesque. She stopped the car and sat still for a smoke ... emptiness, tranquillity, late-night death ... save only for some boozers on the towpath singing themselves off into the dark. Excitement, as she was to aver in the wordiest of her several statements, had faded entirely: the sole question left to her was when would bloody Fatima stop whingeing and keening in her useless incomprehensible language? She turned upon her sharply; the poor girl shrank away and Balkis took mouth from nipple to stare out at Molly with great wild scared eyes. Pointless to be harsh to such a pair. So she opened her own mouth and mimed eating and drinking. 'You stay here. Fatima, Balkis, in car. You stay. I go get food. Okay?' There was a shopfront built in to the lock-keeper's cottage.

Get yr Snack's at Charlie H's Waterfront Deli **open day/nite till late.**

Fatima need not panic, she would see where she was going. She crossed the road and tried the door. It was open: a cluttered little general store, delicatessen only by courtesy. A thickset twisty-shouldered man was up a stepladder with his back turned, arranging rolls of toilet paper on a high shelf. He jerked his head and asked sharply, 'Anything particular, or d'ye want to take a look-see? Self-service: your choice.'

'Do you have packed sandwiches?'

'I do. Ham-and-salad, egg-and-salad, chicken-and-tuna, cheese. Yesterday's, not too fresh, airtight packs, should be okay, good value if you're sharp-set. Driven far?'

The tone of his question was acute, and Molly dithered instead of answering it: 'Oh, far? Not quite. No. That's to say, we didn't have supper ... I think, maybe, egg-and-salad, ah you have four of 'em, I'll take the four. And the Pepsi bottle, big one. You wouldn't, I suppose, have a payphone?'

Charlie H, if that was who he was, came slowly off his ladder, head cocked round sideways to look at her. He wore a dark-blue apron, a grey woolly cap with knitted peak, and asymmetrical spectacles – the right lens clear, the left one tinted. His features appeared blurred, ill-shaven, of indeterminate shape. Spikes of hair under the woolly cap might have been black or dirty grey. There was something unwholesome about him. Like Brady's strange watchman, he communicated a feeling of a wrong time or place, the sound of a wrong voice. Yet he smiled with sufficient friendliness as he took her money and showed her the telephone at the end of the shop. Glancing behind her as she pressed the keys (he seemed not to eavesdrop), she got through to the number Bríd had given her. A man answered, calling himself 'Sam'.

'Sam, this is Molly, d'you know who I am, now? Concannon, Bríd knows me, isn't she there? when *will* she be there? because oh God I'm in a pickle, I need her advice badly, can *you* do it, I don't know you, I wonder should I tell you at all?'

'Ah now, Molly, take it easy,' murmured Sam. 'We heard a piece of what happened this morning. We've had a word from the Guards –'

'Oh Jesus, then they're after us! I knew it, I knew it, I knew it –'

'Ah now, Molly, take it easy. No reason to panic. Where are you?'

'I ... I can't tell you where – but the general direction is Dublin –

can anything be done for us in Dublin? – can you give me a number to ring, or can *you* ring, or – ?'

His phone might be bugged, it might not be him at all but a detective deceiving her. If this really was an Underground Railroad like in the old American slavery days, it could too easily be infiltrated, she thought. And Sam, so it seemed, thought the same. 'Yes, there *is* a Dublin number but ... This line, d'y'see, Molly, it's not ... Tell you what, give me *your* number, I'll ring you back on somebody's mobile. Not more than five minutes.'

She gave him the number of Charlie H's payphone, and stood beside it, waiting. Charlie H peered sideways at her, like a magpie round a tree stump. 'That car of yours,' he asked. 'The Citroën, okay? There's few enough of them around these days, you'll have had it a good few years, okay? I'd call it highly notable. You do a crime in a car like that, ye'd want to be rid of it as soon as y'could, okay? Ditch it and rob a new one, not hard. Like one o'them white vans, scores of 'em all over the country, as facsimile as a nestful of eggs ... There y'are, now, they're ringing y'back.'

Sam's voice, hurried and low, dictating a number; the instant he finished, he rang off. He'd sounded a deal more anxious than before: had something dreadful happened, within less than five minutes? She bolted from the shop, jumped into the car, started it up, sandwiches and Pepsi on her knee, and turned at once into a dirt-track that led round the rear of the meat factory, roughly parallel to the canal. For now she *was* frightened, deadly anxious to be out of sight of discomfortable Charlie H, less and less able to elucidate what she was doing or even her motives for doing it.

There was a chainlink fence to separate the dirt-track from the strip of wasteland beside the factory – a vile region of industrial rubbish, black plastic bags, dead cats, empty oildrums, forklift palettes and so on. Molly stopped the car and put its lights out among bushes and stunted trees between the dirt-track and the canal: they must eat, and after that she needed desperately to sleep, and so must her passengers; impossible to *think* until her eyelids for a few hours had lain closed. It seemed as safe a place as any from casual observation.

And so it was, because clearly the two thieves who arrived in a white van, broke the lock on the gate in the chainlink, drove in and then broke into the factory, at approximately two-fifteen in the chill morning, had no idea she was there within yards and (as it happened) watching them, wide awake from sheer discomfort and very angry at all the world. For sleep had proved as futile as thought, despite overpowering weariness. It took a little while for her to grasp what they were up to. The moon was low in the west and intermittently covered with cloud. But this much she could see: they had forced open a small back door in the blank brickwork of the factory wall; they had opened the rear doors of the van; they were passing at a trot in and out of the building, fetching tottering piles of cardboard packing cases that quite hid their heads as they came. They tumbled the cases into the van: she heard them curse that they found them such a weight.

Her first notion was her own danger. For if they saw her and they knew that she had seen them, why, they might . . . Ah, but if they were thieves, the one thing they couldn't do was report her to Immigration or the Guards, so in that case –

She was to claim that from this moment she was no longer in a state of panic, no longer overcome by her hopeless impetuosity, she was going where she knew she had to go: she was, as it were, under orders, a *fey woman* controlled from without. (Nor was it her own fault. Eamon Brady could so easily have put up his proclamation within sight of her bungalow; he deliberately chose not to; he was the one to blame for whatever she was about to do next. She wondered would he ever accept the fact? Probably not: he was a thug.)

She made a cautious movement, the springs of the seat creaked, Fatima (in the rear of the car) woke up. Molly stretched back her arm to press Fatima's head below the window-rim, ferociously commanding her, 'Sit! Stay! In car! Hide head! Down! Shush your Balkis, sh-sh-shush! Down!' She pocketed the keys, slid out of the driver's door, stooping low, and crept among the bushes toward the gate. Fair concealment almost all the way. One man in the building, the other about to re-enter. Cat-footed, she sprang toward the van, aware as she moved that it carried no name, aware that its motor was humming away. She was in and driving off before she thought about the open back doors. She heard heavy cases crash out onto the ground as she rocketed over a pothole and across a chunk of rock on the threshold of the gate. Through the gate, past the bushes, and she screeched beside the Citroën to a stop. 'In-in, IN!' she yelled, throwing open her nearside door.

Fatima knew something about emergency embarkations, she was aboard the van even quicker than Molly, Balkis tossed in front of her with an exultant ululation: an outbreak of car theft did wonders for Kurdish morale. The rear-view mirror showed Molly the thieves racing to catch up. If she delayed even an instant they'd see enough of herself and Fatima to create an unending peril. So she drove at high speed until she came into the housing estate, where she stopped briefly to get out and shut the back doors. She thought nobody saw her: she had found a black baseball cap on the driving seat, had tucked her hair into it and pulled it well down over her brow. With her jeans and loose jerkin, wizened features, lean hips and flat chest, she might at first sight be either man or woman. She felt 'man': she felt impregnable.

She decided to drive to Galway. Dublin would not do. The man Sam had sounded so nervous and she had only that phone number to go by. Whereas in Galway she could still count upon one or two possible friends, supposing they still *were* friends – at any rate, she knew people. She steered westward by every by-road and bohereen she could find. Upon one of these, between eight-foot high hedges, a choleric hobbledehoy came raucously tailgating her, frantic to overtake; his car overflowed with shaven-skulled drunkards on the last stage of a rural pub crawl. Finally he made his move, surging between Molly and the right-hand hedgerow, absolutely alongside Molly, quite regardless of the blind corners ahead of them. 'Eedjit eedjit!' screamed Molly, 'ya young bloody looderamawn!' He and his passengers screamed back at her, swollen-faced, inaudible.

In the midst of her road rage, from the corner of her eye, as she glanced to make sure that Fatima was strapped in, she saw Balkis (pointlessly playing) pull open the glove compartment and fetch out of it a . . . The child had her little fist round the handle of a . . . Actually turning the business end of it toward her mouth as though she wanted to . . . It was indeed an automatic pistol.

Molly's grip upon the steering wheel was instantaneously lost. The van shuddered off the tarmac, over a soft steep hump of muddy grass, into the flimsiest part of the left-hand hedge, where she stopped it, undamaged, more or less, or at least she thought so. Balkis was screaming with fright. Meanwhile the other car sped away on its erratic course. Within seconds the road was empty: Molly must deploy the strength and cunning of her four wheels to skid herself back onto it. But first, where was the gun? In Fatima's hand. 'Fatima, NO! Please: you must give me. You must give!'

Fatima said, 'Gun'. She said it twice and followed through with an emphatic manifesto in her own tongue – Kurdish? Turkish? Arabic? She was holding the weapon as though she knew how. She was checking the magazine to see was it loaded (she did know how), she found that it *was* loaded, she put it into her bosom. And she grinned like a woman who not so very long ago had lived only for the company of, or indeed had herself been, a freedom-fighter, a terrorist, a black-haired golden-skinned killer – Molly decided it would not be wise to attempt to disarm her, knowing how easy it was to regard murder as a renewable option, once you'd already done it, or thought you had done it. So with no further word, she brought the van out of the hedge and doggedly set herself to find the safest way to Galway.

At last her evasive journeyings fetched her past the small town of Tuam into a maze of scanty townlands that lay to the east of Loch Corrib, no more than a few miles from her old home. She had a notion that those who had bought the old home used it chiefly in high summer – college lecturer and charity-organizing wife, with approximately liberal credentials, name of Rafferty. Molly told herself she wouldn't trust 'em an inch (too much of the Gene Gilmartin breed) but they might be of use to her, supposing they were in the cottage. Supposing they weren't? ah sure, she knew well how to get herself inside without the convenience of a key.

Already, however, she had cause for anxiety. She was almost certain she had seen a Garda car backed up in a laneway as she dodged among the outskirts of Tuam. 'Gun!' she cried to half-asleep Fatima, both hands off the wheel, miming furiously. 'Here, here, gun gun gun! Kill you, they will: kill. You must not have it:

GIVE!' Intensity rather than words made some sort of impression. This time, reluctantly, the pistol was handed over. Ten minutes later she fancied she saw the car again, a good way behind her on a long stretch of straight road; hard to be sure, for she was running into thick wet mist that spread across low pastures from the River Clare. Thereafter a sight of any possible pursuer was shut off by a sharp turn at the junction; and then nothing more until –

* * *

A digression to explain what the Gardaí were thinking of. An anonymous phone call had reported the meat-factory robbery shortly before it took place. A squad car arrived just in time to find the thieves doing their futile best to hot-wire Molly's Citroën, two angry gougers well known to the Special Branch for both criminal and paramilitary connections, and so furious at having been outflanked by unknown strangers that they actually asked the cops, 'who was it had the neck to rob our fucking van and all our fucking gear, wha'?' A query they answered themselves, sure it could only have been 'the Fermanagh crowd', most treacherously employed by their own sleazebag employers. They then confessed an inside job: the meat factory was going into receivership; the directors desperately needed all the files (paper as well as software) which might tell too true a tale; they'd paid these two to purloin them, whereupon some boardroom Judas had clearly paid the other crowd to come and snatch them back. What for? Insurance scams maybe? internal intrigue? blackmail? evidence before a judicial tribunal? The thieves now began to fantasise so broadly that the Guards stopped believing them. But 'Fermanagh' had been a key word.

A check on the provenance of the Citroën gave an M. Concannon as the owner, her address but a few minutes' drive this side of Fermanagh. It was immediately deduced that certain elements from that British-ruled county had stolen the car expressly to hijack the Mullingar robbery. Now they had stolen the white van. Next stage in the investigation: hunt down the same white van and explore the 'fucking gear' – the rest of the stolen boxes and probably firearms as well. Two boxes had in fact been picked up outside the factory; they contained portions of a most valuable desktop computer together with a multitude of files. Prosecutions of respected midland businessmen would very likely follow a close look at those items. Meanwhile, the crucial questions: who was in the white van, where were they going, and why?

By three in the morning a curious new strand had woven itself into the investigation, thoroughly confounding it with all manner of misapprehension. The police near the Border put out an announcement of an 'assault' upon immigration-office informants, a Mr Flynn and his volunteer secretary, followed by the flight of an on-the-run illegal with her aider-and-abettor in the aider-and-abettor's ancient Citroën. So perhaps the ancient Citroën had not after all been *stolen*. Was it possible that Concannon herself was involved in the main plot? An insanely ambitious superintendent on border security duties decided she should be: he constantly yearned for all the kudos that would accrue if only he could lay bare a truly dangerous conspiracy. He had occasionally tried it before, discovering caches of arms which he might well have hidden himself, coercing tendentious statements from vulnerable informants and so forth: but this was the biggest yet. He asserted Concannon's guilt, solely (as would only be revealed after weeks of confusion) on the basis of her overheard 'republican death threats' against the Planning Officer and Gilmartin TD. He interviewed the man Hood from the Greenview site at about the same time as the Mullingar officers were questioning the proprietor of the Waterfront Deli. The combined information (amateurishly run together on a new and untried computer) was eccentric, equivocal, yet apparently incriminating: these women in the white van could be up to no good and were surely not alone.

Whatever the mystery, would it not be prudent to take a look at Concannon's old home? Who could say how far the Raffertys might not also be involved? They'd been noted by Special Branch at an anti-war street demo, 'No Shannon Airport Warflights for Bush-n-Blair!' – just the kind of subversive nonsense that could lead to almost anything.

* * *

Molly galloped the van through clinging vapours of the lakeside dawn, down the bohereen to her old cottage, the last dwelling of all on the very edge of the water, bullrushes indeed at the end of the bit of garden, where the track came to its own end in a tight turning circle immediately in front of the gate. A couple of Garda cars were parked across this turning circle; if Molly wanted to flee, she would have to reverse; but she could not reverse, for the squad car from Tuam was sliding up behind her. Cops were spread out in front of her, uniforms and plain clothes, more than one of them holding what looked like a ... She'd never in real life seen a man with a submachine gun, only on TV, in the films, and such. She spun the van through the privet hedge, onto the overgrown lawn, revolving it right round at the very brink of the water, and back like an angry buffalo into the side of the car from Tuam. There is nothing to be said in favour of this outrage: she seemed to have forgotten any ethical meaning her adventure might once have contained; she ruthlessly hazarded the safety of Fatima and Balkis; she might have hurt or killed an officer, if she hadn't lost quite so much speed on the turn and if they hadn't leapt out of the squad car as soon as she shattered the hedge.

For a wonder, the inspector in charge roared to his marksmen not to shoot. At the very last second he'd seen Balkis behind the windscreen staring straight into his face. No one had told him anything at any time about a child. And terrorists? Who'd started this crap about terrorists? Had some bloody canteen chip-pan gone on fire at headquarters, they were all in such a mucksweat and spasm?

Fatima, paralysed with shock but otherwise unhurt in her seatbelt, clung to her daughter and prayed. (She would stay there for a full half-hour, incapable of movement; they had to fetch an ambulance crew from Galway to get her out.) Molly, on the other hand, literally *fell* out: the driver's door had shot open with the impact, the clip of her seatbelt must have been faulty, she was lucky to be flung sideways and not through the windscreen. She staggered upon all fours. The pistol dropped from the waistband of her jeans. It was only when the Guards had her handcuffed and bleeding, propped up against a gatepost, that they pulled off her black cap and realised she was a woman. They did not quite go easy with her, but relaxed a small part of their fierceness.

The Raffertys at this point were let out into the ruined garden, and stood bleating and wringing their hands. Molly mocked them incoherently and then mumbled she would make a statement. 'Make it here and now,' she said, 'and then shut up my trap for ever.' She said, 'I only took the gun to quench the gun, so that no one could call me killer, not ever again, no. Murder for a view of the green hills of the north, no. What sort of a proportion would that be? Except that this poor girl and the child in her arms had the runaround once too often. Only for the thug Brady with his damn proclamation that wasn't, wouldn't they now be on an aeroplane all the way to the torturers? That much to thank him for, respite, and little he knows of it, the ugly bugger ... Just to ask you, please, I can see you're a decent skin of a man, bluebottle peeler or no, just to ask you after all this, would y'ever leave the creatures alone?'

'Ah, that,' said the inspector gently (he had been listening to his mobile and talking back to it for several minutes), 'that must depend as you know upon the minister's statutory procedure. I daresay from all I hear that her running away with you ditched any chance she might have had of a last-minute appeal. Mind you, if it can be shown that you were holding her hostage, like – you with your firearm and whatever help you might have had from beyond the Border, County Fermanagh – well, there could conceivably in that case by some hope of a mitigation for her. Think about it. We're here to help you, make it easy for you. You tell us what you know, what we want to know, what we *need* to know, and we'll see.'

PERPLEXITIES OF AN OLD-FASHIONED ENGLISHMAN
(1) The Dissident

DAMON & PYTHIAS. Pythagorean philosophers (*4th Cent. BC*). Condemned to death by Dionysius the Elder, tyrant of Syracuse, Pythias begged to be allowed to go home to arrange his affairs, and Damon pledged his own life for his friend's. Pythias returned just in time to save Damon from death. Moved by so noble an example, Dionysius pardoned Pythias.

Chambers Biographical Dictionary, 1997

Spike Oldroyd had heard about Damon and Pythias, having endured during his schooldays a good many hours of Greek and Roman bits and pieces. A grand old-fashioned North Yorkshire grammar school with no nonsense about it, he would say to his Irish acquaintances, the very best possible training for an honest-to-goodness working journalist, he would say. Over and over again he would say it. His generation, he would say, was one of the last generations to be taught as a matter of course about such old-fashioned stuff as Damon and Pythias. 'From which you might deduce,' he would say, 'that I'm quite a bit older than I look.' He flattered himself with this, for when he was at his worst (in bad weather or after three or four hours in a Galway bar boring those acquaintances with interminable self-centred anecdotes) he would look at least seventy-five.

At his best, on the other hand, he might have been thought of as no more than a broken-down sixty (which just about hit the right figure), a cadaverous portentous yellow-faced old jackass nearly six-and-a-half feet tall, with thick bristles of grey hair in his ears and his nostrils and some sparse greasy streaks of it combed forward across his bald crown. His eyebrows were quickset hedges above mud-coloured red-rimmed eyes, his teeth were rotten fence posts in a bog. His posture while drinking was unusual and rather ominous: he would rear himself upward and forward in his chair, looming (so it seemed) over everyone else at table like a vulture prospecting for carrion.

He was said to have quit a good career as a salaried hack in England for reasons of Creative Conscience, a courageous and risky decision perhaps, except that he was also said to have mitigated the risk by settling in Ireland, thereby taking advantage of the national tax concessions for practitioners of the arts, by which token he wrote novels, or was it film scripts? – at any rate he would drop his hints that some sort of masterpiece was always underway and that such and such an agency, or studio maybe, was imminently interested, and so forth. Which might or might not have been so.

In fact he was still busy with quite a quantity of newspaper work, modest work, dreary work (you might say), almost degrading: he was the west of Ireland stringer for several British provincial journals, sending them facetious items about paradoxical verdicts of Irish lawcourts, absurdities of Irish country people in the witness box, linguistic ineptitudes of Irish politicians in the debates of local government – just the same sort of sorry stuff that might have been ground out for the same sort of papers a hundred-and-fifty years ago – but it seemed that there were editors in Norfolk or Gloucestershire or some of the suburbs of London who were still prepared to pay for it: for they knew they still had readers who were happy to laugh at it, and Oldroyd could write it in his sleep. It was never published under his own name, his Irish friends would never know about it, so why should he worry? He was, he always had been, a good old-fashioned working journalist and that was the work that he did. Honest to goodness, and no queasy conscience qualms, right?

Nonetheless he *had* heard of Damon and Pythias, how the one dared to hazard his life for the other, pre-Christian virtue almost

Christian in its intensity, vibrant with the drive of aroused and compassionate affection – to be sure they were very very close friends, highly likely a pair of queers – the schoolmaster who taught him the story had let slip a little embarrassment at the moral implications of the subtext – in any case (modern standards, civilised society, western democracy), was not Pythias a terrorist? – 'philosopher', maybe, but what sort of philosopher was condemned to be crucified for plotting the murder of his head of state, however tyrannical? And what in heaven's name had all this to do with anything? – except it so chanced that one day the ancient tale came suddenly into Oldroyd's mind in connection with a man called McGranaghan, a man he used to know (in an uncomfortable sort of way) but hadn't seen for ages and most certainly hadn't wanted to see.

If McGranaghan wasn't a terrorist, he was surely as close to it as might be a mouse to the cheese. When we say 'terrorism', we mean what was known at the time as Dissident Republicanism; when we say 'at the time', we mean the last years of the twentieth century. The Provisional IRA had declared a formal ceasefire and apparently was keeping to it. So of course there were Republicans who immediately cried 'Sellout!' and would themselves by no means keep to it. Insofar as they inhabited (Oldroyd would have preferred to say 'infested') the remoter parts of County Galway, Martin de Porres McGranaghan would have been one of them. He owned a small public house and general shop attached, up a steep little glen among the hills of the Joyce Country, north-west of Galway city.

Nearly two decades earlier, at the start of the 1980s, Oldroyd had been living only a few hundred yards from McGranaghan; he had rashly purchased a hillside cottage at the top of a precipitous bohereen, a deeply-rutted track turned by every rainstorm into an ankle-deep torrent. The building was all but derelict, incorrigibly damp and very bad for Oldroyd's rheumatism, but its price had been so low that he truly thought he'd found and seized a picturesque bargain indeed. Then he met his neighbour and realised he had doomed himself to dwell (for the rest of his life very possibly) within a furlong of a beady-eyed antagonist. In those days

McGranaghan was a round-faced sandy-haired little whipper-snapper, bright as a cock-robin, quick with suspicion, hopping and skipping in busy preoccupation. He was no sort of Dissident, but a regular Provisional Republican devoid of all doubt as to that movement's own political virtue. It must be said, he did not pursue anything like a *feud*. On the contrary, he made sure to be polite to the English interloper, although never gratuitously helpful. If he hardly ever spoke to him when they passed each other on the road, he would nevertheless duck his head sideways together with a jerk of his forearm, a recognition by body language which could not quite be construed as a gesture of hostility. Oldroyd's attempts to warm up the relationship by buying his food in McGranaghan's shop and drinking of an evening in McGranaghan's bar were not so much rebuffed as ignored, and eventually he stopped trying. He drove into the nearby small towns, Cong or Oughterard, for his groceries, and all the way to Galway for his hours in the pub. Galway had a university, first-class bookshops, firms of gossipy solicitors, two or three local newspapers, a great supply of the sort of people Oldroyd needed for his conversation. McGranaghan and local cronies could go hang.

For a journalist Oldroyd was perhaps rather slow on the uptake. It was ages before it occurred to him that his neighbour's attitude contained a political ingredient. As far as he could see, the root of the trouble was simply that McGranaghan had kept sacks of cattle feed and a disorderly clutter of boxes and barrels and old bottles in the kitchen of Oldroyd's cottage before Oldroyd bought it, and consequently resented his loss of free storage space. True enough, as far as it went: except that Oldroyd did not know, and indeed was never to find out, that twitchy-beaked McGranaghan spent something like a year and a half revolving in his mind the disconcerting probability that 'your man at the top of the bohereen' was not only a snot-nostrilled Brit but a spy for the MI6. He went so far as to concoct several plans for making away with him, but carried out none of them because, well, how could he, how could anyone, be dead sure? If he wasn't dead sure, he'd never be able to act. In his dreams he was ruthless enough, but violent action here and now was something else entirely ... Nor had he clear approval from higher authority. Eventually the word was passed to him, 'Go easy now, Mac, easy – if he really is a spy, just find out what he's spying at – there may be some way we could use him before we *do* him – okay?'

Which meant without doubt he must burgle Oldroyd's cottage and hunt through all his stuff for fragments of evidence, a duty he was none too anxious to perform. What was he after all but the fellow next door? – altogether too exposed for confidential housebreaking. He begged for a face-unknown substitute to be sent from outside to do the job, but was brusquely informed he should use his own wits, what the hell else was he supposed to be there for? (This was at a time when the Provisional Republicans were obsessed day-in-day-out with the horrors of the hunger strike in the Long Kesh prison camp; local units in the south were on continuous standby for mass demonstrations, putting up posters, hanging out black flags, painting graffiti, all on top of their normal task of the guardianship of weapons dumps. Eccentric Englishmen up the western glens were no great priority; and if McGranaghan had at one time looked after a cache of arms, it had long ago been cleared out and transferred to the Border.)

In the event McGranaghan did exert his best endeavours. Upon one wet windy summer morning, at first glint of yellow sunrise through the gaps of the speeding clouds, he awoke with a stab of alarm to hear the roar of Oldroyd's motor as it stumbled down the bohereen. He sprang out of bed, he peered anxiously through his lace curtains just in time to catch a glimpse of the rusty old VW Beetle jerking itself to the right at the entry to the main road, spitting and sparking out of sight towards Oughterard, towards Galway, or even Dublin – odds on, the bloody man'd be away all the day, else why would he leave so early? Mrs McGranaghan, still in bed with the bedclothes over her head, said, 'Name o'God, Mattie, what's the time? who is it making that desperate noise? and where're y'off to, where?' 'It seems it's maybe the Brit,' returned her husband, disguising his tense nerves with a pretence of sleepy vagueness. 'I'd best go see what's up. He might need a helping hand. I'll be back before the breakfast.' In less than ten minutes he'd astonished himself by discovering Oldroyd's doorkey as plain as a pikestaff under Oldroyd's mucky doormat. Almost as though he were *expected*, for God's sake ... He very nearly fled in self-induced panic; but no, he controlled himself, he crept trembling into Oldroyd's kitchen, peering guiltily about for ... what? Truth to tell, he didn't know. A small transmitter or a pistol would have given him a useful clue, but no such luck. There was a typewriter on the table on a ragged piece of green baize, and several bits of typescript scattered about. A couple of hundred books crowding the shelves of the dresser. Some boxes full of old letters. And a very considerable quantity of long-overdue washing-up.

It must have been an hour before he came back down the bohereen and into the back door of the shop, to find his wife up and dressed and ostentatiously at work, sweeping the floor, dusting the counter, arranging a pile of copies of the morning's *Irish Press* only that minute slung down on the doorstep by the conductor of the early bus. She did not bother to look at McGranaghan, but began at once to rail upon him, a scared and resentful crescendo: 'Mattie, you were in his house! you were up to your tricks again! never thought to tell me, did you? never thought to tell me anything beyond a lie, your usual lie? if y're going to have to kill him, are you going to tell me *that*? And what'll *I* do when they come here to give you the orders? Make the tea and butter the bread, boil 'em an egg, will I? boil 'em their usual egg –?'

'What the hell d'you mean "kill"? There's nothing to be done with him but ... but leave him alone with a bloody great cold shoulder. Sure he does nothing in th'ould house above there, but write his dirty slanders to scandalise the Irish and the life we have to lead in these backwards bloody places, it's pathetic. Didn't I read all his jocularities, scattered about there on his table, didn't I read the damfool letters from the editors in England? Jasus Christ, the man's pathetic!'

Which is how it remained for the next four or five years. Oldroyd lived up the bohereen, McGranaghan lived in his pub, and the unspoken cold shoulder lived drearily between them. Would it have been any different if McGranaghan had given himself time to read *all* of the letters from *all* of the editors in England, and if he had not overlooked one or two typescript drafts (stuck out of the way among old envelopes) of newspaper articles not quite so jocular? Attempts in fact at some genuine analysis of Irish society and Irish public life: unsuccessful attempts, certainly, neither completed nor submitted to editors, or maybe the editors hadn't wanted to know. It was, however, just as well that McGranaghan did not find them; the opinions expressed were strongly and none-too-intelligently anti-Republican, and moreover largely based upon Oldroyd's observation of the character of McGranaghan himself.

For the Englishman was trying, in his defeated middle age, to get himself a name as a serious political commentator. In truth he had never been much of a journalist, he had worked for years in Britain for the same sort of papers as those which he now supplied with his silly Hibernian titbits, and he had all that time detested his own triviality. To be sure, he had earned a living: he had no wife and family to keep, his expenditure was very small, his way of life both mean and meagre. His dealings with women were sadly infrequent. Likewise his boozing was far less than it seemed – he would spend hours in a bar gossiping, but he drank only sparingly and found many crafty ways to avoid ordering drinks for anyone else. Now and then, for no obvious reason, he would depart from the pattern and slide into a sump of cantankerous intoxication. You would think him a man well suited to live alone up the side of a mountain; but it did not make him happy, and his writing failed to prosper.

At last he decided he'd had more than enough of ill-considered solitude. He abruptly sold his cottage at a loss to the McGranaghans (both of them quite ready to do that sort of business with him, cold shoulder or no); he moved down to Galway city and rented a flat near the middle of town. It must have been the right decision: little by little he began to discover himself better and better all round. He found more people of his own sort to talk to more and more of the time, not all of them Irish. Their conversation helped him to something approaching a proper understanding of the country, at any rate from a middle-class media point of view, and this in turn helped him to complete a whole series of quite convincing pseudonymous fragments of 'foreign-correspondent perception': two or three of them were printed in the *Yorkshire Post*, one even got into the *Daily Telegraph*. He might put them all together, he thought, into a book, one of these days, why not? – *Connaught Cross-Purposes*, or *The Wink and the Nudge*, struck him as possible titles. In the pubs he was no longer the sullen soak he used to be; he bought his rounds of drink for the company whenever he could afford them; many a night he was quite tipsy and jovial with some style, which is to say he told old jokes and laughed at them himself over and over again, but pleasantly for a change and avoiding the snarls of quarrel.

And so he grew old; he became an accepted character, 'th'ould Spike' they used to call him; he did nothing to surprise anybody; he would always be what he was and none of the men who knew him need look for anything different: until all of a sudden – not just surprise but outright incredulity! – the word began to spread that he'd fixed himself up with a woman. And what's more, it did indeed seem to be an authentic attachment: she was a forty-ish German with long blonde hair in coiled plaits who played the mandolin and kept a New Age boutique in Lower Abbeygate Street. She sold a range of continental health foods, packs of Tarot cards, mystical books, lunar calendars, home-made Celtic jewellery, coloured prints of goddesses from world-wide mythologies, Native American woodcarvings and anything else of a loosely concomitant sort. Her name was Ute O'Reilly: she had been married to a local technical-college lecturer of allegedly 'subversive' connections, who left her stranded in Galway when he skipped off toward the Continent with one of his female pupils and the Special Branch, allegedly, hard on his heels. Nothing had been heard of him for nearly ten years; Ute to all appearance was well established in the town and strongly independent. It was not at all clear why she took up with Oldroyd, save for the obvious fact that he was by no means Irish and there was nothing about him to remind her of the vanished O'Reilly. Or that's what was said, anyway.

One other thing was said: the nice little lump sum of capital with which Uta was able to set up her Lower Abbeygate Street business was part of the proceeds of the very same bank robbery which had caused the sudden flight of O'Reilly.

If so, then the relationship of husband and wife was less fractured than Ute pretended; moreover, in all likelihood, O'Reilly still owed his own lump sum to whatever Republican splinter group he had been involved with; maybe they were after him quite as keenly as the Special Branch. But nobody so far had caught him. And if anyone, police or paramilitary, had tried to put pressure on Ute, it was surely a long time ago and in the end must have been given up as a bad job. She had her shop, comparatively prosperous; she had her Englishman, grotesque and rather disgusting; she had her secrets, whatever they were; and she smiled upon the world from behind her large round spectacles with the sunniest disposition you could imagine.

Oldroyd's arrangements with her were characteristically cautious, as though he really believed nobody knew what was going on and – provided he employed sufficient discretion – nobody would be able to find out. He generally spent his weekends with her in her little flat above the shop. Very occasionally she would come at eight or nine of an evening to his own flat in the Bowling Green – the ground-floor apartment of a matchbox of an old terrace house otherwise occupied by a pair of single men in bed-sitting rooms, post-office clerks, he thought, he wasn't sure, he'd never asked – but he did not want them knowing about any women spending the night with him, so Ute always left before midnight.

In his cumbersome, retarded way, he was delightedly alight with all the symptoms of a man in love, and what's more, he and Ute kept it going for the best part of a whole year, *reciprocated* love, an unprecedented paradise of shameless sensuality at an age when he had no longer dared to expect it. Add to which, a professional bonus: in the midst of the sensuality, indeed (he at first concluded) *because of* the sensuality, Ute used to tell him things, political gossip, unpublished facts, the hilarious secret story of this and that in recent history, most of it almost believable, all of it useful for his writings. She possessed a multiplicity of sources of information, so it seemed, many of them connected with her connection, whatever it was, with the vanished O'Reilly. But then, after a while, it crossed Oldroyd's mind to wonder just why she was so swift to confide in him, for surely she knew that all his newspaper contacts were pretty far to the right and only in the Irish market for material to discredit the Republican cause? Besides, he was pretty far to the right himself.

One night, when they lay sprawled on their bed drinking wine and he had drunk one glass too many for total prudence, he put it to her: 'Why the deuce d'you still say that you love me, still love me, bloody hell, yet you *use* me, you do, *use*! – all the bloody time, you do, to put this stuff into the Tory press and bloody hell you don't say why, and how the hell should *I* know what the fucking hell it's for – hey?'

'Do not please say "fuck" to me, it's fucking uncultured . . . And you know what I tell you is true, always true, you dirty old *Dreckvogel*, scavenger-bird,' she murmured, with the fingers of her left hand tracing a little maze-pattern of red wine stains around his navel. 'Because it is true, it is necessary your Tories should know it; so much of what they think they know has always been lies, which is why such loathsome policy out of London all these years. And the more I tell these things to you, the more *you* believe them, yes? and your opinions, my vulture, month by month become very nearly good sense, *mein Gott* I have seen it happen even between these walls, so why not the readers of your press?'

'But Ute, you do *use* me? don't deny it, duckie, you do. And no, I don't like it, I don't like it at all, you are not just a galloping old whore, you're a whore with a secret agenda, and one of these days, oh one of these days, oh yes.' For all the violence of his language, he was nuzzling in her neck and interspersing his remonstrations with amorous murmurs, love and lust perversely about to rekindle themselves from this unexpected spark of resentment.

She asked him, 'One of these days, my old old bald-head – what?'

The truthful answer would have been, 'One of these days I'll find out just who you think you're working for.' But he shifted aside from it and offered her, instead, a pseudo-philosophical bit of nonsense: 'O dear God, I don't know . . . maybe one of these days we'll both of us find out just who we are and why. Surprise ourselves, the pair of us: ha, that'll be the day!'

He did not raise the subject again. It threatened to spoil his pleasure; and of late there had been so much pleasure – he was not (nor ever had been) a man of such good luck – was it possible the days of pleasure had already lasted far too long? He was beginning to take note he was no longer as fully capable as Ute might require. Dear God! by next year, or maybe the year after, he was bound to have to pay for it, and dear God he ought to prepare himself! But no, he thought, not just yet, let him not spoil the pleasure until such time as he had no choice, and surely he'd be able to see such time approaching?

He thought 'surely', but he was wrong. For indeed such time arrived even before the end of *this* year (which is to say, just a year or two short of the new millennium); it came all in a rush; he could never have been prepared for it (to be fair to him, nobody could); at no period of his life had he been able to cope with emergency, and now he saw with so bitter an insight that had he only been left alone he would never have had to cope, would he? – all because he had fallen in love, dear God was he punished for falling in love?

It began in November, a late evening of unwholesome weather, muggy and moist and too warm for the season, an insidious wet wind beginning to sweep in from the west. Grey rainclouds had muffled the sunset and did their best to do the same for the full moon. Oldroyd had to travel thirty miles out of Galway to the small town of Ballinrobe in County Mayo, a vexing journey on a supposedly main road far too narrow for the traffic that thronged it. In Ballinrobe he was to interview a county councillor with controversial opinions as to forestry in the western region, an important source for an article he hoped perhaps to write for the *Economist*. When he reached the man's house he was informed with many apologies that the councillor all of a sudden had had news of the death of an influential constituent and of course had to hasten to the funeral: would Mr Oldroyd be too put out if the interview were postponed till next week? In a very ill temper he turned his wheels and took the dark road again, south. (He no longer drove the decrepit VW. These days his vehicle was a small Renault mailvan superannuated by the Post Office and put on sale at a low enough price. It was not in good mechanical order.)

He drove about twenty miles, dodging death at every curve of the road – then was able to increase his speed for a long straight stretch across bogland – and then he all but ran himself right under the looming bulk of an articulated euro-juggernaut that without warning lurched out from a side turning. Thoroughly unnerved, he skidded across the greasy tarmac into the car park of a roadside tavern, where he shut off the engine and sat shaking for ten minutes. Never mind the drink-driving laws, a man *must* have a whiskey after a shock the like o'that, out of the van into the bar, lean heavily on the bar counter with his eyes closed lest he fall, order the drink, swallow it, order another one, shake his head, open his eyes, look about him – ah! relax ... there y'are then, fair enough, right.

The place was brand new and spacious, more of a Teutonic beerhall than a traditional Irish pub; at this late hour of a midweek night it was not at all full. No more than half a dozen customers, sparsely distributed along the bar and at the tables, nobody of much interest for Oldroyd to start gossiping with – except? – was it possible that that solitary man in the alcove was Mattie McGranaghan? with his hair gone quite white and a tobacco-stained grey moustache so altering his appearance that you'd have to go and ask him to be sure. Moreover he wore a filthy old scarlet baseball cap with an emerald green peak and 'Miami Hotshots' inscribed on the crown, and he appeared to be dead drunk, lolling disjointedly across the table, forearms and wrists all askew among his nasty mess of empty glasses, empty crisp packets, an empty cigarette carton, a split ashtray and a beer-sodden evening paper. Whether or not it was McGranaghan, Oldroyd did not want to meet his eye; Oldroyd pulled his tweed hat an inch further down on his brow; Oldroyd twisted his body along the bar to the right so that only the back of one shoulder was presented toward the man in the alcove. But the man in the alcove caught sight of the movement. Sharply aware in the midst of his stupor that someone desired to avoid him, he lurched to his feet to express his hurt feelings. Three steps across the floor and he was propping up the bar immediately behind Oldroyd's elbow.

'Begod,' says he, ''tis Mister Spike, how many years,' says he, 'since McGranaghan shook your hand? Begod you never recognised me, and why should you, me life has collapsed. Expelled from th'organisation with ignominy, that's what they said. Slandered at and scandalised through every unit in th'movement. *Ignominy* was the bloody word, and for nothing at all except –' (a quick crafty glint in his bleared eye, as though suddenly he bethought himself about what he was saying and to whom) '– except nothing. That was it. And didn't the bloody Guards compel the closure of me little pub, loss of licence for nothing at all, except . . . except nothing, bloody nothing, that was it! And what the hell for am I talking to *you* about it? I'm in one pub after another for th'whole of three days and not one decent nationally-minded man to listen to me for godsake, and th'ould motor car is banjaxed and sure it's never possible I can ever get home again, and if I do, how the hell can I tell her where I've been? My phil . . . philo . . . philsophical profound opinion, that that woman'll tear me head off.'

Oldroyd did not know what to say to all this. He nodded and smiled and absurdly offered a drink. McGranaghan assured him he was 'a reliable good friend, din't I always know it, always,' but the barman shook his head. 'More than enough already and I told him so, this is the very state he came in with. He said he'd crashed his car, I was sorry for him, that was all. If I knew how to get him home I'd turn him out this minute. You yourself, sir, wouldn't be able to give him a lift? I believe he lives way up at the top of the lake but whereabouts exactly, God knows.'

'I know where he lives, I can't give him a lift, headed in the opposite direction, late as it is for an appointment. No, this much I *can* do: if you ring for a taxi, I'll pay for it.'

The taxi office in Galway said a car would be out there in less than fifteen minutes; in fact it didn't arrive for three-quarters of an hour. In the space of that time McGranaghan failed again and again to keep guard over his tongue, and Oldroyd was treated to a thoroughly confused narration of acrimony and treachery and renegade collusion in what seemed to be the Provisional IRA, or might possibly have been the Continuity IRA or the Real IRA or even, maybe, a further splitaway that had not yet got its name in the papers. None of it was of journalistic use to him, it was all so indefinite; but he did make a mental note to elaborate an analysis of 'a climate of ideological demoralisation as a foreseeable by-product of the Peace Process.' He chewed upon this notion; oh yes, it sounded authoritative enough, no doubt he could fit it in somewhere. He had gathered that McGranaghan's 'ideological demoralisation' had been the immediate cause of his drinking, or was that no more than a cop-out? Might it not be the other way round?

As soon as the taxi came, he slammed McGranaghan into it, stuffed banknotes into the driver's hand, drove rapidly off towards town in his van, and did his best to forget the entire dismal incident. He did mention it to Ute, but only very casually, attaching no importance; she did not suggest it held interest for her.

A month or so later, grim December, a black Sunday afternoon, rain from a broken gutter pouring down just in front of Oldroyd's door and soaking him top to toe as soon as he left the house: he'd promised himself at Ute's at around two o'clock (and already half past four, O God she'd be fuming!) with bottles of wine for their evening – only an evening, alas, the whole weekend not possible. He'd been all the week in Cork chasing a possible story, he should have been back in Galway by midday but his Renault made trouble for him time after time on the way home; as soon as he *was* home, an urgent phone call from the *Telegraph* picking holes in the piece he had sent in a week ago – 'Sorry, Spike, it's not consistent, you say the IRA refuse flatly to decommission and then in the next para you seem to imply that McGuinness might get 'em to make a start with a vanload o' handguns, either they do it or they don't, I've told you before, you ruin perfectly sound arguments with *fudge*!' (The fudge was damn well Ute's fault, feeding him tale after tale and failing to connect them logically, although the tales were all so plausible, why reject one for another?) He was thus compelled in great haste to rewrite and then telephone, his computer had gone wrong, he could no longer click into the internet, all in all a bloody bad start to all that Sunday meant to him, how much the more so when he found the off-licence had sold out of his usual plonk and he must buy another brand nearly one-and-a-half times the price.

He arrived all of a sweat at Ute's side door, slipped on her wet doorstep while he fumbled with the key, within an ace of smashing his carrier bag of bottles against the wall, and then in and up the stairs at a swift stride, pulling off his anorak on the move and catching his left elbow in the armhole like a straitjacket – he plunged into her living-room sideways, crowing his apologies, dumped down his carrier bag, struggled and wriggled to be free of the coat – why wasn't Ute greeting him? Who was the woman in the fireside armchair with her back to the door? How *could* Ute have a visitor when she knew (he'd rung her up!) that th'ould Spike was already on his way?

Dear God and the woman was Julia, Mattie McGranaghan's disquieting wife; she sat there, she turned her head, she glared at him, hideous, the very wraith of that Fairy of Discord whom no one in the storybooks ever remembered to invite to the party. She must have been about the same age as Ute, but she appeared a great deal older, pallid drawn features, dark rims round her dark eyes, lustreless dark hair dragged up tight into a twisted ribbon and some of the strands of it hanging down beside her cheeks. She was never (he recollected) any sort of trim young woman; tonight she was a positive slattern, ominous beyond words. He stammered his recognition; she immediately looked away from him – 'Mr Oldroyd,' in a wan, low voice, 'I'm very glad to see you. Mrs O'Reilly said you'd be here, so I took the occasion to wait. I'm sorry, sir, to occupy your time.'

He was sorry, too; but what could he say? What he did say was something quite flimsily hypocritical about how was Mr McGranaghan and he hoped he was well? Julia burst into tears.

Ute put her arms round her and murmured words of comfort into her ear. At the same time she fixed her eyes upon Oldroyd with meaningful intensity, and of course no explanation of just what the meaning might be. Oldroyd stood and looked stupid. To ask was ridiculous, as either he would be told or he wouldn't; and in any case (after his recent unspeakable encounter with McGranaghan) he was in no damned hurry to know. But he had to speak, hadn't he? He couldn't stand here all night, so why must Ute make it so damnably difficult? 'Eh duck, I didn't know you knew Mrs McGranaghan? Did you know her for a long time?'

'Not important how long: all that matters, I know her now, I have told her we will help.' Ute was brisk and businesslike, employing the tone of voice with which she would take hold of the business of her shop, to telephone, perhaps, a complaint to a supplier that a consignment of joss sticks was faulty, blazing up like fireworks instead of smouldering; she herself being quite liable to erupt into a firework-blaze if she got the wrong answer. Oldroyd felt she was expecting *him* to give her the wrong answer; her tone of voice was a warning he'd do well not to ignore. But 'help', had she said? For God's sake, help how? McGranaghan, he supposed, had gone off once again on a bender: did they seriously plan to trawl every pub in the city and county, on the off chance of finding him?

No, that wasn't it. What it *was*, was perfectly horrifying.

Julia McGranaghan thrust her words through gritted teeth with poisonous force, conquering her own sobs single-handed. 'Why, the bastards had him here in the Guards' barracks in Galway forty-eight hours before I even knew of it, pulverising him with their truncheons till I'm told in the shops at the far end of Dominick Street they heard the roars that came out of him, what else could you do but pity him, drunk though he was and the biggest bloody fool, bloody fool, bah.' Rage rather than pathos, no more moaning but verbal excoriation, with emphatic slaps of her flat hand against the arm of the chair. 'And the instant I did know, hadn't they carried him to Dublin, will they tell me where they have him in Dublin? – they will not.'

Ute's contribution: 'Offences Against the State Act, they can keep him as long as they want, so many hours to start with, then renew it and renew it beyond next year's *Walpurgisnacht* if that's their need, no visitors, no lawyers, *incommunicado*, until he's up before the Special Court, politically-chosen judges, no jury, what chance you think he has? And so, what are *we* to do when he's totally innocent, *ja*?'

Oldroyd, bewildered, took refuge in pedantry: 'Offences against the State? – no, they certainly can't keep him as long as they want. I don't know offhand the legal length of time, but –' (Ute snorted her contempt; he changed tack directly) 'You haven't told me what the charges are, why *I* should be so sure he's innocent, or what help can you or I give that a good lawyer can't? Can we not cool it down a minute, you're bound to be all upset, but –' (two pairs of glaring eyes burning into him from left and right; he subsided into anticlimax) 'But I mean, you haven't told me; look, I've only just come in; look, why don't I open a bottle?'

To be sure he opened the bottle, but no drinks were poured directly, the explanations came too thick and fast. Both women talking at him, now alternately, now together, surges of angry counterpoint, Julia's voice biting the air like a chain-saw, Ute's in a ceaseless rush, a foaming millrace over the weir.

As he gradually picked it out from amidst all the fury and fluster, it was the tale of an armed robbery something over a month ago, just after dark, at a road junction in the middle of Ireland, the outskirts of the town of Athlone.

(Yes indeed, Oldroyd had read all about it in the newspapers, a notorious outrage, yes; so why hadn't he paid more attention? Fact was, he couldn't be bothered with every armed robbery, they'd lost all significance, they were happening all the time. And no doubt he'd had other things on his mind.)

The full story went something like this:

A gang in balaclava-masks hijacked a truckload of cigarettes on its way from the Dublin docks to . . . well, there was uncertainty here: it seemed as though the cigarettes were smuggled, which seemed to imply some species of internal gangland feud, which could nonetheless include 'political subversion', 'dissident paramilitaries', almost anyone able to lay hands on a gun. Two of the balaclavas leapt off the motorbike that drove into the path of the truck, the third sprang from a mud-splashed Toyota that pulled up behind the truck to cut off any chance of its reversing. A fourth balaclava kept the Toyota's engine running, and stood upon guard with one foot in the car and one on the tarmac, a pistol in his hand, bawling threats to the passing traffic.

'So keep it going, you fuckers, keep fucking going, don't you fucking look at *me*, keep your eyes on the road if you know what's fucking good for you!' Such traffic as there was – three private cars in approximately four minutes – did indeed keep going: who would have been fool enough to stop?

The driver of the truck was alone in the cab; he had his door locked against the balaclavas but it did him no good; they shot off their pistols with insensate abandon into the lock and the panel and the window of the door, until the driver, screaming for mercy, flung open the opposite door and jumped down. They chased him and caught him and pistol-whipped him into unconsciousness for daring to try to frustrate them. They took bolt-cutters to the padlock at the rear of the truck, shoved the motorbike in among the cases of cigarettes, crowded into the cab, the three of them, and drove off at great speed in an approximately northern direction.

The fourth balaclava, left with the Toyota, adopted a more leisurely style, a practicable sigh of relief, as it were, that the heavy stuff was finished and done. He supposed there were no witnesses. (He failed to see a farmer in a nearby pasture crouching down among his bullocks, peering terrified through the moonlight from between their legs.) He unrolled his disguise from his head and replaced it with a parti-coloured baseball cap, checking his appearance in the mirror; he considerately made sure that the truck driver was lying on a bit of grass verge where he wouldn't get run over; he backed his car into a by-road to turn it round and get out towards the west; he failed to see that the headlights hurtling at him down the by-road were those of the Garda Síochána.

Cars full of pain-clothes cops, right on top of him, while the gear-change of his stolen Toyota suddenly decided to throw a thrombosis – on top of him from *behind him*? – how could they have got there? – from an ambush in the housing estate the far side of the fields? – they must surely have had a tip-off, inaccurate tip-off, and of course they were just too late, they were furious, they were flourishing firearms, they were shouting incomprehensibly. He staggered out of his useless motor, scrambled over the hedge, turned and fired his pistol to the right and to the left, and then ran.

One of the shots hit a detective sergeant, grazing (as it seemed) the inner edge of his thigh inside the skirt of his fleece-lined leather coat: 'I'm grand!' he shouted, 'Go go go! – all of you, damn your eyes! – jump the fucking ditch and catch the bastard – GO!' He lay wide-armed and face down against the bonnet of his car, out of breath for the moment (as it seemed), and there and then he bled to death from the puncture in his artery.

The light of the moon, already dimmed by shifting cloud, now disappeared completely behind a thick dark rain-squall. The sergeant's killer ran and ran through grass and thistles in the gathering storm; in a minute he was out of sight; in two minutes his pursuers came up against a barbed-wire fence and a ditch too wide to jump; they scattered to this side and that, but no result, nothing; all this time the rain was pelting, within five minutes they'd no option but to tell themselves they'd lost him.

In short, little more than was known to the country at large from the news media in general – Oldroyd realised that he himself had already absorbed most of it, more or less subliminally, vaguely aware that the hijackers had so far escaped arrest, but not at all aware until this evening that one of them – the cop-killer, *that* one – had gone on the run in a parti-coloured cap, conceivably red and green – too old (jeered the police at their press conference) for a top-notch car bandit, with his unkempt grey moustache, his hunched-up short stature – to say nothing of his great mouth like the grin of a rabid terrier (this latter sharp titbit passed on to the *Sunday Tribune* by the man from among the bullocks); if it wasn't Mattie McGranaghan, could it be his twin brother? But he had no twin brother. And the date of the murder was the very date McGranaghan had turned up on his own doorstep in an alcoholic stupor, tipped out from a pre-paid taxi with no recollection of where he had been for the whole of three days; only the name of Oldroyd, as given to the cab driver, made any sort of sense to Julia; so now herself and Ute needed to hear what Oldroyd knew.

Grudgingly, he told them. Why grudgingly? He did not quite understand why; he just felt that this was something he'd do better to keep to himself; at this stage not allowing himself to follow the thought through to its logical conclusion. Ute had no such inhibitions. 'Spike,' she cried, 'what *is* this? Don't you know, you are his alibi?' She said it as though she accused him.

He spluttered a little, unwilling even yet to accept the fact. 'Am I? Are we sure? Was he *really* drunk in that pub, or was he putting it on? It's not more than an hour's drive, hour and a half at the most, from Athlone to where I found him, if he had another car at the back of the robbery somewhere, he could easily have done it, easy.'

Julia lost her temper, she flew at him and screamed. He fell out of his chair sideways, knocking wine bottle and glasses from their tray on an occasional table; it all fell into the hearth; crashing of furniture, clanging of tray, shattering of glass. Ute caught hold of Julia and pulled her back. Ute began to shout, ruinous knife-edged words to interpret and augment the unarticulated cacophony still pouring out of Julia: how dared Oldroyd doubt the man's innocence when Julia swore to it? how dared he prevaricate like the glued-up-arseholed Brit that he was? how dared he attempt to evade his undoubted, most obvious, immediate duty? how dared he aspire to drink and to eat and to laugh and to talk and to fuck with a woman who despised him as much as Ute did this night?

How dared he indeed? The upshot was, he *didn't* dare.

'All right,' he mumbled, 'Right. So let's have a bit of quiet ... And the pair of you can tell me what you think I ought to do. Go to his lawyer? Has he got a lawyer? Who is he? Where?'

'Dublin,' gasped out Julia, catching her exhausted breath. 'I rang up a man in Dublin but there's nothing he can do before they've finished the interrogation. And then they've got to charge him, and the lawyer says, so he does, if they charge him with murder of a Guard no way will they grant him bail, oh it could be two years before they bring him to trial, if there's any sort of question he might be acquitted the Guards'll string it out as long as they bloody well can, so he gets at least that much of jail time, he's a fair-enough suspect, for thirty years a known subversive, oh the poor small man! Innocent or guilty they'll never let him go scot-free, says the lawyer, so he does.'

Ute broke in with direct practicality: 'Here too is what the lawyer said: this alibi (he has said) must essentially be presented to the Guards before they charge him. If it does look to them like an alibi of strength, then maybe they don't charge him at all.'

'O God, I want him home, I want him home, oh the biggest bloody fool, in his own home safe and sound!' Julia had launched into a type of meandering keen, no stopping her; Oldroyd and Ute would have to sort it out on their own.

Even though he still believed that McGranaghan's alibi might well be a mendacious construct, even though he considered that McGranaghan deserved all he got, Oldroyd thought it best to show willing with a good grace, he said that very likely he should travel to Dublin tomorrow, early-morning train at – dear God! *half past five*! – but he'd yielded to his duty, and he smiled to say 'half past five', smiled to hide the grinding of his teeth . . .

Right then, very good, fair enough, and he'd yielded; from Ute he might well expect praise. All he got was a cry of astonished remonstrance: had he not heard a word that anyone had been saying? So stupid! did he not realise that tomorrow first train would be too late?

For despite her earlier rhapsody about Offences Against the State suspects kept *incommunicado* for ever, Ute knew all the time that McGranaghan must either be charged, or let loose, or re-arrested with a judge's warrant, this very night, Sunday, midnight and no later. He had, it appeared, 'been already three days in police hands. If you, you fucking bald-head, had not been on your useless wanderings all of this past week, all this foul nonsense could be finished and done, *ach Gott, ach Gott, Schurkerei*! Do you not understand?'

So there it was. Somehow, to get himself to Dublin overnight. No time for preparation: just go.

Question: his own little van or the train? He might have to drive all over Dublin, looking for the lawyer, looking for the right police station, in the middle of the night when buses no longer ran and taxis were impossible to find; so it had to be the van, but could he trust it for more than five miles? The garage in Limerick had sworn they'd put right whatever had gone wrong with the steering on the road out of Cork, and indeed he had managed from Limerick to Galway without further disaster; so maybe he might take the risk.

Julia, thank heaven, was not going to come with him; Julia was not going to go anywhere near a police station; Julia, besides, had a shop to attend to, as had Ute; they left it all to Oldroyd, *not* in complete confidence, but as a sort of forlorn hope – there was, they assured him, nothing in his record to cause the Special Branch to look at him dangerously, whereas, if either of *them* were with him ... '*Ach Gott*,' muttered Ute, 'I do wish I could trust you – dear Spike, do not lose your temper when these *Stasipolizei* will try to put up your back, you know? For I tell you they will not want to hear what you must tell them.'

And then she reminded him that until only a few years ago the killing of a Garda automatically incurred the death penalty; whereat Julia moaned and wailed and cursed between gritted teeth.

All this on Ute's doorstep. And then, at the last moment, he had Ute's strong round arms tight about his neck and her lips upon his lips, fiercely, almost despairingly, as though she said goodbye to him for ever – 'Oh but I know you will get it right,' she breathed. 'For oh when you must do it, then you do it so well, don't you, my love, don't you?'

She pushed him away from her, caught Julia by the arm, and turned abruptly to go back into the house. He must not waste time: he pulled his hat-brim as low as he could, to keep the rain out of his eyes (it was turning already to hail); he ran heavily up the street with his long-legged see-saw gait, out of sight of her doorstep towards the corner where he'd parked his van. Ute brought Julia upstairs into the living-room. The two of them settled down to get drunk on Oldroyd's wine: there did not seem much else they could do.

When he tried to start the van, it refused to respond. He called for help from a crowd of young fellows out on the tear, builders' labourers or university students, hard to tell which; they were shouldering each other along with cuffs and kicks and exclamations, as boisterous as colts in a paddock; they enthusiastically flung themselves at the vehicle (quite excessive enthusiasm; it was only a quarter to six and already they were half-cut); they swung it out from its parking spot into the middle of Mary Street and a stream of one-way traffic, diagonally across the traffic, wildly attempting to deposit it on the opposite pavement. Oldroyd began to panic, bawling at them to leave off. In the nick of time his engine broke out into life; he had, it seemed, been holding up every car in the city. Every motorist was enraged, every horn was being blown in a long line behind him all the way back to O'Brien's Bridge. He drove grimly up the street into the wide space of Woodquay (once a market square, now a blighted parking lot); at the far end of this expanse lay his shortest way out of town.

The rain and hail came harder and harder. However would he get to Dublin with such impossible visibility? He'd never known it pelt so hard. No: but of course, that wasn't it, was it? – he'd forgotten in his panic to switch on his windscreen wipers. No: but they *were* switched on. Switched on and not working. They'd been perfectly in order on the road home from Limerick, so how had they – ? Oh, what the hell did it matter now *how*? If he could not wipe his windscreen he did not dare drive through night and rain and hailstorm one hundred and twenty miles; he was sixty years old and night-driving scared him. He was not going to do it.

(Oh certainly not for a bloodthirsty tick like McGranaghan. He was sure that when he lived up the side of that damned mountain, McGranaghan used to prowl among his private papers. Ute once implied, in a casual throwaway, which she immediately tried to pretend was a ghost of a joke, that McGranaghan would be the sort to have somebody come and shoot you if he thought it might make him, she said, 'enormous, you know what I mean, big, hard, nobody-fucks-with-me, *ja*!' But then again, had she not whispered to him, only just now, as she paused upon the staircase leading down from her flat, 'You must know why we know he can never have shot this *Polizist*: such an old rotten rascal, no one among the Republicans – *any* of the Republicans – will trust him, not ever again, with anything, least of all to be part of a shooting group. Some question of some money, disappeared. He paid it back, *jawohl*; so slow he paid it back; no trust for him, not ever again.'

He was not going to drive. He was too late to catch a train. Thank God then, the journey was off. Finished, aborted, *kaputt*.

No: but it wasn't. Dear God! by what ill luck did he chance to have these time-tables in his wallet? Dear God! by what ill luck was he afflicted with such a conscience? For on Sundays (of course, of course!) the 17.55 train did not leave until 18.15. If he dumped the damned van now, over there in that gap amongst the parked cars in front of the estate agent's, he had time, if he ran, to get to the station and catch it. So off he went, running, to the station.

The train did not leave at 18.15 but hung about in the station until 18.35. The passengers had been warned, fair enough, in large letters chalked on a blackboard beside the entrance to the platform:

WEEKEND DELAYS.
WORK IN PROGRESS FOR TRACK IMPROVEMENT MAY CAUSE
MINOR DELAYS TO SATURDAY AND SUNDAY SERVICES.

At the second stop, Attymon, a decrepit country station in the middle of empty fields, where nobody got on or off, the train stood stock still for very nearly half an hour, the only sign that it was ever going to move again were a faint throbbing from the diesel engine and an intermittent flickering of the carriage lights off and on. If the heating system had been active at the beginning of the journey, it was certainly no longer so: Oldroyd was already feeling most uncomfortably chilled. The guard wandered through the carriage, checking tickets; Oldroyd asked him about the heating and received a helpless shrug and an even more helpless reply, 'Sure we're doing our best for ye, but Sunday night, d'y'see, not a car on the rails that wouldn't be forty years old. And begod every Sunday this train'll be seven days older. Ah sure, 'tis a terrible system.' He added lugubriously that the buffet car was closed because the barman was ill with the flu and his substitute hadn't turned up. 'There would be a chance that we pick up a man at Athlone, but . . . d'y'see, Sunday night, ah 'tis not very likely.'

Despite the cold and the lack of refreshment, Oldroyd was not seriously anxious. the train was due into the Heuston terminus, Dublin, at 20.56; even were it an hour or two late, he would still, he supposed, have time to do what he had to do. He crouched shivering over his notebook, jotting down the heads of the business. What was the shortest possible time he would need? He first must make contact with Julia McGranaghan's lawyer; Ute had phoned this character before Oldroyd left her flat, but he wasn't at home;

she left a recorded message to tell him to expect Oldroyd; Oldroyd would ring him from Heuston and arrange how and where to meet him, and then they would both go to the Garda. Simple enough, speedy enough . . . provided that the lawyer did in fact return home in good time from wherever he was, and provided that he did not live so far out in the suburbs as to make it impossible to meet him before midnight. If Oldroyd had a mobile phone, of course it would be easier, he could ring the fellow up from the train. But he had always despised the mobile as an over-hyped fashion accessory. And if this nuisance of a lawyer was still recklessly out upon town, all types of phone would be equally useless.

No, he was not anxious. Not, that is to say, until the train rumbled wearily out of Attymon, moved snail-like to Woodlawn (another rural halt officially nine minutes up the line, in fact twenty-three minutes; Oldroyd by now had his eye on his watch continuously), and remained at Woodlawn, flickering and throbbing, until 19.55. Dear God, at 19.22 they should already have been leaving Athlone! And Athlone would be – what? – twenty miles away and more – at this rate they wouldn't arrive there much before nine, and then after Athlone there were still one and a half hours to Dublin: dear God, how many chances for further delays ('*minor* delays', no problem!) in the course of those freezing ninety minutes?

According to the timetable there was a two-minute wait at Athlone. It had spun itself out into a quarter of an hour when the guard came down the gangway, very apologetic: 'Sorry, lay's genem'n, the tannoy's on the blink, I'm after making me anouncement three times over before it came to me no-one could hear it. Fact is, we're held up with an incident between here and Clara, there's cattle all over the line and the devil's job, I can tell yeh, to get 'em offa the line into the fields, Sunday night, don't y'see, no way can they locate the farmer.'

There seemed little point in Oldroyd asking him how long he thought the delay might be; clearly it depended on the skill and good fortune of the nameless heroes of the cattle drive; clearly the arrival of this train into Dublin had entered the realm of astrology as an unprovable future consequence of circumstances invisible to the naked eye, albeit acceptable to the inner eye of faith, no question it was not good enough, no question he would not put up with it, not one moment longer. Then, most charmingly and obligingly, the ticket collector remembered the last bus for Dublin; he announced that it left Athlone at nine o'clock exactly; it was already one-and-a-half minutes to nine; the bus station, he stated, was in the railway-station yard, no more than fifty paces from the train. Oldroyd all of a sudden was out of his seat with the peremptory energy of a latter-day Spring-Heeled Jack, out of the carriage, down the platform, off the platform through the barrier and into the bus without once taking breath. He tossed the cash for his ticket in the general direction of the driver, staggered up the aisle to the nearest vacant seat and plonked himself down in it, gasping and collapsed.

The bus did not start in accordance with the timetable. Instead, the driver left his seat to hold a whispered conference with an inspector on the steps of the entry-door; they talked for fifteen minutes, looked wisely up at the sky, and shook their heads in concert. The inspector stepped back onto the pavement. The driver sat back in his seat to operate the door-closing mechanism, and then he stood up again and turned to his passengers. 'Isn't y'r man just after telling me,' he observed, in casual, almost throwaway, tones, 'that there's a good probability of black ice on the roads east, no guarantee of an arrival in Dublin at the stated hour or anything like it, sure I'm taking no risks wid y'r blood and y'r bones, nor would yez expect it, yeh? O'course, if we're later than midnight, God knows what'll be the upshot ... yez'll all have heard your radio, yeh?'

This last was double Dutch to Oldroyd, who (as it happened) had missed out on the news media that day. He could not bear to exert himself by demanding an explanation...

The driver made a rapid count of the empty seats, scribbled the result on a notepad on the ledge beside his ticket machine, adjusted his cashbox and waybills (or whatever they were) and finally sat down at his wheel, for the third time. He started up his engine. He carefully waited until he heard that it ran to his entire satisfaction.

He put the vehicle into gear; he steered his way, carefully, between the ranks of parked buses and cars to the exit from the yard and so, by slow degrees and intense deliberation, to the main road out of Athlone towards Dublin. The rain and hail had been left behind along the west coast; a gibbous moon and a sprinkling of stars now shone as though behind the gauze curtain of a stage set, indeterminate patches of silver blurred by the cold mist that crept up from the bogland, frost indeed, black ice, omens of failure and grief ... Oldroyd checked the 'stated hour' in his timetable: eleven o'clock. It *ought* to be possible. But then so was the train journey potentially possible and look at what had happened. He closed his eyes and tried to sleep; at least this bus was warmer than the railway carriage ... possible ... *ought* to be ... *ought* ... His anxious thoughts merged themselves imperceptibly into a dream.

He saw himself arrived in Dublin in black-and-white freezing weather, two o'clock in the miserable morning, not a taxi on the street, not a portion of the River Liffey flowing free from the clinging ice, all the windows blind and dark along the Quays, only the traffic lights were active and awake, changing their colours like treacherous politicians, green, amber, red, and then out of all order red and amber over and over again, what had happened to the green? And yet did it matter? for no one could catch them at any one colour for long enough to cross the road, so slippery was the frost-bound tarmac you'd have to go on all fours to stop yourself falling full-length to a broken hip-joint – did they not realise he was almost an old-age pensioner? Why could they not grit their damned surfaces?

He saw himself knocking at ice-sheeted doors up street after street through the labyrinth of Temple Bar, crying out for this lawyer he'd never even talked to on the telephone and couldn't remember the name of – 'Solicitor!', he was bawling. 'Solicitor for rat-face McGranaghan, I know what you are and I know where you are, you're hiding away on purpose: come out of it, man, and face me! I will give you ten minutes, not a second over the ten; and then it's done and gone, I'm out of it, finished, go scrape for your damned alibi in the ice of the gutter, go scrape!'

And then somehow he saw himself in the ante-room to the jail, amazingly hot and steamy with a great glowing stove, whitewashed brick

walls, brief shards of black winter sky just visible between the streaks of
filth on the window-panes, and something like fifty men crowded in there
together, red-faced, sweaty, foul-breathed, laughing and cursing and
disgustingly breaking wind, in warders' uniforms, policemen's uniforms,
soldiers' uniforms, strangely archaic – red tunics and spurred riding boots
for the troopers, bottle-green capes for the peelers, cheesecutter caps for
the screws, riding crops, swords, bristling moustachios, whiskers like
blacking brushes. The lawyer, if it *was* the lawyer, crept mysteriously
under Oldroyd's elbow, a pursy little shape in an ankle-length black
greatcoat, with a blank faceless face of what appeared to be white dough;
he was pressing against Oldroyd's hip and whispering hoarsely out of no
visible mouth, or rather, out of a *sort* of mouth like a knife-slit in the
dough (horrible!): 'This alibi's no good, y'know, they've already done
their sums – driven five different makes of car at five different average
speeds from Athlone to beyond Galway, against the stopwatch, mark that!
– and afterwards checked it on that new yoke of a computer they're after
installing at Garda Headquarters – your man could have been in the pub,
easy, easy, no more than a few short minutes before *you* were there, sure
the barman couldn't state within an hour or an hour and a half what time
the silly bugger staggered in.'

' "Silly bugger"?', bellowed Oldroyd, outraged. 'Your *client*, your
unfortunate *client*? By God, but I've not come here all this way (I'd have
you know) to hear him made a monkey of by you!'

'Oh hush, will you hush,' begged the lawyer. The sockets in the dough
that might have been his eyes were full of what might have been tears.
From the slit of his mouth crept a miserable drooling. Oldroyd had to
stoop to him with one hand cupped over his ear, the hoarse voice had now
sunk to such a dismally low register. 'Every word that you say will be
heard by all o'these and don't you believe they won't use it against us. But
here you are anyway like Pythias just arrived to surrender his bail and
fetch his friend Damon out of it, an act of bloody virtue, considering the
circumstances, I could never praise too highly – God, you must have
bloody loved him, silly bugger that he is too, but matter a damn for that! –
when you write up his case for the newspapers, will it be in the style of a
grand old-fashioned erotic ode with no nonsense about it? There's some
of us at any rate hope that it will . . .'

He snuffled into silence and wobbled swiftly away into the thick of the sweat-and-leather crowd. They shifted aside a little to let him through, but without any obvious awareness; it was as though he moved in some dimension quite outwith their notice. Instead, they were staring contemptuously at Oldroyd, spitting their squirts of tobacco juice onto the flagstones, snorting through their nostrils; but none of them spoke to him.

He endured their scornful company for as long as it seemed to take, which is to say his sense of time was gravely deranged and he could not stabilise it. Was he there for ten seconds or a whole hour? – and how was it that such a gang of intimidating louts did not succeed in scaring him? Well, he *was* conscious of a most powerful sense of virtue, overcoming his natural timidity; and also was he conscious of a strangely sexual warmth pouring into him like whiskey from a jug – inexplicable anticipation of scarce-believable ecstasy was throbbing in the very air of this guardroom – in the fug of the stove, the stink of the guard, the reek of the muck on the floor – his loins grew quivering strong for it – any minute now its fulfilment would be clustering upon him so exquisitely sweetly – and at *his* age, moreover! (for he could not deny that the loving lecheries of Ute no longer inflamed him quite as fiercely as they used to) – yes indeed, at his age, these government ruffians could not possibly prevent it: he was calm and intrepid in their midst, he endured them, he despised them, and they knew it.

He saw himself pass through them, with nobody leading him; doors opened before him and shut themselves after him, clanging and banging with nobody's hand to cause it; locks, bolts, cages and gratings, down stairs and down stairs again; and a final clang behind him, louder than all the others. He saw himself in what must surely be the condemned cell. A dank narrow space twice as high as it was broad, lit by one small lantern through an opening in the spring of the vault. Below the vault the walls were lined with baulks of blackened timber like railway sleepers, studded top to bottom with huge-headed nails.

Mattie McGranaghan, deep inside there, sat cross-legged on his plank bed. He had to his hand a pitcher of water and the heel of a stale loaf, his bare feet were thrust for warmth into a bundle of straw. His only garment was a sort of shirt that barely covered the top of his thighs: but on his head he wore his baseball cap, rakishly back to front, and the curly forelock that flopped out of it was neither grey nor white but the abundant sandy-ginger of years ago, and thank heaven! he'd got rid of that mildewed moustache. He looked up at Oldroyd and smiled, a smile of joyous friendliness, the smile of a boy of fourteen. 'Aha! dearest Pythias, oh I knew you would come,' he cried. 'Oh I knew you would not be too late. I'm afraid they have me chained, though, my right hand, d'y'see, to the staple in the wall here, if you want to make love to me you'll have to do most of it yourself. But I do have the other hand free, so why don't I start by unfastening a few of your zips – God, but this anorak is a robe and a half too much! Come on,' he murmured, 'closer! come on, dear old friend, dear old uncle, and cuddle me, God but this cell is so cold . . .'

Whereupon Oldroyd saw himself lying tightly with this smooth-limbed slender-hipped juvenile new McGranaghan stark naked in the straw of the prison. 'Damon,' he breathed, 'my darling little lad, and at last! after all these barren years, such delight I cannot bear it, oh your skin and your fingers and the soft little twists of downy red hair just beginning to sprout in your crotch . . .' It was cold and it was hot and his heart beat faster and faster for lust and for longing, for solidarity and comradeship, indeed for a weird sense of fatherhood, and at the end of it all (oh why not?) for true love.

Without doubt an erotic ode, grand and old-fashioned, the rich consummation of an honest-to-goodness grammar school. At the climax of it, he awoke; better to say, he half awoke, for the dream was still surging inside him, and for an instant he felt could he fall back asleep again, he would carry on deliciously from where he left off; then he realised he couldn't, the bouncing of the bus put a stop to all such business. He gave a deeply regretful sigh, and came fully to his daytime self (the bus driver blared his horn, the bus skidded and pulled our sharply from the brink of a deadly accident, Oldroyd all but fell from his seat into the aisle), no dreams any more, no drowsiness, only piercing stabs of horror that his subconscious could run away with him into such queer and secret places. He had often enough played host to vidid dreams of carnality, but not as a rule dreams that abraded his privities with images of men or of boys or of men who mutated (as in this case) into boys even as he groped them. Or at least, not since he himself was a boy, an uncoordinated broomstick of a masturbating fourth-former . . . he began to remember things he had hoped he had forgotten ... oh no, this WOULD NOT DO! For after all, he had his Ute, he was therefore (so he believed) as entirely heterosexual, and as thoroughly satisfied with it, as would keep him in good standing with his own particular corner of bar-room opinion, *nem. con.* So he believed: but what would *they* believe, if ever they found out what went on within the slumbers of th'ould Spike? 'Enough to make a man throw his dinner up,' he muttered into the wool of his scarf, 'mucky murky nonsense, how *could* I have invoked it? – ugh!'

And yet he had invoked it, created it, even: and now he knew no trick to dismiss it from his mind. He huddled in the creeping bus and brooded, morose and prurient, surging with neurotic self-aversion.

Beside the village green of Tyrrellspass, a full hour after leaving Athlone, the bus skidded yet again on a streak of hard ice – the driver trying angrily to swerve clear of a white van that had itself skidded across him – the man in the van going far too fast – the flat nose of the bus bashing slap into the side of the van – both vehicles ending up half on the road, half on a stone curb between the road and the edge of the green – all the passengers in the bus thrown hither and thither like coffee beans rattled in a jar. Nobody hurt, not even the white-van man.

Arrival of the Garda, strenuous three-way argument between cops and the two drivers with passengers chipping in to denounce the white-van man, snarling conversations on various mobile phones, and an announcement (eventually) that a relief bus was on its way from Athlone, and might be with them within the hour. Once again the bus driver was pleasant enough to throw away a few words, possibly portentous words, having to do with midnight; but Oldroyd did not hear them.

He *had* heard 'within the hour', and there and then, in explosive dudgeon, had taken himself off to warm himself and soothe his rage with what he thought of as 'a brisk walk, therapeutic'.

So brisk that after no more than two- or three-score paces he had reached a public house at the corner of the green. He was the first into its doors, and before any of the others came in he had bought himself a hot whiskey with lemon slice, sugar and cloves; a surviving lunchtime sandwich; a packet of crisps. Quite contrary to his normal pub manner, he avoided conversation. He bought another hot whiskey, and then two more. He was still tinkling his teaspoon in the remains of his fourth, bitterly glowering at the grease smears on the bar counter, when a voice called out from the doorway that the bus was already up there, didn't they hear the man hooting his horn?

The relief bus might have been superannuated from the rural school-run of the 1970s, no heating, slashed upholstery, three broken windows. The driver was a surly greybeard within a year or two of his pension, and no longer giving a damn; he kept his thumb jerking on and off the horn button until all his passengers were aboard (he'd been bequeathed his colleague's note of their number); he started away without one single word to them, good or bad. The nearer he drove to Dublin, the thicker the mist, the more frequent the traps of black ice. At Kinnegad, just beyond the junction with the main road from the north-west, he suddenly slung his wheel over, and dragged (rather than steered) the bus into a parking lane along the frontage of a flashy bar/restaurant. Two buses were parked there already, passengers unaccountably standing around them on the road. The driver pressed the button to open the door; a man in busman's uniform jumped in; the door slid shut behind him. It closed in the faces of a tetchy little knot of apparently protesting persons; their mouths and arms were in violent motion, their words were inaudible, and Oldroyd, at a loss, could only stare at them through the window.

The newcomer spoke rapidly and forcefully to the driver; the driver stood up and confronted the passengers; he twisted his lips in what might have been an attempt to ingratiate, to detract from the straightforward brutality of his speech: 'Okay, okay, you don't have to like it! because dammit, y'know, I don't like it, I don't live in Kinnegad, how d'ye expect I'm going to find me way home tonight? Fact is, it's gone midnight: industrial action – as the company's been well warned, as the public's been warned, all branches of the media from first thing this morning – industrial action was declared to commence at midnight in default of negotiation, not a sniff o' negotiation has been offered to this union all day. So there y'are, it's as we promised, I'm on strike; *he's* on strike, just come in all the way from Sligo, ages late on the bloody ice the same bloody game as me; the feller up the front in the bus from Ballina, *he's* on strike – so we gather up the money to make sure that nobody loots it, and the ticket machine, *here*, and all the rest of the clutter, and we go.'

As he spoke, he was collecting his regulation moveables. He opened the door again and stood to usher the passengers out. 'It's no good to re*mon*strate, no good at all at all,' he added, with more disdain than sympathy. 'There's many a worse place to be stranded than Kinnegad. Th'establishment here's kept open all night for the survival of travellers, the bar'll be likely closed, but they say there's a fire in the lounge: given the circumstance, there may well be some young straps o'waitresses to boil ye up y'r pot o'tea.'

The passengers – in contrast with those from the other two buses – gave vent to no complaint beyond stoical moans and groans. Apart from Oldroyd, there was only a dozen of them, they were chilled to the bone, and Kinnegad, they seemed to think, would be near enough to Dublin to make it easy to continue their journey; moreover the well-lit lounge and the thought of the fire in the lounge were powerful inducements to good temper.

At last and at last, a taxi was discovered, whose owner was prepared to roll out of bed and risk the black ice to get Oldroyd to the capital city. He was not a Kinnegad man; he had to be called from Mullingar, eleven miles off in the wrong direction. But at last and at last he came. Thereupon, without warning, a whole platoon of stranded passengers demanded to be accommodated. The taxi driver refused to accept more than five, or else, he declared, the bastards above there'd have his licence off him soon as look at him. In the end Oldroyd agreed to take a four-year-old child on his knee in the front seat. The child did not sleep, nor would it heed its worn-out mother and 'hold its sodding noise'. She herself, in the back seat, between two massive Scandinavian tourist-youths and all their raincapes, wallets and water bottles, had a two-year-old on her lap and a baby in the crook of her arm.

When, at last and at last, they drove into Dublin, at something like half past three in a biting new squall of sleety rain, blown in from the east and possibly turning into snow, they must first deliver mother and children to a tower block in Ballymun, upon the far edge of the city. After that, the Scandinavians began to quarrel, nag and fret about a particular hostel – they had its name but not the address, and no other place would do, for had they not arranged to meet the rest of their party there so they could all take the same plane to Oslo, one of the very first flights in the morning, 'important, most important, you must find it, please!' Oldroyd asserted himself. He demanded to make a telephone call before the taxi went anywhere else. There was a kiosk just across the road – 'over there, man! *there*! stop!' He dialled the number of the McGranaghans' lawyer and waited and waited for someone to roll out of bed and reply.

At last and at last, blearily and resentfully: 'What's that you say? Oldroyd? ... Yes of course, Mr Oldroyd! from Galway, are you not, sir? And what *have* you been up to, Mr Oldroyd? My client seemed to think you'd be with me last evening. I can tell you here and now you're more or less too late for any useful immediate purpose, but begod you've woke me up, amn't I barefoot on the lino in a freezing cold passage? so before you yourself decide to rent a bed and go to sleep, you'd best come straight round and we can talk. Where are you? ... *Ballymun*? God save us, God preserve us, listen here, sir –' He rattled out a baffling slew of most complex directions. Oldroyd (without apology) passed them on to the taxi driver – all the way across the city to some hard-to-find cul-de-sac hidden away behind Dalkey in the far south suburbs, let the Norsemen wait their turn, no way would they need to be connecting with their party before half past five at the earliest, they had bucketfuls of bloody time, let them stop their bloody croaking.

Before they reached the lawyer's, Oldroyd had to demand another stop, this time beside a bank to activate the hole-in-the-wall for a couple of hundred pounds. Sheer chance and good luck he had his card in his wallet, more often than not he left it at home: and it certainly did look as though his share of this taxi jaunt would cost him near enough a month's earnings.

* * *

Mr Cornelius Collopy, solicitor, still in pyjamas and dressing gown, in a pokey little study built out beside the kitchen of his pokey little semi-detached (a roaring gas fire turning the room into a brick kiln), gave a guarded and dubious welcome to his client's unlooked-for alibi and the queer-looking old fellow who had brought it. This Collopy was queer enough himself, not at all the uncanny dough-face of Oldroyd's dream, but a black-muzzled, sharp-jawed pickaxe of a man, something between forty and fifty, an intermittent nervous uptilt to his chin which strove in an odd way to rhyme with Oldroyd's constant stoop, rimless glasses attached to his neck by a strip of ribbon, and three fingers missing from his right hand. His shiny black hair, newly oiled and brushed straight back from the brow, might well be a wig; it was at all events more smoothly arranged than seemed entirely natural for a character who had not bothered either to shave or to put his clothes on.

'You'll take a cup o'tea, Mr Oldroyd, I've dropped a dash of whiskey in it. Fierce cold out o'doors this early morning, and you all the way from Galway. God preserve us, in the midst of a bus strike. What will you be thinking of this country at all? I daresay you can put it all into one of your pieces for the London *Telegraph* – what is it then, the name you write under? "Captain Macmorris", is it not? and that's a good one, Shakespeare, ha! I'm told you have a mordant pen.'

This was intolerable. Not a person in the whole of Ireland was supposed to know Oldroyd's *nom de plume*. But at least one person did, of course! and good heavens, she'd been talking. Why, his trustworthy Ute had talked to that bitch-weasel Julia, and Julia had talked to Collopy, and Collopy without doubt was giving him warning that if indeed he was a British agent, he was already blown, and nothing he might say could be taken at face value.

Mr Collopy continued: 'Only for your connection, at some remove, with a certain roving rogue of the name of O'Reilly (d'you take my meaning?), I would never have considered paying heed to your evidence. Not that I don't believe it; but be assured, Mr Oldroyd, I'm damn sure the Special Court wouldn't. There's rumours going around already that whoever robbed that truckload were neither straight criminals nor honest-to-goodness idealist Republicans, but a class of United Kingdom hitmen on hire, d'y'see? from certain unknown corners of a supposedly unknown department – MI5, would it be? or is it 6? And the unfortunate McGranaghan is supposed to be one of 'em. Of course the man's a renegade, why wouldn't he be one of 'em?'

'What the hell are you talking about? How dare you suggest that I – ? What the devil d'you mean by O'Reilly? And in God's name, on hire to do what?' Oldroyd was beginning to panic. This quixotic peregrination, for the honour of his name and the love of his lady, was collapsing all about him like a DIY bookcase. He had hated his mission most ferociously all night long: yet now (so very strangely) he was beginning to *enjoy* it, and now was it going to be ruined for him?

'To do what, d'you ask me? Why, to foul up and sabotage whatever useful talks may currently be in progress between a brace of prime ministers, an assortment of unionists, and – well – all the pack o'them the far side of the Black Pig's Dyke. Now if that's the case – take note, sir, I say "if" – if that should be the case, you in the witness box with your highly significant *curriculum vitae* ("Captain Macmorris", God preserve us) coupled, my dear sir, with your conceivably significant accent (would it be Sheffield, or County Durham?) – to be frank, Mr Oldroyd, our judges are not idiots. Most certainly you'd be taken for a man with an agenda, a most sinister agenda, perversely determined to liberate the guilty and set the Garda Síochána on the trail of the innocent.'

Oldroyd in his fluster harked back to his first question: 'Why don't you damn well answer me? I asked you what the devil did you mean by O'Reilly? I have never said a word about O'Reilly. There is nothing in my story to even *hint* at a man called O'Reilly. This is sexual scandal for the sake of discrediting not only my reputation but *hers*!' He did not know what on earth he meant; only that himself and this unforthcoming Collopy were wildly at cross purposes.

He lay back exhausted deep into his chair and wondered, was he falling asleep? If so, the solicitor was not about to allow it. 'Will you pull yourself together and stop wasting my time! The fact is, the man O'Reilly, wherever he may be, is by way of being a voucher for your own *bona fides*, I'm surprised you don't see that, I'm surprised you should resent it. But as for poor McGranaghan, I've no notion what we can do.' Mr Collopy all of a sudden seemed stricken with total despair. He helplessly allowed his uptilted head to droop till his glasses slid down from the bridge of his nose to the tip; his hands were spread out on either side in front of him, clutching aimlessly at piles of papers. 'Didn't they charge him on the stroke of midnight with capital murder,' he moaned, 'and a judge around the corner in his nightshirt (I suppose) rolled straightway out of bed to agree that he shouldn't get bail, so that one-two-buckle-me-shoe the unfortunate ould devil's banged up in Mountjoy Jail and they'll not let him out till he's dead. For he not only murdered a Garda but he damn nearly murdered the entire Provo ceasefire, they'll never forgive him, not ever.'

'But I'm here to tell you that he cannot have done it.'

The solicitor straightened up again, shot out his chin toward Oldroyd, and fixed him with a glare of implacable antagonism: 'I'm here to tell *you*, sir, that the more you say that, the more they'll believe that he did. O God.' He rattled his fingertips on the top of the desk, baring his teeth into Oldroyd's face. 'Oh God, let me see: what to do, what to do, what to do?'

Was it simply a result of the man's apparent collapse, that Oldroyd (at last and at last) felt able to tell himself he had found himself a real reason for his crackpot involvement in this seriously discomfortable affair? No, he was not here because Ute had put the pressure on; no, he was not here because Julia McGranaghan had somehow contrived to spook him; no, no, *he had his reason*! – in a venomous vindictive world, what else could it be but a reason of self-preservation? 'Mr Collopy,' he growled, 'I've not come to Dublin just to make things easy, not for me, not for *you*. Your client is in jail. Your nasty little client, if you want me to be candid. As far as I'm concerned, I'd be happy for him to stay there (as you say) till he's dead. I've lived in this country for the best part of twenty years; I had hoped I could bide until *I'm* dead. I've not had any trouble with the Garda Síochána, I've left 'em alone and they've left *me* alone. But what sort of place is it, for a man who earns his living by expressing his opinions, if police force and judges through political paranoia, to say nowt of damned laziness, leave a desperate little runt in the bowels of Mountjoy who ought never have been put there at all?'

'You suppose it hasn't happened in England?' Mr Collopy's national feelings were rubbed on a sore place. 'D'you never hear of the Birmingham Six, or the Guildford Four, or the –'

'I said, what sort of place is it? *This* place, here, now? The only bloody place I'm concerned with at this moment. The fact is, I am frightened, shit-scared, bloody terrified. For if I had the chance look of a twin brother of a wanted murderer, could you tell me would *I* have any more hope than you seem to hold out for McGranaghan? If I'm prevented giving the evidence that'd clear him from that prison, I'll never sleep another dreamless night.'

'Night . . . dreamless . . . how?' Mr Collopy was caught off guard by the anticlimax. 'What's wrong with having dreams? I'm always having dreams. All the poetry of a man's soul comes out in his dreams, let alone the satisfaction of his unfulfilled desires . . .' He realised he was talking more to himself than to Oldroyd: he cleared his throat abruptly and rapped his desk. 'Oh very well then . . . For you, dreams are bad. We'll leave it at that.'

'They never used to be bad. Tonight, on that bus, though, I had a terrible one, disastrous. In God's name, no repetition. If you won't go with me, I'll go to the Guards myself. And I'll tell them, straight up, straight down, who I am and where I stand. I'll tell 'em what you tell me about what other people *think* I am, so they'll know I'm straight and truthful with 'em. If you choose to go with me – why, *you* can tell 'em as well. Tell 'em frankly, don't you see? – yes, I do write for the Tory press, nothing strange about using a pseudonym, and my articles (as far as possible) are never owt but straight and truthful.'

Mr Collopy shot his lips out with a harsh derisive bark. 'Ha! straight and truthful? He believes it, he really believes it? In which case, he's as innocent as a hoar-headed baby, and of course it isn't him that has the sinister agenda, but the editors that pay for him, oh yes! Oh yes, I daresay it'd be *possible* to argue it . . .' A long brooding silence: then at last and at last: 'If only I could be sure I had a witness that *I* could trust, never mind the cops and the judges. And what about this alibi anyway? I mean the time it'd take a motor from Athlone to the pub where you found him. Couldn't your man have been in the pub, easy, easy, no more than a few short minutes before *you* were there? ... God preserve us, whatever's the matter? Are you having a heart attack?'

'No. No. Leave me alone. I do *not* want your whiskey forced into my mouth, no!' Oldroyd was staggering upright from what had looked like a violent fit: retching and writhing and jerking all four limbs; he knocked away the alarmed solicitor as though he were swatting a fly. 'The exact words of that terrible dream, disastrous! – am I sure I remember it, or do I take the words from you now to insert them retrospectively? I mean, was the dream sent me in order to warn me off, or do I reinvent it as an excuse to go no further? Oh, Mr Collopy, I beg you, just sit and shut up ... I'm perfectly all right, except I'm tired, I'm growing old, I cannot cope with nonsense. Do you mean to come with me to talk to the Guards, or not?'

From one police station to another, the length and breadth of Dublin, Collopy was led by a fuming Oldroyd like a dire old dancing bear on the end of the bear leader's rope. They started off the very minute they had finished what Collopy called breakfast – burnt bacon, fried eggs the consistency of suede leather, stewed tea out of yesterday's teapot (there seemed to be no Mrs Collopy) – and kept on and on, street after street, in taxi after taxi (all the buses of course on strike), until long beyond a normal person's lunchtime.

In none of the police stations did they find a single detective who was prepared to admit knowledge of, let alone responsibility for, the Athlone cop-killing case. They all stared very hard at Oldroyd, their eyes agleam with insensate hostility, they all pulled their mouths into rigid furrows of rage and distaste, but the most any of them had to say was, 'We are in no way privy to that matter in this place. It was handled as an investigation of the highest security category. I am not at all empowered to furnish details. I suggest you get a chit from the office of the Public Prosecutor. Sergeant So-and-so, like a good man, will ye show these – ah – citizens out. Goodbye t'ye, so.'

Collopy was spluttering that there was of course no such thing as a Public Prosecutor's chit: it was no more than a device to keep them running in circles, the sort of trick the Guards always pulled when they wanted to hamper Republicans. No more than twenty-four hours ago, Oldroyd would have contemptuously dismissed such a statement as sand-blind subversive persecution-mania. Now he began to see that the man knew what he was talking about. His sturdy-Yorkshireman confidence in his own manifest integrity, his untroubled reliance upon civil rights in a democracy, were taking a battering. At about three in the afternoon, as they left yet another police station, yet again dismissed with contumely, somewhere in the council-house deserts of Artane, the desk sergeant beckoned them over. 'Psst,' he whispered. 'Mr Collopy: mind you, I've said nothing, but you did help the young son of a lady-friend of mine last year, he was in trouble wit'the drugs, know what I mean? Why don't you try Clondalkin? They might just say "no" to you, if they do y'd be no worse off than y'are. But 'tis always conceivable they'd be bound to say "yes".'

Collopy had no chance to enquire further or even thank him: an inspector at that moment came through from the inner offices and the sergeant's face became as lifeless as his own rubber stamp.

Oldroyd asked (out in the street), where the devil was Clondalkin? Collopy told him, pretty damn nearly halfway to Athlone. The taxi they had arrived in was still waiting for them at the corner, the driver only too happy to quote an exorbitant fare.

'Are you sure you can afford it?' Collopy was getting worried, not only by their official mistreatment, which he had not felt able to resent in proper terms, but also because he had an uneasy notion that his companion was no longer answering to his helm, was going off his head, up the wall, round the bend, *non compos mentis*. For every time they'd been given the brush-off Oldroyd had insisted on trying somewhere else regardless, he wouldn't stop to eat or drink, he poured out his money into the grabbing mitts of taxi drivers like a sailor on leave, he didn't even seem to want to go and have a piss.

And then that crazy business of his dream, half past four in the morning, hawking and whooping and throwing his feet about? There was more than enough hardship from a client like McGranaghan without his one and only witness running stark mad. Collopy decided: okay he would go to Clondalkin, just the final definitive trip; after that, he'd pack it in, nothing came from nothing, they were finished and fucked, they might just as well accept the fact.

Clondalkin is a vast new suburb, practically a new town, stretching out into the countryside to the west of the city. The taxi driver did not know where to find the Garda; he wasted a great deal of time taking directions from passers-by and misunderstanding them. At last (and at last) he deposited his passengers in front of the long-sought premises, and asked, should he wait? Oldroyd said, of course he should. The driver said, 'You're the doctor. Jayz, you must be in need of a good long dose o'th'law-n-order, okay. What are ye, a pair o'touts outa work and seeking a contract?' He was vexed because they had not told him the reasons for all their journeying. They ignored his jocularity, went up the steps, in through the door, put their everlasting question to the Guard at reception, and astonishingly received something like an answer; moreover, in a tone of voice that suggested they were half expected . . .

'Ah, you want Mr Donovan, so. The Chief Super's just in to see him, he ordered no calls for twenty minutes, but I'll ring him and tell him you're here: I don't think he'd thank me for not letting him know.'

Almost at once they were ushered along into the recesses of the building, up the stairs, into a very small office almost totally filled with two very large men, together with all their tobacco smoke – a plain-clothes detective (presumably Donovan) and a uniformed chief superintendent.

At the end of a lengthy bout of consequential explanation, first by Collopy, then by Oldroyd, with the Chief Super and Donovan listening attentively, almost *too* attentively, there was a pause, a profoundly silent pause, impregnate with sceptical menace. The two officers were staring significantly at each other; Collopy and

Oldroyd stared anxiously at the two officers ... Then Donovan, with a quiet smile, put a few quiet questions to Oldroyd, getting him to repeat various points from his statement, and making little scribbles in a notebook. Another silent pause; and then the Chief Super heaved himself up from his chair. He cleared his throat and gave utterance with some apparent physical difficulty, a deep-seated emphysemal wheeze: 'I'm in no doubt you know what you're going to do with this, Patrick,' he said to Donovan. 'No need at all for meself to hear any more of it; I'll be away back to the Phoenix Park directly; let me have your report in due form.'

He padded to the door, and then turned himself heavily about. 'Oh,' he gasped, 'oh. I shouldn't leave without a mention of it. Your client, Mr Collopy, gave vent to a confession. And that was why we charged him.'

'Confession? Confess? Confess *what*? I don't believe you.'

'Oh it's not, not as yet, a very complete confession. And not all of it entirely adds up. It's possible Mr Oldroyd's – oh – *alibi*, when carefully analysed, will help to confirm it. Shall we see?'

He went out.

Donovan looked at his notebook, then up again at Oldroyd, a cautious, speculative survey from little shoe-button eyes between heavy folds of eyelid. He lit a cigarette from the butt he had just discarded, sucked on it noisily, blew out the smoke in a cloud. His eyes through the cloud remained fixed upon Oldroyd. He clucked his tongue in apparent indecision: did he know or didn't he what he was going to say next? When he spoke, it could well have been at random, yet it probably wasn't. Oldroyd had a sensation as of cobwebs falling softly around him, cobwebs with the strength of nylon nets.

'Will you tell me, Mr Oldroyd, did Mr Collopy here ever tell you just how he lost his fingers?'

'That's quite enough of that!' blustered Collopy, unpleasantly taken by surprise. 'My God, you have no right to –'

'Mr Oldroyd's the man I'm talking to, thank you very much, sir. Mr Oldroyd, would you care to answer?'

'I certainly will answer. No, he did not tell me, nor did I ask.'

'Ah well, your curiosity was no doubt on the simmer, so why

don't I satisfy it, now? Mr Collopy, I'm warning you, be quiet or I'll book you! Solicitors, in this office, do *not* have immunity if they choose to be obstructive . . . Now, Mr Oldroyd, how much will it surprise you to hear that those three fingers were taken off by one pistol bullet each? Your friend here was so misfortunate as to incur the righteous wrath of a particular virulent crowd of paramilitaries (oh less than a year ago, wasn't it?): they were under the impression he was safeguarding their interests and then they discovered he was already retained by quite another crowd altogether – you'll be familiar with the phrase, now, "an Internal Republican Feud"? You journalists are always using it; which of course doesn't mean it's not true.'

The solicitor, to Oldroyd's astonishment, sat and sulked in defeated silence.

This was hopeless. It was only too clear the man Collopy was nothing more than the creature of his own terrors; what possible good could such a one ever do for McGranaghan? Oldroyd nonetheless remained resolute, indomitable, determined; he had already made his statement as strongly as he could; he would make it again and again; by sheer force of his character, by God he would compel this cut-price 'tyrant of Syracuse' to accept his good faith.

But as soon as he thought of Syracuse, he thought of something else: Pythias, who had raced against all odds to redeem his friend from crucifixion, was the terrorist-subversive, not Damon, Damon was innocent; somehow the ancient story had got twisted the wrong way round . . . For the first time in all this adventure, Spike Oldroyd felt personally imperilled.

There was a small knock at the door. A second detective, a slightly built young fellow with a shaven head, slipped into the room and took his place behind Donovan, on a chair in the far corner. 'You got the doings?' asked Donovan, without looking round.

'I have, sir. Here it is.' The newcomer stretched his arm out and laid a small tape recorder on the table.

Donovan spoke into the instrument. 'Clondalkin Garda Station, Monday the fourteenth of December, five thirty-five pm. Present at this interview, Detective Superintendent Donovan, Detective Sergeant O'Malley, Silas Witherington Oldroyd (aka Spike Oldroyd) and Cornelius Collopy, solicitor. I am about to charge Mr Oldroyd with obstructing the Garda Síochána in their duties by providing a false alibi for Martin de Porres McGranaghan who was himself charged last night with the murder of a member of the Garda Síochána. I am warning Mr Oldroyd that further charges may very well be brought, accessory after the fact in the murder of a member of the Garda Síochána, conspiracy to commit the murder of a member of the Garda Síochána, conspiracy to carry out an armed robbery – the list could go on all night, but we'll keep it up our sleeves, which is dependent on what we get from you in the way of a revised statement, a very heavily revised statement; if you want to hear *my* advice, you'll tell a new story altogether. Or maybe you'd prefer not to tell us a story at all. And maybe the latter would be best.' And then, with a sudden and quite appalling shout: 'Because you've really gone and run yourself nose-deep into the shite, have you not, you bloody old eejit?'

Mr Collopy was twittering rather than talking straight out. Oldroyd thought he heard him say, 'Do you not need a good solicitor? oh I'd say that you do ... Tell you what, I have a colleague, not at all political but very good at this class of a mix-up, I'll give him a ring, why don't I? He could come and fix you up with some bail. Mr Oldroyd? oh yes: I daresay.'

All Oldroyd could offer was, 'Dear God. Oh dear God. However could you think that I ... Dear God it's inconceiv ... Oh dear God I'm dead and gone, and I've not had a sandwich all day. Nor even a cup of ... Oh dear God.'

EPILOGUE

Was Oldroyd brave enough to stand by his statement?
He certainly was. He was resolute, indomitable, determined; and so furious at their refusal to let him have a cup of tea that he shut up his mouth on them as tight as a child-proof pillbox. He knew he

had seen McGranaghan where and when he *said* he'd seen him, and no further word would he vouchsafe.

Did they charge him as an obstructionist, an accessory, a conspirator – all the fearful things they threatened?

They did not. They badgered him for five hours and then they let him go. After all, as Donovan said to him, just before they let him go, they were not in Indonesia nor even in Belfast, and sure a man like Oldroyd should think himself damned lucky.

Did he give evidence at McGranaghan's trial?

Indeed he did, straight up, straight down: he told them who he was, he told them where he stood.

Was McGranaghan acquitted?

He was not. The prosecutor made it clear to the judges of the Special Court that if Oldroyd was not the dodgy old foreigner with a sinister agenda that perhaps he might seem to be, he was at least a heavy drinker and his memory was unreliable. The judges thought this to be good sense: they ignored Oldroyd's evidence altogether. They accepted McGranaghan's confession with all its inconsistencies. They refused to accept that it might have been coerced. They swiftly found him guilty and sent him to prison for life. Oldroyd, ever since, has been working with Ute to try and secure a retrial. An almost impossible job; and a number of English editors have in consequence become unwilling to accept his contributions. They have told him, in effect, that they no longer know where he stands.

PERPLEXITIES OF AN OLD-FASHIONED ENGLISHMAN

(2) The Crawthumper

Crawthumper: two definitions.

(1) *Dictionary of Buckish Slang, University Wit & Pickpocket Eloquence (compiled by Capt. Grose, 1811).*

'Roman Catholics, so called from their beating their breasts in the confession of their sins.'

(2) *Collins' English Dictionary (2000).* 'An ostentatiously pious person. [Irish informal].'

I

City Pensioners' Day on the Water

The Waterfront Residents' Association will hold its Last-Summer-of-the-Old-Millennium pensioners' outing next Saturday week, afternoon and evening. The *Connacht Queen* pleasure-boat (licensed bar and cold buffet) will leave Woodquay Pier at 4.30 pm for an upriver trip into Loch Corrib, and a picnic at Annaghdown (if weather permits).

On return there will be a two-course supper with dancing and cabaret in the Corrib Oarsmen Clubroom from 8.30 pm till late (licensed bar). All local pensioners welcome, bring your grandchildren if you have any! Names to Mrs Kate O'Curry, 'Agnus Dei', 41 Bowling Green, telephone *etc etc* . . .

She had pulled out the *Galway Advertiser* from the loose heap of last week's papers she kept stowed beneath her bedside armchair. Now she thrust it in a kind of miniature fury into Oldroyd's reluctant fingers, rattling her own fingers hard against the small announcement at the bottom of an inside page – 'There you are, look at it, "Day on the Water", damn your eyes, you are already of bloody near pensionable age, why do you not put down your name and go?'

He read the announcement aloud, slowly and with sour incredulity.

'Spike,' she continued, her speech heavily German on top of her acquired Irish accent – whenever she was angry or disturbed, or felt a need for persuasive energy, the half-buried indigenous utterance came insistently to the fore – 'Spike, will you listen please! You have a problem, you know it, and you know that your problem is this: you call yourself a writer, a commentator, journalist, essayist, fictionist, whatever it is, *ja*? And yet you make no trouble to know people whom you do not know. It is timorous, it is selfish, it is most bad for your imagination. Last Thursday in this *Advertiser* I saw this something that *you* should have seen. You have read it, *nicht wahr*? and now, you think about it. Will you think please, about it, Spike, now!'

She strode around the room between the bed and the window, the window and the door, stooping to pick up and put on her clothes, bits of them here, bits of them there, exasperated.

'Dear God, I know you're vexed with me, but to ferry me out, Mrs Ute O'Reilly, with all the ancients of Galway City on a sodding ship-of-fools through the whole of next Saturday evening? Dear God it's what the Yanks'd call a cruel and unusual punishment.' He cowered among her tangled bedsheets, like a ferret in a poacher's pocket. '*Grandchildren*!' he snarled. 'Dear God in a Christian Heaven.'

'And what is so wrong with grandchildren? *I* have got grandchildren.'

'What? you've got *what*? Dear God, you never told me. O'Reilly, I suppose: the far-departed Irish husband. But you never even told me you had –'

'A daughter? Well I do. Twenty years ago, more than twenty. Not here but East Germany, *die DDR, nicht wahr*? And not at all O'Reilly. None of your business who. But I tell you what *is* your business, Spike. And because you are in my bed when you should be at your desk at this time on a workday morning (*hoch lebe der Kaiser*! it is all but nine o'clock), you make it into *my* business.'

He was a Yorkshireman and proud of it, but he no longer knew where to turn. He was trying to write a novel; he had never written one before – or at least he had never finished one – it was taking him ages; he was not at all sure his choice of plot was workable, or maybe his characters did not fit the plot, or maybe neither plot nor characters were of themselves interesting. It was taking him ages and he had to earn a living. Yet how? For whatever about his incapacity for fiction, as a freelance political journalist he was (he had to admit) more or less finished and done, oh dear God! *dead*. Which distressed him but scarcely surprised him.

He knew what he looked like to his profession at large. He was too old: he was already sixty. He was too far away: he had lived for years in the west of Ireland and yet still expected his work to make easy sense in England. He was ideologically blown upon: his regular old-fashioned right-wing notions were of late most drastically compromised – like an Edwardian juvenile half maddened by some fantasy of the Honour of the Old School, he had volunteered an alibi for an obvious terrorist accused of the murder of an Irish policeman; and then, when the man was convicted and jailed he had launched a quite futile campaign against the verdict. Who after that would take his views seriously upon any public issue, to the right or to the left? 'Emotionally unstable,' said shocked editors who had thought that they knew him. Furthermore, he was often drunk. His boozing, they said, must assuredly blemish not only the worth of his writing but also the practicality of any business arrangement any one of them might care to try and make with him.

And again furthermore, he had been so careless with his finances that he had somehow failed to entitle himself to either a British or an Irish pension. There was of course his German lady, between whose Sunday sheets he had just spent the night, indeed a disappointing night: liquor enough, to be sure (empty bottles and glasses were all over the carpet), but an adequate fornication only halfway achieved, his own fault, he couldn't deny it, his libido was not what it was. For three years this sensual Ute had been modestly subsidising him; she was generous, and she loved him, and he had taken her for granted. Dear God, no more than a week since – he had scarcely come to terms with it yet – she so casually let him know that her occasional little loans might very shortly be coming to an end; she wouldn't say why; he knew better than to ask; he suspected that her husband – an IRA bank robber (men said) on the run somewhere in Europe – was secretly in touch with her and issuing demands.

To forget his problems he would make believe to bury himself in the endless complications of his novel. It was all about German spies and Nazi sympathisers in neutral Ireland during the Second World War and he couldn't make up his mind about the salacious bits – they were clearly essential if the book was to sell, but just how *perverted* ought they to be, given the perverse politics of most of the characters? Did nasty Nazi sympathisers necessarily display their nasty Nazi habits in bed? Or would the readers be put off by too much sadistic squalor? This was something else he did not care to ask Ute about: he was far from sure what her elder relatives had been up to during the Hitler years and it would scarcely do just now to make a coolness between him and her.

Yet if all this, this bright Monday morning, with the sunshine through her windows dazzling his crapulous eyes, was not to be called a 'coolness', what the devil *could* it be called? She had positively determined to upbraid him, and her musical sweet voice became as harsh and as Nazi as you could wish. 'Since McGranaghan went to jail,' she ranted, 'you find you cannot sell your political analysis, so instead you waste your talent with secondhand exposures of civic corruption, ecological, ecclesiastical, commercial, *ja*? And you cannot sell that either. Why not? You have no proper sources, your research is only halfway baked, you write down nothing but rumours from silly people who should know better. At least, when you wrote political, your sources and your rumours came from *me*: don't pretend, my gobbling turkey-wattle, they were not authentic.'

She had indeed furnished him for months at a time with all manner of first-rate material from mysterious paramilitary informants. But he was now in no mood to admit it. 'And so what, so bloody what? One of these days there'll be a turnaround, there's always a turnaround, it's a matter of supply and demand, which is why – '

'Which is why you can get no persons of well-reputed public status to support you in your call for a new trial for Matt McGranaghan. You do not *supply* them, or not with any stuff they can trust. McGranaghan's poor wife is out of her mind, he himself in Portlaoise prison, has the cancer of the colon, and no hope at all for him unless you by some means become acceptable, respectable, a wide-published writer with influence, Spike, *influence*! If you want to be of use in this issue of national justice, then at once you must improve yourself and this is how you do it. You must forget all your solicitor friends, your local journalist-hack friends, your public-bar Goethes and *jawohl*! your Victor Hugos and James wouldbe Joyces; you must mix with Irish citizens of no repute nor ambition whatever, no pretension, no stupid rumours, no fallacious inside stories of this and that in planning department or bishop's palaces or university. Make yourself over into a quiet underween-ing individual man who can talk to fellow people without giving them a lecture; and then you will learn from them; you will all of a sudden write like a new-blooming flower. Is all I have to say. This Mrs O'Curry's house is in the same small street as your house. You should have met her years ago. Go talk to her tonight, join in with her pensioners' treat. *Teufelsdreck*, Spike, it is already half past nine, I have a craft shop to attend to, will you not go! Trousers at once onto your hairy old legs, downstairs with you, man, and OUT!'

Clutching a ticket in his rheumaticky right hand, Oldroyd arrived on the pier at a quarter to five, accidentally-on-purpose fifteen minutes too late, breathing heavily as though he'd run all the way, hoping hard that the *Connacht Queen* would already be in midstream, and going over and over in his mind the explanations he must make to Ute. Maybe he was not well, he had pains in his chest sometimes, coronary angina, perhaps? The doctor at the hospital had been vague but had prescribed some pills. Oldroyd hadn't told Ute, he'd kept it in hand for a useful excuse. It would certainly have slowed him down, and anyone with potential heart trouble could be forgiven for missing a boat.

But he hadn't missed the boat. Clearly the trip's organizers did not expect their ageing guests to be punctual. With a grunt of resignation (it sounded more like a death rattle), he handed up his ticket to a smiling young woman in a CONNACHT QUEEN T-shirt and baseball cap, a water-hostess presumably, and allowed her to support him by the elbow onto the gangplank as though his legs were collapsing under him. 'Steady down the steps,' she warned, as he descended to the saloon. A dozen or two tables, like the lounge of a hotel, wide windows on either side, a further flight of steps leading up to the sundeck (he wouldn't bother with the sundeck, a drizzle of rain was just beginning) – so where was the . . . ? aha, there it was: the licensed bar! and another smiling T-shirt and baseball cap behind it, already serving drinks to an assorted scrum of . . . well, he supposed they were citizens of no repute whatever, elderly and crumbling without doubt, but most of them seemed jolly enough and not at all humiliated by mixing with their coevals in such a . . . well, such a deadly overt fashion.

It was even quite possible he was going to enjoy himself.

But not to the extent of being allowed all on his own to delve for compatible company. (This boat was not one of those pubs he used to frequent, where professional men and littérateurs propped the bar in sardonic detachment, mouthing their malice and scorning the world, waiting anxiously to be approached; but never to be approached save by tentative crab-like motions, one step at a time.) As soon as she saw him, Kate O'Curry came bounding toward him with her secretarial clipboard, hospitable, enthusiastic, all a-bubble with good works. A neat little black-eyed widow-woman, employed in the Bank of Ireland, by no means a pensioner – scarcely older than Ute in fact – fifty, fifty-five at the most. Now if he could spend the trip chatting to *her* – his recent life with Ute had, after all, thoroughly loosened him in regard to such juicy and agreeable ladies – but no! that was not her intention.

'Ah, Mr Oldroyd, how glad I am you could come! How extraordinary you've lived in the Bowling Green all these years and we never met! A shy man you are, sure you would be a very shy man, from England of course. And a Protestant, no? so we'd never run across each other at mass. Now, who do you know here? Ah sure, you wouldn't know anyone I daresay. All on your own and I wonder now is there somebody else all on his own, another of your shy men, that needs to be pushed and dragged ... Ah, there is of course. The bould Ignatius.'

And there and then, not a moment's delay, he was forcibly introduced to Mr Ignatius Tumulty, a small-town bachelor iron-monger from the wilds of County Mayo, who had (it appeared), not a sixmonth ago, been compelled to sell up his business before the DIY supermarkets bankrupted it, and had come to Galway city to live among strangers – the saints alone knew why, because to be sure Mrs O'Curry didn't.

'See can you get it out of him, Mr Oldroyd – did you say Spike? – he'll not say a word to me or to anyone else, will you, Ignatius? – a man of mystery entirely, but I always tell'em "no! let it out into the open and all the demons fly away", which was good Christianity long long before psychiatry came slithering into the country to leave us all on the roof with no ladder, wouldn't you agree with me there, Spike? Enjoy yourself, it's all laid on.' And off she went, not a moment's delay, bright and swift as a house-martin, to greet the next arrival.

'A lovely lady, Mrs O'Curry,' said Tumulty, looking at his toecaps. Wet lips, Oldroyd noted, toothbrush moustache not as well trimmed as it should have been, a cloud of white soft hair. 'Amazing,' the old fellow went on, 'the good deeds that she does for us all. D'you know I'm seventy-five if I'm a day? D'you know, until this last year, I never missed a year of the pilgrimage to Lourdes? There's many a one of my age would never have kept the strength up.' His soft voice was suffused with gloom. But then why wouldn't it be? thought Oldroyd. Hadn't the man just said goodbye to his livelihood, against his will and at a loss, no doubt – why the devil should he be *bounced* like a child in the sulks in the playground? Kate O'Curry was very kind, but she clearly lacked something of an intuitive sensitivity.

He offered to buy Tumulty a pint of beer or stout, but this was refused in favour of lemonade – a modest touch of the finger to the Pioneer pin in the lapel – yes indeed, he might have guessed it, he was up against a wretched crawthumper. Lourdes every year indeed, absolutely the class of veteran with whom that wretched Ute would expect him to hobnob – what, for all evening? – "till late", had the press notice said? Out of the question . . .

Nonetheless, he must be polite, must be sociable, sit to table (one of the few tables with only two seats), and allow some sort of conversation to develop – aha, the boat's crew were casting off the mooring ropes, should they talk about the landscape of the river as they passed along it, maybe there'd be a heron on a rock among the bullrushes, arrogantly posing in a fine heraldic attitude? Somehow, however, the interest of the riverbank failed to create an adequate sequence of speech – Oldroyd stammered a few useless syllables and fell silent – Tumulty didn't even stammer. Shy man with lemonade opposite shy man with pint of stout; what *was* to be said, and by whom? Until Oldroyd, driven by duty, absolutely had to start things off.

'So Lourdes, you said? Lourdes?' – in a peremptory bark. 'I'd not want to pry, but d'you go there for a cure? If you do, do you get any benefit?'

'Not for a cure in my case, no. Oh no, no.' Tumulty seemed instantly pleased at this choice of subject, his whole countenance lit up, he lifted his eyes, he looked into Oldroyd's eyes, he launched into explanations with no inhibition at all. 'I'd go as a volunteer; they always need the volunteers, pushing the wheelchairs, handling the stretchers, stewarding the crowds . . . 'Tis interesting work in itself, you meet so many dear people, devoted people, so you do, and there is what you'd call a great spiritual dimension. Believe it as you will, sir, you *do* witness miracles. Why, I could tell you stories . . .'

And then without warning his voice fell away, as though suddenly he was overcome by some terrible tragic reflection and all his hopeful stories were mere dust and ashes in his mind. Useless to attempt to revive them: they would only add despair to a heap of grief. Oldroyd had said already he did not want to pry; when he said it, it was true enough, he was just trying to improvise discourse; but now there was a new situation. Something concealed here? something perhaps shameful? something not quite consistent with Mr Tumulty's devout simplicity – journalistic instinct *compelled* him to pry, but dear God he'd have to do so with caution, or he'd scare the man off altogether.

He pretended not to have noticed anything untoward, he casually picked up on a previous remark, he spoke without show of particular concern. 'You never missed a year until this last year, you said? Any particular reason why you didn't go to Lourdes last year? I mean, did you find it too much of a strain? Seventy-five's a grand age, right? but even so – I'm only a bit over sixty myself and *I* wouldn't care to be – '

Mr Tumulty ignored the question. Instead he once again spoke direct into Oldroyd's face, once again no inhibitions, but a dark tense anxiety that dreaded to be rebuffed. 'D'you know, sir, Mrs O'Curry, d'you know what she said about *you*? She told me in as many words you were a journalist and no Catholic, an atheist very likely, and so I thought, sir, to my disgrace perhaps, you were the very man for *me*. You of all men, so I thought, in this religion-riddled country of ours, would be least likely to serve up to me a ... why, a dose of cowardly humbug. I beg you, sir, don't tell me I have made a mistake.'

What else could Oldroyd say to him, but – 'Eh nay, there's no mistake, I don't *think* I'm a humbug, there's a lot o'rude things said of me but that was never one of 'em. And it's true, I write for newspapers – now and again – I don't know how Mrs O'Curry found out, I'm sure *I* didn't tell her ... What was it you wished to talk about?' Whatever it was, he knew he had to hear it, diffuse no doubt, and wearisome, but exactly what Ute, with all her cranky intuition, seemed to think he should take pains to elicit. *An Irish citizen, of no repute, speaking direct from the heart: pay attention! learn to write like a new-blooming flower.*

2

Direct from the heart very possibly, but direct in fits and starts, and so slowly that it looked as though they would chug forward the length of the river and up into the lake and be already at their picnic before Mr Tumulty could bring himself to the core of his narrative.

Small apologies, self-deprecations, continual reiterations of the fact that a mere ironmonger should not be giving himself airs as a storyteller in the presence of a real professional – but at last, at last, the solid business. (The rain was now so heavy that an announcement from the skipper came over the tannoy, regretfully no picnic, they'd just glimpse Annaghdown and turn around; Oldroyd was glad of this, an interruption might be fatal to old Tumulty's confidence, and something quite strange, even important, seemed finally about to emerge.)

Oldroyd made fluent shorthand notes in his pocket book; he ought really to have brought his little tape recorder, but whenever he tried to use such a gadget, something technical was bound to go wrong with it; in any case Mr Tumulty appreciated the pocket book, he could see what went into it, he kept pausing to interject, 'You do have this down, sir? – now be sure you have it down!'

Later on, when his shorthand was edited and clarified into a draft of a fair copy, Oldroyd's version of the first part of the old man's story went something like this:

He remembered (that's to say Tumulty remembered) that I (that's to say Oldroyd) asked him why he hadn't gone to Lourdes the last year. He hadn't wanted to answer me, the whole thing too painful, now he saw he *must* answer, because unless here and now he could get it off his chest, impossible to tell the story, because that's what it all hung from.

He couldn't afford it, was the simple answer, because he'd decided to make a pilgrimage elsewhere, on the strong recommendation of a very very prayerful priest from Boston, Mass., whom he'd met in fact at Lourdes the year *before* the last. 'Elsewhere' was hugely costly (at least in comparison with his usual package via Aer Lingus to the south of France), almost all the poor devil's savings – but for spiritual benefits, so this Father Scallion persuaded, 'worth a whole small-tradesman's lifetime of cents and dimes at the store counter'. The cost being the travel cost, vast distance by long-haul jet at full commercial rates, the final 1250 miles by private jet (at far more than commercial rates) and not just any old private jet, but a very special holy jet, blessed by a cardinal, used for no other purpose but conveyance to ... well, 'Elsewhere'! He could hardly bring himself to tell me just where 'Elsewhere' might be. Not exactly a secret:

Father Scallion had told *him*, but then *he* wasn't *me*, and *I* wasn't a Catholic, and all of a sudden he was feeling cold feet.

But unless here and now he could get it off his chest, those feet would be frozen the rest of his life, he'd carry them with him into the 'dark frosts of purgatory' – *his* phrase, not mine; *I'd* always thought of purgatory as a place of searching fires – and he'd rather tell an atheist than a priest. No, he *had* told a priest and all the priest had said was – no! he'd save it for later to tell me what the priest said. Too painful for just now.

'Elsewhere', he at last blurted it out, was an island in the Indian Ocean. He gave me the name: São Sebastião, St Sebastian bare and beautiful with all the arrows stuck into him, I've seen his picture often enough, an erotic emblem rather than a holy one, that's what I always thought – but never mind, the Portuguese named the island, how long ago? say 450-odd years, their own business how they saw that particular saint, and Tumulty, it's quite clear, discerned no ambivalence. Nobody living there when the Portuguese found it, nor did they ever put a colony on it. Nowadays it belongs to ... well, in theory, still Portugal, so Tumulty was told. And Portugal gave permission for all these *immeasurable* monks. 'Immeasurable', Tumulty's word, immeasurably serene, compassionate, comforting, sweet-natured, forgiving – healing – he said 'healing', even more so than Lourdes, he said, though not so much the body as the soul. He gave me to understand he'd had his turmoils of guilt and sin, living unmarried in the County Mayo, anyone's guess what they could have been; but that's why all his crawthumping, incessant, almost hysterical, I didn't ask for details, not entirely germane, or seemed not to be, already I had told him 'I did not want to pry'.

Of course at this Sebastian Island, in contrast to Lourdes, no vision of the Blessed Virgin, no canonised personage, no miracles. Only the unending presence of a handful of mortal men, sometimes cheerful, sometimes grumpy, sarcastic, men who got irritated, and yet, so said Tumulty, even more so than Lourdes, all the healing they brought to his spirit! – 'immeasurable,' he had no better word. 'Unbounded,' if I preferred it. 'Unsurpassed, unsurpassable,' all equally true, so he said.

I said, too much waffle, couldn't he give it me straight? 'Monks' he'd said, what monks? why? whence? and how? Did it signify I'd never heard of 'em? In the western parts of Ireland even a Protestant agnostic learns more than he can stomach about Catholic devotions, cults, apparitions, eccentric communities – it's in the very air of the place, let alone every shape of the media, press, radio, TV, little posters in shop windows, leaflets through your letter box, unavoidable surely – so what was the mystery here?

This much, at any rate, gleaned from his rambling diversions. Sebastian, solitary rock in the vast ocean, out of sight of anywhere, due north of the Seychelles; used by the Missionary Order of St Brendan the Navigator as a place of retreat and, yes, healing since – Tumulty not sure of exact date, but whatever year the order obtained its first small steamboat that could go the distance, just after World War I probably. Nowadays, the private jet; it's based at Nairobi. St Brendan Brothers in every English-speaking African colony since – Tumulty not sure, probably end of nineteenth century. Members of the order few, but carefully selected, highly zealous, highly professional, running schools, hospitals, undercover anti-apartheid cells (where necessary), some of them imprisoned and/or assassinated by S. African security forces, Rhodesian ditto, Idi Amin's ditto, and such others of similar species; they made no great song about it.

Order both contemplative and hands-on activist, unusual combination; contemplative Brothers dwell on Sebastian all the time, activists pay regular visits to recoup exhausted energies.

Order founded by a priest from Mayo (hence Tumulty's instant enthusiasm), a Father Daniel Rogan of Ballina, harsh old greybeard, who made an absolute point of 'NO VAIN TALK AT LARGE' (in effect, no publicity; that's how it was, is, that's why so few have heard of these Brothers – or 'Brethren', more probably? – I need help with the technical vocab., didn't ask Tumulty, didn't want to distract him) – 'THOSE WHO SHOULD KNOW OF US WILL BE TOLD OF US BY GOD' – so you ask, as I asked Tumulty, 'Where did they get their funds from?'

At which Tumulty began to weep; but only for a moment. Blew his nose explosively, apologised for the desperate cold he'd caught, rapidly started to talk (of all things at this juncture) about how dismal was Loch Corrib in the grey of the rain, if he'd known it'd be so wet, he'd have surely stayed at home. The end of his revelation? Looked like it. Finished and done.

Connacht Queen had just then made her turn in the bay to take up moorings at the pier of Annaghdown. Thirty minutes wait, and no more, announced the skipper, time enough for any passengers who might feel like braving the rain to take a look at the monastic ruins.

The water-hostesses, fussed over by Mrs O'Curry, began to hand round plates of ham sandwiches, hard-boiled eggs, lettuce, and cups of tea. This would have been the picnic, if the picnic had been able to take place: as it was, it was briskly rechristened 'the onboard tea' and a surprising number of wet people came down from the upper deck to take their share of it. Oldroyd, trying to pretend he didn't notice Tumulty's misery, cracked a joke about Irish rain being as good a preservative for old age as Irish Guinness, but he got no response. In some disgust, he shoved his face into his teacup and considered leaving Tumulty well alone for the rest of the day. But there didn't seem to be room for him to move his tea things to another table without giving the impression of intruding himself into someone else's party, so he stayed where he was and crunched lettuce without comment. In the meantime, some sternly mackintoshed elders, vaunting their hardihood, skidded down the gangplank and scurried off along the lane, crying, 'Keep us a cup and a bit in the hand, Kate!' as they went. At which Oldroyd grasped at straws and asked Tumulty if he wanted to go; there was perhaps a chance that the sight of a monastery, a monastery founded by St Brendan indeed, might rekindle his reminiscences, but the little man shook his head, 'Oh no,' he moaned, 'Oh no no, no'.

A violent crew of small children – the 'grandchildren', no doubt, so dangerously predicted in Mrs O'Curry's advertisement – were tearing up and down the stair that led to the upper deck. In fact they had been doing this ever since the boat left the Woodquay Pier, but with the shutting-down of Tumulty's narrative, they suddenly became a damned nuisance rather than a mild distraction. They ran among the tea things, bouncing from table to table. One of them, a lion-hearted little girl about five years of age, flung a scowling young Napoleon rather older than herself clear out of her way into the narrow space between Tumulty's legs and a steel column that held up the saloon ceiling. Tumulty dropped his teacup and only saved his plate of sandwiches by a scarce-credible swiftness of reach. (His emotional state had by no means deterred him from his share of the refreshments.) In some shock, he just managed to articulate, 'Now, now, no need to be bold, aren't we all friends together, so we are?'

The children reared back in alarm, staring at him as though they didn't believe him. For why should they? – his attempt at an avuncular smile was more like the grin of an ogre, and he flapped his sodden handkerchief at hot spilt tea all down his trousers. Whereas Oldroyd made no pretence at friendliness with the little monkeys: he thrust down his face to their level and hissed in a flurry of rage: 'I'd sooner eat a brat like you than a sandwich any day o'the week: get out of it before I take me fork to you!'

They fled. Oldroyd laughed. Mr Tumulty laughed too. A cantankerous pair of old hoar-heads at last in an agreement of mood; and Tumulty, almost merrily, exclaimed, 'Children! Not a child upon that island. Perfect peace, Mr Oldroyd, I thought "God's peace and no disturbance!"' He laughed again, and then his voice changed, a shrewd spurt of vinegar dissolving his good humour. 'D'you know, Mr Oldroyd, that was *not* a Christian thought. And I think now, that that's where the mistake was. I should never have wanted it, and neither should anyone else. Children of course are vicious demons, all of them, how can they not be? Are they not just ourselves, a smahan smaller, that's the truth, but no more wild than we are. At my age, if you like, all the blackguardism's deep inside, no intelligent man could pretend otherwise. You too, it's inside of *you*. If you could, you'd be roaring end to end of this boat, upsetting people's cups and plates, hurtling and scratching, I know you, I can see you, don't try to deny it!'

Oldroyd lost patience. It was his job to probe Tumulty, drive drill-bits into Tumulty's guts, and dammit not the other way round. He heaved himself upright, out of his seat into the aisle of the saloon. 'Now look here, Ignatius, I have had enough of it! – *more* than enough of your nonsense. If you really want to tell me what happened on that island, I'll give you ten short minutes to get the heads of it into me notebook, and after that I'll shut up shop. Finished, deaf ears, no story, d'you get me? Just you think about it, will you, while I fetch meself a whiskey ... dear God yes, a whiskey ... whiskey ...'

Spitting the word out over and over between closed teeth, he pushed his way to the bar, secured his glassful and came back again, to find Tumulty sitting blankly just as he'd left him, sandwich in hand with one bite taken out of it, just like the Mad Hatter, catatonic, all but lifeless; until he uttered a long slow sound: 'Ah,' focusing his eyes neither upon Oldroyd nor anything else. 'Ah.' And then in an instant he was no longer all abroad. He spoke out once again like a rational being. 'Mr Oldroyd, there are two things: first is what happened, that's not too hard to tell, now I know where the mistake was. Then what happened afterwards; and there, you see, the terror. Begin where I left off; your question, the funds . . .'

Such a puzzle why that question had upset him so fearfully. Puzzle increased as I heard him dispose of it in little more than a half-dozen sentences. Thus: to start with, the Order was richly endowed by a Victorian-era Irish barrister, a strong Catholic in practice at the London bar. He accrued great torrents of money from a multiple libel action – he'd appeared for a gang of colonial sharks in the rubber trade; they'd enslaved certain villagers in the King of Belgium's Congo and sued a radical newspaper for saying so. After he'd won their cases for them he remembered his religion; he thought about hell's pains for murderers, torturers, slave-drivers *and* their collusive advocates; he handed over the cash (or some of it, most of it? who could say?) to Father Rogan. More crucially, he instructed Rogan how to invest it effectively; inserted himself into the inner counsels of the Order, a sort of high-finance lay brother. He was able to prise successive donations from a succession of similar rich hypocrites (my word, not Tumulty's: Tumulty kept it factual, non-judgemental, circumspect). Again, successive investments, effective, and more or less secret. The Order, meanwhile – in a humble enough low-key style – sent its preachers into Irish and British and Irish-American parishes to run retreats, novenas and such, and to rattle the collection box for good people's shillings and pence and quarters and cents; that was all the world at large knew, all it *needed* to know, seemingly – quarters and cents and shillings and pence and good people doing their best.

Tumulty was aware of these historical facts because the monks of Sebastian told him. If he thought there was anything not quite – what should one say? candid? – about the Order's two-tier system of funding, he kept it to himself. Took the whole thing for granted, indeed, which only made his earlier emotions the more opaque.

His account, transparent, straightforward, about the island itself, how he got there, what went on:

... he booked, as per Father Scallion's advice, at a travel agency in Knock that specialised in charter flights to Medugorje, Santiago de Compostela, Loreto, Fatima, Lourdes (not Tumulty's own Lourdes trips; they'd always been via his parish priest and a diocesan organiser). He found himself flying Ryanair from Knock to London; then Air France to Paris; change airports in Paris for a curious multi-national outfit called Air Proche-Afrique, to Kinshasa; and from there to Nairobi by Askari Adventure Flights, adventure indeed, the pilot (an apparent Australian) 'strolled out among the passengers, drinking God knows what out of a bottle (excuse the Holy Name), said he'd warn us the intercom wasn't working so 'twas better he'd tell us in person there might be a "pancake-landing" on account of defective undercarriage. Not to say he killed us. Sure we got there safe and sound, but –' All this supposedly cut-price, tho' Tumulty didn't think so, prices were exorbitant, thought the agency had conned him, should have challenged them from the start, but their shop so 'very sanctimonious, Mr Oldroyd, so like (if you like) a repository or a funeral parlour, holy pictures and all – why, I didn't have the nerve.'

At Nairobi, all quite different. A young lay brother in white cotton habit and straw sombrero at the customs barrier with a placard – Tumulty's own authentic name, and moreover correctly spelt – Mr I. L. TUMULTY *from* KNOCK, IRELAND – everything without question just so and all prepared for. Led to a small sleek two-engined jet across the runway, Chi-Rho symbol on the tailplane. Couple of dozen pilgrims already aboard, Americans, Germans, Poles; three or four Africans in traditional multi-coloured togas. All men. No women, ever, on Sebastian. No nonsense with the Brothers re chastity; old-fashioned, and wise with it, thought Tumulty; on an island, mid-ocean, God knows what might happen ('excuse the Holy Name'), some of these monks very young, he'd been told – and so he was to find. But most of them grey-haired, lined faces, hard voices, men of deep and dark experience.

Didn't tell me much about the full six weeks he spent there. Except what he'd already said: immeasurable serenity, compassion, comfort, the sweetness of the nature of the monks he had dealings with, the unutterable sense of forgiveness and healing. A daily rule, as I gathered, of old-fashioned discipline, gatherings at fixed hours for worship, prayer sessions, Gregorian chant, sermons, private meditations and spiritual reading, one-to-one discourses with a spiritual director, penances, and every day a round of work – not, for a man of Tumulty's age, hard work exactly, but deliberately monotonous: they had him chopping vegetables in the gadget-free kitchen, pushing fruit through sieves to make a purée, grating potatoes for the 'boxty' (a species of Irish potato cake which the monks ate every day, a tradition, as I gathered, dating back to old Rogan: the island grew an abundance of spuds). Tumulty – as I gathered: he was far from precise – had tried to shift his long years of inner turbulence both at Lourdes and at his parish church, and no success: now at last the Brendan Brothers made the road for him. He thought about joining them for the rest of his life, even. Taking vows, all of that. Maybe they'd have accepted him; told him, though, he must first go back to Mayo, settle his affairs entirely before formal application; sell up his business, dispose of his property – nephews and nieces, lawyers' conferences, all of that.

Nonetheless, that was his intention. Right. The day he left, on the island's airstrip, all aboard the private jet for Nairobi: oh yes, that's what he meant. Shook hands with the guestmaster monk, a mild-eyed soft-voiced Zulu from Durban: 'God bless and go with you, friend Ignatius; very shortly by Heaven's Grace we'll meet again.'

What else he had to say about the island, outside of his religious meanderings – sharply observant, with spurts of vinegar – an old ironmonger's practicality:

... that most of the buildings are utterly 'up-to-date modern', 1970s, or 1980s, superbly equipped (except where deliberate austerity obtains, as in the kitchen), adorned with the 'queerest' works of religious art, the most avant-garde styles, and no expense spared ('avante-garde' my own guess, not Tumlty's diagnosis: Tumulty no art expert).

... that the monks' farming operations, cutting terraced fields out of the steep mountainside, building cisterns and a complex irrigation system, sending out plane-loads of produce daily from the airstrip, plus regular trips of cargo boat to Mombasa, clearly show how Sebastian is *business*, for the Glory of God (no doubt of that), but as businesslike as Guinness's brewery and no expense spared.

... that about 30 per cent of the monks are Irish; the rest are African, American, European, Indian; talk Latin amongst themselves; the ones who deal with the pilgrims are not at all those that run the farm, still less are they those in administration, at computers, on the phone all day long, a sharp eye for the office TV (not available in the pilgrim quarters) where CNN news rolls endlessly hour after hour.

... that the abbot is a tall rawboned black-avised Donegal man in his fifties, Dom Peter Chrysologus, stalking alone across the slopes of the mountain, along the rocks of the ocean shore, standing for hours brooding darkly, arms folded, in a corner of the chapel; never spoke to the pilgrims individually, but blessed them with great ceremony on arrival and departure – 'a distant man, concerned for great matters', Tumulty's phrase, very solemn, had somebody perhaps put it in his mouth?

So now came the core of his story, the 'Terror', had he not said? – the only reason for his telling the story – the only reason why he found it so hellish hard to tell. But once he got into it, he fairly let fly with it, all in a run and no hiccups. Too important to summarise; I made a good grab for his exact words, as well as I could get 'em all down, my shorthand was never speedy.

'All aboard, that's how it was, the private jet for Nairobi, at nightfall, if you please, and the weather blowing up for a storm. "Never mind," says the pilot, "We'll get above it in a brace of shakes, but there might be some bumping." Well, we bumped and we tore and we hurtled and roared, so we did, oh I'd say full ninety minutes of it! and outside the cabin windows I saw the lightning flash like gunfire. "Never mind," says the steward – he was that lay brother in his white habit, a young Croat, I do believe, white as his own gown with the fear that was on him, sure he tried to be confident, "Never mind," he kept onto it, "here is an airplane was blessed by a cardinal!"

'Just as he's saying this for maybe the twelfth time, such a wallop and a thump and up we go, down we go, and the pilot's voice comes over the intercom – "something-or-other emergency landing" – *emergency*? and to land on another island, is he telling us? "Yes, for your reassurance, there *will* be a proper airstrip but ... glory to God hasn't one of our engines gone and we're all over lopsided, so why don't we all say an –" *Crackle-crack*! and the last portion of the poor divel's speech has slipped away from us altogether, but the steward boy comes in on the uptake with a yell like a County Clare hurler – "act of contrition!" at the top of his voice – we'd been saying nothing else for the past half-hour but now begod we *knew* we were banjaxed.

'All right, all right, the Holy Name, I can't apologise any more for it – after what happened that night I call it out in my very sleep: I'd say 'tis pretty nearly the least of me offenses, so ...

'I saw flame fifty feet long shooting out of the left-hand engine ...

'So I suppose at that stage we must have hit the ground. I'd me head between my knees as instructed, didn't I get a fierce belt on the edge of me temple from the corner of the seat in front and I wasn't in me senses till ... till I found they were after pulling me out of the smash and laying me on a stretcher – a great blaze of atrocious fire, and then an ambulance, there were floodlights, rows and rows of chainlink fence and the floodlights on top of it, and a siren I heard screaming like mad.

'I came into consciousness in a class of a hospital. That's to say a hospital bed, in a narrow little room with some other beds, I'd say there were four of 'em; but the walls, Mr Oldroyd, were corrugated iron, rotten – would you believe? – with rust, the roof as well. And it must have been raining, the roof thundered like a railway train. Stifling hot with an electric fan that seemed to make no difference. No windows except well above eye level, you'd have to stand on a bedside table to see out, supposing, that's to say, the casement was open, for every pane was ground glass, the sort of glazing you'd put into a toilet.

'Now three of the four beds had men in them, bandaged and plastered, on the drip-feeds and oxygen, not one of 'em conscious, or if they were, they didn't talk. I guess they were pilgrims who'd been in the plane with me. I knew who it was in the next bed, clear enough: the steward boy, Croat, Slovenian, whatever he was, Brother Wenzel, they had his name on a card about his head. He was able to respond to me, of course he couldn't move, two broken legs, and in traction, the poor divel. Meself, I soon discovered, I was better off entirely. Contusions and lacerations and a shoulder that didn't work, something wrong with me eyesight, hammer-and-anvil *clang-clang-clang* in th'ould brainbox; but otherwise, I was more or less meself. I saw neither nurse nor doctor for an hour or two, that's a fact. So all I found out, I had to find out at that stage from Wenzel. Did his best to tell me, but couldn't keep it up, y'know, hurt him too much to talk, he said. Maybe he didn't want to talk.

'"What happened?" I asked him.

'"Emergency landing," says he. "Catastrophe."

'I knew that. I said, "To the people. Passengers and crew. What happened to the people? We can't be the only ones survived – what, five of us, just in this room?"

'He says, "Correct. Oh, terrible, is true, yes it *is*." He says, "Oh, here this *is*. Everybody dead. Or so bad hurt they *must* die. You and me not so bad. Praise God."

'"Where are we then?"

'"You ask, where? Oh," says he, "King George Island. Three hundred kilometre away from St Sebastian."

'"King George? I never heard of it."

'"Very empty island," says he. "Sand and stone and no mountain. Named by an Englishman."

'I said, "We're under the British flag, so," thinking that would explain why this hospital looked like the back of a garage, Westminster penny-pinching, notorious all over the world. The last days of empire, old rope and a stink of kerosene.

'"Correct," he says. "Was one time. But no, you see, no! – is not British government now. Is private corporation, which is best you should not ask. King George not good place, not place for God's work, I tell you. Just hope they get you well, send you back to St Sebastian. Meantime," says he, and he suddenly dropped his voice right down to a whisper, "keep quiet."

'He had his head turned to look beyond me, over across toward the door. I turned to look likewise: there was a doctor feller just come in there with th'ould stethoscope, y'know; another one in a white coat – a male nurse, I daresay – they were both of 'em white men, but they weren't talking English to each other. German, maybe? Could have been Dutch. They were bent over the bed nearest the door doing something to the feller in it, hard to say whether or not they'd heard our conversation. Clear enough that young Wenzel was in hopes that they *hadn't* heard. They did know Wenzel and I were conversing, fair enough; and the next thing they did, when they'd finished with the first patient, was to come straight across to me and the doctor feller stoops right down to me so he's muttering into my face. "Ha," says he, "you talk?" The very divel of a thick accent, near as bad as Wenzel's. "You talk to your friend, yes? Now, he is not well, it is best he should not talk. And for you, Mister Tew-*mu*lty, we bring you out of this ward into convalescent room, yes? Where with a stick you can walk about, sit down, go to bathroom, eat off table, read magazines, watch TV, yes? Much better for you, much; and then we send you safe back to the island of the holy men, yes? – you say your prayers in peace and give thanks."

' "Island of the holy men"? – a crude bit o'discourse, wouldn't you say, for a doctor to give vent to? To be sure, he was a crude class of character altogether, more like a man behind the counter of a betting shop, add to which I was certain I was not really fit to be moved; but there and then they put me into a wheelchair and moved me, so fast I'd scarce the time to say more than "God bless!" to poor Wenzel. Direct out of that hutment into the stifling hot rain, tropical rain, Mr Oldroyd, no foyer or porch; they wrapped a plastic sheet over me, themselves they had great brollies; they absolutely galloped me down a set of narrow passages between more of their tacky ould hutments, jolting and splashing that wheelchair through puddles, if you please, of red mud, till they got me indoors again and slammed the door behind us, another back-of-a-garage, but this one had more furniture than beds – chairs beside a table, magazines (as he'd said), *Newsweek*, *Time*, and so forth, and – aha! the TV.

'They put me out of the wheelchair, sat me on a bed, furnished me with a walking stick, told me there'd be an orderly coming along with a bit of dinner, if I felt I could eat. All I felt was terrible. Contusions, lacerations, hammer-and-anvil – *eat*? I'd as soon run a marathon. But I didn't want to say so. Didn't know *why* I didn't want to say so. I just could not bear to tell that doctor a damn thing, Mr Oldroyd; all I wanted to do, if you see what I mean, was to *boycott* the bloody man – oh and his hospital too.

'Here am I swearing as much a blackguard as any of 'em – wash me mouth out with soap and water! – and that's the effect they had on me, I tell you no lie, sir – oh, something wrong, something badly wrong and rotten with that island, oh yes! Brother Wenzel had it taped. I couldn't say exactly what it was that was wrong, but I knew there was a duty for me. Begod, I'd not been building me spiritual resources for all of six weeks without –

'The doctor was just leaving. I plucked up th'ould courage, I refused to let him leave. Stuck me stick against his chest, and I asked him a quesstion.

'"What *is* this place?" Quite simple.

'He gave a simple answer. I didn't believe it. He said, "Is a trading station."

'"Trading what, if you please?"

'"These questions I cannot reply to. Is matter of national security."

'"Oho? That sounds serious. Whose nation would you be thinking of?"

'He chewed upon this one for more than a moment; and then he said, "The alliance. Of all the free nations," he said. "You have heard," he said, "of NATO? Of SEATO? Of Partnership Euro for Peace? Very good. Upon King George, by an arrangement, to prevent, deter, aggression. Do not ask more questions. I have told you: security."

'I think he thought "security" would shut me up entirely. A good religious Catholic, he thought; obedient, he thought; fair play to be intimidated. He didn't know much about the views of the Irish – at least the Irish of *my* age – on a word like "security", to say nothing of the notion of NATO and such. I let him conclude what he wanted to conclude, said sorry for me curiosity, said I'd lie down and rest until dinner. So he went, and the nurse went with him. And then comes in this black man, dressed in a sort of blue boiler suit, puts down a tray of soup and bread, goes out without a word. Oh I tried to talk to *him* all right; but nothing, not a word.

'Nor yet when he came back, to pick up the empty tray – except it wasn't empty, I hadn't been able to eat of course, too confused, too upset, and I'd made a discovery: the bloody door was kept locked. Hospital, Mr Oldroyd? Or a prison, what would *you* think? And I needed to go to the toilet, damn fast – we do when we get to our term of years, as you'll know – I'd been hollering for this orderly for twenty minutes, can you imagine? All he did was point out a class of cupboard at the end of the room, I'd thought it was for buckets and brooms and that – not at all, there was a jakes inside of it, why *couldn't* they have shown me at the beginning? It did flush, I'll say that for it.

'Once the orderly was gone I'd nothing to do but worry. So weak and exhausted, no initiative left, what else then but switch on the telly? It worked, I'll say that for it, reception like a snowstorm, but no worse than a hotel in Castlebar. Only thing was, though, it had but the two channels,

CNN perpetual news, and what they called the video channel – would you believe? 'twas sheer porno. Why, I'd never seen such a thing in me life, not only disgusting, but 'twas all in a foreign language, Portuguese, I'd say it was, and very very bad from the point of view of morals – not alone the sexuality but the *cruelty*, Mr Oldroyd; I suppose it was possible they were acting, pretending, just playing at their wicked game ... But I'd say those girls there were really getting hurt. I'd prefer to tell no details, it doesn't bear thinking of.

'And yet I can't *help* thinking of it. I saw it for just ten minutes, if I'd been any younger I'm sure I'd have polluted meself. It'll stick in me memory the rest of me days. I sometimes wonder, did it turn me into a filthy corrupt old man?

'Be that as it may, I forced meself to switch it off, I forced meself to take my mind off it, I forced meself to think of something else. Like what, would you suppose? Like how to look out of those damnable windows, frosted glass and eight feet up. Set a chair a-top of the table, that'd raise me up four feet, it ought to be enough. But was I in a fit state to do it, to *clamber*, Mr Oldroyd? when the best I could do was to stagger with a stick? I needed the second chair to get meself up on the table and from there – well, sir, I fell down, brought the top chair down with me, every injury from the plane crash set throbbing once again till I knew I had to scream but didn't dare. So I tried it again, and again, Mr Oldroyd, it was either climb up there, or murder my soul with staring at the telly screen, those piteous girls stark bare naked, flagellated with whips until they agreed to –

'Again and I tried again, sir; and thank the good Lord, I got there. Oh I tottered and wobbled but me face was up to the window and me hands groping along it, the frame all black with dirt, trying to find the catch to open it. I found it, I couldn't shift it, it was rusted as fast shut as though that doctor or one of his men was after welding it, ridiculous. I'd done everything up there I could: nothing left, so, but to scramble down again and pretend, if it was possible, that I didn't know the switch to get onto the video channel, after all there was nothing wrong with CNN, I could sit and look at *that* programme, could I not? could I not?

'Would you believe, at that moment, just on the point of scrambling down, I suddenly saw what, if I'd had but half an eye, I'd have put me eye on half an hour ago! One of the panes of the window, no more than nine inches square, had been positively broken, I couldn't tell you how – did somebody fire a stone? – a hole in it the size of me fist, and all they'd done was to mend it with paper – a sheet of paper pasted over – would you believe I was able to get me thumb under the corner of it and peel it off? And there, sir, I was able to look through that hole and see . . . was able to see *what I was not supposed to see*. Totally and utterly in breach of security, ha!'

He talked at great length, inordinate detail, about what he'd been able to see. Nearly all the way home to Galway across the lake and down the river, he elaborated his quick glimpse – for it had been nothing more than a glimpse – nit-picking at his memory till Oldroyd longed to toss him overboard.

Once again, it's easier to summarise:
The downpour had come to a stop. No sunshine, swollen dark monsoon cloud over everything. Clear view nonetheless, save for obstruction by gables of adjacent hutments. Between two of these hutments, a short access road blocked off by a chainlink fence twelve feet high. Tumulty looked out through the fence into an open space – more than an open space – great expanse of rock and scrub all the way to the ocean. Something at the edge of this, might have been a mile away, he could only see a corner of it, seemed to be the head of a mineshaft, sprawl of lower-level industrial structures at its foot, tall chimneys ejecting yellow fumes. Procession of trucks on a tramline, loaded with red-coloured earth, diagonally crossing his field of vision, from mineshaft in the right-hand distance, thence to disappear on the left behind the hutments, close to the hutments; far side of, parallel to, chainlink fence. Each truck pushed by a couple of men, bowed down by the effort, sweating, straining, slithering in mud – white men and black men, emaciated, wearing nothing but shorts, and a headcloth, what Tumulty called 'a half-counterpane', twisted into a turban-shape. More men, same appearance, lined out in a gang beside the tramway, resuming work halted by rain, baling water out of a ditch, digging at the ditch, toting lengths of pipe to be laid into the ditch.

All these men were chained: a leg-iron to each of them, on one ankle only, connected by long links to the iron on the next man's ankle. Truck pushers were chained in pairs, ditch diggers in clumps of five or six.

Guards and taskmasters stood about, along the tramway, along the chainlink, some had rifles, some had whips, rhinoceros-hide sjambok whips. (Tumulty knew about sjamboks, saw them in a museum of African slavery kept by the Sebastian monks; one of the Brothers talked to him of apartheid days in Jo'burg and the police there.) More guards, with a machine gun, in a tower beyond the hutments, Tumulty could see the top of it sticking out above nearby gables. Guards and taskmasters all black men, blue boiler suits and baseball caps. Tumulty didn't see them *using* their whips; didn't need to; he'd seen that video (ten minutes of it anyway, maybe more than ten, he'd told me of it like a man unable to tear himself away); no sort of possibility that anyone here could be 'acting, pretending, just playing at their wicked game'; this was real, this was hell, this was hell in the real world, inexplicable and right in front of him; he was seventy-five years old, what on earth was he going to do?

He might have fretted about it all day; he wasn't given a chance. The door was flung open, doctor and nurse came charging in, Tumulty still up on top, a-tremble with fear and horror, turned to try to speak to them, excuse himself somehow, foot slipped, chair fell down, Tumulty fell down (third time in an hour), broke his leg and lay shrieking on the floor. Doctor and nurse stood dreadfully over him. He was a dead man, so he thought. *I'd* have thought so, too.

In his terror, it suddenly struck him that doctor and nurse were terrified too.

They were not going to kill him, they had no authority. Instead, the picked him up, dumped him on his bed, moved table and chairs (in a bustle of panic) back to where they belonged. Nurse pointed out uncovered hole in window-pane; doctor spoke hastily to nurse; nurse ran out; doctor stood beside bed, staring at Tumulty sidelong; two guards arrived breathless (in a bustle of panic), rifles at ready; stood against doorframe, staring at Tumulty; doctor ran out. Tumulty saw badges on the guards' caps, a monogram logo G&D; not a word from either of 'em. From Tumulty, moans, groans, pathetic pleas. Deadlock, thereupon, for excruciating half-hour.

Next man into the hut, a white man, officer of sorts, wore well-pressed khaki uniform, blue gold-braided baseball cap with red-and-gold badge, G&D under a horseman jabbing his spear into a reptile. Pistol at his belt, swagger-stick in hand. Rimless spectacles, intellectual appearance, crew-cut fair hair, gold teeth in his mouth when he smiled. He smiled now at Tumulty, glowered at the guards, sent them off with a harsh order (African language?), and sat beside Tumulty's bed, a concerned hospital visitor. In behind him came doctor and nurse, began to put splint on Tumulty's leg. While they worked, their hands were shaking.

Tumulty opened his mouth – lurched his body toward the three of them in a surge of senile fury – groaned out just the one word, 'Torturers!' They dragged at his leg and he screamed.

'Mr Tumulty, I have to apologise.' Very polite, spoke English with not much accent; wasn't English himself; more likely South African? 'The doctor should have told you. Should you not, doctor?' Doctor writhes, serves up a greasy grin.

Officer was no end candid. Too damned candid to be credible, some would say. Tumulty reports him with what seems to be total recall. Says, 'Total recall, yes, that's just what it was. I can only account for it by the very queer state I was in. Is it true or isn't it? There is the problem . . . Oh dear.'

Tumulty goes on to say that the officer then said: 'This doctor, between ourselves, is an idiot. Despite appearances, we have no secret here. No need at all for you to peep from the window by subterfuge. You will have observed the obvious fact: King George is a penal colony. So of course strict precautions, security considerations – by which you were perhaps misled. As I say, we have no secret; nor do we have visitors. So your aeroplane disaster, in the middle of the night, necessarily caught us on the wrong foot. You are in pain, sir: don't try to talk. I will answer all your questions before you even ask them.

'You would ask first, who are we? We are George-&-Dragon Special Services plc, a multinational, head offices in London and Brussels. We own and operate the whole island. It contains a most valuable mineral deposit. Now here there *is* a secret: I can't tell you what *sort* of mineral. Commercial confidentiality, I'm sure you understand? But let me hint that it has unprecedented uses in state-of-the-art high-tech., wasn't even known about till twenty or thirty years ago. We pay regular market prices for the importation of dangerous and irreconcilable convicts – all of them serving life sentences – from the penal systems of many nations, Eastern

Europe, ex-Soviet republics, Africa, South-East Asia. They are our workforce in the mine, as you have seen; women as well, whom you haven't seen, for whom we have other employment, our ancillary chemical plant, for example, plus the ... plus the essential subsistence work of the community ... and so forth. We are, more or less, self-supporting.

'You would ask, how can it be we have never been exposed in the media? Surely prisoners' friends and families must demand where they've been taken? For my answer, consider the countries which send us the prisoners, consider who the prisoners are. Ethnic elements obnoxious to the majority population – Gipsies in Eastern Europe, so-called Tribals in Indonesia and Burma, Kurds from all sorts of countries. Political elements equally obnoxious. Fanatical religious elements. Disruptive *secular* elements obnoxious to majority religion. Miscellaneous asylum seekers, unwanted by anybody anywhere. And for the rest, what shall I say? – dysfunctional bloody bandits, Mr Tumulty, whoever would wish to see them again? They have effectively *disappeared*; who will care, who will dare, to enquire for them? and yet they have not – as in Chile or Argentina – disappeared into their graves. For through the enterprise of G&D they are re-discovered, re-created, re-constructed: they can prove themselves now as a human resource, commercially viable for the first time in their lives, for nothing less than the world-wide benefit of free-market civilisation.

'Let me tell you, Mr Tumulty, without their labour, without their produce, half the computers across the globe would stop working. Not a telecom tower, nor an air-defence missile project, nor a genetic modification lab – not even a simple spacecraft – would be capable of business from Tokyo to Turin, from Irkutsk to Bangalore, from Porton Down to Houston, Texas.'

As he said all this to Tumulty he kept looking at him for response: no response: disconcerting. Tumulty in fact *unable* to respond, could only lie and stare – 'in a class of a trance' – post-traumatic stress following the plane crash, intense disorientation following what had just now happened, the TV, the hole in the window, the riflemen. Tells me he was not deaf, could hear the officer, every word (*remembers* indeed every word with utmost clarity); but could not cope with the words' meaning, could not register the 'good or bad' of what he heard.

Officer seems to have sought for a more insidious argument; the old bugger, he must have concluded, required to be *coaxed*. He tried again:

'And let me tell you something else. There's a by-product to the ore that we dig. Minute batches of it are processed in our chemical plant. And let me tell you, we can create therefrom a pharmaceutical ingredient for an entirely new drug for heart disease, maybe cancer if research continues, maybe even AIDS.'

No response. The officer ground his teeth, became waspish.

'You would ask, I'm quite sure you would ask, does Ireland send prisoners here? The answer is, not yet ... But it's under discussion ... Governments will prepare for such developments very quietly, very much behind closed doors, wouldn't do to make it the subject of ill-informed public controversy ...'

Still no response. The officer smacked his swagger-stick hard against the headrail of the bed, snapped at the doctor, 'Just do it!' and stamped out of the hut. Tumulty saw the doctor take a needle from his bag, saw him inject God knows what into Tumulty's arm, felt nothing, understood nothing, saw the ceiling above him dissolve into an appearance of 'kidney beans,' so he tells me, 'boiling in a pan'. He passed out.

Unconscious for three days at least.

Tumulty's own words again, verbatim:

'I came into consciousness on one of those wheeled hospital trollies, in the first-class lounge of a British Airways jumbo jet, a flight from Nairobi to London; I'd a kindly young Kenyan nurse-girl beside me, she looked after me hand and foot, I couldn't ask for better care. At Heathrow we were met by a couple of nuns with a private ambulance, and away with me to a Catholic nursing home, somewhere at the back of Hampstead, they said. I have a card from the place, easy enough to check up if you wanted. They said the St Brendan Brothers had arranged the flight and the Kenyan nurse. They didn't know anything about King George Island; they said they thought I'd come straight from St Sebastian – hadn't the plane crash been at take-off on the St Sebastian airstrip? They said I was the only survivor. Brother Wenzel, they said, was dead.

'I'd say they were very good nuns, but someone was telling them lies. On the other hand maybe not. I didn't know, so I didn't argue. I just let those nuns look after me. Very peaceful, very quiet. Except I was fearfully agitated. My memory, Mr Oldroyd. Why, my memory was *collapsed*, like a bursted balloon. I could pick up not a thing that happened since I boarded the Brothers' jet for Nairobi. The nuns said it was normal, bit by bit it would start coming back.

'Bit by bit, that was right. Fragments of that officer, his sentences in no sort of order, but each word of each sentence – what you said, like – total recall. Bit by bit, in fits of horror, I gathered it into my head – all of it, the guards, the prisoners, the whips – and that plug-ugly damned doctor, that *torturer*, what else could I call him? Now, I didn't say a word to the nuns.

'Because something else came into my head, and I found I couldn't place it at all. It must have been after the officer did all his talking. But if so, it was after I'd had the injection. When I was totally knocked out, which is mad. I'm not even sure whose voice it was. It might have been the officer, but the accent was not quite the same, the accent was almost Irish – oh good God, an Irishman, in all the filthiness of King George, it doesn't bear thinking of. In the heel of the hunt he said to me – whoever it was, he said to me – in hard, grating, sneering tones, like you'd imagine a statue talking, one of those devilish gargoyles you'd find on an old cathedral – he said:

' "I'll add a thing to all you've learned since you *fell upon* King George. This is not told to everyone; closed information; privileged: so listen to it. St Sebastian and the monks and all the work of the monks is eighty per cent paid for by George-&–Dragon Special Services – it's one of our most cherished good works – the Order, quite utterly, would have faded away, if it hadn't been for us. Have a hour or two's contemplation about that fact, you dotard at death's door, and adjust your tangled conscience in accordance. It's what we call Living in the Real World, understand me. The monks do it; so should you." '

3

Oldroyd decided not to bother with the pensioners' supper at the clubroom. He felt wildly disorientated by all he had been told; and in any case, Ignatius Tumulty wasn't going to be there. Disembarking from the *Connacht Queen*, the old fellow had appeared quite suddenly very frail, very tired; he said he would prefer to go back to his bed-sitter – above a café in St Anthony's Place, a crooked little side street not far from the Woodquay Pier. Escorted thither by a solicitous Oldroyd, he paused on the threshold to exchange addresses and phone numbers, then swiftly disappeared upwards, round the bend of his narrow staircase, like a little boy sent to bye-byes after an over-exciting day out. Oldroyd wandered for a while in the town and called in to a public house or two. Throughout the whole afternoon Mr Tumulty had taken him over with such permeating thoroughness that there was nothing he could do now but think, brood, soliloquise, all on his own: impossible for him otherwise to reconnect with Ute. Moreover (with a shudder) he believed he was actually scared. Scared of what, he did not know; perhaps Tumulty's fear on that island had somehow infected him? Ridiculous, but this *thing* that had come upon him was almost certainly much too large for him; how far could he go with it before he was most dangerously embedded? For Ute would surely insist upon –

In the event, before the pubs shut, he began to feel capable of Ute. He cut himself off, heroically enough, from additional drinks at the bar; he bought a couple of bottles of wine; he went straight to her flat, by way of a fish-and-chip shop where he picked up a takeaway (she would expect him to have fed with the pensioners, she wouldn't have got any grub in). He found her at home waiting for him. He told her the whole tale.

'So he wants you to write it up for him, to publicise, to expose – why, Spike, this is wonderful, did I not say to you, here is your chance!'

'I thought that you said my exposures were no damned good.'

'I said they were second-hand. But this one – this is new! Spike, it is original, it is shock-horror beyond our dreams. Not only shock-horror – the most profound political dissection – never so shameless a humiliating striptease of the pseudo-idealism of the global economy face to face with the material reality! *Mein Gott*, it will make you famous! How shall you start? Research, research, Ireland, Great Britain, Africa, everywhere, you must worm it to the very fundament!'

'Ah. But there's a problem.' Best to conceal his dread behind traditional Yorkshire pessimism; a pessimism that thrived upon the enthusiasm of others. 'I don't know if any of it's true. Tumulty himself don't know if any of it's true. It could all have been an illusion, hallucination, couldn't it? a three-act *delirium* while unconscious after the crash.'

'Of course,' she said sharply. 'Then you as the writer must study all ways and means to *find out* if it is true. If not, then is no harm done – but if *yes*, then – oh Spike, can you not see the enormity of the implications?'

'Such bloody great enormity there'll be no one dare to publish it ... You know, I'm not the first that Ignatius has been in touch with. Old crawthumper that he is, it's only natural he was well in with bucketsful of senior men in the Church. Monsignors and such, and one of 'em fetched him up to a bishop. Oh they listened to him, fair enough; but each of 'em told him flatly that he'd dreamed the whole affair. Threatened him in the end with a mental home. Which is why he left Mayo and all the folk that he knew. Word got about he was half-mad and breathing scandal. He couldn't bear to look his neighbours in the eye. Galway's a town big enough for him to put his head down, live anonymously: he says to me he'd determined to keep quiet for evermore about these Indian Ocean islands and whatever goes on there or doesn't, he's given up all pilgrimages, he still goes to mass (he says) but breaks off his prayers to mutter "humbug! high-pocracy! religion-riddled omadhauns!" at intervals throughout the ritual, particularly when the priest gets up to do a sermon. He says to me he'd started to wonder whether he *was* going mad. It was only by pure chance, the O'Curry woman introducing us, that he heard my profession and that set him off again; up to now he'd only tried clerics, he'd hated the very notion of the "media", sensational and godless pornography, you know the way they think in the backwoods. But the clerics all betrayed him (so he says), and now – with the likes of Oldroyd – he'll do his best to betray *them*. Oh aye, he's dead vindictive. I want no more to do with him.'

'You are afraid,' she said. 'Of course, of course, and it is true it is too extraordinary for you not to be afraid of it. Eat, eat! we will reconsider.' She poured him another glass of wine, and brought the fish-and-chips out of the oven where she'd been warming them up. She put the two portions on a communal serving platter; they sat over them at a low coffee table, crouching on bean-bags; they splashed the vinegar on, and the tartar sauce, and the salt; they devoured the oily victuals with relish – eating with their fingers, smacking their lips, uncontrolled exhibition of middle-aged and elderly greed, all the worst possible table manners against which their parents had striven hard to indoctrinate them. They were now both so shaken with their own different forms of nervous excitement, they just had to be self-indulgent. Oldroyd's excitement was absurdly contradictory: he was demoralised, in shock at this ill-omened notion of 'shock-horror', worried indeed to death – yet a little bit hopeful that Ute's 'reconsider' denoted some measure of caution – added to which, behind all of it, he was incongruously proud, as proud as a rat at a baited trap, to have found out (all on his own) something truly new to be worried to death *about*. Ute's excitement also contained its ingredient of pride: she was proud of her ageing lover, she had known he could do it, she had known he was not a loser, he just needed to be goaded, that was all.

Wiping fat from her lips and fingers, she swallowed some wine, belched, and returned to business. Her first words briskly reminded him that 'reconsider', in her personal usage, never quite meant what it said. 'Let us suppose that for once in your life you refuse to give in to your fear. So how shall you start the research? My opinion is: do not go to the clergy. Your Tumulty has gone there already, a pious man, a discreet man; if they were disposed to admit things, they could have done so to *him* most persuasively, kept him still a loyal worshipper. But they did not. Which means they are most certain to give you the scornful brush-off. Which means, I think rather, you ought to go through London, this corporation, G&D, discover if in fact it does have a head office. After that, to Nairobi. Discover these Brendan Navigator priests, discover who may know about the island of King George – ask questions of Kenyan officials, customs, immigration, department of trade – it is an ex-colonial society, native bourgeois and police hegemony, corruption ha! endemic, none too strange when you come from Ireland – I wonder, how can we find you the money for bribes?'

'Aye and well you *might* wonder. If there's anyone in Nairobi knows owt of any value they'll be paid bloody thousands to keep their knowledge to themselves. Far more than *we* could match, square it up whichever road.'

'You don't want to go.'

In fact he was appalled at the very idea of a visit to the equator. Hot weather, even in Ireland, made him dizzy and sick. He hated the thought of the ex-colonial Third World, massacres, diseases (AIDS just one of many, not even necessarily the worst!), venal and brutal police, stench of a poverty that'd make a man spew. Moreover, and despite all of Ute's most strenuous efforts, he was still (dammit) more than three-eighths of a right olde-English racist. All these Irish Catholics were difficult enough, but to have to go and deal with a crowd of black Africans – well, he just didn't want to. And of course, he must not say so.

'Oh no,' he answered airily, 'I'd go, never fear. I am not, never was, a skrimshanker ... But I do strongly feel you were right first time, and that London's where all of it starts. First London, then Brussels. There's men on the business pages of half the Brit newspapers'd be glad to give me some feelers, if I'm careful not to let on to 'em just where it is I'm coming from. That is, if I think fit to take up the story at all. *My* story, isn't it, duck? mine, all o'mine and nobody else's.' He gave vent to some chuckling croaks, suddenly convinced that he *could* do it if he needed to; with his own undoubted eye for a colossal opportunity in an unexpected place, he'd stumbled right in upon this one, why shouldn't he handle it? He was suddenly quite tipsy and deliciously engorged with an access of amorous warmth. He really thought it likely, in the delight of his achievement, that tonight, for a wonder, sexual congress would be hot and strong. He said as much to Ute – 'Hot and strong, girl, what d'you think then?' – he growled it into her ear with a noise like central heating afflicted with an air bubble.

She responded to his mating-call with her usual murmur of a fag end from Goethe: '*Warte nur, balde ruhest du auch* ...' ('Wait a little, soon you'll be at rest, so you will ...' She'd taught him enough German to understand the sleepy syllables.)

She gently moved him away from her and began to unwind her

thick plaits of waist-length hair, pale as stubble of wheat and shading imperceptibly into a delicate silver-grey – 'I have the colours of a Persian cat,' she had whispered to him, the first time they ever made love, 'today I shall purr, tomorrow I scratch and tear.'

He'd shed his tweed jacket already, to give himself elbowroom to eat. Now he pulled off his loosened woollen tie and stood up to release the heavy leather belt round the top of his trousers that was always so damned awkward in a hurry – the buckle had been distorted by misadventure several years ago – he had trodden his drunken boots onto it while trying to re-accoutre himself underneath a dud light bulb in the boghouse of a pub.

Clutching the join of the belt with both hands, tugging it this way and that, he sank to his knees beside the coffee table. Unaccountably, he leaned forward, stretching right across the table, all six-foot-four of him, scrawny old scarecrow, knocking over the wine bottle, pressing his face into the platter among fish-skins, stripped backbones, congealed fat. Ute was indignant: '*Ach*, why is it never possible you get drunk with some decency?'

'God, girl, this is not *drunk*! In my jacket, in my wallet, there's a pill, quick, oh quick! ... Dear God, let her keep me alive!' In urgent terror she scrambled for the wallet, found it, found the pill (in a sachet of foil), broke it out, put it into his mouth, held him tight in her arms as he slowly let it dissolve under his tongue. He straightened himself up again, breathing heavily, looking ghastly. More to himself than to her, he groaned out a few short words of miserable remorse, 'He said, don't drink, don't smoke, don't fill your gut with grease ... he said. Not any more for Oldroyd, fish-and-chips is bloody well barred.'

'*He* said? – *who* said? *Ach Gott*, you careless bastard, you have been to a doctor for this, he treated you, gave you pills: you did not choose to tell me?'

'Last year it was, you were away, shut up shop for a month and gone to Leipzig. For whatever reason ... It's only intermittent, it's not got any worse since. All I've got to do is take it easy on the fish-and-chips, once a week the absolute maximum ... Mind you, that just proves it, a trip to Nairobi is not, bloody not, a viable thought just now – all the tropical stress-and-strain – and the more so, it's more than probable I'd end up in jail there, after all the funny questions I'd need to ask.'

'It would be a risk,' replied Ute, very soberly, her soft palms folded over the yellow-tinged backs of his joined hands. 'You are not that kind of writer. No "thrill-seeker", is that the word? – not you. We shall have to think things through, find a different way to do it. Meanwhile, at least tonight. I do not recommend we try to fuck. A dead corpse inside my bed, thank you no.'

So he did not attempt any thrill-seeking in Kenya. But London, he conceded, was probably within his powers. The doctor to whom he referred the question (at Ute's most anxious importunity) told him brusquely that such a journey was less dangerous than a packet of twenty: 'You are still on the fags, I take it?'

'Not just this week . . . I have these patches on my arm . . . But I – ah – I –'

'But you're longing for the day when the patches are finished and you can suck at th'ould bonfire once again? All I can say to you, Mr Oldroyd, is . . . oh! do your best, man, you cannot do better than that. And watch yourself in London, didn't they call it at one time "the city of dreadful night"? – every variety of trauma and stress – but you won't need any telling – sure you've been there a hundred times.'

The doctor was not quite right about that. Oldroyd's experience of the metropolis was in fact rather limited. Before he came to Ireland he had lived and worked almost exclusively in his own Yorkshire. Moreover, he was less acquainted with those 'men on the business pages' than with their letters informing him of their 'regret that they were unable to make use of his contribution'. But when he needed to, he could be brave: he hired taxis with a great show of confidence; he strode into people's offices, he made assignations in bars; and in the end he did get something of what he sought. To start with, he discovered G&D. It was not quite a simple discovery. There was no such company in the phone book or any other of the more obvious listings. The stock exchange disclaimed all knowledge. In the end it was no more than a process of elimination: after groping his way through a week's useless litany of the wrong questions in the wrong places, he stumbled at last upon the line he should have taken at the very beginning, and the one man on Southwark Bridge who would certainly know the answer. (Number One Southwark Bridge, as he explained in a gleeful letter to Ute, being 'the majestic address of the *Financial Times*: Anglo-Saxon allegory, right? – all knowledge of our wealth and poverty poised perilous above a rushing river!') Furthermore, this 'man on the Bridge' was an old colleague from the *Barnsley Chronicle* dating years and years back, almost a friend as much as a colleague, and not at all spoiled by success. 'He really is interested, really does seem to take me seriously; and he don't only write for the *FT*, he moonlights for *Private Eye*, anonymously, mind you. I might have to give him a share in what eventuates, if owt *does* eventuate. Sat here this afternoon, I'm dead hopeful.'

Some portions of Oldroyd's notes upon the progress of his investigation:

Hadn't realised just how deftly one company can find ways to hide itself inside another. Excavations by C.B. [i.e. Charlie Bones, the 'man on the Bridge'] have uncovered G&D like a djinn in a bottle – the umbrella company is Hanover Holdings plc, which sounds German but is merely monarchical – King George, of course, of course! – see it written down & it's hardly a disguise, but it fooled *me*, fair enough.

Tumulty got it garbled, or was he misled on purpose? G&D is *not* a plc, but a mere subsidiary of Hanover H., subcontracting for the 'security programme' (sic) on the island.

With C.B. to Hanover H.'s offices – a whole floor high up in the Canary Wharf Tower, very posh, very smooth; exquisite PR woman, only too anxious to help.

For the background: Hanover H. have mining interests worldwide. Even in South Yorks (privatised coal, result of M. Thatcher's whirlwind).

Yes, they do have a concession from Colonial Office to dig minerals on King George.

Yes too, there is a pharmaceutical by-product programme.

And yes and yes again: Hanover H. has most certainly made donations to the Order of St Brendan. Proud of it, very; but they don't boast. Exact amounts confidential. Why not ask the monks? she challenged us.

As to Tumulty. 'This very unfortunate gentleman' was sole survivor of air disaster last year. Hanover H's medical staff transferred him to monks in Nairobi as soon as possible. Still unconscious? May have been, but was certified out of danger. Documents available, if need be.

(But Tumulty says the nuns said that the plane crash was on Sebastian?)

Perhaps to change the subject, she gave us a pile of brochures. They seemed, at a glance, to deal with every aspect of the corporation's doings, *except upon King George*. 'No,' she said, 'oh dear me, no!' – they cannot give out details about mines, chemical plant or anything else on that island. Confidential, sensitive, high-security classification. Hanover H. has contracts with government departments worldwide, military considerations, peacekeeping, solidarity against 'rogue nations', terrorism, industrial espionage, the latter is a permanent danger. Implication that ecological activism is included in 'terrorism' (Greenpeace, etc.).

And no (in some dudgeon), King George is *not* a penal colony. Migrant labour, of course, how else get the workers there? – the island was always uninhabited. Many of the migrants maybe moved from countries of origin by offical order – stateless refugees, nomadic ethnics, aliens who've served jail sentences & deportation on release. Great benefit for such to be employees of Hanover H. Saving their lives, basically. Human rights agenda (sic). Hanover H. only wishes that more corporations would take pattern.

No possibility of press being allowed to visit King George. 'Security' – see above. Do the likes of C.B. and myself not live in the Real World? Appalling risks everywhere, political, economic, cultural: precautions *must* be taken. Even pinko-liberals can see that, surely.

PR woman didn't in fact *say* 'pinko-liberals'. Meant it though, and no error. For thirty seconds the mask slipped.

At least I'd like to think it slipped. C.B. not so sure. Said my hectoring would aggravate a saint. And didn't I know my breath smelt? Poor woman sitting directly downwind of me, no wonder she showed us the door.

I said, 'She said, ask the monks. Let's see if we can do that. Let's aggravate an *authentic* saint.' C.B. not so sure. Walks wary of the clergy. So do I. But I think I'm tasting blood. Let's see what we can find.

With C.B. to the monks: i.e. London representative of Order of St Brendan. Order's HQ is in Armagh but they have a house in South Ken., just behind the Brompton Oratory. Use it as a sort of staging post for novices from the wider world (i.e. not Ireland) en route to Africa. Not an obvious monastery, just a tall gaunt 19th-cent. stucco terrace house, statue of St Brendan in a niche by the front door, a cross perched ungainly on the portico entablature.

Great contrast with Hanover H. Monks not at all anxious to help.

After long wait, sniffy permission for an audience with their London 'sub-prior' – whatever rank would that be in overall hierarchy? – bald-headed Belfast bruiser in chocolate-brown habit, plus something like a long white poncho hanging front and back from his bull neck. (A 'scapular', in fact: went to Crouch End public library, 200 yds. from my dismal digs, looked it up in *Catholic Encyclopedia*.) His reception room light-years from the 'up-to-date-modern' of Tumulty's description of Sebastian. Chocolate-brown lino, lime-green distemper, chocolate-brown dado, dark-varnished holy pictures (hysterical-baroquish style) in gilt frames thick with dust.

Sub-prior wades into me the instant we sit down. 'We take it on board you're not to be considered a man free from bias. We take it on board you've been exploiting the mental derangement of a poor afflicted soul, who was never on King George Island at all.' (So the sub-prior agrees with the nuns, and not with Canary Wharf. I hadn't time to ask him why: he came so wildly at me with his verbal harpoons, leaning forward across the table, eyes like red-hot lasers.) 'We take it on board you are to be considered a ... a ... in short, Mr Oldroyd, a political leper.'

C.B. can't believe his ears. *I* can. This can only mean the McGranaghan case, dissident IRA, vicious little cop-killer (alleged), enemy of the Northern Irish Peace Process. Northern Irish bloody monk strongly in favour of said Process. So who the hell's been talking to the censorious old bugger? Talking about *me*? And all within the last few days ...

If indeed there is blood to be tasted, I'm beginning to perceive it might be *my* blood.

Dear God.

In the upshot this monk spoke only to C.B., feigning not to know I was even in the room. Bastard. His spiel much the same as Hanover H's (leave aside the discrepancy of where was the plane crash). Excellent relations between company and monastic order; human rights agenda on King George Island; saving migrant workers' lives, basically. Most generous donations from the company toward the development of Sebastian, and why not? Exact amounts confidential: let not your right hand know what your left hand doeth, etc. Throughout history businessmen have made great gifts to religion. Money does not need to be *soulless*. Here is proof of it.

'I wish you a very good day, Mr Bones. It's a pity we cannot invite you to Saint Sebastian, but you do understand our accommodation must strictly be reserved for bona fide pilgrims. Neither the media nor the tourist trade would cohere with the Order's priorities. You do understand . . .'

C.B. said not one word to me except he was late for an appointment in the City, off he rushed for a taxi. I took the tube to Finsbury Park and bus to Crouch End, ate in a chip-'oyle, drank in the King's Head, went to bed feeling thoroughly fucked up. Bastards.

Horrid row with C.B., no shouting or threats, but quiet, and dead ugly. Had no idea of his suggestibility, his bias, his bloody bigotry, damn his eyes. We'd met in a wine bar in Thames Street (prior arrangement) to coordinate tactics, consequent on meeting that monk. He's very 'off' with me before we've even ordered drinks. Distant tone of voice, chillingly avers that Hanover H's story and monk's story are mutually consistent, does not regard plane-crash discrepancy as important (simple issue of one of them having been badly briefed, kind of cockup not uncommon in corporate institutions). Does *not* agree that both of them are lying, *must* be lying. Asks, how can he be expected to agree when he hasn't met Tumulty and can't possibly assess how reliable he is? Asks, what are my motives for standing over Tumulty's testimony when nobody else believes a word of it? Asks, how can he be sure that the whole thing's not a ploy to discredit a sound British-led company doing wonders for the economy in a hard and competitive world? Let alone my unaccountable Irish-based anti-clerical agenda, which he don't pretend to understand. Asks, how can he be sure I'm not an agent for some faction of Irish terrorism?

So who the hell's been talking to him? Talking about *me*? And all within the last few hours! The monk? no, the monk did no more than hint: someone else has put chapter and verse to the hints ... I try to explain the contradictory pressures of that wretched McGranaghan case: waste of breath. C.B. retorts, simply, flatly, finally, that from what he used to know of my 'overall perspective', he'd have expected me to support Hanover H. up to the hilt against any sort of pan-leftist attempts, neo-anarchist attempts, Zapatista attempts, 'Good God, Spike, *Seattle* attempts! – all the globalised chaos of the down-with-the-globalisers: can you not comprehend the enormity of the implications? Whatever has happened to you? Who the hell have you been talking to in Ireland?'

I said, 'Nobody but Tumulty'. He whipped up his briefcase and went out of the bar in a black sulk. Leaving me to finish his ploughman's lunch. And pay for it.

4

Disaster, undiluted. Without the willing guidance of his 'man on the Bridge', Oldroyd could see no way to make further enquiries in London. So what was he to do? He could, to be sure, write up everything he'd already garnered; but unless Hanover Holdings or the Order of St Brendan could somehow be induced to deviate from their stories, no reputable publication would look twice at his material. (Could he catch them out over the plane crash? Not a chance: already heads would be together, holes plugged, narratives homogenised.) He had thought Charlie Bones might have found the inducement, but Bones was now an enemy, Bones was obsessed with his anti-Irish fantasies, Bones all of a sudden had become the great defender of exploitative global capitalism.

No question but Oldroyd would have to go back to Ireland, and what on earth would he say to Ute? Mind you, it was all Ute's fault. Ute was the one who had got him involved less than two years ago with McGranaghan and his hopeless alibi, Ute was the one who less than two weeks ago had fed him all this shite about *research, research, research* and *worm it to the very fundament*. If anyone was an agent for a faction of Irish terrorism, it was nobody else but Ute, and dear God hadn't he always known it! He was a doddering idiot of a love-lorn pantaloon, an old rotten rascal sunk deep into the enthralment of a blatant and manipulative trollop. Nonetheless his heart turned over every time that he thought of her, every time that he pictured her full-fleshed glowing cheeks, still free from the wrinkles of middle age, and set between coils of tight-plaited hair, one above each ear; her smooth round throat with its two slight horizontal creases, astonishingly voluptuous; her wide-lipped pouting smile, the right-hand corner of the mouth turned up, the left-hand corner just a little bit down; her piercing greeny-yellow eyes (feline and watchful) that could suddenly seem to blur with affectionate warmth, comradeship, competence – oh above all, maturity and *competence*, without which he was just nothing, neither a writer nor (God help him!) any sort of a normal denizen of what they called the Real World.

Yet before he met Ute, he had been so very fond of expressing his contempt for all those who refused (wilfully refused) to live in the Real World, all the socialists, pacifists, humanitarians, rentacrowd do-goodery offal. To say nothing of Irish nationalists – why, a *Daily Telegraph* features editor actually told him that his articles on the latter were just what was needed, 'no more and no less, to put the boot into Irish pretensions with military precision and the right British breed of scarifying humour'. And to be sure, at that time, he truly believed what he wrote. The question was, did he still? Despite Charlie Bones's resentful accusations, he thought that he probably did.

In which case, why ever had he chosen to destroy his credibility by insisting on the innocence of McGranaghan? It surely was not just Ute. All Ute had done was to point him – *insistently* point him, oh yes – towards what he knew deep down inside him was the only fit and proper thing. In other words, the McGranaghan case had no political ideological significance, it was an individual human issue of justice and truth. Although of course justice and truth were in themselves political, ideological; that is to say, to a certain degree . . . it was all very difficult. And then again, this Tumulty business: he had been convinced by the old man's tale, at any rate enough to promise him to explore it as deeply as possible, which is what he had done, wasn't it? (What he *still* should be doing. Could he honestly say he'd finished?) An individual human issue of justice and truth.

It was perfectly preposterous to call him a Zapatista. He was sure, if he were a Mexican, he would oppose those scruffy rebels tooth and nail. And as for Seattle ... disgraceful and terrifying collapse of public order, had he been State Governor he'd have sent in the National Guard with live ammunition: plastic bullets and tear gas were no sort of answer ...

Back in Galway he found Ute to be grimly and perversely sanguine. She said, 'Go and write it. All you've done so far is take notes. Get out of my flat and go to your own and sit down at your word processor. If you need to, walk round the corner, make more chats with Mr Tumulty. The very fact that the man Bones (your old friend, did you not say to me?) has now turned against you, surely shows you have touched at something real. You did say to me he is from the *Financial Times*? Ha-ha! you could not make an enemy in a more significant place. Already you have hurt them where they live: we do not despair, we continue!'

He postponed walking round the corner. Instead, he sat alone in his flat and settled down to some serious drinking. He drank slowly, until the small hours, blearily watching a rubbish film on television, Chicago police, drug dealers, car chases and crashes galore. His telephone rang. He answered it, blearily.

'Mr Oldroyd? This is Tumulty here, Mr Tumulty, you remember me, sir, of course?' Tumulty had not hitherto used the phone on him. Either good news or very bad, and from the tone of the old fellow's voice, he suspected bad. 'Mr Oldroyd, would you mind, would you mind coming round to see me? I know, sir, 'tis very late, but I've a matter on me mind, like; I'm going to have to talk to you – please!' It certainly did sound bad, but bad might be good for Oldroyd, it might mean that Tumulty was about to confess the whole tale was a pack of lies, in which case all the danger was over, the obligations, responsibility, and no blame to himself, no angry recriminations from Ute, he hadn't exactly failed, old Tumulty had failed *him* – as anyone could have foreseen, but Ute wouldn't listen, not her.

Tumulty opened the door to him in what appeared to be an old-fashioned nightshirt with a raggedy grey dressing gown worn over it. Bare ankles, thick and shapeless, protruded from purple slippers. 'Oh thank you for coming, sir; come up, come up, do! But please don't make a noise, th'ould woman beyond is very sensitive to the noises at night.' He gestured vaguely toward the party wall of the house next door, and led Oldroyd on tiptoe up a very steep stair into a sloping-roofed garret little larger than a horsebox.

He gave his one chair to Oldroyd and himself sat down on the bed. He was gasping from the effort of climbing the stairs, and he winced as though in pain. Pain in his back, it might be, from the way in which he writhed against the bolster. Then he remembered to offer a cup of tea, and began tortuously to unwind himself; but Oldroyd prevented him – 'No no, nowt to drink, not at this time o'night, I'll be up every hour with me bladder if I do.' Duplicitous excuse, with all the whiskey already inside him, and the glass left half-full beside his television, but – 'Very kind of you of course, but I *was* on me way to bed and I'm anxious to get down to brass tacks, if you would? Right.'

Tumulty nodded. 'Of course, of course, yes.' And then, with none of his fits and starts but direct asseveration: 'I'm after thinking, Mr Oldroyd. I'm after thinking all night since I came into the bed here – from nine o'clock onward till now – four hours of it, sir, five, and at last, sir, I've made up me mind. By the same token, I'm not at all well. So I've called you, sir, to ask you to take this thing no further, I mean proceed with your writing no more, whatever your researches; I simply, sir, don't want it done.' He seemed pretty calm about it, offensively calm, in view of the implications. Let alone his posture, as though carefully rehearsed – how to convey that your decision is immoveable? conceal apparent pain with an obviously monumental effort, set your mouth downturned and rigid like the edge of a pruning knife, and leave the ensuing angst to be dealt with by the other party.

Oldroyd, with an equal effort, kept his angst well reined in. He should have felt relieved, he was amazed he did not feel relieved, he was in fact unexpectedly outraged. He saw no point in throwing things or stamping up and down the room; the space was too confined, and Tumulty was too old. He took a deep breath, he opened and shut his mouth, he said no more than, 'Why not?'

'I had a look at it, d'you see, from the point of view of the confessional, as if I were the priest and the monks were the penitent – I don't quite know how it came to me to see it like that – y'might say it's a sort of blasphemy, like, putting meself in that position – "presumption", I dare say, would be the name of the sin. But in the heel o'the hunt, sir, that's what I did. And here's the conclusion I came to. The Order of St Brendan, all over Africa, has done more deeds of good than I've ever ate the Blessed Host, and that's into thousands and thousands. Now if at the same time they've been practising the deeds of ill by allowing themselves subsidies from this George-&-Dragon wickedness – very likely inadvertently, at any rate, to begin with – we do have to ask, do the ill deeds outweigh the good, or vice versa? Now just suppose it *should* be vice versa, Mr Oldroyd, just suppose there's more good than bad – isn't it as well, then, they're after taking the company's money to accomplish all the good they've done? Isn't it just as well, like, that they're Spoiling the Egyptians?'

Oldroyd opened and shut his mouth again, endeavouring to frame an effective counter-argument. But Tumulty forestalled him, holding a hand up palm outward, a clear sign that all argument was over. 'So you see, I'm quite determined, I do have to give them the benefit of the doubt. The only reason I didn't think of it before, I was so broken up entirely by that video I had to look at on the island . . . the way it stayed with me . . . all my judgement of right and wrong; why, 'twas all thrown about, sir . . . I couldn't tell the proper shape of it at all. So therefore, please don't write, or if you *have* written, don't publish. Leave the knowledge of their guilt, if indeed guilt there is, to be decently mediated between themselves and our Blessed Saviour.'

Tumulty spoke this last sentence with a degree of downcast piety amounting almost to sanctity, hands clasped upon his breast. Then, all at a blow, an intolerable access of pain, he shot his fists out into the air, he flung his torso left and right, his soft voice abruptly switched into a guttural scream.

'Oh Holy Mother, let me offer it up! oh for the sake of your own

Beloved Son! – sure, I'm crippled, Mr Oldroyd, me chest and me back and me loins, a class of pleurisy, the quack said – I had him in this morning, Mrs O'Curry made sure that he came – she's ringing up County Offaly to see will me widowed sister be prepared to look after me, that's the one that married the Garda sergeant until he was killed in the road accident, not the farmer's wife in Roscommon with the six children and one of 'em disabled – would you believe leg-irons and a wheelchair the whole of her life, that poor little girl, I'd say she must be near twenty already or twenty-one, you'd never know it ... Will you listen to me talking? And I've not yet left you time, sir, to respond to me proposition. Only for the pain, it might never have occurred to me, but as I said, sir, I'm determined. So what do you say?'

Oldroyd tried once again not to shout, couldn't help it, shouted. 'You know what you've done, don't you? you ... you ... you distressing little bugger! You've conned me, you've coneyed me, you've fucking well *conveyed* me – weeks of my time, wasted, poured out into the London gutters – let alone the sodding expense – d'you think a man o' *my* class, *my* experience, do you? an honest-to-goodness working journalist, forty shitty years of it, nose-down arse-up at the coalface, d'you think I'd *expect* to have to do my work buckshee?'

Tumulty stared up at him, thunderstruck there on the bed, a streak of a tear out of each round eye, a little dribble of dismay from the corner of his mouth.

Oldroyd went on, not quite so loud, but loud enough. 'I don't think you do know what you've done, not the half of it, so I'll put it to you bluntly. By telling me the tale, and then telling me not to tell it, you have made me an accomplice, just the same as the monks made *you*: and I'm not going to stand for it. I am *not* an accomplice, not with Hanover H. or G-fucking-D or Saint Sod Sebastian and all of his arrows! *Quod scripsi scripsi*, that which I've written, I've bloody well written, even though as it stands it's no more than bits o' shorthand: I daresay you'll recollect a certain biblical curtain line?'

On his way through the door at the head of the stairs, he turned briefly around and added, 'Don't get the wrong idea, I'm truly very sorry, right? to have found you as poorly as this. It's very good of Mrs O'Curry, and I do hope your sister can come.' He was vaguely aware of an angry knocking on the wall ('th'ould woman beyond', no doubt) and a diminuendo wail from Tumulty to the effect that foul language was quite out of order in what was after all a religious situation . . .

He ran breakneck down the stairs and out into the street in no more than four or five leaps, he felt so ashamed and disordered.

At all events, his boats were now thoroughly burnt. After what he'd just said, he'd no choice but to continue. One stupid surge of (oh yes, justified) ill-temper, one jump of wounded pride, and he was well on the way to reshape his whole life. He shuddered at the thought, and yet –

And yet he knew that if Tumulty had *begged* him to continue, he'd have tried every which way to find an excuse to dissuade him. Ute could go to hell.

Dear God, this thing would kill him . . . Over and above his immediate central problem (i.e. was it even *possible* for him to tell this tale effectively, and where, to whom, how?), he began now to discern another most burdensome problem, a problem of psychology, or maybe pathology, rather than fact: the actual content of Tumulty's account. For stretch a point and suppose every word of the tale to be true, there were nonetheless complexities in it he had not fully appreciated, and he had to bundle his head round them, now, at his desk, tonight, or he'd *never* be able to start! Tonight, and no more whiskey. Get the notes out, get the pencil, don't just narrate it, analyse.

Out of the blue it had come to him: the accusation of 'accomplice'. From the look on his face, Tumulty seemed to know what he meant; and indeed to accept it, if all he could muster in the way of remonstrance was a plea against Oldroyd's swearwords. The difficulty was that Oldroyd himself was not sure what he'd meant; but he *was* sure that this was a thread he should pursue, pick and pick at it until the ravellings one by one might come undone. Of course Tumulty from the beginning had been ambiguous, ambivalent, self-entangled in his meshes of obscure Catholic guilt.

And it seemed too that all those monks must be more or less entangled. How far were they in the know? Even the most obviously innocent – Brother Wenzel, for instance – appeared to be curiously tainted. If Tumulty had heard him aright, Wenzel had more than an inkling, but only of the doings on King George Island; he was surely not aware of the Order's involvement. Perhaps the fact was, the monks in general *did* know there was something that they *ought* to know but could not bring themselves to ask? Perhaps their very religion, so infused with impalpable mystery, made it fatally easy for them to accept without question a material mystery in their everyday life? Nonetheless, he had to wonder, how could such men live as they obviously did, at once efficacious and spiritually authoritative, if they even half comprehended the truth? (Or what Tumulty claimed was the truth?) There must be *some* limit to collective hypocrisy, right?

But the abbot on St Sebastian who never spoke to pilgrims and the South Kensington sub-prior who fired abuse at total strangers ... no doubt best to defer judgement upon those two.

And then there was another matter. He began to scribble notes:

A difficulty here I've only just thought of, I haven't even started to solve it. If I'm not able to solve it, I can't see how the psychology, all of its aspects, can fit into place.

This convict colony, right? Hanover H. will not admit its existence to me, but their security officer did admit it to Tumulty, why? And they do admit their cash for the monks, and admitted it too to Tumulty: isn't that above all what hit him so hard?

You'd have thought, given the vile criminality, nowt less, of what Tumulty had already seen, it would have been more economical, more rational, indeed *safer*, to – let's not say murder him – but 'allow him to expire from his ordeal', plane crash, fall from chair on table, general trauma, etc. Easy. So why didn't they?

Spike's guess, for what it's worth:
Tumulty says it was full half-hour from doctor finding him on chair on table, peeping, to arrival of security officer. Officer angry with doctor,

angry with guards, treats 'em like dirt, why? Because during the half-hour, somebody had a phone chat with higher authority – with Canary Wharf head office? Could be. Could be a sudden realisation that tight-arse security surrounding the island was bound in the end to leak. Monks' private jet smash-landing on its airstrip decisively proved the point: suppose *all* of the pilgrims and crew had survived? Too risky to terminate all of 'em, far too hard to cover it up.

So therefore, change of policy, final decision only just taken, only passed on to island security during the crucial half-hour? Sudden new orders to officer. (Not the sort of man to make a U-turn easily; feels loss of face in front of doctor and guards; brazens it out by bullying them; standard little-Hitler behaviour, right?)

He's been told to relax security, admit everything needful to account for what Tumulty's seen, but make sure by the time he's told it that the wretched old codger is – dear God, didn't I hit it, without even knowing what I hit? – an *accomplice*.

All the spiritual grace-and-blessing he'd imbibed on Sebastian was the fruit of cruel slavery & he'd blissfully received it, found his soul healed of worldly torment:

Ignatius Tumulty at last at one with his Creator.

But his Creator was at one with abominable G&D.

So Tumulty and G&D were intertwined like man and wife.

He went to St Sebastian full of mysterious guilt, gets rid of it, comes away via a gut-wrenching odyssey that fills him once again with mysterious guilt.

They're employing a two-pronged strategy. (1) to work through Tumulty's conscience, and (2) if it *don't* work, flat denial all round – Tumulty's mad! End of story . . .

The old crawthumper, they were sure of it, would come home so messed up, that whatever tale he told, there'd be nobody in charge of anything who'd be bothered to believe him. In the mindset of these multinationals, those who are *not* in charge (e.g. the likes of Spike) simply do not count.

(Unless, that is to say, they're a huge Revolution, which, thank God, I am not.)

Am I able to show that that mindset's all wrong?

Yes, if I've solved the difficulty. I'm not sure that I have. But at least I've discovered a hypothesis. Not good enough. I'm living in the midst of the most litigious nation upon earth and I sit here vivisecting (by guesswork, can you credit it?) the soul of an old man so I can put it all out in print after he told me he didn't want.

By God I'm just asking bloody Tumulty to sue me!

Or if not him, his family. County Offaly, County Roscommon, rural attorneys like ogrish leprechauns homing in on the greedygut trail, fee-fi-fo-fum, they'll all smell the blood of an Englishman. Didn't I know that this thing was bound to be too large? Whichever way, I'm ruined. If that bastard Charlie Bones hasn't ruined me already.

Dear God, of what value were his journalistic skills when he couldn't even use them to convince another journalist, not even when he ... but then he'd always said, he was not a bloody journalist, a penny-a-line hack with neither soul nor breadth of vision, nor ... that's to say, not *just* a journalist.

Dear God, it'd have to be *fiction*.

It was ten in the morning when this brand-new notion burst upon him; he had left his notebook down and gone to bed at around five, trying desperately 'to sleep on it, to let it lie fallow a few hours', a technique that in the old days he would recommend to young colleagues, 'no better way', he used to say, 'for an honest-to-goodness newspaper man to get all his wild thoughts in proper order'. Which in this case was exactly what happened: he sat immediately bolt upright, as wide awake as ever he was, both feet with a jerk out of the sheets onto the floor, as he stooped for slippers, fumbled for dressing gown and scurried into his sitting-room. (For why *not* fiction, after all? How else was he to test the plausibility of his hypothesis? Why, it might even pass the test. How could he know, until he'd done it?) He switched on the word processor, clicked into the file already labelled 'novel', and without hesitation began. He had saved, in this file, twenty-three-and-a-half pages of sex-obsessed, envenomed Irish Republicans and contemptuous Nazis, all that was left, after one dire revision upon another, of the twelve vigorous chapters which months ago he believed had taken on their final shape. He deleted the whole lot with a drag of the mouse and a finger tap on the keyboard – the slightest possible movements for so profound, oh so perilous a decision – yet they felt as though he'd caught himself round the neck from behind and stabbed a murderous dagger deep down into his own heart. Repellent deed! but he had done it. Nor had he quailed. Indeed he triumphed, in proud spirit, like Brutus upon the death of Caesar.

And then he changed the title of the file. No longer 'novel', but 'story'. He could not think he would need more than, say, 25,000 words to wrap up Tumulty and his nightmare into acceptable literary form, now that he knew he could *construct* what he did not know. All sorts of different names, different details, get it well out of the way of a libel suit. He rattled at his keyboard for three hours before he realised that he *must* go to sleep: when he wrote at such speed he invariably ended up with an interminable slew of nonsensical verbosity. So he stopped. Let it lie fallow once again, sleep on it once again, and then tomorrow he would see where he had got to . . .

Tomorrow did not reduce the heat of his creative fury. Nor the next day, nor the day after that. A whole week he kept to his task, scarcely leaving the flat, except to buy his basic food and newspapers, and every morning his cigarettes – dear God, this was no time for *patches* – were he to kill himself by this neglect of his bodily wellbeing, he didn't at this stage care, for would he not be dying in harness? Just so long as he was able to reach the end of his text before he pegged out. He did have the sense to leave the hard liquor alone. A glass or two of cheap red wine in the evening; for the rest of his working hours, coffee, cup upon cup. He telephoned Ute to tell her he was hard at work and wouldn't be able to see her. He did not say what sort of work: she would surely have begun to nit-pick about his writing a mere tale (a Grimm Brothers *Märchen*, she would probably call it) instead of a precise analysis. She had never shown enthusiasm for his novelistic aspirations. But she was sensitive enough not to ask too many questions; she congratulated him on having got his teeth well stuck into the job; she said he and she would celebrate – 'orgiastically' was the word she used – once it was finished and done.

The mere tale, as it continued and expanded and curled its way round unlooked-for corners, developed into an intense psychological speculation about the nature of pilgrimages, the nature of the guilts assuaged by them, the nature of the bliss, grace or peace provided by them – not only the effects upon the pilgrims themselves but also upon the clerics who hosted them. Through these vast generalisations, he was seeking to convey the sidelong collision of the strange character of Tumulty (as he himself had fragmentarily observed it) with the collective personality of the monks (Tumulty's far-from-consistent account of them, plus Oldroyd's own sheer guesswork). As for the alleged experience on the penal island, he took a leaf from E. M. Forster, *A Passage to India*, the Marabar Caves outrage. Forster never stated whether there was in fact an attempt at rape within those caves – the importance of the incident was its political and social consequence. And the consequence was devastating. The novel had annoyed Oldroyd years and years ago (had he even finished it? – he couldn't remember) exactly because of its evasiveness; but now he began to think there was something to be said for Forster's shuffling.

So the island must remain in his tale a giant question mark. Maybe the disguised Tumulty-figure was tipped headfirst into evil incarnate, maybe there was nothing but the phantasma of delirium. But either way one question sat waiting for an answer: did this Tartarean vision of an international profit-making gulag carry any sort of conviction, given the desperate state of the so-called New World Order? Oldroyd, only a few years ago, with weary complacence, would have smiled and murmured, 'No'. But that was before his life was so startlingly disrupted, sexually by Ute, politically by the McGranaghan case; nowadays he could only say 'Yes'. Or at least, 'Yes, probably'. Or even, in the flurry of his swift-inflamed emotions, 'Yes, probably, God damn it! and why the hell did it all have to fall into *my* lap?'

(Because even as he wrote, he was more scared than he had ever been, more scared than the worst time in his life up to now, that drear black winter's evening when the Dublin Special Branch had announced they were about to charge him as an accessory after the fact in a terrorist murder.)

On the eighth day of his labours he came to the conclusion that if he didn't finish this minute, he would never finish at all. Ridiculous to go on and on till the last bloody trumpet. Let him type a row of dots across the page to mark 'The End', and then let him – let him rest, for God's sake, before deciding what to do with it. At his stage he'd no idea whether the writing was first class or worthless. Nor would he have, without a second opinion: but whose? Should he show it to Ute? Or perhaps it would be better to ... He drank down his glass of wine, poured another and drank it down, poured another and –

5

Oldroyd to Ute the following evening: 'It don't matter what I've written; he's refused to let me publish. Bloody crawthumpers, they're all the same.'

'Don't be silly,' she said. 'You know nothing about craw-thumpers. This man is an hysteric, his opinion changes daily. But if he plays such tricks with you, best you should not see him again. So: show me your article, show ... You are coy, which is infantile, why do you not show? How else can I tell you what I think?'

So he showed her his fiction and, remarkably, she praised it. She fully understood, she said, why he'd had to write it in that form; it demonstrated, she said with a grin, a deal more political cunning than she'd given him credit for. 'And of course you must publish. It's not *his* story, it's not *yours*, it belongs to ... why, Spike, it damn well belongs to *me*, now that I've heard it, and any of my friends I choose to tell it to. It's as much public property as ... as Auschwitz or Hiroshima – and never mind the Blessed Saviour; if he happens to exist, the one thing he won't want is garbage-trash cover-ups. For who is this Tumulty to speak on his behalf?'

The orgiastic celebration might now be appropriate: she had not cared to mention it earlier, suppose she had not liked the work? So that's how they spent the night, a Saturday night, no haste to get up tomorrow. A muted sort of orgy, she had acquired a snuffly cold and Oldroyd's stomach gave him trouble: nervous indigestion, he guessed. But he erected himself to some short purpose and moreover he did not die.

'Right,' he said in the morning, 'the question now, my pet, my duck, my chuckey-egg, the question now is: where am I going to send it?'

'Ireland, I think no good, you need serious circulation. I don't know the British journals so well. But if you do want money – and I know you want money – you need to find pretentious glossy. Will you bite off my head if I tell you, send to Germany?'

'Eh?' He gaped at her vacantly over the cheese and salami she'd thought fit to serve him for breakfast. 'A month ago such a notion would ha' stuck in my throat. But after that bastard Bones, all I can say is let's try it! . . . Who'll translate it? You?'

'*Jawohl*, for who else?' Cheshire-cat grin at his diffident delight (she had never before made him so useful an offer in regard to any aspect of his work); she went on to explain that the quarterly publication she had in mind would print in several languages, the author's on one page, German on the opposite, no mere magazine but a literary/political/global forum, two hundred pages each number, certainly pretentious glossy but also strongly radical, and no question they would *pay*. 'It is a publisher in Heidelberg, granddaughter of a Nazi-era slave-labour profiteer, inheriting his foul fortune and turning every pfennig to the cause of extreme left. She was taken over lately by some octopus multinational but they leave her her independence – as a means of . . . *ach Gott*, as a means of the same motive for Hanover Holdings to pass money to the monks. Ironic. Some things no doubt they would not wish her to print, but this is a fiction, I am sure they will make no trouble. And Spike, I am more than sure that this woman will love your work. She and I, we have old connections.'

The German quarterly was called *Til*, after Til Eulenspiegel, the traditional trickster. Within six months Oldroyd's story was in it, printed in two languages, 'loved', so Ute declared, by 'this woman', the publisher, and paid for with a handsome enough cheque. Ute took care of all the business arrangements; for one of her mysterious reasons, she did not want Oldroyd dealing direct with the Heidelberg people, preferring always to work under a cloak, even when there was no apparent need.

Less than a month after the story appeared in print, a letter came to Ute, posted in Heilbronn. It was written in English on the headed notepaper of Longbeard Films (Independent Co-operative), with a PO Box number in London, an e-mail address and two phone numbers, one in London and one in Germany. It said:

Dear Friend,

For the attention of yr client, Capt. Macmorris [Oldroyd's professional sobriquet]: our minds are quite blown by his tale in the latest *Til*, 'An Island and Another One.' It is an imaginative fiction, OK? So how come it ties so neatly with all the buzz that's gone the rounds of *global resistance* underground through the past 2/3 years? We are a TV/documentary/ investigative/agitprop outfit, and we'd like v. much to follow up the Macmorris story on a factual basis. Check us out, if you don't know us. Our camera-cred can be vouched for by *Til's* editorial board; we have sold stuff to Channel 4 as well as TG4 in Ireland. But the theme is a dodgy one, so be careful how you get in touch, walls have ears, no letters please at this stage, ring the London no. (above) between 6 & 8 am. Don't ring the German one. The e-mail is safe enough, I guess. You're surely on-line, no? *Til* says you still use snail-mail, which anyone can intercept. But do let us know if Macmorris can come in with us on this, he seems to have hot antennae.

Yrs in solidarity
(on behalf of the collective),
Mo Mischief, chief programmer.

PS: Let's agree in principle and then we can rap as to who owns what rights and how can they be paid for.

'Longbeard?', was Oldroyd's immediate comment when Ute brought him the letter. 'Rings a bell somewhere. Wait, I've got a book.' He rummaged in his shelves, found a broken-backed Victorian history of the City of London, riffled through the dog-eared pages till he found what he wanted. 'Aye, here we are. William FitzOsbert, nicknamed "Longbeard", twelfth-century insurrectionist, made riots all over the city till the feudal lords had

had enough of him, the Archbishop of Canterbury ordered him dragged at a horse-tail and hanged on a butcher's hook in Smithfield. It says that folk called him the "King of the Beggars". A film company of that name'll never make anyone rich, and I don't like the tone of their letter. Mo Mischief, indeed. Can't even tell is it a man or a woman.'

Ute said, 'You would be most foolish to throw this chance away. I have heard of these people, they are damn good professionals.'

'Right then, give 'em a call. You're the agent, aren't you? So it seems. First *I'd* bloody heard of it. But if they're seeking hot antennae, they're going to have to go to Tumulty, and *he* won't want to talk to 'em . . . Nay nay, lass, I'm not in the sulks. Just you do what you think right, and don't tell me till you've reached – whatever. I'm keeping at arms' length on this one. No more Charlie Bones for me.'

'E-mail?' murmured Ute. 'If that's what they wish for, that's what they should have. I did not use it with *Til*, for sending a manuscript, receiving a cheque, no good; but with these people . . . You will ask, why do I not have my e-mail code on my personal notepaper? So I tell you, it is because –'

'I didn't ask nowt o't'sort. As it happens I know the answer. Your e-mail's your secret bit. "Let not your left hand –", etcetera etcetera: just like the monks, isn't it? Which most of us'd call perverse. Any road, go and use it, "if that's what they wish for". Piffle.'

He'd said he was not in the sulks, but he was. Things were getting out of hand again. He couldn't spread his story as it needed to be spread unless he had good help. And now that it seemed that he might have good help, he feared and resented it. Jealous old crab, he was; and Ute told him so.

Two more months went by. Ute and Longbeard sent and received constant e-mails, a harassment of messages for the reclusive Captain Macmorris, whose response was quite simply – 'If you think that's what you need to do, then do it. It's *your* film, when all's said.' And of course they were trying all ways to discover Ignatius Tumulty and no doubt to descend upon him and crowd up his sickroom with cameras, sound equipment, clapper-board doxies and all manner of odd bods with coffee in cardboard cups, a snarl-up of wiring under every piece of furniture and the domestic electricity fused into the bargain. On this matter, alas, Oldroyd was unable to assist them.

For Mr Tumulty was dead. He had suffered a severe stroke at his sister's bungalow in County Offaly, in a townland not far from Tullamore. Mrs O'Curry brought the news, said she was going to the funeral, would Oldroyd like to come with her? He hurriedly exaggerated the embarrassing effects of his perennial gastric trouble as a pretext for refusal. It was true that he loathed the funerary culture of the Irish, and avoided its manifestations whenever possible. But in the case of Ignatius Tumulty there were heavier considerations. He foresaw he'd be roped in, helpless, and to everyone's discomfort, amongst the ins and outs and comings and goings of a whole clan of mournful Tumultys, and who could say what they'd want to know about how he came to meet Ignatius, and what Ignatius told him about Africa and the plane crash and the good monks and the good nuns? Such potential for queer emotions that he knew he was not to be trusted with: he would get drunk, he would pick quarrels, he would thoroughly disgrace himself. Much better he should stay in Galway.

He bought a mass-card for Tumulty's sister ('the least I can do'), and continued to spar with the film-makers, alternatively fending them off and egging on Ute to encourage them on his behalf. He went so far as to fax them every page of his notebook, much against his better judgement: he thought it not at all the sort of thing a responsible journalist ought to do; but this was, was it not? an odd set of circumstances, and surely, as Ute put it, now was the time 'to twist and turn, dead flexible!'

Longbeard's e-mails were full of zest; their research seemed to be vigorously on the go; they already had 'a guy out in Kenya, safari-wise, supposedly filming wildlife, he'll know what to look for'. And then a long silence.

Ute's e-mails to Longbeard were not replied to. Her phone calls to London met a constant engaged signal, whatever time she rang, and the operator told her that as far as could be known there was nothing wrong with the apparatus. She then tried the German number (dialling-code Heilbronn), strictly contrary to Longbeard's instructions; and this time she did get an answer, one that drove the blood from her face: '*Sicherheitspolizei, wer ist das?*'

At once she rang off and telephoned Oldroyd. Thank God he was at home, and thank God he could recognize the panic in her voice and so uttered no stupid remarks. 'Spike,' she cried, 'Spike! Longbeard Heilbronn is all in a swarm of cops, secret cops, spooks, *Stasi-Gestapo-CIA, Gott!* – I do not know *who* they are, and if we are not smart, we are into the same trouble!'

Oldroyd bethought himself. With Ute in a state, he had to be calm; he was a Yorkshireman, he *could* be calm. 'Right,' he responded, slowly and heavily. 'Heilbronn? Am I right to believe that that's pretty close to Heidelberg? Am I right to believe that these Longbeard people told us if we had any problems, check it out with your *Til* woman, right? So why don't you do that? She might know what's going on. It might, after all, have nowt at all to do with us, why there might just ha' been a car in the forecourt improperly parked, you know what your German law-n-order can be?'

'Spike, these are not, I say *not*, Spike, the criminal police, but security branch, horrible, and altogether different. But I think you are correct, I think I *will* ring Lise.'

Lise rang back in the middle of the afternoon; she had driven straightaway to Heilbronn, Longbeard's small office there was closed, a policeman on duty outside, he didn't know what it was all about, his business only to keep people out, it was not his opinion that anyone was arrested; the occupiers, he apprehended, were all inside their premises 'undergoing discussion' with special officers; the special officers, he apprehended, were undertaking a search. 'Here they are, *gnäd'ge Frau*, why don't you ask the Inspector?' A couple of detectives had appeared from the building carrying boxes of files and computer discs to their van round the corner; when they saw Lise, they wrote down her name, address and car registration, told her nothing of what they were doing, and warned her (if she persisted) they would run her in for 'nuisance behaviour'.

Ute had just finished taking the call when Oldroyd came round to see her. He was no longer calm; rather he was working himself up into a cold sweat, in hope against hope that the *Til* woman would have said that nothing was wrong, they were a pair of bloody fools, so now they could just sit down and have a laugh. '*Nein nein*,' insisted Ute, 'here is news to be taken with the utmost earnest thought. This story of yours is a scorpion that has made its nasty den in the depths of your underwear. On the other hand,' she added – and now she did laugh, harshly and quite scarily – 'ha! yet it goes to prove you can really do them damage ... Now then, earnest thought: first thing we must do, you bring, Spike, your notebook pages and your printed text from *Til*, and we make of them photocopies, and deposit them in the bank. At once we do it, at once; the bank closes in an hour.' Then she caught hold of him, gripping his wrists and pulling him to her. 'It is not the weekend, Spike, but please, I don't know why, will you stay in this flat tonight? Do you feel me, Spike? – I tremble.'

That night, while they lay together, trying in vain to go to sleep, his own flat was ransacked. His computer and many discs were stolen and a bunch of his books and papers. The Garda Síochána refused to agree that the motive must be political. But if it was, they opined, it was very likely some Republican effort in connection with McGranaghan. They seemed to suspect Oldroyd of God knows what. Ute came round to help clear up the mess and sort out the remains. While she was doing this, her shop and her flat above it were also ransacked. Money was stolen and some Celtic-style jewellery, arty-crafty stuff of no great value. She told the Guards that the theft was no more than a cover: it must be political. They seemed to suspect her of unspecified subversion in regard to her IRA husband; it served her right (they implied) to have her home and her business turned into a knacker's yard. It was obvious that neither break-in was about to be taken seriously, let alone solved.

Oldroyd and Ute spent the next two weeks pretending not to be frightened; but they were. Partly it was physical fear. There was a savagery about the way their dwellings had been roughed up that made them feel that those who did it would as freely expend their violence, gratuitous, unrestrained, against individual persons, a middle-aged woman, an elderly man . . . (And who *did* do it? Police agents? Irish? British? Some new-fangled undercover Europol? Or private-hire bullies on the payroll of G&D?) The moral fear was even worse: hideous to realize that not so very far away an indeterminate cohort of strangers was all the time on the move toward you and around you, unseen and silent in half-darkness, swollen with malice, knowing far too much about you, where you lived and when you were at home, who your friends were and where *they* lived – it was a wonder that the pair of them did not sign themselves jointly into the psychiatric unit of the University College Hospital, it was a wonder that Oldroyd did not have another heart attack.

But in fact nothing more happened, until at last there came a letter from Longbeard, a three-page hectic document, sent by registered post from London and signed as a round-robin by five members, no less, of the collective. Their experiences in regard to the film project had been appalling.

Their London offices (in a Clerkenwell converted warehouse) had been ransacked; a whole rake of computerware and documents was missing or befouled with ink and excrement or scattered about in complete confusion.

A dignitary known as the Abbot-Primate of the Missionary Order of St Brendan the Navigator (address in Armagh) had instructed a high-powered London firm of ecclesiastical solicitors to enter an action for criminal libel against them in the event that they were to publish the Macmorris story, or any speculation in relation to the story, 'whether by film, video, audio-tape, print-media or internet-technology.'

An officer of the Special Branch had cropped up, making enquiries as to possible breaches of the Offical Secrets Act. He said he had no doubt that one of the two anonymous islands in their film treatment was intended for King George Island, a territory subject to an information embargo upon grounds of national security, the severest prison sentences could result.

Their insurance company had issued a warning, that unless Longbeard Films dropped all idea of doing anything with the story except to send it back to *Til*, the insurance cover would regretfully be terminated.

Their people in Germany had had all their material confiscated by units of the special police, acting in accordance with anti-terrorist legislation. Nobody told them why; they were casually informed that there might or might not be a prosecution. In the meantime, they were as free as any citizen under suspicion had a right to be.

The man they'd sent to Africa had been killed in a motor accident on a trackway in the bush: a common occurrence, according to local police. 'Drunken miscreants drive too fast; regrettably no sense of duty to the nation.'

The letter wound up with a battery of apologies, explaining that Longbeard had to 'Live in the Real World'. They could hardly put themselves out of business for ever, for the sake of a piece of fiction which turned out to be not so much 'true', as 'rather too damn close to the truth'. Ute (and no doubt Captain Macmorris) would see the political imprudence of taking the matter further. Beneath the five signatures, a handwritten postscript: 'Strategically ill-judged, tactically a total fuck up'.

Thus the attempt at a film was irremediably finished and done. Very probably Oldroyd and Ute were out of physical danger. They would try, so they assured each other, to keep a low profile – until they saw 'how things stood'. And until they could replace their stolen gear. But Oldroyd, inconveniently, grew most anxious to read and reread his luckily preserved script. It was almost as though he were deranged: Ute had to beg him to quieten down, and on no account to fetch the papers out of the bank.

She herself, without warning, took one of her trips to Dublin, and beyond Dublin to the Continent. She left a note in Oldroyd's letterbox to say she was already on her way to the station, it was too late for him to see her off, but she'd ring him as soon as she returned. She signed with 'many kisses, you old vulture, & yet-to-come good fucks! & you are *not* to have heart attack!', so he concluded that nothing more had gone wrong over there. Despite her absence, therefore, he kept up a semblance of good cheer (at least during the daytime), endlessly rewriting his story in his mind, augmenting it, *improving* it. 'Murder will out!' he'd cry to his shaving-mirror every morning with hysterical emphasis. And then he would whimper, 'There's bound to be a turnaround, one of these days, if only a man can have faith!' Were Ute to hear him, she would take him for a shape-changer, slowly mutating into Tumulty. But Ute would not hear him until she came home; and for that, he could do nothing but wait.

After nearly three weeks his patience was rewarded by a breathlessly laughing Ute ting-tinging upon his doorbell to the rhythm of 'Lili Marlene'. 'Oh to think of it!' she cried, bounding into his living-room, throwing her shoulder bag onto the sofa, an unspoken indication she'd run straight from the train. His home before hers! – he'd never known her so demonstrative. 'Unbeliev-able good news,' she exulted. 'Matt McGranaghan, new evidence! Even possible a retrial within months, *Gott sei Dank*! oh to think of it, Spike, we vindicate after all of this time!' She explained, with certain evasions, how the hijacking near Athlone of a smuggler's cigarette truck (in which McGranaghan was supposed to have taken part, and which led to the shooting of a detective) had caused a most serious feud among groups of Republican dissidents: some of these now were prepared to shop the others, and men from associated non-political criminal gangs were to be put up as State's Evidence to secure the convictions of the real killer and his fellow-hijackers. 'Super grassmen,' she snorted, 'demeaning, disgusting, they are cowards of no principle, but we say *nichtdestoweniger*! – for McGranaghan it is transcendental – better still for his wife – I never met the man, you know, before he went to jail, but his Julia was always a good woman, distressed and most loyal, you remember her well – Spike, you do know how she had the nervous breakdown? – still in hospital, of course yes, and now there is hope.'

Oldroyd guessed at once that Ute had been with her husband. The fugitive O'Reilly. Assuredly the information was his. He might well be the moving spirit behind the whole scheme, supergrasses and all. There was no point in asking her; she would not explain further; in this sort of business she never did.

Instead she took it for granted that Oldroyd already understood everything; she jumped forward to immediate practicalities. 'What we have to do, and we will do it first thing tomorrow, is connect once again with the lawyers and make sure, certain sure, that we keep them to their work.'

'Aye, and that's to say that *I've* got to work twice as hard as *they* do, don't tell me. We've been there already, pet. By God, but it wore me out, as well you know. And I wonder can we afford it?' He suddenly depressed himself, remembering all the futilities since McGranaghan was arrested.

But Ute was not depressed. 'Oh!' she called out, with a sudden spurt around the room as though commencing a hurdle race. 'Oh Spike! and I have more good news! Insurance for the burglaries has not been enough, but cash flow *glücklicherweise* is suddenly so much better than two-three months ago – here!' She dragged at her shoulder bag, unfastening a zip on the side, and pulled out a long leather wallet. Out of this a sealed envelope. She tossed it to Oldroyd. 'Take it!' she laughed. 'Open it, it is not a letter bomb. Only no, you don't ask where it came from.'

He was holding at least two thousand pounds in sterling fifties: not a fortune, but more than he'd been able to set his hands on at one go for quite a long time. That revealing trip to London had all but broken his bank balance. Right, he wouldn't ask where it came from. She had her sources, she had her silences, she was generous and she loved him.

'I'm not giving up on old Tumulty, you know.' He said this to her afterwards, in the midst of confused talk about lawyers. 'I've still got to vindicate *him*. I categorize his death as the unmitigated result of those shitbags in the Indian Ocean, all of 'em! monks and bloody doctor and jailhouse screws combined.' He was, as it were, leapfrogging the arduous duties he foresaw.

He sat and chewed his lower lip with his long yellow teeth. He spat out a few grim sentences, with equally grim pauses between them. 'I just wish, though, that McGranaghan was a fresher bit o'haddock; unwholesome little bugger, that's all he ever was. Oh aye, we'll get him out. Because things like that do happen, even in the Real World. I want to see those judges' faces when he comes. Prosecuting barristers, Garda Síochána and all. Aye aye, I'll see their faces.'

PERPLEXITIES OF AN OLD-FASHIONED ENGLISHMAN

(3) The Fagsucker

In the late fall of the year 2000, a most violent fire broke out at a fifth-rate motel in an Oregon seaside resort, possibly caused by a careless cigarette butt. An entire terrace of timber and tarpaper bed-shower-and-toilet units was totally destroyed. A small number of people perished, two, three or even four, it was never made clear how many or who they were, foreigners probably or out-of-state tourists, and all of the corpses unrecognizable. The management had kept no proper register of guests, the investigation and inquest were slovenly, the county sheriff blamed the fire department, the fire department blamed the coroner. One of the firefighters, more conscientious than his colleagues, did attempt a detailed search of at least part of the wreckage. He made an odd discovery: a heavy steel dumpster on the corner of the verandah was full of all sorts of everyday trash that had lain there sheltered from the flames; deep among the bottles, cans, supermarket bags, old newspapers and dollops of discarded junk food was a laptop computer, wrapped in a blanket, not entirely wrecked. A police technician (husband of the sheriff's young sister) was ordered to explore what might be in it. He was able with some difficulty to retrieve and print out a highly revelatory document, a sort of impudent memoir addressed to the world at large.

If we don't get clear of this damned America, we're both going to get killed. Killed, do I say? Dear God, I mean murdered. That bouncing bloody pickup truck that ran the red light at the intersection of Meriwether Lewis and Frémont, and missed us by the thickness of a steak knife, was no sort of accident. And if it had hit, wouldn't they say it was all our own fault: we were new in from Ireland and fixed into a moronic mindset of left-of-the-road traffic? We'd without doubt have disappeared from the ken of all and sundry, in an obscure crematorium, no ceremony, not even a secular one, ash scattered (but by whom?) on the rim of the Pacific and no one in the wide world to give a ragman's fart. Except maybe for her, Mrs Ute O'Reilly; she has at least a grandchild, I've no idea where; she has a shadow of a husband whom nobody ever saw, a renegade terrorist, it's been said, which is why she's my mistress, not my wife.

At all events, we both agree we write down here and now the reasons for this idiotic mess. How we got here. Why they're after us. I'm tapping at her keyboard on the minuscule bedside table which squats between our meagre twin beds. There was a time we'd have shared this room for love. Now we only do so in order to save money, and maybe for an illusion of mutual security. (I write 'maybe' advisedly. I've seen enough movies to know an American cheap motel is no safeguard against hitmen; the joker at reception with his alligator-hide countenance, and his dribble and his stammer and his drug-addict's dark glasses and his front-to-back baseball cap, would be bound to be an accomplice.)

Write it down. Right.

Barely four or five years ago, we were a pair of affectionate hoar-heads who had suddenly enkindled one another's carnal frenzies beyond all expectation. But nowadays I'm pushing sixty-five, direly lumbered with a sick old heart (tobacco-sick, I still can't give up the fags after a lifetime of sucking at the little bastards, dear God), and taking no fewer than five stultifying pills per day for it. She, on the other hand, nigh two decades younger, is more lecherous than she's ever been. Okay, right, I'm well aware of it, I ought not to call her 'mistress': far from correct, but so what? – I'm an old-fashioned newspaperman, no damn nonsense, none of this 'partner' rubbish, 'close companion', 'permanent personal assistant', 'meaningful relationship', I won't have the words in the house.

It is a fact that as a newspaperman (in-depth political commentator, don't assume I was a hack reporter) I am more or less superannuated; but can you believe, I'd scarcely noticed, so infatuated I was with her? and besides, at her best she's so damnably flattering, plausible with it moreover, dead lovely. We lived in Galway in the west of Ireland; even though *I* came from Yorkshire, never mind why I never went back; even though *she* was a German, never mind that sly O'Reilly long gone and no trace of him, both the Brits and the Provos allegedly after his blood. I like to suppose she stayed because she'd met *me*. Wishful thinking, you'll likely say. Never mind: because anyroad it's finished and done and I'd certainly not have mentioned it if I didn't think a summary was requisite background knowledge to the Good Old Caitriona Twohig phenomenon, which I hate to describe, but I have to, so here goes.

'Some say *Good Old ****, and others tell the truth!' – to recapture a form of words much used by pre-pubescents in the Wharfedale of my schooldays: you'd insert the name of any friend thought ready to be taken down a peg, and shout it out at them in chorus as soon as they came close.

Good Old Twohig was a literary scholar, D.Litt., Ph.D. and Lord knows what else, from University College (Dublin), Girton College (Cambridge), Columbia University (New York), and Lord knows where else. Specialist in the theatre of Sean O'Casey and Boucicault and the Irish characterisations of the first Tyrone Power (great-granddad, apparently, of the film star; migrated to America in 1840; you'd learn these things immediately when introduced to Caitriona; I can tell you, she wasted no time.) Last year she came to Galway to earn her bread at the university there, associate professorship and very warmly hyped, profile in the local press, public lecture to the local intelligentsia: Ute and I made the serious mistake of taking out an evening to go to this lecture.

Nothing wrong with it at all as a piece of agreeable instruction. Straightforward common-reader stuff to show the roots of O'Casey in nineteenth-century melodrama and traditional ethnic comedy, easily and wittily delivered. The only clue to the lecturer's hidden heart was the flash of quite savage and needless contempt with which she dealt with a questioner who disputed her indulgent view of Boucicault's stage-Irishmen. Afterwards there was a reception, hosted by the Eng. Lit. Department, with wine and savoury titbits and malicious academic gossip for those of us with friends on campus. I shuffled myself through the throng to get near Dr Twohig; I won't deny I was struck with her; things were not good between myself and Ute just then and it did cross my mind that – no of course it didn't bloody cross my mind: I knew perfectly well that sex, even with an exciting stranger, was out of the question. And no error, she *was* exciting, a complete contrast to Ute, being surely no more than thirty-five years old, slender and tall, nearly as tall as me (which is to say at least six foot), with astonishing long legs in loose-fitting red-and-black striped trews, black hair cropped quite short above an astonishing long nape, and dark golden skin that made you wonder had she a parent or grandparent from Asia or North Africa? Whereas Ute was short and plump, pale blonde until she began to go grey, round-bosomed, round-buttocked, and most notably round-faced.

I should add that this Caitriona had the profile of a meditative kestrel. They've more than once compared *me* to a vulture; we might have made something out of it, had other things been different. As it was, she ignored me, she ignored almost everyone, she drank glass after glass of wine, she shamelessly chainsmoked the most acrid untipped Gaulois, she fastened herself beak-and-claws onto Ute, and Ute writhed and purred with languorous satisfaction.

Walking back across the river into town, I'm ashamed to say I bellowed at Ute. She refused to deny that she was struck with Dr Twohig. She demanded to know in what way it was any of my business, and I couldn't find an answer.

It very soon became obvious that Good Old Twohig's Sapphic urges were ruthless and predatory: she simply did not care whose wives, chums or concubines she might decide to launch herself at. My difficulty was, I had had no idea that Ute would respond to such an initiative; when I saw that she did respond, when I saw with what coarse enthusiasm she replicated Twohig's oglings, I was frankly bewildered and couldn't see how to deal with it. (Bellowing was out. I'd tried it that night on the Salmon Weir Bridge, nearly lost Ute's friendship for good; never again, no.) I was still dropping in every Saturday to her flat to drink, eat, smoke and natter; now and then to lie in her bed all night in an affectionate and technically chaste cuddle. But Twohig kept dropping in too. She never seemed to give forewarning, and Ute was always delighted to greet her – ostensibly surprised, but complacently ready to offer all the hospitality she used to bestow solely upon me. No, I should say *almost* all: I don't know about the bed, I didn't ask, I'd make a point of leaving early, I tried not to speculate.

Twohig on these occasions was cordial enough toward me, although she never called me 'Spike', always 'Mr Oldroyd', a careful formality that made its own point. And yet she was good fun. She'd sit cross-legged on a bean-bag in a swirling cloud of smoke, laughing and swearing and blackguarding the reputations of her university colleagues, in the most reckless and profane fashion – for if Ute was coarse, this woman was *barbarous*. I will admit that in their company I would thoroughly enjoy myself, until suddenly, inevitably, some small phrase, some trivial gesture, destroyed my careless pleasure with its hint of secret intimacy: and that's when I'd get up to go. Upon those occasions, no bed for Oldroyd.

This continued for six months. I was able to endure it because I was hard at my writing work; a series of short stories delving one at a time into the diverse types of sexual desire I could remember from the phases of my own life, smut-talk at school or in the army, conversations with odd characters in pubs, or (more often) books I'd read, pictures I'd seen, films. It was the first time I'd made a stab at serious pornography; I found it a challenge, strain and stress to the imagination, not nearly so easy as one might think.

And then Twohig, with no forewarning, went off to the United States. Only for a month or two, it seemed, a series of seminars and lecture dates at various seats of learning from one side of the continent to the other, the sort of thing she was always doing. But Ute was put out. A careless phone call from Shannon airport while waiting for the flight to be called was not what she'd expected in the way of an *auf Wiedersehen* from her warm-hearted pal. I didn't tell her what *I* thought, didn't remind her that she herself had frequently disappeared out of Galway, out of Ireland, travelling on her own concerns without ever letting me know why, where or for how long. At least Twohig promised a weekly postcard. And for five weeks the postcards came. I used to see them on Ute's mantelpiece, written in some damnable erotic code, which I'm sure I didn't want to decipher.

The sixth message to Ute was not by way of a postcard, nor was it in code. It was a crackly, garbled, gasping cry on the tape of her answer-phone, 'I've been shot, I'm in hospital, intensive care, I'm fucking dying . . . Ute, sweet pussycat, do you not realise? it's only because of this fucking America, where they . . . Ute, you *must* come to see me . . . Oh God you need to know where it is, Wyeth's Creek Campus, University of Oregon, check with Professor . . . Professor, oh what the fuck is her name? Maelstrom, for Christ sake . . . Christ I can't remember, Professor Maelstrom? Theatre Department? Ute, you've to check with *her* but for shit sake, pussycat, *come*!' This arrived on a Thursday morning – i.e. about one-thirty a.m., West Coast American time, a proper hour for European reception, had not Ute just left her flat to catch the Dublin train, one of her arbitrary business trips, closing her craft shop and giving no reason; she did not pick up the message until a pretty late bedtime on the Friday, and she reacted with understandable dismay. She immediately rang for me, guessing correctly I'd be watching late-night telly; she ordered me round to her place without delay; I made haste and discovered I was to find phone numbers for her, fax numbers, e-mail addresses, airline reservations, whatever crossed her mind in her immediate panic.

'Spike,' she beseeched me, 'O Spike, in the name of God, *heilige Sakrament*, Spike: I truly am not capable to listen and speak sense to telephone flunkeys just at this moment, shock, I am in fucking *shock*, so please please for *me*, Spike, ring Directory Enquiries Overseas, get me this campus, get this professor, you can, Spike, I *know* you can! – American time, *ach Weh*! I do not know the differences, it will not be more than teatime, they cannot *all* have gone home? *Um Gottes Willen*, not *all* of them?'

After an overplus of ill-mannered snappings and snorting, I found the Wyeth's Creek campus switchboard, who put me through to the Theatre Department, who in turn let me know that there was no Professor Maelstrom. I had striven to give this Nordic-sounding name a plausibly Ibsenesque dreariness, which might have misled the department secretary or whatever she was; so now I did my best to anglicise it, at the same time losing as much as I could of my Yorkshire accent (which Americans can find baffling). I also kept repeating, 'Emergency, it's a serious emergency!', until the interlude of cross-purposes was able to resolve itself: there was no Professor Maelstrom, but Professor *Millstream* did indeed exist, Professor Rosalind Millstream, who was not in her office 'at this point in time' but could possibly be 'accessed' at home. Clearly Twohig was still Twohig, even in intensive care (I remembered an obnoxious Father Proinsias Kissane of Galway's university chaplaincy and how she'd relabelled him 'Pontius-Pilate Kiss-anus'). At any rate, after some demur, decidedly ice-bound demur, I was given Millstream's home number; I dialled and found a fruity female voice with a deeply concerned twang to it and more than a hint of botheration. When I said where I was calling from, she knew at once *why* I was calling; she began indeed to hyperventilate, but before she could embroil me in the swift-gathering nightmare, I handed her at once to Ute and retreated discreetly into the corner of the room. It was, after all, the bedroom; I should on no account have been there, given the anomalous circumstances, but if my help was required it was not for me to turn stuffy.

As she listened to Millstream, Ute wailed and ejaculated, and groaned and ground her teeth, and carried on in a spate of furious German mutterings, a running commentary upon what she was hearing which conveyed to me nothing beyond a sense of unspecified tragic accident. I had to wait until she was finished and then I had to wait until she had made a good number of further calls – one of them to the Wyeth's Creek hospital which left her blankly frustrated by total lack of information – another to Aer Lingus asking how could they get her there and then to Portland, Oregon – and others to Oregon police authorities with variant jurisdictions. She was rapid and efficient at all this business, once she'd sorted out what had to be done; she hadn't really needed me, save perhaps to give her strength to begin to think straight. After which I had to wait until the hangover of her emotions would allow her to express herself in proper order. Then at last she condescended to transmit to me Millstream's self-exculpatory and blubbering narration. By now it was past five in the morning and neither of us had had any sleep. I'll just give the main points of the story, plus some bits of it I found out later.

Twohig had gone to Wyeth's Creek to read a paper at a seminar organised and chaired by Millstream. The theme was 'O'Casey, a Playwright's Politics'; sessions began on the Tuesday afternoon and concluded the next evening with a restaurant dinner hosted by Millstream. Millstream had offered Twohig the hospitality of her home for the two nights. In the course of the seminar, Twohig several times crossed swords with a local scholar, one Buzz Hackenbush, an iron-bearded Brigham-Young-type patriarch who had been blacklisted in the McCarthy days: in recent years he had gained great credit for this martyrdom and the Theatre Department gained credit for maintaining him on the faculty. He interpreted O'Casey after the sternest left-wing pattern, as a socialist-realist writer with a straight-line revolutionary agenda. He was particularly incensed to hear how Twohig described the Young Covey in *The Plough and the Stars*. 'A narky bit of self-caricature,' she had said; whereas Hackenbush insisted that the character was a serious object lesson in the errors of vulgar Marxism; there was no way (he argued) that such an educative playwright as O'Casey could conceivably have considered himself to be that sort of person. Not even in joke. Hackenbush did recognise that O'Casey made jokes; but they were always politically *positive*. This one, if Twohig was right, would be thoroughly *negative*, therefore Twohig could not be right: QED. He went on to accuse her of expounding O'Casey from a theatrical rather than ideological point of view. She replied by asserting that a playwright's theatricality and ideology were one and the same. In his disgust at what he termed her 'dialectical cop-out', he brought all his arguments to the restaurant, growling at her resentfully from the far end of a long table. He thereby irritated everyone present (his habit upon these occasions, according to

Millstream), and Twohig would no doubt have won their general sympathy if she hadn't lost her temper.

She yelled and she swore, she called Hackenbush 'Fuckingbutt', she called him a 'sodding Stalinist', she stormed out of the restaurant as though she had done with them all for ever. In fact she was going mad for a cigarette – she had found nowhere under a roof in the whole of Wyeth's Creek where smoking was allowed, not even Millstream's house, not even its porch – she just walked a few paces in the rain and lit up her fag on the sidewalk. But the damage had been done. The assembled scholars pursed their enlightened lips over their ice cream and coffee, looked down their liberal noses, made vaguely racial excuses for the manifest 'Irishness' of Twohig, while Millstream felt hideously embarrassed. She excused herself abruptly and ran all of a fluster after her guest, wondering where the woman could possibly have gone without a car and without the key to the house, indeed without a street map to discover how to get there. When she saw her loosely propped under the penthouse of a bookstore, extruding smoke from her nostrils like a fairy-book dragon, embarrassment was redoubled.

'O Caitriona for heaven's sake, you can't smoke in the street, don't you know you're in violation of a regional ordinance? – heaven's sake didn't I tell you? – Nat Wyeth County has the most progressive anti-smoking enforcement of any community in this state and let me tell you that's not peanuts! – if a cop car comes round the block, you'll be thrown in the slammer and indicted – heaven's sake, we can't have that!'

She hustled her down an alleyway and so to the restaurant car park and plonked her straight into the back seat of her vehicle like a long bundle of shopping – new drapes for the living-room, perhaps – bending the feet in last and slamming the door before they could slide out again. Millstream was stout and muscular, Twohig was fuzzy with drink, it was something between a kidnap and an ambulance rescue, and (despite Twohig's foul protestations) Millstream uttered not a word until she stopped at her own front door.

'Okay, Caitriona, here we are, you know where your bedroom is, if you want a cup of cocoa, stuff like that, you know where the kitchen is. Meantime, I'll drive back to the restaurant, finish with the people there, come home again and we can rap, how about that, okay? Or maybe, you'll have gone to sleep. Heaven's sake, I guess you need to. Okay.'

With that she bustled down the steps of her porch, heaved herself once more into her driving seat and swung the car into an illegal U-turn. Now she'd got Twohig indoors, she was past caring about the police. She wove her way at a most dangerous skid-provoking speed through blinding metallic gouts of Hollywood-style rain (flung along the empty streets as though from high-pressure hoses); she raced across the car park, a plastic shopping bag over her head, splashing through new puddles that already resembled foaming lakes; she plunged into the restaurant with a gasp of something like utter despair – 'Heaven's sake, heaven's sake, gimme a long strong cognac, don't tell me I'm driving, I gotta get myself good and drunk, the waiter can call me a cab . . . Buzz, my man! where are you? you and me have gotta talk. Where is he? Where the hell is that sonofabitch Buzz? How *could* he have let himself go in that godawful ridiculous way? Heaven's sake, didn't I ask him, if only for *my* sake, not to do it? Does nobody know where he is?'

The man Hackenbush, it appeared, had left the restaurant only a minute after Millstream. He was very upset, it appeared.

For the next ninety minutes she sat with the remains of the seminar as they soaked up brandy and bourbon and talked academic shop, delaying their departure until they were sure the cloudburst was over, tactfully avoiding any mention of the evening's contretemps. Millstream guessed they would save it for later, gathering in twos and threes in various bars where her presence would not inhibit their sarcasms. She herself would go home alone, hoping against hope that Twohig would be asleep when she got there.

But Twohig was not asleep. Twohig was not even in the house. Instead, there were police cars garnished with multicoloured flashing lights parked all up and down the sidewalk, and the porch and front yard were full of cops, male and female, uniform and plain-clothes,. A lieutenant informed her brusquely that a foreign national named Twohig had been reported shot to death in a street half a mile away; the patrol car that answered the call found her lying against the roots of a tree on the lawn of an untenanted house, losing blood at a great rate but still alive; although the rain had stopped an hour ago, her clothes were soaking wet; documentation in her shoulder bag included valid ID (an Irish passport) and a letter of invitation from Professor Rosalind Millstream ('I guess that would be you, ma'am?'). A man found standing beside her was believed to be the assailant. He had a large dog, a German Shepherd, on a leash, a cellphone in his fist, and an ancient Colt revolver in his pocket, from which one bullet had been fired. He admitted that he regularly carried a concealed weapon. He was aware it was against the law, but 'Survival, lieutenant, is the name of the game in this twenty-first century; you know it, I know it, the old Wobblies used to know it; one of these days America will come to understand it. I'm not talking redneck fascism but good old radical good sense. Thomas Jefferson would have approved: that was a guy knew all about bloodshed for the greater good of the human race. I'm only sorry it had to be a woman. I was raised to be chivalrous, but –' Whereupon, said the lieutenant, the suspect had burst into tears.

A search of the suspect's person had turned up ID which gave his name as Brotherhood deLeon Hackenbush. The lieutenant had reason to believe Ms Millstream might know who he was. Ms Millstream was beyond coherent speech.

And so, by now, was Ute. White-faced, deadly silent, and moving with intense rapidity to sort out her luggage, her travel papers, her laptop computer, her financial bits and pieces, she made a point of hearing none of my stammered remonstrances; she booked herself out of Shannon on a flight for Chicago that left that very morning; she ordered me to fetch my car and drive her there. She herself had 'no wheels, my ignition (as you know) is *kaputt*; you must get me there by nine o'clock and I beg you not to talk as you drive. It is crucial, Spike, that I do not at this moment fall into a nervous breakdown. *Verstehen Sie?* Let's go.'

So we went.

I heard nothing from her for a week and a day, and then she sent the oddest e-mail I'd ever received. I should say I didn't receive it myself: my computer was very nigh as *kapputt* as her ignition. It was unaccountably refusing all internet functions; although it did now and then do its business for me as a word processor, so I found it just possible to continue my venereal little stories. Which took my mind off Ute and the strange fate of Twohig; dear God, I couldn't bear to think of either of them. The more so as there'd been quite a degree of bewildered coverage in the Irish media, reporting what was guessed to be a random 'drive-by' shooting, typically American. *I* guessed that somebody out there was doing their best to hide something, but at this stage it did not occur to me that a hot potential *scoop* might indeed be in the offing, a startling refurbishment of my career.

The e-mail came to a man called Duffy who owned a betting shop at the top end of the Bowling Green a few doors from my flat. He and I sometimes drank together in an adjacent lounge bar, and once when his computer had broken down I'd allowed him the use of mine to attempt to keep up with the turbulent world of the horse race. After that we exchanged e-mail addresses, in case of future emergencies; Ute was sharp enough to make a note of the arrangement. As a result then, this Duffy came knocking me up out of bed in the middle of Sunday morning to tell me it must be for me, I was the only man he knew 'by the name of Spike, and would it maybe be something to do with writing up a film story?' (It was often assumed in Galway that I worked for mysterious movie people. I never took the trouble to contradict.) When I read Ute's message I could see why he thought what he thought.

O Spike – she WAS dying, no she's dead, she did have to die, and only because of her desperate love for a beloved woman who could not until too late comprehend – why else did the surgeon renegue? while as for the D.A. – how bring him to book over prosecution of this murderer? – coverup, corruption, political interference, you name it, this script has it – your narrative-skill ESSSENTIAL here, you must at once come, all expenses PAID, Spike! Airticket arranged from this end. [Flight Number so-and-so, such-and-such date & time] Pick it up at airport desk. Change planes at Chicago, madness, blood, revenge, can only hope this reaches you, telephone impossible for such a hellbrew: Jesus-Christus, my voice would fail, BUT YOU ARE NEEDED, you slow old man. To meet you Portland – U.

The plane in question left on the morning of the next day, Monday: the connection from Chicago would bring me to Portland in the late evening, local time. The message gave me no clue as to how long I might expect to be away, or even why she wanted me. 'ESSENTIAL', she wrote, 'NEEDED', she wrote, which meant bugger-all when you looked at it. (Her capitals implied hysterical yelling, *by no means the proper thing* in internet etiquette.) And what was all this about 'she did have to die'? I found it ominous, even allowing for Ute's perennial over-excitement. I did not want to go. My stories were NEEDING me too. I perhaps ought to argue that they found me ESSENTIAL. I was planning a round dozen of them; no more than three were completed, plus two-and-a-half pages of a fourth. How could I at this juncture go flapping away to America?

I suppose it slowly came to me: for the first time I must recognise that she *loved* Caitriona Twohig, fathoms deeper than just lust, far far beyond infatuation. And I loved *her*, didn't I? How could I then stay when she implored me to move? This was a journey of heartbreak, inescapable: double heartbreak, hers and mine. Whichever way things went, there was no happy ending. I had never set out from my door on a bright sunshine morning with such gloom and uncertainty and foreboding in my mind. And yet, at the Shannon passport desk I smilingly told the official that my motive for travel was 'tourism'. 'Have a good holiday,' she said, and gave me my smile back again. 'Take care now.' Dear God, how I wished that I could.

(And yet, and yet ... Had I not, for year upon year, been describing myself as 'journalist'? *Coverup*? *Corruption*? How could I ignore such electrifying words? Heartbreak, to be sure ... why not also opportunity?)

Ute met me, as promised, at Portland. I saw her at once as I came out of the baggage hall: she stood there quite alone, keeping her distance from the usual clutter of people at the barrier.

Other people, strangers, damned ciphers upon two legs each, with faceless bloody friends to meet and relations and regular business colleagues, nowt to do with her and me, nowt to do with our *business.*

Her feet were firmly planted astride, her hands clenched behind her back, her chin cocked a little upward. She was wearing clothes I had never seen on her, an ankle-length black skirt, a drab black sleeveless waistcoat over a high-necked black sweater, thick-soled clumping black ankle boots, and she had tied up all her hair into a red-and-black scarf. She looked like a Balkan peasant not far from a massacre, waiting for terrible tidings. Except that *I'd* come to hear *her* tidings, and she didn't seem to know who I was. For as I approached her, wheeling my baggage with one hand and waving to her with the other (a sadly sympathetic wave, I hoped, even though I was no good at the body language), I realised that her eyes were out of focus, blurred, a species of translucent film veiling their cat-like green sharpness; had I been told she was blind, I'd have believed it; had I been told she was heavily drugged, I'd have believed that too. Her cheeks were no longer plump and rosy but sagging, pasty-grey, as grey as her lead-coloured lips.

I said to her, 'Ute'. I said, 'Ute, I'm here'.

She was looking through me, not at me; but she was after all aware of me. She spoke like a child reciting a lesson, as though she had prepared herself to say what she needed to say and had no capability to give voice to anything more. 'The funeral was this morning, crematorium. Very swift. They all put on black. So did I, but not with the headscarf; I had to choose the red because of my rage. I said to them nothing of my rage; but I saw they saw the headscarf. They know.'

She turned and started walking, very fast, toward the car park. I had a difficulty, with my baggage trolley, keeping up. She talked as she walked, faster and faster.

'It's as well you have come. There is nothing you can do, but you are here and you will take note. We must go to that Millstream for dinner. Important you meet her. She asked me to stay with her, but she is, I think, a liar, and she will not let me smoke. Neither does the motel, except in a small yard, but they are commercial, it's not personal, I can live with it. That Millstream offered to drive me here to meet you. She is, I think, a liar, did I say so? so I refused. She would not let me smoke in her car. I have, instead, hired a car. Here it is. I think I must not smoke in it, *neither must you smoke*, it's as well I make this clear, you will very soon understand why.'

After hours and hours of economy class I was as mad for a fag as poor Twohig in the restaurant, but Ute snatched my packet of Superkings out of my hand and elbowed me intolerantly into the front passenger seat. She drove through the car park carefully enough – her queer style of speech had made me afraid she would go tearing into a tree or under the wheels of a truck – and she moved into the highway traffic with an automatic skill that did not quite reassure me. She was aware of the other vehicles, just as she was aware of me, but I was not persuaded she could actually *see* them. She continued to talk.

'Caitriona had no next of kin we immediately could discover. On her passport she gave the name of a cousin in Australia, but he is not at home, or he is dead, or he does not wish to answer his phone and the police there have never heard of him. Millstream thought that strange. This city, this county, this campus, is a tom-thumb police state: of course she thought it strange. But in Australia, why *should* they have heard of him? I suppose he is a good citizen. By telephone, a wreath, from Galway, her university department. A reporter at the incineration, as stringer for the *Connacht Sentinel*, *Irish Times*, I don't know what. They told him nothing. *I* told him nothing: he would not have written it, Millstream would see to that, he is a Wyeth's Creek man, young, in need of preferment: *you* will write it, no?'

And then suddenly, in a harsh new tone of disagreeable surprise, angry menace almost, '*Gott im Himmel*, you had better, I paid hugely for your airfare.' She turned her head and gave me a quick, perilous glance. The film had cleared from her eyes; I saw them bright and alive, but could not read them. Then she turned away again and drove in silence for an hour and a half, perilously fast, ignoring all my efforts to talk.

'Now,' she said, 'Up here is a lay-by. I pull into it, so. We get out for a few minutes, so. Now: you may smoke. Me too. Our last fag until we are done with that Millstream, therefore make it two, three, five if you want. While we smoke, I will tell you something, this and that, of what has happened. To understand the real business, you will need to hear Millstream. Okay?'

'Okay,' I said, and sat waiting, on a log bench beside a picnic table for tourists. There was a splendid tourists' view of the ocean on one side of the ridge and of the distant Willamette Valley on the other, but this was no time to think about landscape. I had to hear her and hear her carefully, which was going to be difficult because what with the air travel and the inrush of tobacco I felt thoroughly doped. (I commonly feel doped after a long flight, but today it was out of all proportion.)

'Understand first, Spike, she was purposefully murdered. I mean her, I mean Caitriona, I mean my beloved; he had no one else in his mind, he has admitted, little by little, every bit of it to the police, she was his chosen target, he came upon her all of a sudden where she sat in the rain under shelter of a tree, and he saw what she was doing and he shot her. So you ask me what was she doing? She was doing what we this very minute have begun to do, she smoked.

'He does not approve of smoking; he has given the police pages and pages of statistics of smoke-related deaths and illnesses, he calls them his bible, more vital to his present life than the works of Karl Marx for which he suffered so much when young, more *electric* to his temperament than even the plays of O'Casey, his academic specialty – he is an American, he says "specialty" not "speciality" – he talks and thinks like a man from Mars. He does not approve of smoking, and neither does the city ordinance, which might have been created in Mars. My beloved Caitriona had made herself a criminal to sit smoking under a tree in the rain and so – as I understand it – he instructed himself to punish her.

'Where, he has enquired, were the police when they were needed? It should not, he has protested, have been left solely up to him.'

I noticed she was leaving out her usual jerks of exasperated German, so helpful to her when in a state. Instead, she ran on swift and quiet, a deliberate rhythm, formulating the flow of English with the same automatic deftness she had applied to her driving. It was all quite out of character, it could only mean severest shock; I did not think the death of Twohig, however atrocious, would have caused such a shock, not to Ute, oh no; she was excitable, emphatic, pragmatical, emotional, but at all times resilient. Oh no; summat more, summat deep, summat downright bloody deadly.

Wait on: she'd have to tell me, be bound to, why else was I here? All I could do was let her take her own time.

At any rate, here came a piece of it: 'She would not be dead if that man had dared to cut. In the hospital, that man, the surgeon, I said in the e-mail. The bullet was in her chest, in her lung, approaching the heart. He said it would move into the heart with the pumping of her blood and then she would die. Unless, so he said, he could cut and take it out. So he said, but then he said he could *not* cut because her lung was so ruined by all her tobacco all her life, she would infallibly from the cut lose blood, breath and life. Her death, he said, infallible, whether he cut or did not cut, he staked his reputation. For if he dared to be a surgeon he could be sued by her next of kin; if he renegued and did nothing there was nothing could be done against him. Because, stupid woman! she had smoked, it was all in her lung, he would prove it; not a jury in the state could gainsay.

'Ah, and then this. The telephone call. Telephone call to me, because she loved me, as soon as she came to her senses in that hospital she insisted on a telephone; somebody – ward-orderly, woman with a cleaning mop, with a tea tray, not a nurse, not a doctor – found her this telephone, the way they have them on wheels, no? to bring to the bed, and helped her to call to me so she called and I knew and I came. And then that man, the surgeon, said that only for the telephone, the bullet would never have moved. She was, he said, forbidden the telephone, whoever brought it her must be fired; therefore she has died, therefore some poor kind woman has lost her job, therefore I am to blame for both of them, ah and then this –

'The man who shot her is in jail, but . . . I try to say, Spike, that the man who fired the shot is in jail, and they really do think that . . . There is no doubt he is in jail, yet even so . . . No I cannot speak of it. You shall hear it from Millstream. She tells lies but I can sift, detect, out of them something of truth. Fag finished? So into the car, no more than ten miles ... Ah yes, my good friend, you shall hear.'

As soon as I saw Rosalind Millstream flying out onto her porch to greet us, I understood why Twohig had at once thought of 'Maelstrom'. She was enveloped in a sort of chintz tent purporting (I daresay) to be a 'dinner gown for the fuller figure'; it billowed about her like the spinnaker of a yacht changing course. She at once exclaimed 'For heaven's sake!', and thereafter she must have uttered it at least a dozen times before she had us sat down in her living-room with unspecified stiff drinks on-the-rocks. She whirled about all over the place, overflowing with favourite-aunt solicitude; but I noted that her eyes did not whirl. I thought they were cunning eyes, half-hidden by her bifocals. Tight little black puckers in a big soft slab of a face. But would I have thought so if Ute had not said what she'd said? The whole tale was so bad, I'd surely have had *some* suspicions ... As it was, I decided to hate her.

She made a great fuss – a whirlpool, a maelstrom – of the dinner she served us – an 'Oregon' dinner, she reiterated over and over, compulsively naming the dishes, outlining their provenance, losing her spectacles and then hauling them up again on the end of their finicky gold chain every time she swung a tureen onto the table; I was in no state to appreciate (or even recognise) the bill of fare, what could it have been? – I can't even guess at it now – a peculiar west-coast fish dish (chowder?), hominy grits, huckleberries, hashbrowns, waffles and whatnot? – every bit of it out of tins or packets and she'd done it all up in a microwave: dear God, throughout the entire meal she talked like a waterspout, a whirlwind, a maelstrom, an endless bloody flux of apology, justification, equivocal explanation and now and then the most spiteful little barbs.

'Unforgiveable, for heaven's sake!' she cried, excoriating and excusing the man Hackenbush all in the one outburst, 'He has put the department, put the whole university, in a disastrous position, it is not as though he hadn't threatened so often some equal absurdity, oh thousands of times, but never quite made it! – he was always an oddball, disastrous, who could *tell* what would set him off next?

They called him a Marxist but of course he never was – a naive libertarian gullible guy, if you gave him a dogma that in any way seemed to interface with individual liberty, he'd just turn himself around, open his big silly mouth and heaven's sake fix his teeth into it like a dog – and wow! from then on it was *his* dogma, never let go – isn't that just wild? a dog into dogma – like his very own dog, because I surely do believe that that dog was the very first cause – heaven's sake, she never did cotton onto the species, did she? –

'I mean your Dr Twohig, the dear lithe-limbed creature, Caitriona, your "cat-woman", isn't that what you called each other, okay? – heaven's sake that must have been exactly what happened. Caitriona blew smoke into the eyes of the German Shepherd, and poor Buzz he just went wild. You know, since his wife, the dear yearning creature, passed away – cancer of course and tobacco-related, his own passive smoking, he smoked and she didn't – he has *lived* for that dog; it was previously registered with the county as her Lifetime Canine Companion and she willed it a whole third of her estate, an honorary trust as recognised in state law, and poor Buzz became trustee? Wow, wasn't that something?'

Ute had endured the dinner in a dark oppressive silence, fork poised as though she was almost immediately about to eat but in fact eating hardly anything, eyes half-shut, ears seemingly deaf to the crescendo-diminuendo crackle and fizz of our distressful hostess. Or not so deaf. 'As recognised in state law' tripped, as it were, a switch. She brought Millstream to a sudden halt by commencing a monologue of her own, addressed solely to me, for my better understanding (I supposed) of the context of Millstream's discourse, but unhelpfully low-voiced and directed at the rim of her plate.

'Spike, you must comprehend, this is the State of Oregon. Where the dogma of the Ku Klux Klan for so many years held pride of place, where no more than five per cent of the population is as a result non-white, where state troopers have traditionally been called in to even the smallest little labour fight, where the beauty of the landscape and the hospitality of the inhabitants are conserved and controlled by such a multitude of legislations, such pedantry, prudery, pettifoggery, pomposity, pusillanimity, as have never been known since the highest old days of dynastic imperial China. To say nothing of trust funds for over-indulged, over-fed, over-bred under-exercised hounds. All this I have unhappily within one week learned ... Rosalind, I shall smoke. Out of your *back* door, so of course out of sight, so carefully out of your legal responsibility, out of all of your neighbours' responsibility and concern. You'll excuse me. Ten minutes.'

She blundered out of the room and thence out of the building as though she was drunk, but I knew she wasn't. Millstream looked at me in consternation and then shrugged, with the snide implication of 'heaven's sake, what can you *do* with her? – even worse than dear lithe-limbed creature Twohig!' I was saved from having to comment, whether by gesture or word; for the front-door bell at that very moment rang, sweeping Millstream up from her chair to fling herself across the house to answer it. 'Heaven's sake,' I heard her exclaiming, 'Hello hello, *Taft*! – right in the nick of time for de-caff and cupcakes.' So saying, in she came again, possessively ushering a prim little suit with a briefcase and a crewcut and a mouth like the slit in the stopper of a bottle of pure lemon juice, unsweetened.

She sat him down effusively with his briefcase on his knee, and effusively let me know who he was, Taft Q. Steunenberg Jnr, of the District Attorney's department, and wow, wasn't it just great of him, so thoughtful and considerate, to take time to come meet with me – and heaven's sake, with Ms O'Reilly as well, when she came in from the yard – just to 'put us in the picture', wasn't that what the English say? – despite all the wrong-handed rumours that maybe I'd already heard? – or hadn't heard? – or maybe ... maybe –

Taft took over. 'If she *is* here, I'd be sincerely more than glad, sir, if only as a mark of respect for Professor Millstream, to take this opportunity, because – well, wrong-handed, wrong-headed, wrong-spirited, I guess, is just what's been happening, and whereas as a foreign citizen Ms O'Reilly could be excused for misunderstandings, nonetheless our department must hold her in part culpable for –'

'For, you say? For what? *Gottverhasste Scheissmaul*: so *tell* me for what?'

Ute was amongst us, fire-eyed in the kitchen doorway, as German as all-get-out, and a smouldering cigarette stuck outrageously in the corner of her face.

Taft looked at the cigarette, looked at her quite terrifying Medusa face, looked down at his slim fingers on the handle of his briefcase. His posture was diffident; his words were low-toned but as precise as a fishmonger's gutting knife. 'Ms O'Reilly, she will forgive me for saying, has talked to the sheriff's office, has talked to our office, has talked (I believe) to a state senator's secretary, and moreover has talked to the media and all at great length, indiscriminately asserting incompetence, negligence and/or political bias in regard to the prosecution of the alleged perpetrator of the homicide. Until this point of time the proper authorities have chosen – and the media, I am happy to say has also chosen – to ignore her assertions in the general public interest. However, it has been put to me' – a brief inclination of his stiff little head toward Millstream – 'that a new factor has been introduced by the arrival in Wyeth's Creek' – inclination of the head toward me – 'of a prestigious professional columnist from Europe. Mr Oldenrod, he will forgive me for saying,' – not a hint here of irony, though with this brand of jack-in-office you could never be sure – 'may be unaware that Wyeth's Creek campus is by no means our only institution to require an unsullied reputation. We have also the adjacent oceanside resort of Wyeth's Bay, where the conservation of natural beauty, pioneer architectural heritage, and pollution-free environment are essential ingredients of the community's prosperity. Our citizenry therefore regard any breach of statutes against tobacco abuse as heinous in the extreme.'

'More heinous, d'you say, than murder?' I had not meant to intervene, at any rate, not yet, but I sensed that Ute was upon the verge of flying at the man's eyeballs with her red-hot fag and her fingernails. She had to be headed off.

'The comparison, Mr Oldenrod, is inappropriate, nor has it been made by any of our law-enforcement personnel. The fact, sir, remains, that the state has yet to decide how, or to what degree, it will be possible to allow Mr Hackenbush to cop a plea. His counsel insists that the homicide was carried out in self-defence, and as such may be deemed justifiable.'

'You see, you see, you see. *Scheissmaul*!'

Ute spat the words as though she'd found a rat's foot in a hamburger. Millstream, with a sudden access of rage, rose up and lurched towards her. 'How dare you in my house, you bitch, you *woman*!' she roared. 'Out of your mouth with it, NOW!' Ten seconds of eyeball-to-eyeball: and then Ute, with a horrid grin, plunged what was left of the cigarette into Millstream's coffee cup and sat down on a chair in the corner.

Taft waited until all was still. He continued his dissertation unabashed. 'Statistics will be introduced, and proven by expert evidence, as to the lethal effects of passive smoking not only upon *homo sapiens* but also upon many domesticated species, dogs for example. Defendant himself wrote a pamphlet on the subject, claiming that in 1989 in the State of Oregon 70 per cent of deaths of non-smokers (human or animal) were tobacco-related. Forensic search of the crime site has revealed three of Dr Twohig's discarded corktips, admittedly rain-sodden, but smears of lipstick upon them have been found to match up with her mouth; it follows they will be introduced in evidence, defence counsel being firmly of opinion that no jury in this state will convict Murder One once it is shown that defendant's life and the life of his beloved canine companion were placed under threat by the toxic fumes illegally emanating from the late Dr Twohig. Maliciously emanating: for defence will produce testimony as to threatening language uttered against Mr Hackenbush by Dr Twohig earlier in the evening. "Stalinist" was the most significant pejorative, an attempt (it will be argued) to incite political hatred and thereby to induce discrimination against defendant in regard to his academic employment. May I say, a profoundly ignorant attempt. In no way is this a bigoted community: indeed it is a widely recognised and widely approved fact that Mr Hackenbush's alleged radicalism has in recent years been solely directed against the malignancy of the tobacco manufacturers and their mendacious political lobby. The prosecution, you'll forgive me for saying, has a very considerable problem here. In short, Mr Oldenrod, the guy's gonna walk.'

'Walk! You mean *acquitted*? Dear God, it's not credible, I refuse to accept –' A pointless outburst, really, as Ute made clear from her corner by further reiteration of 'You see you see you see,' while Taft went spikily onward, his jurisprudential syllables punched out *sotto voce* like staples from a staple-gun.

'Not exactly acquitted. If he pleads to a lesser charge, he will receive a lesser penalty, conceivably a term of community service. Which will necessarily depend upon the judge. But I am sure that you will now be prepared whole-heartedly to recognise that any apparent leniency toward Mr Hackenbush' – rising from his chair and beginning to back out of the room – 'is the totally proper result of all due process of American law, impartially and candidly administered. I am glad,' – bringing his speech to a rapid end as his haunches bumped into the door and he had to twist himself around to pull it open – 'extremely glad to have had this small chance of setting your minds at rest, Ms O'Reilly, Mr Oldenrod, Professor, I thank you –' He was out of the door and closing it behind him before 'I thank you' entirely left his mouth. He need not have worried. Ute was not about to rush at him; she sprawled in her chair as though falling asleep, still muttering 'You see you see'.

Millstream stood and stared at the pair of us; she had never before encountered such dreadful words and deeds in her well-cared-for little home. It seemed cruel to compel her to throw us out. So I took Ute by the wrist and *pulled* her out, main force; unprecedented rough-stuff, but I did have to shut down the evening somehow.

She would not let me drive to the motel; she said I'd never be able to find it and moreover I was drunk; she got there in the end without crashing the car, even though it was pitch-dark and raining, even though she screamed and cursed behind the wheel with utterly scary abandon. Wyeth's Creek was all up and down, steep little switchbacks between the hills and the sea; the motel was no more than a mile away along the coast road, looking out across Wyeth's Bay. I guessed that tomorrow morning there'd be a breathtaking view. 'D'you think so?' said Ute. 'Strange to say, I have not noticed. And now, if as I do, you need once again to smoke, out into the back. Do not deprecate the rain. It is sent to make addiction as discomfortable as possible: you and I are virtuous people, we submit. *Scheissmaul*! *ach Gott*! that fucking little prick with his briefcase! I vomit.'

Next morning, even before daylight, I was awoken by Ute tramping barefoot up and down between her bed and the bathroom door. When I asked her what she was up to, she replied, 'I am thinking. First, of what has been. Then, what is next to do. Spike, when I arrived here, that sweet woman was still alive. I say "sweet", though you do not think so. You do not think *I* am sweet. You take both of us for yelping yahoos, yes you do. You are superficial, you mistake people, I beg you, dearest man, think deeper, please. For me.' She knelt beside the bed and put her arms about my shoulders, burying her head in my neck. 'To my Caitriona, for a few minutes between drugs and intravenous and coma and hospital horror, I was able to speak and she understood. And *she* spoke. To *me*, Spike, haha I gave thanks, for she knew me. She said, "Now you are here, dearest pussycat," she said, "the horror is gone. All is quiet, no more nightmare. Alas," she cried "alas" like a poor girl in a ballad poem, "alas, that man Fuckingbutt, he made a big fucking error. I know he thinks I hate him. I do not; all I hate is just what he is. So rigid." She was gasping, she began to try for too many long words. "So rigid, so fucking possessive. He is *not* the proprietor of my unfortunate cigarettes. Nor yet of unfortunate O'Casey." After that, she muttered "unfortunate" three or four times, and never any words any more, so I kissed her, dearest Spike, just like this, and that was it.' In fact, she did not kiss me, it was more of a demonstration kiss, a quick little pretend, as of an actor at an audition.

She stood up, began once again to walk. 'As I said, what is next to do. You will, please, Spike, get out of bed, you will open my laptop and write down all of the words of last night; for if not, we will forget them.'

Dear God, I felt tears upon my face, unwonted and unwelcome; but if she wanted the subject changed, I was fit-and-fettled fair enough to go along with her. I said, 'By which token, what the hell was all that about a prestigious bloody columnist, hey?'

She actually laughed, very nearly an ordinary laugh of quite ordinary amusement. 'Boost. You know boost? Before you came here it was important I gave you a boost, which I did; and they shall *shake*. Now then, when you have written it, I think best we should once again to go see this sheriff. No, he has not been helpful; but I am pierced with the impression that that is not his real wish; I am stabbed in my very womb that he resents the district attorney imposing his politics, the way the D.A. is *Grosshandelspolitiker, unumgänglich*, ineluctable, *nicht wahr?*'

She was of course quite right; the written record at this point was the only thing, goddammit, the essential beginning of *all* the great things I could do with it, dear God, I had a story! I might at last become marvellous, an honoured veteran, an aged achiever, could I believe it? a made man! So I did what she asked, and tapped out words. Add to which, it was apparent she was back into her normal conversational mode, an ally as of old, a collaborator. Yippee. I did make the point that – 'isn't the sheriff political too?'

She said, 'Maybe yes, *jawohl*; but maybe the opposite party. Who the fuck cares? We go see him.'

At the police station the desk sergeant brought us into a waiting room to confront an inner door with an inscription on a ground-glass panel:

State of Oregon, Nat Wyeth County
JOHN JOAB CLAM
County Sheriff

The sergeant knocked at this door, opened it while he was still knocking, put his head in, and announced in a voice like a chainsaw (I really believe he believed it to be an undertone), 'Them two from the cigarette-slaying to see you, John Joab. The Irish Kraut with the old Limey we was warned about, raggedy grey'n'yaller *mus*-tache, famous newspaperman, okay? Send 'em in or ship 'em out?'

Somebody behind the door grunted 'In,' and in we went. Sheriff Clam at his desk in his shirt sleeves with a large mug of morning coffee held up to his face in both hands. A soft-looking smallish fellow, younger than you'd expect for a police chief, uniform informally crumpled, reddish curly hair going bald over the brow, a soft pleasant smile on his well-shaven face. The only wrong note was the pair of sunglasses. Quite as wrong as those worn by the baseball cap at the motel. For a sworn public servant to affect such an item on a dripping-dark autumn morning, and *indoors*? – I was at once upon my guard; this bogey could be dangerous.

'Guess I know what you've come for,' says he, without preliminary. 'Sit down and I'll tell you.' His tone was genial, his expression (as far as one could deduce, give or take the sunglasses) did not lack good humour. I recollect only too vividly a vicious afternoon I had spent with the Dublin Special Branch, no more than a year or two since. It is true they had reason to suspect me of covering up for a murderous subversive; but the same sort of superficial blandness, behind the same sort of curiously blank-faced desk in the same sort of mean-minded office, rang some very unpleasant alarm bells. 'You had an evening session with Mr Steunenberg Jnr, and he told you the score, okay? Like, unduly legalistic, a little chill, a little lacking in the friendly amenities, yeh? But then you haven't met Mr Steunenberg Snr, district attorney in person, head honcho. Both of the Mr Steunenbergs are well known, well admired, and avoided as often as possible; you, as a pair of strangers, it's not hard to know how *you* feel. You want me to do more than I've done. You want me to do more than it's possible for me to do. With the best will in the world. *Which, let me tell you, I do not have.*'

His final sentence was such a drastic change of tone that it quite rocked us back on our chairs. The geniality had fallen away: he was hard, hoarse and hostile, he stood up from his swivel chair, thrusting his head forward against us like a compact and ill-conditioned little bull. This abrupt change of posture brought his armament into sight above the desk, two huge revolvers in elaborate holsters, one on either side of his belt, plus a night stick and a pair of handcuffs all a-jangle around his hips.

'So just let me clarify, Mister and Mez from Ireland, though neither of you Irish as far as I can see. You come here smoking cigarettes all over this clean little town, and you try to pollute our justice system as well as the air we breathe. I don't go so far as to say, ma'am, you actually offered a bribe, nor delivered any four-square threats or menaces. You simply brought in a prestigious European columnist and aimed him like a shotgun at our educational excellence and our small-scale but burgeoning tourist trade. And that's what I'm not gonna have. So first, Mr Oldroyd – and Oldroyd *is* your name, okay? – this "Oldenrod" was by way of an alias to confuse the agenda – ?'

'Wey-ey!' I expostulated, 'Ey-up no, the mistake was young Steunenberg's, I –'

He overrode me with gobsmacking rudeness. 'Zip it shut, grandpaw, I talk, you listen. And here's what I was about to say: – Mr Silas W. Oldroyd, aka Spike, you will leave this jurisdiction within twenty-four hours, and before you leave you will sign your name to this paper I've prepared for you here.'

He shoved a sheet of typescript across the desk. It was the draft of a guarantee, a most sweeping guarantee, that nothing I had heard or seen in Nat Wyeth County, Oregon, would be communicated, either orally or in writing, to any form of news media in any part of the world. I looked at it, Ute looked at it, we looked at each other. Both at the same time, as though exhaustively rehearsed, we shouted out, 'No!'

The sheriff smiled, a good-humoured smile. 'Like, I guess you're gonna tell me this inhibits your freedom of speech. Sure does. I guess you're gonna tell me it would never stand up in court. Maybe so. But how long would it take for you to get it into the court, let alone heard and determined? In the meantime, who's got the power? You with your pissy little laptop or me in my office with *that*?' He shot his hand out towards his own state-of-the-art technology, computer, radio-and-tape deck, CD player, video player, gleaming cream and silver on a shelf system in the corner. 'Through the early hours of this morning,' he said, 'me and the two Mr Steunenbergs sat together in that corner checking out a few electronic trailways. Our network extends far beyond these United States. We discovered, Mr Oldroyd, that the Irish police have you heavily marked down as a determined propagandist for some criminal-political shit which won't exactly prove you a terrorist, but it don't go too far from it. Ms O'Reilly, the same police, combined with the German police, would seem to know more about *Mister* O'Reilly than you've ever cared to give to the world, okay? Now, if you were arrested and detained incommunicado in my executive-class county jail, prior to proceedings for deportation as undesirables – why, I doubt very much if you'd even make bail. Once again, you might in the upshot beat the rap; but how long would it take? Like, hot-diggety-dog, old man! d'you reckon it's worth the hassle?'

No, in fact I didn't. I looked towards Ute, and decided from the clench of her teeth that she shared my opinion. Without a word I took out my ballpoint and scribbled my wretched name, unheroic bloody name, on the bottom of the sheriff's little chit. The desk sergeant, who all this time had been leaning against the frame of the open doorway, stepped forward and signed as a witness. The sheriff slammed the document with a huge rubber stamp, and laid it away in a drawer. The desk sergeant moved politely out of our way. We left the room, we left the building. Nobody said a word, and outside in the street the fog from the Pacific had suddenly come in so thick we could scarcely see our way to the car park.

Of course we should have defied him: *Live in the Real World, Sheriff Clam! You force us to go through the courts, who knows what'll be revealed about you and your Steunenbergs and your sleazy little cover-ups? Dear God, you'd never dare.* But somehow, in a strange country, such an arbitrary strange bloody country, we didn't seem to have the confidence. And a damn sight less confidence when we got the car back to the motel, after half an hour creeping it in low gear through the fog like a terrified woodlouse, only to discover we'd been robbed. Our suitcases were where we'd left them, in the bottom of the wardrobe, and still padlocked, but some sneaking clever devil had slit each of them along the seams and made his lucky with everything of value. Which was not very much, no; just our travellers' cheques, air tickets, and Ute's special body-belt with most of her cash and her credit card. I did have my own card safe in my jacket pocket, but its credit was a busted flush. (So why didn't Ute wear the belt to the police station? Because it was giving her a rash round her waist, that's why; and no more of your *Dummkopf* questions.)

Ute's laptop, thank God, was in its shoulder bag, on her shoulder.

So what do we do? Go to the police? Go to *Clam*? Would he not say it was all a trick to avoid getting out of town? All he'd do is lock both of us up.

Dear God, this needed thinking about.

Outside, take a smoke, take a walk, we couldn't sit still, the fog was too dank, every surface was too sodden, what the hell were they playing with us? Don't tell me, she yelled, this is all a coincidence? Did she try to make out the *police* had robbed our stuff? We'd have to have a word with the twitch-and-stammer baseball cap, would you trust him an inch? We kept stopping as we walked, to shout at one another, blame one another, wave our angry arms like windmills.

Even in a fog when there appears to be no traffic, you should watch out while you're crossing a road. But even in a fog when there appears to be no traffic, you do not expect a pickup truck to be tearing straight at you at sixty, seventy, eighty miles an hour at the very least.

We ran, no, we scurried, we scuttled back into the motel room, we locked the door, we latched the windows, pulled down the venetian blinds, kept our cigarettes alight regardless of rules (how else can we summon our energies?). Ute dictates, and I write – or rather, I write without reference to what she's dictating, because dammit I am the professional, and the way she wants to present the whole sequence of events is absurdly paranoiac and frankly all over the shop. And even as I write, there is someone outside, on the verandah, soft shoes, a crafty hand to try the door knob: no, fair enough, we have it all fastened, they're creeping away. Shift the blinds to take a peep. All there is, what did I tell you? just impenetrable grey layers of thick wet shadow of fog.

Dear God, but I'd stifled the smoke alarm with my aerosol shaving foam, it can't be that our fags have at last set it off? No it's all down the block, not alone in this room, NO. Screaming and the stench of fire, real fire, smoke, crackle, glare. The whole place is shoddy clapboard. Ute is screaming at me, she can't open the door, did we jam it when we locked it? Or did someone outside – Sirens in the fog and revolving bloody lights through the gaps of the venetians: is it the fire brigade, or the cops, or both, or is it maybe the blood-wagon from the morgue?

*Windows no escape, burglar-proof bars fixed outside, cemented into lintel and sill. At least beside the transom at top of the door there's a gauze-metal ventilator, just to burst it with the computer, just to shove the computer through? Maybe it'll be all smashed up with the fall, but if not – Dear God, whether we do or we don't get clear of it, **we have got to be believed.***

The sheriff read the print-out from beginning to end just once, very carefully; he no less carefully lowered it into the shredder beside his desk. He took the computer away from his brother-in-law and nobody's seen it since. The brother-in-law assured the sheriff that only the one copy had been made. Maybe so.

AFTERWORD

I wrote these nine stories at irregular intervals from 1996 onward. The first of them was *Molly Concannon & the Hag out of Legend*; to begin with, I called it *The Stealing Steps*. It was printed under that name in 1996 in Issue 3 of *Asylum*, a very elegant literary magazine published in Galway, and now, alas, defunct. The late Pat Sheeran, novelist and scholar, was an associate editor. He specifically asked both myself and my partner Margaretta D'Arcy to contribute to Issue 3. I need to record our debt to him here because of his recent sudden death, quite unexpected and carrying him off distressingly young; we seemed, one way or another, to have found no opportunity to show him our appreciation while he lived.

It was not until I put the stories together to form a volume that it occurred to me that each of them, in its own fashion, dealt with the approach to old age, the vagaries of old age, the 'rage against the dying of the light' that might have been in the mind of Shakespeare's gravedigger when he sang the queer little garbled ballad I have used as a title-page quote. This was not a deliberate choice of theme. The tales came up one by one into my mind, with gaps of many months between them, apparently entirely disconnected, except insofar as three of them are about Spike Oldroyd and two about Molly Concannon. I suppose my own age – sixty-five when I began the stories, seventy-two now that I've finished – had something to do with it, but it was odd, nonetheless, and positively demanded *The Stealing Steps* as the overall title of the book.

Another odd thing: I am startled to realise just how acutely some of the stories have been overtaken by events.

In the case of Spike and *The Dissident*, this was merely comical: during the late autumn of 2002 I had to travel by coach from the west of Ireland to London, leaving Galway at 4 p.m., a rapid drive to Dublin and straight onto the Holyhead ferry, and thence along the motorways, to arrive at Victoria coach station at 9 a.m. the following day. The run across Ireland should have taken about four hours; in fact it took seven. Huge deluges of rain all along the east coast had flooded every road into Dublin except the one on which we rode; all the city-bound traffic from everywhere else was accordingly diverted onto it; we sat for three hours in a blocked stream of vehicles intermittently jerking forward twenty yards at a time; when we finally reached our terminus it was only to be told that the ferry was long gone and the national bus company was prepared to accommodate us with what an inspector lightly described as a 'hostel situation'. We were to take the first boat the next morning, but it arrived late from Holyhead because of storm winds in the small hours, and therefore left Dublin even later. We found the motorway across north Wales shut off by police for something like thirty miles. It seemed there had been a smash-up. The fire brigades were on strike, replaced by unpractised soldiers; and the officer in charge had doubtless thought fit to demand total elbow room for his experimental rescue operation – 'nothing, for Godsake, from either direction, keep it absolutely clear: my men must work out what they're going to have to do here!' – the entire long-distance traffic into the English midlands had therefore to snake through a succession of narrow country roads and residential suburbs just as all the cars of all the north Welsh mums emerged from every side-turning to fetch home the children from school. We never made up the time and we ran into London long after dark. Half asleep in the bouncing coach, I toyed with the thought that here was the basis of a new story – if I hadn't already written it, two or three years before. And when I was writing it, had I not wondered was it perhaps a bit over the top?

Spike's meeting with *The Crawthumper* might have had a different emphasis had I foreseen the depth of asylum-seeker hysteria in the tabloid mentality of Britain and Ireland, dredging up the most morbid deposits of envy and spite from the sump of popular prejudice, and squalidly debasing so many politicians. The story as I conceived it derived chiefly from the zeal of the lunatic parliamentary right wing (nowadays mutating into left-of-centre mainstream) for a privatised penal system on the model of *Beggar's Opera* Newgate. To be sure, I did mention asylum seekers; but they were not the main thrust of the tale. Then, a year or so after I finished it, came the astonishing events in Sangatte and the Channel Tunnel – to say nothing of Australia, where the Woomera concentration camp was assailed by a task force of conscientious amateurs out to rescue its asylum-seeker inmates. Whereupon I had to recognise that what I had thought of as a grotesque gothic sensation-narrative was in fact so run of the mill it would scarcely cause raised eyebrows in the *Irish Times* or the *Guardian*. But I prefer to leave the story as it is: it arose from a dreadful dream I had in 1999 or 2000, and such a source is best not tinkered with. Startling first notions are usually the surest notions, despite all niggling afterthoughts ... In any case, my second Molly Concannon adventure made up for the omission.

If I'd also foreseen the lurch into public view of al-Qaeda and the quasi-mythological Osama bin-Laden, the prison island manifesto (as delivered to Spike Oldroyd by the Canary Wharf PR woman) would have had to take account of their ramifications. It now seems that they must have existed, indeed without my knowledge, as undefined, indefinable shadows behind the events in the *Fagsucker* story – a tale prompted by a visit I made with Margaretta D'Arcy to an American university drama department, toward the end of 2000, just at the time when George W. Bush and his vote-faking gang of oilmongers and Enron-rats were fixing the presidential election. There was deep dismay on campus, talk of the Constitution subverted by a legalistic *coup d'état*, overriding anxiety about loss of civil liberties, reactionary legislation, religious fundamentalism from the depths of the Bible-belt, only too probably war. And yet in sharp contrast to this fear for the common decencies, we found also a kind of fury against – of all things – tobacco, that went way beyond the rational. (I should say that I used to smoke, quite heavily, for many years; I don't any more; a rational decision, my health will not tolerate it; it's as though I have cast off an old and cheerful comrade, Henry V expelling Falstaff, oh it's sad.) The second morning of our visit, we were to meet a professor at the campus theatre, to read some of our work and talk about it to the students. We were a little before time, and surprised to discover a large portion of our prospective audience defiant in the sunshine, puffing away at cigarettes like bandits in a canyon carousing. They were drama students, they told us, and therefore they smoked. They implied it was a token of bohemian independence, of rebellion indeed. Hardly anyone else, they told us, in any of the other departments would share their depravity. Tobacco, mind you, not pot: oh it was sad ... The next morning Margaretta got up before dawn to take a stroll through the tree-lined lawn-bordered streets, and take a smoke in the open air – she had promised not to do it in the house where we were staying. She felt very uneasy: almost as though she were out there to commit a crime, plant a bomb, rob a bank, shoot a policeman. She felt deadly vulnerable to goodness knows what vigilante attempt. She suggested I make a story: the puritanical fundamentalism of the United States, sometimes religious, sometimes a substitute for religion, as fierce in its own way as the Taliban: even the good guys are infected.

So we went home and I made the story, neither of us thinking how very soon our paranoia would be consummated. On the 11th of September next, day of murder, day of valour, day of hideous hypocrisy, fundamentalism met fundamentalism in a black toxic mix of God and geopolitics. Bush found his fulfilment, and everything since then has proved itself far worse than our drama-department friends could have possibly guessed. Just before I wrote this, I watched Colin Powell on TV as he lectured to the United Nations: he projected onto a screen the alleged words of a strange dialogue between two alleged Iraqi officers. Translated from the Arabic by someone with a most creative and flexible English vocabulary. One officer says, 'Yeah, yeah.' The other one replies, 'Yeah.' The first one says, 'Yeah?' The other one elaborates, 'We have this modified vehicle.' The first one can think of nothing to say but 'Yeah'. Then, later on, someone else says 'Yes,' and a fourth speaker indulges himself with 'Okay okay'. What was it but a rejected script for a 1930s gangster movie? Edward G. Robinson and Jimmy Cagney swopping snarls. And it was supposed to make us believe we'd no choice but to slaughter an indeterminate number of Iraqis? What on earth was going on?

Oh yes, and the Irish government has just announced it intends to ban all smoking in all pubs, cafés and restaurants, the strictest set of such regulations in Europe, matched only by certain states in the USA. Fundamentalist infection spread from continent to continent.

I really cannot think of anything else to add to this pessimistic afterword, except to mention that the story *Breach of Trust* won the V. S. Pritchett Memorial Prize in 1999 and was later published in *News from the Royal Society of Literature*.

J. A.
Galway, Ireland
2003